The Sun Shines over the Sanggan River

Ding Ling

FOREIGN LANGUAGES PRESS   BEIJING

First Edition 1984

Translated by

Yang Xianyi and Gladys Yang

ISBN 0-8351-1008-7

Published by the Foreign Languages Press
24 Baiwanzhuang Road, Beijing, China

Printed by the Foreign Languages Printing House
19 West Chegongzhuang Road, Beijing, China

Distributed by China Publications Centre (Guoji Shudian)
P.O. Box 399, Beijing, China

Printed in the People's Republic of China

Contents

Foreword

It may be of some help to the reader if I give a brief account of how I wrote this novel.

In July 1946, I joined the Huailai land reform work team. Later on I left for Zhuolu, and returned to Fuping at the end of September. There was no chance to summarize this stage of our work satisfactorily. However, since I had no other work to do at Fuping and my mind was full of the people I had seen, I decided to start writing this novel. All I hoped to do at that time was to describe this stage of land reform and give a fairly faithful picture of a village with all its troop of living people. I would feel satisfied if I could just avoid making them too abstract. My original plan was to divide the book into three parts: the struggle, the distribution of land and the peasants' voluntary enlistment in the army. While I was writing, I received some very moving materials about the land protection corps in the Sanggan River area. The leader of the corps is the original of Comrade Pin, the county propaganda commissioner in the novel. I had travelled over that county several times too, so I hoped to go back there in order to be able to write the second part. Thus, while I was writing, I made constant allusions to material that would be more fully developed later. The manuscript was half written when the final checkup of land reform work came in 1947. That made me hesitate to go on with my work and wish to go back again to the countryside to make good the deficiencies in my experience of life and in the novel by taking some part in the mass struggle. According-ly, I set my manuscript aside, and went with a team to Xing-tang in central Hebei, then came back to Fuping. This experience of life proved of value, but failed to provide me with much actual material for my book, so I went on writing for another three and a half months, till the summer was over. I devoted most effort to writing the first part, about the struggle, and was just about to start on the second part when the land reform programme was promulgated, and I took part in the land reform conference. As a result, I felt renewed doubts about going on with my writing, and decided to go back to the country first to take part in the distribution of land. I worked in a village in Huailu for over four months, and as a result of this experience made certain changes in my original plan. I felt there was no need to write the second and third parts I had originally decided on, because the distribution of land and the join-the-army movement the previous year had been somewhat superficial and carelessly carried out. This was a result, of course, of war conditions, but still these working methods were not good enough to be worth describing. So, after thinking it over, I decided to compress the book, and since there was no way of adding other relatively new material, my first plan had to be modified. I did not, therefore, develop the two later topics. Just at that time, too, I was to take part in the Congress of the Women's International Democratic Federation; thus I had to bring this work to a hasty close. If there is time in future, I hope to be able to revise this book further.

June 15, 1948

Characters

OLD DONG *chairman of the district trade union*

COMRADE PIN (ZHANG PIN) *propaganda director of the county Party committee*

WEN (WEN CAI)

YANG (YANG LIANG) } *members of the land reform work team*

HU (HU LIGONG)

YUMIN (ZHANG YUMIN) *secretary of the Nuanshui Party Branch*

QUAN (GUO QUAN) *Yumin's uncle, a poor peasant*

VICE-HEAD ZHAO (ZHAO DELU) *vice-village head of Nuanshui*

YOUNG CHENG (CHENG REN) *chairman of the peasants' association*

SECURITY OFFICER ZHANG (ZHANG ZHENGDIAN) *son-in-law of Schemer Qian*

SWARTHY GUO (ZHANG ZHENGGUO) *captain of the militia*

ORGANIZATION ZHAO (ZHAO QUANGONG) *Party organizer in the village*

3

CO-OP TIAN (REN TIANHUA) *chairman of the village co-operative*

FRECKLES LI (LI CHANG) *Party propaganda officer in the village*

BUGAO (ZHANG BUGAO) *organization officer in the peasants' association*

GUI (DONG GUIHUA) *Vineyard Li's wife, chairman of the women's association*

YUE (ZHOU YUEYING) *the shepherd's wife, vice-chairman of the women's association*

TEACHER LIU

TEACHER REN (REN GUOZHONG)

LANDLORD LI (LI ZIJUN)

LANDLORD HOU (HOU DIANKUI)

SCHEMER QIAN (QIAN WENGUI) *chief of the village racketeers*

TRADE UNION QIAN (QIAN WENHU) *chairman of the village trade union, Schemer Qian's cousin*

YI (QIAN YI) *Schemer Qian's son, in the Eighth Route Army*

QIANLI (QIAN LI) *Schemer Qian's son*

DANI *Schemer Qian's daughter*

HEINI *Schemer Qian's niece*

WENFU (QIAN WENFU) *a poor peasant, Schemer Qian's brother*

LANDLORD JIANG (JIANG SHIRONG) *village head*

4

OLD GU (GU YONG) *a well-to-do middle peasant*

YOUNG GU (GU SHUN) *Old Gu's son*

DA *Old Gu's elder daughter*

ER *Old Gu's second daughter, married to Schemer Qian's son Yi*

HUTAI *father-in-law of Old Gu's elder daughter*

SHENG'S MOTHER (GU CHANGSHENG'S MOTHER) *a middle peasant*

TENANT HOU (HOU ZHONGQUAN) *nephew of Landlord Hou*

YOUNG HOU (HOU QINGHUAI) *Tenant Hou's son*

TENANT GUO (GUO BOREN) *tenant of Landlord Li*

YOUNG GUO (GUO FUGUI) *Tenant Guo's son, tenant of Landlord Jiang*

YOUNG WANG (WANG XINTIAN) *a poor peasant, tenant of Landlord Jiang*

ORCHARD-KEEPER LI (LI BAOTANG) *relative of Landlord Li and his hired hand*

LIUMAN (LIU MAN) *an ex-Party member. His family has been ruined by Schemer Qian*

LIUQIAN (LIU QIAN) *Liuman's brother, a former ward chief, now mad*

VINEYARD LI (LI ZHIXIANG) *a poor peasant*

SHOU (LI ZHISHOU) *Vineyard Li's cousin*

OLD HAN *a poor peasant*

YOUNG HAN (HAN TINGRUI)   *Old Han's son, former-ly a soldier of the Eighth Route Army*

EX-SOLDIER ZHANG (ZHANG JIDI)   *formerly a soldier of the Eighth Route Army*

RED-NOSED WU   *primary school cook and town crier*

WHITE SNAKE   *a loose woman who acts as a medium and quack to deceive the villagers*

I

THE heat was sweltering. Although it was only about four miles from their starting point, Bali Bridge, to the river Yang, White Nose's chest and flanks were soaked with sweat. However, she was Hutai's best mule, and pulled well, though the cart track was so muddy. The sun hanging in the west was hidden by a clump of roadside willows, but the heat was still intense, and the muddy water spattered into the cart from the wheels felt warm against bare legs. At last leaving the flooded road, the cart came to a dry place. Only then did Old Gu, who had been urging on White Nose continuously, relax. Sitting up straight, he reached for the tobacco pouch behind him.

"What a downpour there must have been, Dad! Look at the state this road is in, like a muddy stream!" Da, his elder daughter with her son on her knee, was sitting to the right of the old man, a little further back. She wore a new cotton gown with blue flowers on a white ground. Her hair had been cut and hung straight down at the back, combed up high in front. She was looking about her cheerfully, for to be going home with her father was a piece of rare good fortune.

"The river's in flood, you sit still!" The old fellow beat a rat-tat-tat with his pipe. It was proving a difficult journey.

When they started across the river, the two cart wheels were practically submerged, and all that could be seen of White Nose was her big spine which seemed to be writhing through the water. Old Gu's daughter held her child more tightly and gripped the side of the cart, while water from behind spattered forward. The old man flicked his whip, calling out encouragement to the mule as the cart rocked from side to side. The stretch of water in front of the cart, lit up by the sun, dazzled the eyes so that the old man could not see clearly, and sweat poured down his wrinkled face. The cart bogged down, then was extricated again, rocked violently, then righted itself again, till at last White Nose emerged from the river, and slowly planted her four hooves in shallow water. On the river's south bank, the cart once more reached the road and a gust of wind rose, delightfully cool!

As on the north bank of the river, rice was growing here in great profusion. Millet was thick and tall, the height of a man's shoulder. Kaoliang screened everything else, its leaves as wide as maize leaves. The soil was moist and black, and a rich odour emanated from the thick growth. Then there came vegetable gardens encircled by irrigation ditches, the land neatly divided into patches of dark and light green. Each time Old Gu passed this way he felt an inexpressible longing to own such a fine piece of land. He could never have enough land, and he could not resist saying to his daughter: "In the section north of the river the land round Bali Bridge where you live is the best. In our Zhuolu County this Sixth District is the best. See how rich this soil is. Every three years a crop of rice, and a bigger harvest in one year here than in two years elsewhere."

"Planting rice one gets more out of the land, only you have to put more work into it. The water has to be changed every other night, and you have to keep at it all the time. . . . My father-in-law says the orchard land in our village is good. I hear this is a bumper year." Thinking of the orchard trees at her old home, laden with bright red fruit, Da recalled how she and her family used to burn piles of weeds in the orchard and

8

pick fruit there, piling it up into little mountains, then packing it into baskets to take to market — what fun it had been! But that reminded her of the pear tree which had been crushed by a neighbour's willow tree.

"Has that willow of Uncle Qian's been cut or not?" she asked, frowning.

The old man shook his head without saying anything. "Humph! And we're supposed to be relatives!" she said impatiently. "But couldn't you ask the village cadres to settle the matter? Or if it's beyond them there's always the district court."

"I'm not quarrelling with him over that. One tree can't ruin me, and I can make it up by sweating some more in other ways. Besides, only half of it was torn down, and we're getting quite a few pears from it this year." He sighed. Last spring when Old Gu's son was digging an irrigation ditch he had grazed a willow tree belonging to Schemer Qian and growing on the ditch. Later the tree fell in a high wind, coming down across the ditch and crashing into Gu's pear tree, tearing half of it off. Qian wanted the Gu family to pay for the damage to his willow and would not let anyone move it. Young Gu wanted to argue it out with Qian and ask why he didn't look after his own tree. But his father would not let him. The whole village could see quite well the pear tree was slowly dying. They thought it a shame, but only discussed it in private, not wanting to meddle in other people's affairs.

Now the old man turned to look at his daughter with eyes that constantly watered. Only after a long look did he wipe his eyes, turning round again and saying to himself: "Young people have no sense!"

He devoted all his attention once more to the mule. The cart had passed Baihuai Village, and the Sanggan River could

9

be seen ahead. The sun was sinking towards the western hills, and from the fields on both sides of the road rose swarms of mosquitoes. They bit the little boy so badly that he cried. His mother flapped her handkerchief to drive them off. Pointing to the trees at the foot of the mountain on the other side of the river she soothed the child: "We're nearly there, we're nearly there. Look, all those are fruit trees, filled with red and green fruit. We'll go and pick it, and it'll all be for you. There, there. . . ."

Once more the cart was rocking through the river. This was in the lower reaches of the Sanggan River; five miles further on, at Hezhuang, it joined the river Yang. The Sanggan flowed from Shanxi to southern Chahar, carrying prosperity with it, and here its lower reaches were even richer.

Now Old Gu was giving all his attention to White Nose, mentally thanking his stars for such a good beast and for Hutai's strongly built cart with its rubber tyres. It would have been no joke travelling that muddy road and fording two rivers without it.

Once more the cart gained the river bank. When it reached the farms, the peasants who were still hoeing the fields stared at both cart and passengers and wondered: "Has the old man bought another cart? The crops aren't in yet, where could he have got the money?" But they had little time for speculation. It was getting dark, and they bent again to their painstaking weeding.

Gradually the ground began to rise. Slowly the cart passed fields of kaoliang, millet, flax and mung beans, and reached the area of orchards. Both sides of the road were thickly planted with trees surrounded by low mud walls, some branches overhanging the walls. Most of the fruit was still green, but some of it had already turned an inviting red. Voices could be heard from the orchards, for people liked to go there to look at the fruit growing riper every day. Passing the orchards the cart turned into the street. Idlers were squatting outside the gate of the primary school in front of which was a stage, while a group of villagers were sitting beside a wall. Others were leaning against the window of the co-operative keeping up a desultory conversation with the people inside, while watching the street. The rubber-tyred cart attracted the attention of these chatterers, some of whom came running over. A few called out: "Where did you get that cart? What a fine mule!"

With a mumbled reply Old Gu jumped down from the cart, took the bride and hurriedly turned off at the crossroads in the direction of his home, giving his daughter no time to greet her friends.

2

OLD Gu was fourteen when he came with his brother to Nuanshui. He had been a shepherd while his brother worked as a hired hand. The two of them had toiled for forty-eight years, their blood and sweat dripping into the barren land to which their hopes were fixed. As year after year passed and the country changed hands repeatedly, their hardships began to tell on them. However, thanks to their hard work they gradually acquired land and became able to hold up their heads. Since their family grew fast they needed more and more land. Because they had many hands and the whole family of sixteen, men and women, old and young alike all worked on the land, they were able to conquer it. Their acreage increased until they had to hire a number of day labourers. People in need of money sold their land to Old Gu, and spendthrift sons of ruined landlords' families after a bout of gambling made over their title deeds to him too.

At first he used paper to wrap up these title deeds, then a piece of cloth, and finally a small wooden case. He also bought a house with two large courtyards from Landlord Li, and everybody said that in recent years his was the only family to prosper, since both his family and fortune were increasing.

His third son was lucky enough to attend school, and brought home a primary school's graduation certificate. He could write and calculate, and was a hard worker. Being a straightforward youngster who took part in village activities he was made vice-chairman of the Youth Association. And so long as this chairmanship did not interfere unduly with his work, his father raised no objection.

Gu's elder daughter Da had married into Hutai's family at Bali Bridge. Hutai's family was quite well off. In the past two years they had bought carts, and owned a mill. Bali Bridge was on the railway, so the Hutai family did some business in trading too. As the women in the family did not have to work on the land they gradually grew a little sophisticated, liking to dress in foreign materials. Da was in her late twenties. Old Gu's other daughter Er had married Yi, younger son of Schemer Qian who lived in the same village. Qian was one of the most prominent men in the neighbourhood. When he sent someone to arrange the match, Old Gu, fearing to offend him, had to agree, although he disliked Qian because he was not a proper farmer. After her marriage Er often came home and cried to her mother, although the Qian family led a comfortable life, the women doing little work and not cultivating the land. They depended on rents and, even more, on Qian's other activities. Hence, although they owned little more than sixty *mu*[1] of land they lived better than most people.

---

[1] One *mu* is about 1/6 of an acre.

The previous autumn the village cadres had urged Gu's second son to join the Eighth Route Army. Old Gu considered that since the Japanese had surrendered, his boy would not have to stay in the army long. The farm could do without him because the family had been fairly well off the last few years. Since he had three sons he could very well let one go. And he had not asked for any compensation. His son, stationed in Zhuolu County town, often wrote home. As long as there was no fighting Gu felt easy about him. He would wait for a while and see.

That spring Schemer Qian had sent his son too. The young man wanted to join the army, but his wife, Gu's daughter Er, was unwilling. She dared not say anything, however, seeing that her father-in-law approved. Qian said he was supporting the Eighth Route Army, that the Communists looked all right to him. He also reasoned with Gu: "It's better for him to go. Nowadays things have changed, and to have people in the Eighth Route Army is all to the good. You know, we're called 'army dependents.' "

3

THE arrival of Hutai's rubber-tyred cart gave the Nuanshui villagers something new to talk about. Nuanshui and its neighbouring villages were in the mountains, off the main line of communication, and none of them could boast of so fine a cart. In the past, Landlord Li had only owned an iron-wheeled cart which he had sold to Landlord Jiang two years ago, and this year the co-operative had bought an old cart from Li's brother. Now how had Old Gu got hold of such a fine cart? Some of the more curious made enquiries and found there was no mystery. It was because Hutai at Bali Bridge was ill and could not use the cart, that he had let his relative borrow it for a few days. Sure enough the next day and the day after Old Gu made two trips with the cart to fetch coal, whereupon all were satisfied and asked no more questions. The only person in the village not to believe his story was Schemer Qian.

Schemer Qian came of a peasant family, but during the past years the villagers had virtually forgotten his origin. Although they all knew quite well that Wenfu, who cultivated two *mu* of vegetable garden, was Qian's elder brother, Qian himself seemed like a rich man from another world rather than a peasant. Though he had only studied with a tutor for two years he behaved like a city gentleman. All he said and did was premeditated. In his youth he had liked to travel. He had been to Zhangjiakou and even to Beijing one year, coming back wearing a big fur cloak and hat. While still in his twenties he grew a moustache. He knew all the ward chiefs and was on very familiar terms with them. Later he got to know the members of the county government, and when the Japanese came he established contact with higher circles. It had come about that if any of the villagers had to be chosen as ward chief, made to contribute money or act as porter, his word was law. He never held office either as *xiang*[1] leader or ward chief. Neither did he engage in trade. Yet everybody treated him with respect and sent him presents and money. He was spoken of as the man behind the scenes and wielded great power. His family lived just like city people, with wine and fragrant tea every day and white flour and rice as regular fare, not seeing a kaoliang or maize dumpling from one end of the year to another, and they all dressed fashionably.

---

[1] An administrative unit composed of several villages.

Now that the Japanese had gone and the Communists were in power, with the arrival of the Eighth Route Army people on all sides were settling old scores. The previous year the villagers of Nuanshui had given Landlord Xu, the former *xiang* head, a public trial, and confiscated his property. He had fled to Beijing and his family had gone to Zhangjiakou. That spring they had also tackled Landlord Hou and fined him one hundred piculs of millet. But Schemer Qian sat at home not doing a stroke of work, smoking cigarettes and fanning himself. Because his son had joined the Eighth Route Army and Qian had found a village security officer to be his son-in-law while many village cadres were his friends, no one dared to lift a finger against him. When villagers met him they smiled and greeted him politely. But they preferred to keep out of his way, because if he took a dislike to you he would take secret steps to injure you. He only had to say a few words, and you suffered without even knowing it was his doing. Behind his back the common people called him a "racketeer," the foremost of the eight racketeers in the village.

When Qian heard that Old Gu had borrowed Hutai's cart he chuckled to himself: "A straightforward fellow like you, Old Gu, learning to tell lies too? If Hutai were really ill, would he let his daughter-in-law come home? Isn't it time to get in the garlic? Hutai must have planted at least four or five *mu* of it this year, for this is the year for them to grow vegetables at Bali Bridge. And the women in his house alone couldn't string all the garlic. There must be more in this than meets the eye." Qian felt he must get to the bottom of the business, for he was incorrigibly inquisitive. It upset him if he could not get to the bottom of any secret at once. He set about investigating this matter which everyone else believed to be plain and above-board.

15

At breakfast time he watched his daughter-in-law careful-ly. After hurriedly setting rice and dishes on the table on his *kang*,[1] Er turned to go. She was very afraid of her father-in-law.

"Have you been home?" he asked her.

"No." Er stopped, and glanced suspiciously at Qian. She was a grave-looking woman.

Eyeing her glossy black hair, her father-in-law went on: "Your sister is back."

"She came back yesterday evening with your father. People say she was dressed very finely. After all Bali Bridge is a big village, all the women there like to dress well." The speaker was Qian's wife of nearly fifty, who had already lost two or three teeth, and yet wore a wig to which she often fastened flowers. She had just begun eating, and now joined in the conversation.

Qian's glance had fallen on the silver bracelets on the woman's wrists. His searching scrutiny made her feel her rough hands very awkward, and she crumpled the corners of her dress till her snow-white tunic hid the ruddy hands from sight. When her father-in-law took up his winecup she made another attempt to leave, but he spoke to her again: "After the meal go home and have a look. Ask your sister how the harvest is there."

When she left the room Er hurried to the kitchen where her sister-in-law and nephew were eating, and her cousin Heini was boiling water to make tea. In her excitement she could not help exclaiming: "Heini!"

Everybody in the kitchen stared at her. Heini blinked her great black eyes, then broke into a laugh: "Er! Whatever's the matter with you?"

---

[1] An enclosed brick platform through which heat is piped. It serves as a bed at night.

Er was about to tell her when Qian called for Heini from the northern room. Heini hastily made the tea and took a tray with two cups and the teapot in to her uncle. Er followed her out, then stood looking at the two pomegranate and oleander trees in the courtyard. A butterfly was fluttering among the flame-coloured flowers.

Qian told his niece that he wished her to accompany Er home to see the visitor from Bali Bridge. She should ask what illness Hutai had and what news there was, because living by the railway they heard all the news quickly and were the first to know of any changes. He was worried about the Kuomintang troops and the possibility of civil war.

"What does that matter?" said Heini. "I shan't ask. It's nothing to do with us." But she was scolded, and dared not protest any more. Still she thought to herself, "Uncle just likes to poke his nose into other people's business."

But when she had had breakfast and changed her dress she went with Er to the Gu family. She meant to be sure to ask the questions her uncle had told her to, without necessarily telling him all the answers. She had grown a little fonder of him, because she felt he had become more understanding recently, and seldom scolded her. Indeed he sometimes showed signs of sympathy.

4

AFTER leaving her father-in-law's home Er felt like a bird released from its cage, grown younger again. She was only twenty-three. Like a wild date tree she loved the fresh morning wind and blazing sun. She was not pretty, but sturdy and strong, with something charming in her awkwardness. However, since her marriage she had changed. She

17

had never worn the complacent look of some brides, but seemed like wild grass torn from the earth and wilting. She got along all right with her husband who was a simple young fellow. They made a respectable couple and did not have to use wiles or ruses to get along with each other.

That spring she had been unwilling for Yi to join the army, and cried for some indefinable reason — not entirely because she would miss him. Yi too had felt rather reluctant to go, because she was so young and had no children. But since his father insisted, he braced himself and left. She had wanted to live on her own, because that spring her father-in-law had divided fifty *mu* of land between his two sons and registered them as separate families. But in practice he did not let them separate. Schemer Qian said that if the family separated there would be no one to cook for him, and that he was now one of the proletariat and could not afford a servant. As she came of a peasant family, Er enjoyed working in the fields. She liked hard, simple labour and felt thoroughly bored just cooking, sewing and waiting on her in-laws. She had asked permission to go with Heini to the literacy class, but had been refused. Actually none of these things accounted for her uneasiness, which was due largely to fear. Fear of what? She dared not admit it, even to herself, but she feared her father-in-law.

Coming out of their lane they reached the centre of the village. The primary school occupied the best building in the place, the former Dragon King Temple. Usually clear, well-conducted singing and happy laughter could be heard from here, and only in the evening did things quieten down. Under two big trees outside the school gate where some stone benches had been set at random, men often came to enjoy the cool and smoke. Women would sit a little further off sewing shoe soles or minding children. In the space opposite the school was a big, empty square platform, the remains of what had once been a stage. In front of it were two large locust trees, their dense leaves intermingling to weave a natural canopy over the space before the platform. An occasional pedlar or melon vendor often rested here. On the left behind the stage was the co-operative, and on the right a beancurd mill. Beside the co-operative a big blackboard news had been set up, and on the beancurd mill wall was written in large characters the slogan: "Follow Chairman Mao forever!" A wide road ran south, with brick houses on either side where the rich families of the village lived. To the west were small lanes where all the houses were of mud, squalidly packed with people.

Coming out from the northeast corner of the village Er and Heini took the road leading south. Old Gu's family had moved several years previously from the west section to this central street, and were living in a house that had belonged to Landlord Li whom the villagers called "Money-bags."

Mrs. Gu and her grandchildren were at home, and Da was washing her nephews' and nieces' clothes. In the morning half the courtyard was in shade and it was not too hot. Mrs. Gu was sitting beside her daughter stringing runner beans, the two of them chatting together. The children were dragging a stool which they had set upside down in the yard. On the front they had tied a string, and inside placed a brick.

As she rounded the gate-house Er called out a greeting. Da looked round, and seeing Heini's tall figure behind her younger sister she stood up, holding out her wet hands, and went to meet them. After looking one another over from head to foot they started chatting, and Mrs. Gu said: "Heini! What good wind blew you here today? Have you had a letter from Yi recently?"

When they had sat down in the shady part of the courtyard Da brought a fan from the house for Heini, who opened it and looked at the picture on it.

While Er helped with the beans, Da described to them how someone in her village had changed into a wolf. It was all hearsay, but the people who told her believed it was true, and it made a good story. Then she talked about a well-known Mr. Ma in their village, an old scholar who had written a petition to the county government accusing the village cadres of "ruining the country, injuring the people and plotting high treason". He had denounced them as puppets. When the village cadres brought this letter back from the district nobody could understand it, but all asked, laughing, "What are puppets?" Now nobody in the village would have anything to do with him. Even his son refused to talk to him. Formerly it was because of him, the lecherous old brute, that the son's wife had run away. He really was the limit: although over sixty he couldn't keep his hands off women. He had a terrible reputation.

After Da had hung her washing out to dry, they went in to the northern room. The screen window was broken and Mrs. Gu had never had it mended, so the room was full of flies. Even Mrs. Gu admitted they had spoiled a good house.

Mrs. Gu took the stringed beans to the kitchen and brought back a pot of tea, and they went on gossiping. Da described an opera she had seen recently, called *The White-haired Girl*, in which a tenant's daughter was ill-treated by the landlord. The girl's father was driven to commit suicide, after he had been forced to sell his daughter to repay debts. Then her mistress beat her and the landlord raped her. When she became pregnant she dared not face people, and finally they wanted to sell her again. . . . Da said this opera was so well acted that many of the audience were moved to tears. A woman living next door to them had cried the most bitterly, because her life had been much the same. She had been sold like that too. When the opera was over no one wanted to leave.   And on the way home all cursed the landlord, saying, "He got off too lightly. He ought to have been beaten to death, but they just arrested him and took him to the county court.   Who knows when he'll be shot?"

After a while Heini grew tired.   She said good-bye and went home first.   Forgetting her uncle's orders, she had not asked a single question, and the others did not detain her. After she had left they started discussing her, her age and her misfortune in having no parents.   Because even though she dressed fairly well, nobody cared for her, and she was not married yet.   What would become of her no one could tell.

Last of all Da spoke of all the rumours at Bali Bridge. Their village cadres had attended a meeting in the town of Ping'an where everything was humming with daily meetings to share out property and divide up land.   It was said things would start moving soon at Bali Bridge.   Her father-in-law was worried because last year when a mass trial was held, someone had been killed and his property confiscated.   And now they wanted to share out property again — plenty of people had their eyes on Hutai's land.   Her father-in-law intended to plead with the cadres.   If they wanted to share out land, well and good, but they shouldn't try him at a mass meeting.   Because he was afraid they would take both carts he had let her father bring one back.   He would tell people he had sold it until this trouble blew over.

Then miming her father-in-law, Da said: "The communists are all right, but they only help poor people. Anyone with a little property is in for trouble.   The Eighth Route Army doesn't beat or curse people, and what they borrow they return.   The last half year or so we've made a little money

21

in business and, frankly speaking, life is much better than when the Japanese were here. There's just one thing — they're always telling poor people to stand on their feet. But a man can only stand on his feet if he himself works hard for a living. The poor can't get rich simply by dividing up other people's property."

5

HEINI'S father had died when she was five. Her mother struggled along for two years, but they had little land. Things went badly, and having no son she was forced to marry again. At first she wanted to keep her daughter with her but Schemer Qian would not agree to it, saying the child was his brother's flesh and blood. And so Heini went to live with her uncle. Neither her uncle nor aunt was fond of her. They decided to bring her up as a maid-servant, and hoped later to make money out of her, because even as a child she was good-looking, with a pair of clear limpid eyes.

Qian had a daughter older than Heini called Dani, who was not pretty but artful like her father and fond of bullying people. Heini could not get on with her. Her aunt had no will of her own, and though not exactly bad, she acted largely as an echo — whatever her husband said was right; she always agreed with him. This agreement, however, did not arise from any real similarity of outlook. It merely served to cover up her lack of intelligence and ability, and to remind others of her existence. Heini's two cousins were uninteresting too, but she was not influenced by them. She was warm-hearted, hard-working and innocent. She liked her Uncle Wenfu, a market gardener who was Qian's brother. She often went to his allotment to play, and did as he told her.

This honest man was a widower who would have liked his niece to live with him, but Qian would not hear of it. From the age of ten Heini attended primary school for four years with Dani, and proved a good student. After going home she often went out again to play, and liked to help people. The fact that she was Schemer Qian's niece made some people want to have little to do with her, but after meeting her once or twice they realized she was a good girl and forgot her family connections. She grew taller year by year and became a beautiful young woman, but did not realize it, and paid no attention to the young men who kept stealing glances at her.

When Heini was seventeen her uncle hired a man named Cheng to do the cooking. He had been a tenant of Landlord Li, but when Li sold his land to Old Gu, the latter cultivated it himself, not needing any tenant, so Young Cheng went to Schemer Qian's family as a cook. Seeing he was young and strong Qian made him do all kinds of jobs. At that time Yi and his brother were still cultivating five *mu* of vineyard, and Young Cheng had to work on the land too. With him in the household there was no need to buy firewood any more, nor to go to Xiahuayuan for coal. His wages were low and he was a distant relative, so the schemer said he was looking after him, whereas actually he was exploiting him. After Young Cheng had worked here for a year he became Qian's tenant, and was now working eight *mu* of his irrigated land.

Since Heini found no warmth in the family, it was quite natural that this newly-arrived sturdy and grave young man should become her friend. Sympathizing with him she often stayed in the kitchen to help tend the fire and wash the dishes, and sometimes stole up the mountain with him for firewood. Young Cheng was down-trodden too, having been fatherless since childhood, and forced to sell his labour power to support his mother and himself. This friendship meant a great

23

deal to him, and the longer they were together the better the understanding between them. However they were found out and separated. Schemer Qian was not going to let his niece marry a poor man. He stopped Cheng's job and found a piece of land for him to cultivate. Because Cheng was an honest fellow with few friends or relatives he had to depend on his employer, and Qian was still able to get him to do various odd jobs.

After Young Cheng moved out of the house, Heini felt all the meaning had gone out of life. At first she did not dare, but later she secretly made shoes and socks and took them to him. Although Young Cheng was afraid too, he could not but respond to Heini's encouragement. They met in secret, sometimes under the vine trellis in her Uncle Wenfu's vegetable garden, sometimes in the orchard. He often promised her: "I'm determined to save money, and once I've money I'll come and marry you."

At such times she hated her uncle and felt how unfortunate she was to have no parents. She would stand behind Young Cheng, leaning close to him and swearing to be true, saying, "You know, not a single person cares for me except you. If you aren't true to me, I shall become a nun."

A year passed, but there was no hope for them. When Schemer Qian began to arrange matches for the two cousins, Heini was worried and cried, and Young Cheng could only hold her hands tightly, unable to think of any way out. Just then the situation suddenly changed. Japan surrendered and the Eighth Route Army came to their district. The villagers who had done underground work came into the open, everything was reorganized and the peasants clamoured to settle accounts with the landlords. Young Cheng threw himself into the movement, and it made a new man of him. He joined the militia of which he later became an officer, and

24

that summer when the peasants' association was set up he was elected chairman.

By liberating the village the Eighth Route Army also liberated Heini. Her uncle dropped his match-making and changed his attitude to her, appearing much more kindly. The increased respect with which Young Cheng was regarded in the village delighted her, for although they were seeing less of each other she did not think he was fickle. She failed to realize Cheng's new dilemma. As a matter of fact he was deliberately keeping his distance. He knew that all the villagers hated Schemer Qian, that although the latter had escaped mass trial twice he was none the less the worst enemy of the poor. Now as chairman of the peasants' association Young Cheng ought to identify himself with the masses and not go marrying Qian's niece, while an affair with her would be even worse. He feared this connection might damage his position and set tongues wagging, the more so since the marriage of Qian's daughter Dani to the village security officer had caused general displeasure. Hence he must harden his heart. Although his deliberate coldness to Heini was very painful to him, and he felt not a little ashamed of it, still he was a man, he could set his teeth and stick it out.

Some of the village cadres, however, saw Heini in a different light. They considered her one of the oppressed, and invited her to teach the women's literacy class. She made a patient and conscientious teacher, obviously doing her best to show that she wanted to identify herself with the new regime and that she was progressive. But in spite of the good impression she made, she could not recover her old footing with Young Cheng.

Gradually Heini realized the danger confronting her. The more she wanted to hold him the less confident she felt of doing so. There was not a single person she could turn to in her trouble, yet now her uncle seemed to understand her wretchedness, often showing sympathy. While unable to understand his motive, Heini felt rather grateful to him, and the girl lapsed into a melancholy out of keeping with her simple and carefree nature.

6

ONLY when Heini reached home, and saw through the branches of blossom smoke wreathing out from her uncle's window, did she remember the points he had told her to find out. But she thought: "Oh, it's just because he sits at home with nothing to do."

Voices could be heard from her uncle's room. Pressing her face against the window Heini had just caught sight of Teacher Ren sitting opposite the *kang*, when her aunt called from the western verandah: "Heini! When did you get back?"

Coming away from the window Heini looked sulkily at her aunt, then gave a little snort and went to her own room. "What's the point of sneaking like that?" she thought scornfully.

Schemer Qian tweaked his moustache, narrowed his eyes and glanced sidewise at the primary school teacher. Ren puffed at his cigarette, then went on relating the news: ". . . The paper reports this as Sun Yat-sen's idea. A good deal has been done at Ping'an. All the rich have been forced to produce their title deeds. Probably Zhuolu won't escape. None of the places under the Communists or the Eighth Route Army can get out of it."

"Of course, that's the Communist way, or rather their — their policy. What's that policy called? Let's see, what did you say just now it was? Oh, yes, 'Land to the tiller.' That's it, 'Land to the tiller.' That's very good, an excellent way to tempt the poor! Hah, very good indeed. . . ." By now Qian's eyes were reduced to two slits. After pausing for a moment he went on: "Only — well, world affairs aren't as simple as that. After all, Old Chiang has American backing."

"Humph, the Communists always say they are working for the poor, for the people, but that's just so much fine talk. Mr. Qian, you should go to Zhangjiakou to see. Hah! Who live in the best houses? Who ride in cars? Who are always coming in and out of the best restaurants? Aren't they the ones who've grown fat? Mr. Qian, nobody wearing an old-fashioned long gown can get anywhere nowadays." So saying Ren looked searchingly into the other's long face.

Qian gave his sleeves a shake, brushed the ashes off his light jacket, and said with a slight sneer: "A new dynasty uses new ministers. Are you complaining, Old Ren? You're a teacher in primary school, you should serve the people!" He laughed.

Being laughed at like this caused Ren some embarrassment, and he could not help saying, "Whatever happens I have to earn my living by teaching. Always, everywhere, I have to take my cue from others. I can't afford to complain. Only I feel they are going too far. Look, we teachers have to be guided by the so-called Commissioner of Popular Education. That doesn't matter, Mr. Qian. But you know as well as I do the so-called commissioner is no other than that Freckles Li. The bastard knows a few easy characters, but he's a fool. Yet without any sense of shame he keeps coming to issue orders for this, that and the other." He sighed.

Qian went on laughing. "Freckles Li had eight *mu* of land himself, and last year after the struggle against landlords he was given more, so now he has ten *mu*. He and his father and that adopted child-bride of his can live quite well, yet

27

they're still considered as poor peasants. In your case, how much land do you have? ... Ah, but you are not a labourer!"

"Each month I get a hundred catties of grain, no more, but that hundred catties isn't easily earned. In addition to the 'capital' put in past studies, nowadays one has to learn folk dances too. They like that low-class stuff. Tao Yuanming[1] would not stoop for half a picul of rice, but for one hundred catties of grain I have to put up with Freckles Li's insolence. Ugh!"

"Well, a hundred catties of grain a month is not bad. Never mind, if they are sharing out property or dividing up the land you may be sure they won't touch you. Just as in my case — I'm not afraid of them. For instance, this spring I gave fifty *mu* of land to my sons. Now there are only we two old people left and Heini, with just a little over ten *mu* of land for the three of us. Each year we only get over ten piculs of grain, so we're neither poor nor rich, simply a borderline case. Let them make all the trouble they like. We see through the vanity of this life and mind our own business."

Ren was a graduate of the rural normal school who had come to teach in Nuanshui two years before and the longer he was there the more superior he felt to everyone else. He had no friends. In the beginning he had seen a good deal of Landlord Li, but later considered that fallen landlord too much of a weakling. There was another teacher named Liu with whom he should have had much in common. Ren did not mind that Liu's standard was lower than his own, but Liu relied on flattering the village cadres and always led the school children in singing, "Without the Communist Party there would be no New China," or writing posters and shout-

---

[1] Tao Yuanming (372-427), famous Chinese poet, gave up his government post, with its meagre pay in terms of rice, rather than bow to his superior.

ing slogans. Because of this he was trusted and regarded as superior to Ren. This made Ren feel aggrieved, and gradually Schemer Qian came to be the only person he could talk to. Sometimes he felt Qian was a real friend, who recognized his ability and could help him. Whenever he heard any news, he liked to discuss it with Qian to work off his depression, for although there was nothing to be hoped for here, and he sometimes left feeling even more depressed, he sometimes derived comfort. Today he had come in looking rather pleased. But when Qian received the news he brought so coolly, without any sign of disturbance, Ren felt a little put out.

It was noon of a summer's day, without a breath of air. Inside the house it was oppressively hot, and Qian told his wife to brew another pot of tea. Ren was fanning himself with a little fan plaited from rush leaves, staring vacantly at the photographs on the opposite wall and at the scrolls with pictures of beautiful women. Guessing how bored he felt, Qian offered him another Sun cigarette, saying, "Old Ren, it's a good proverb that says, 'Dreams can't be trusted.' I wager Old Chiang won't let the Communists have it all their own way. Wait and see to whom this village belongs eventually. Do you imagine this rabble can control the country? Take Yumin, who's one of the top people asked to decide big and small matters. That's a good cadre chosen by the Communists! Bah — Landlord Li's hired man! In the old days he had to bow to everyone. Or take the chairman of the peasants' association. I know everything about that Young Cheng. He was in my household. If these riffraff are allowed to manage affairs they're bound to mess things up. Now they are simply relying on their guns and their numerical strength. Another thing, why must they always start the struggle and never finish settling accounts? I suppose this is the only way to tempt the poor — this talk of giving them land and grain naturally pleases them. As a matter of fact, they're fools. Who can they rely on later when the Kuomintang army comes and the Communists make off? When that happens the old status quo will be restored, and the old rulers will take charge again. As for you, Old Ren, no one in the village has your education. Even though you can't be given any office because you weren't born here, at least you won't have to put up with these insults for nothing."

"You must be joking. I'm a plain teacher and I don't want to be an official. Only I don't like seeing good people oppressed, Mr. Qian. That brings us back to the same subject — in the land reform this time I advise you to be on your guard."

When Qian saw the conversation had come back to this, he tried to change the subject. "I'm not afraid of land reform. If they make a thorough job of it I may even get given a little irrigated land. When my son Yi left I didn't ask for any compensation. Only we should advise the poor it's better not to take land, so that they won't suffer later. In school you can sometimes teach the poor children to tell their parents when they go home the Communists won't necessarily stay long in power! That would be a good thing to do."

Ren thought this an excellent idea. Now he had something to do, he would carry it out very secretly. However, he still believed Qian to be over-confident, and thought it his duty to warn him again: "That fellow Yumin is very cunning. Don't be deceived by the respectful way he talks. Another thing, you never know when one or two people with a grudge against you may come into the open."

"Oh . . . don't worry, don't worry! I'm not going to let those fools get the better of me. You go back and be on the lookout. If there's any news, come here. If the papers report any Kuomintang victories, tell people about it. It doesn't

30

matter even making up a few. They're not all fools in the village, and everybody has to think of the future!" As he was speaking he got up from the *kang*. Ren, who had put on his shoes and was feeling very pleased, took another Sun cigarette from the table on the *kang*, and Qian promptly struck a light for him. They heard the bamboo curtain in the room opposite move, and involuntarily exchanged glances. Then Qian called out: "Who's there?"

"It's me, Uncle!" came Heini's voice. "I'm chasing the cat. She's such a nuisance here."

Ren involuntarily sat down again. Qian understood the young man, and knew why he kept coming to their house and trying to win his favour. But he gave him a glance and said: "I won't keep you. The children will have finished their lunch and be ready for class. Come again when you have time." He parted the Japanese-style gauze curtain patterned with flowers, and Ren had to hurry out. In the central room were the ancestral tablets and god of wealth; on the red lacquer chest gleamed polished brass sacrificial vessels. The whir of a paper fan could be heard from the room opposite. Qian immediately lifted the bamboo curtain leading to the courtyard and the two of them went out together, to be met by a gust of hot air. A few bees were buzzing about in the sun, blundering against the window. Qian saw Ren to the gate-house where once again they exchanged significant glances.

7

IN the stifling noonday heat Old Gu's daughter-in-law took advantage of the midday siesta to go home to see her sister-in-law, Gui. The latter lived at the west end of the village in a mud house with a little courtyard fenced in with kaoliang stalks. The courtyard had a vine. House and courtyard were small but neat as a new pin.

Gui had just been taking food to her husband, and was washing dishes by the stove. Her young sister-in-law stood by her side panting, keeping a secret watch from the window.

"Is all you're telling me true?" asked Gui, catching hold of the girl, while the two of them turned and leaned against the door. "Oh, I warned your brother against it. Look how he got into debt for ten piculs of grain to buy five *mu* of vineyard! Oh, if only we'd known, we shouldn't have bought so much land." The news was so sudden she did not know what to fix on first. It sounded advantageous but at the same time she was afraid they might lose by it. Taking a ragged cloth off the wire she mopped the perspiration on her face, then sat down on a stool to think it over again.

Before Gui had finished thinking or had time to discuss it with her, her sister-in-law hurried off. Old Gu's daughter-in-law was sorry for her brother and his wife, because apart from this little house and the five *mu* of land they had bought they had nothing else but debts. Moreover, Gui was a village cadre who had been pushed into the position of chairman of the women's association, which was, in her opinion, a piece of bad luck.

This chairman of the women's association had come here as a refugee from the north over four years previously, and after an introduction from a fellow villager had started living with Vineyard Li. He wanted to marry her because it would cost nothing, and she saw he was a straightforward fellow, so with both parties agreeable they got married without much ceremony. She was an intelligent woman of nearly forty, not a bad match for a bachelor of over thirty. The two of them got on well, and gradually began to look like a respectable household. People thought Vineyard Li lucky to have such a good wife, who was used to hardships and knew the difficulties and cares of life. She managed the house well, and was good-tempered. All the occupants of the mud houses in that western section spoke well of her, and the previous year when Nuanshui was liberated and they wanted to set up a women's association they proposed her. In vain she pleaded ignorance and the fact that she was not a native of the village. She was elected, and whenever there was any business she summoned the others to meetings. Later she organized a literacy class, and took charge of that very conscientiously too.

Still sitting on the low stool she looked up at the sky above the courtyard. There was not a cloud to be seen, all was azure blue. She felt there might be a storm. One day Nuanshui was bound to be stirred up again, when everybody would seem to go off their heads once more. She recalled the previous year and that spring, and how hard she had worked, going from house to house to fetch the women. When the men called them backward, the women said: "We don't understand anything! We can't make head or tail of it!" At meetings no one opened her mouth, nobody voted for anything. She knew no more than the others, yet she had to stand on the platform and shout. But later when some people were given land she and her husband received nothing but a little grain which lasted less than four months. They had bought five *mu* of land cheap, but they owed ten piculs of grain which they had been allowed to borrow as a favour on the part of the village cadres. And now the village was to be stirred up again. She felt this might be a good thing as far as she was concerned. If only they could pay off that debt of ten piculs. . . . Still. . . .

She was just going to think it over again when the bell for the women's literacy class sounded. At once she stood up to comb her hair and fasten it firmly, then changed her tattered blue cotton jacket for a new white blouse and, without waiting to wash the bowls in the pan, locked the door and hurried off to class. She wanted to find someone to share this news with.

The literacy class was held in the big hall of Landlord Xu's house, a large building which had been divided up the previous year among six or seven families with no homes of their own. It was a fine building, originally well furnished but now in a state of disrepair and disorder. A number of tables had been left in the hall for the class. The few young women who had arrived had clustered together to look at an embroidered pillow-case, and were talking with such animation of the prices of threads and laces, it was impossible for them to notice how upset their chairman was.

More and more women came, chattering like magpies. Babies at the breast had been brought too, who had to be amused. Then Heini, who was their teacher, arrived. At her arrival they started studying, but some women at the back kept whispering or passing remarks about their teacher.

Gui sat on one side by herself, no longer eager to speak to the others. Looking from one to another she realized that the women left in the literacy class — about half of the original number — were comparatively well off. The poorer ones simply had no way of coming. If she insisted on it they put up a show for a few days but then stayed at home again or went into the fields. That only left these young wives and girls without a care in the world, who enjoyed the literacy class and came for two or three hours a day to learn a few characters. By coming to this lively place to exchange news of their neighbours and joke together they could throw off their family yoke and boredom. The spring had slipped past this way, and now the summer was nearly over. Now it was

34

Gui, chairman of the women's association, who seemed different from the rest. For the first time she realized with amazement how out of place she was here. Although neither old nor withered, she was coarse and weather-beaten. Good as she was at dealing with people, still she lacked interest.

All of a sudden she wondered just why she was there. These young women certainly did not need her, and she was not sure they did not despise her, yet she wasted three hours a day sitting here. Yumin had told her that women must organize themselves before they could be emancipated, and be able to read before they could have equality with men. But that was just fine talk. She looked at the women again. They did not need emancipation, nor want equality. Neither did she. She and Vineyard Li were a poor couple, quite content with poverty. She in particular, who had many times been on the verge of starvation, ought to be satisfied with their present life. Of course she was not entirely content, there were still things to hope for. With a debt of ten piculs of grain they needed a little prosperity, for if they failed to clear themselves after harvest life would become even harder for them. What was the good of her sitting here? It was all very fine for Yumin to talk. He had insisted on dragging her into this women's association, with all his talk about serving the poor. But they were not serving the poor, while she herself was even growing poorer.

" 'Prosperous' — means rich. If you are prosperous you have a lot. It means you have more than you need. 'Clothes' — the clothes that we are wearing. . . ." Heini pointed to the blackboard, speaking in clear, silvery tones.

"Do I have more clothes than I need, damn her!" Gui stood up, cast a look of dislike at Heini with whom she was usually on excellent terms, and went out into the courtyard.

This was the first time Gui had ever left the literacy class early. She felt as if she had had a surfeit of something, and at the same time an emptiness as when she had gone hungry too long. The lane was deserted except for a couple of dogs lying there with their tongues hanging out. Reluctant to go home she decided to go and see Yue, the shepherd's wife, who was vice-chairman of the women's association but had not attended the literacy class for a long time. She felt sure Yue would be pleased to hear what she had to say, and they would see eye to eye.

8

THE whispering that had started when Old Gu brought home the big cart gradually spread from within doors to the fields and streets. Of course there was more comprehensive and reliable news from other quarters which people also spread, interspersed with their own wishful thinking, until there were many versions of the facts. But on one point all agreed, namely: "The Communists are coming again to help the poor stand on their feet, and the rich are in for it!"

Resting during the midday siesta under the trees, looking across the river and thinking of the flames of vengeance raging on that plain, the peasants would count over on their fingers the names of despots there. When they heard of local tyrants being punished and their property divided up they did not conceal their delight. There had been two trials in their village prior to formal land reform and some had had their revenge and received shares of grain. But some were still dissatisfied, bearing grudges in silence because they dared not express their grievances openly. Some were grateful to the Communists but were dissatisfied with the cadres, whom they accused of unfairness and selfishness. They wanted another settling of accounts, hoping to see real justice done this time.

They liked to talk like this, group after group drifting together on the land during the midday siesta, and later in the streets and lanes in the cool of the evening.

Other groups, however, were rather afraid, and these were the people who were comparatively well off. They were afraid that once the landlords had fallen the masses would attack the rich peasants, then the middle peasants. So they often gathered in threes and fours to exchange news, hoping for reassurance. If only things were not carried too far, all would be well! They always spoke in low voices. If any newcomer joined them they would turn their heads and start tapping their pipes, or change the conversation to the weather or to women. In a short time all became remarkably sensitive, so that if anyone arrived from the district government or if Yumin, Young Cheng and the other cadres disappeared, they would say Nuanshui's land reform was about to start and that the cadres had gone to meetings or a training class. They would come back early from the fields, trying by hook or crook to find out what was happening, thinking anxiously: "If it must happen, then the sooner the better!" The heat got on everyone's nerves.

With these discussions came rumours that the railway had been cut. The Kuomintang had brought up many divisions of crack troops, armed with big American guns which were even better than Japanese artillery. The Eighth Route Army had never seen the like of them. That American official, Marshall or whatever his name was, had come to mediate, asking the Kuomintang to "take over and reorganize" the Communists. But now he was displeased, so there was no hope of peace. The Americans had brought over countless tanks, big guns and aeroplanes, and were helping the Kuomintang run an officers' training school. The Communists couldn't possibly beat them, their guns weren't good enough and they had too few troops. Thus the Eighth Route Army couldn't last long, any day they might sling their packs over their shoulders and go. Then Nuanshui would change hands again, and those who had shown themselves red would have to risk their necks or abandon their families and go with the Eighth Route Army. . . .

By whom were these rumours spread? Apparently by the peasants themselves. They did not want the Communists to be defeated or the Eighth Route Army to leave, yet they spread these rumours on the sly.

Even after Yumin and Young Cheng came back from the district, nothing happened. They went to work on their land as usual and people settled down again. About the third time for hoeing, rain had made the weeds grow very quickly. The peasants found their work cut out for them and turned all their attention to their rice, millet, kaoliang, flax, orchards and vegetable gardens. They had been humming like bees, but now all their hopes and fears passed away like a summer shower. Since their wishes had come to nothing, they turned all their energy again to their daily tasks. Joy and fear alike abated. Rumours were no longer listened to, nor spread. If the railway were cut, it was a long way from Nuanshui. If Kuomintang troops came, there was the Eighth Route Army to stop them, and anyway the Kuomintang were Chinese too. The peasants lived by the sweat of their brows, not wanting to be officials. They had better carry on as before. For now there was peace, there had been enough rain that year, their crops and fruit trees were not doing badly. Better wait for the prosperous autumn which lay ahead.

9

TWO years before this, when the Japanese still occupied

fortified garrisons, one snowy evening in 1944 just after the lunar New Year, Landlord Jiang, the ward chief, had crept out of his house wearing a new sheepskin jacket. With shoulders huddled in the biting wind only his darting eyes were visible. When he saw the street was empty he went stealthily to the door of White Snake,[1] as the villagers called her behind her back. The door was unbolted, and softly pushing it open he went in. A bright light in the western room made him pause in the courtyard to listen to the sound of dice rattling in a bowl, and a harsh man's voice bawling: "Flush! Flush! Two, three, flush!" At the same time a husky voice called: "Three into six, three into six . . . aha! . . . Seven, seven!" As the dicing stopped there was a moment's clamour followed by the sound of money being counted, and human shadows moved on the window. Then Jiang hurried to the northern room which was quite still. He could smell the familiar odour which he loved seeping out from under the wadded cotton curtain of the door.

White Snake was lying on the *kang* straightening out the opium-smoking utensils under a small lamp, but when the ward chief burst in she immediately got up and invited him to be seated. Taking his new sheepskin jacket and assuming a look of pleased surprise she asked, "What, is it still snowing? Are you cold? Do get on the *kang* and warm yourself. Did you go to the west room? It's so cold, not many people have come. There are only a few poor devils there."

Jiang removed his cap to wipe the snow off the fur, and sat down on the warm *kang*. White Snake brought a tea-pot from the little stove at the head of the *kang*, slowly poured out a cup of strong tea, and suggested: "Let me prepare a pipe for you."

---

[1] A snake in Chinese folklore which could change itself into a seductive woman.

"Is Yumin in the west room?" asked Jiang as he lay down.

"He's just come in. He's been drinking somewhere."

"Fetch him here." He took the pin from her, speared a small piece of opium, and held it over the lamp flame while White Snake went out.

When she came back she was preceded through the door by the sturdy figure of Yumin. His wadded gown was unbuttoned, and he held an old fur cap in his hand. Afraid he was in for trouble, he put a bold face on it.

"Ah, elder brother! Come on the *kang* here! I'll prepare a pipe for you." The ward chief actually greeted him first, convincing Yumin that something was up.

"Thanks, I don't go in for that. I'll have a cigarette." Yumin sat cross-legged on the edge of the *kang*, his head against the wall. Taking a cigarette from his pocket he put the cigarette White Snake had given him back on the tray.

Jiang had to sit up. He took the cigarette Yumin had declined and lit it over the lamp, then said smiling: "Well, elder brother! We're old friends, we can talk frankly. So you come here too to amuse yourself, eh! How has your luck been the last few days?"

Yumin replied half in jest and half in earnest: "The last two days unfortunately I've had a bad stomach. People say 'Lord White' answers the wishes of his worshippers, so I came to consult him. I don't know whether he really answers or not." He laughed.

On the sideboard opposite the *kang* was a shrine with a red silk curtain. In the dim lamplight the image behind the still curtain looked embarrassed.

White Snake pretended not to have heard, but raising her head reached for a water pipe from beside the shrine to smoke, and having lit it leaned against the sideboard and pulled on the pipe until it gurgled.

"Seriously," said the ward chief becoming grave, "I need your help. You'll just have to help me."

"Right, say the word!" answered Yumin cheerfully.

Jiang gave White Snake a look and waited till she had gone out, then cleared his throat and explained the difficulty that had recently arisen.

A month ago he had received a polite letter from the Eighth Route Army, but before he could report it to the Japanese some Eighth Route Army men had come to his house. They were fairly young, but hard to deal with, being polite one moment and firm the next. What they said sounded very fine: "You can't be blamed for being ward chief, but you're Chinese and should have your heart in the right place. All we want is to borrow a little grain from your village. If you let us have it, well and good. If you don't, we won't kill you, we'll just inform the Japanese garrison that you're in with the Eighth Route Army. We have men in the garrison."

Frightened almost out of his wits for fear they would kill him, Jiang signed an agreement promising them grain; and after they had gone he felt he could breathe again. But what was to be done? He could not report it, because they had an agreement in his own writing in their hands. Yet if he did not report it he was afraid the Japanese would find out and kill him. Schemer Qian, whom he consulted, said they were only bluffing and he need pay no attention. However, another letter had come from the Eighth Route Army and he had been visited again. Something must be done. Now Qian was blackmailing him, threatening to inform the *xiang* government that he had dealings with the Eighth Route Army, so he had to give him money. He had also had to collect a few piculs of millet and a few dozen pecks of flour to send to the Eighth Route Army — but who could act as messenger for him? It must be someone with his wits about him, who wouldn't let the garrison know, and it must be someone brave to confront the murderous incendiaries of the Eighth Route Army! If the job were bungled it would mean at the least prison, and nobody wanted to get into trouble. He had thought it over for several days before thinking of Yumin. Yumin, having just had a disagreement with Landlord Li and lost his place, must be very hard up. He was brave but at the same time cautious, just the man for the job. So Jiang had come to White Snake's today specially to see him. While telling this story Jiang naturally made up crimes of the Eighth Route Army, saying it was right to send grain in order to avert calamity from the village, for otherwise the Eighth Route Army would certainly come to burn and massacre.

As he listened in silence Yumin understood the ward chief's scheme, and formed his own plan. But instead of saying anything he just punctuated Jiang's narration with "Oh," "Really?" "Ah," "That's too bad!"

"You're the only one, elder brother! You're the only one who can do it, so please make this trip as a favour to me! I'll see you have everything you need. We're old friends, how could I let you down!" The ward chief raised the question quite frankly.

"Well —" Yumin took another cigarette, then shook his head, saying, "It's not that I don't want to help, but I really couldn't pull it off. I'm a rough fellow, I can't read a word and don't know how to talk. Sending grain oughtn't to be so difficult, but then it's like relations between two different countries. Just can't be done. There are plenty of clever people in the village with the gift of the gab. You've picked the wrong person. If you wanted someone for rough work, to use a hoe, carry wood or drive a plough, I wouldn't mind helping you out. Ha ha!..."

Jiang told White Snake to bring wine dishes, and she sat

by them to keep the guest company and help flattering him. All this time Yumin was laughing up his sleeve, because as soon as he heard of this errand he was delighted. To visit the Eighth Route Army was just what this hero-worshipping youngster wanted. He did not believe that talk about burning and killing, and as a poor bachelor he was not afraid. He knew even bandits worked for justice sometimes. Nevertheless, he made himself appear very reluctant, realizing that Jiang was not to be trusted, and would shift all the blame onto him if anything went wrong. Besides, this was a fine opportunity to make him eat humble pie. Finally Jiang had to write a letter in his own hand and seal it with his private seal. He also had to give Yumin sufficient travelling expenses, and even fetch his uncle Quan to witness that if there were any trouble he guaranteed to ransom him. Only then did Yumin consent, with every show of reluctance.

That same evening Yumin, wearing Jiang's new sheepskin jacket and driving two big mules, set out for Nanshan. Late the next evening he reached a village of some forty families and found the man he was looking for. The Eighth Route Army soldiers were dressed just like the peasants, with the addition of a short gun in their belts with a piece of red silk tied to it. They were very friendly and kind. After greeting him they gave him wine to warm him up while they prepared noodles. He listened carefully as they talked, and felt that they had a sense of justice — to fight Japan and overthrow traitors was right. They also attacked the rich and helped the poor, which he entirely approved. And they advocated equality and showed themselves very friendly. Accordingly he told them how things were in the village, cursed Ward Chief Jiang as a running dog of the Japanese and one of the village "racketeers," and warned them to be on their guard against him.

This trip made a great impression on him, but he said very little about it to Jiang, whom he forced to come time and again to beg him to go, until gradually he became very friendly with the Eighth Route Army.

When Yumin was eight his parents died and he had gone with his little brother to live with their grandmother. Since then nobody had shown him any affection. All day long he worked on the land with his uncle Quan, a simple soul ground down by poverty, who could endure hardships like an ox but had no idea how to look after his nephew. It was simply a working relationship between them, like that of plough and harrow. His grandmother could not look after him either, as she often went with his brother on her back to beg in the neighbouring villages. Since all the grain his uncle harvested went in rent, even if it was a good year and other families ate meat, flour and millet, they were lucky to have a few square meals of kaoliang. He grew up like a little ox, able to thrive as long as he had grass to eat. When a youngster of seventeen he set up house for himself and his brother, and the latter, a lanky boy, became responsible for gathering firewood, cooking and other jobs. He recognized only one rule: Poor people must rely on their own strength to make a living. If a day came when they couldn't take it any longer, they would fall in their tracks and that would be the end of them. Hardened by sun and wind, he had grown strong. Rich farmers liked to hire him, and he was able to make a living by his hands.

When he met the Eighth Route Army, they made him tell the story of his life. As he described to them the past that he seldom liked to think about, he realized for the first time how unhappy he had been, how lonely, oppressed and downtrodden! It was very comforting to have found friends for the first time in his life, and friends who were so concerned about him. Knowing that he was loved he felt happy and eager to live a better life. The fact that others had confidence in him made him want to live more purposefully, especially when he realized that his difficulties and those of his uncle and many other poor people were all owing to the oppression of the rich.

After this Yumin stopped going to White Snake's. He had only gone there in the first place because he was depressed after losing his job. But now whenever he felt low he went to see the poor youngsters who were his friends, and would tell them how he had seen the comrades of the Eighth Route Army, whom he was proud to know. He emulated the Eighth Route Army in arousing their indignation at the injustice of their lot. Why should the poor have such a hard time of it? Was it decreed by fate that they should toil like beasts all their lives? In him Nuanshui had its first Communist that summer, and later he persuaded Freckles Li and Swarthy Guo to join the Party. That winter he had procured one blunderbuss and one local-made rifle, and secretly formed a militia. Then the Eighth Route Army began to visit the village more often. Sometimes they called on the ward chief, and Jiang was forced to protect them. Sometimes they stayed in the western quarter, where the militia stood guard for them.

But the work did not go forward easily. There were eight notorious "racketeers" in the village, whom the common people hated and feard. Jiang, a representative of the eight "racketeers," was only allowed to hold office because he flattered them, and by now he had acquired quite a fortune. He used the Japanese as a pretext to oppress the people, and the Eighth Route Army as a pretext to extort money. There might be more sinister characters than he in the village, but for the present he was the most obvious. The Eighth Route Army comrades helped Yumin arrange for a reduction of rents

45

and rates of interest. The people accepted their ideas in principle, but dared not put them into practice. It was not until the summer of 1945 that a meeting was finally called to reorganize the village government. One evening the militia and comrades of the Eighth Route Army took charge of the village, setting a watch, while they assembled all the villagers in the school for a mass meeting. When people saw Jiang was tied up they felt bold. Because it was night-time and faces could not be seen clearly they dared speak out, and for the first time expressed their hatred, shaking their fists. Jiang was overthrown and Zhao elected.

Zhao was a poor man but an able one, who knew how to deal with the Japanese. At first he did not want to be village head for fear the old powers would make trouble for him, but when he saw how many people raised their hands he was pleased at being elected. After his election, the Eighth Route Army cadres from the district helped him, and he discussed with Yumin and others how to cope with the Japanese. The Japanese had no idea of the real situation in the village, and believed Zhao implicitly. The rich and powerful families in the village were given different treatment, the villagers cooperating with some while isolating, dividing or warning others so that they dared not make a move. Thus for the time being not even Landlord Xu or Schemer Qian could think of a way to retaliate, and from this time on the power in Nuanshui was in the hands of the people. Soon after this the Japanese surrendered and Yumin, chairman of the Resistance Union, came out into the open as a responsible figure in the village. Twice he headed mass trials, and poor people brought their difficulties to him, saying delightedly: "He's done well, the Eighth Route Army has made an able man of him!"

Some secretly despised him, because they had known him as a poor child, and wanted to make trouble. But when they met him they called him "elder brother". In the past the only people to call him this were those who wanted a job done, or his gambling friends when he won money. Now however this form of address sounded quite natural.

<h1 style="text-align:center">10</h1>

YUMIN and Young Cheng brought back from the district a lithographed booklet published by the propaganda department of the county committee of the Communist Party. Neither of them knew many characters, but late at night they would get hold of Freckles Li and the three of them sitting round a little oil lamp would read line by line aloud. Freckles Li also copied out the chief facts in a small notebook. He had many precious things in that notebook: the oath on entering the Party and the minimum qualifications for membership, such as (1) To devote one's life to serving the poor; (2) To face danger together and obey all orders instantly; (3) To pay Party dues; (4) To reveal no secrets to non-Party members, not even to parents, wife or children. . . . All this was copied out. Whenever any problem cropped up Freckles Li would look up his notebook, and could often find an answer there. This homely-looking young Communist was a great talker and a good singer.

The three of them studied *Questions and Answers on Land Reform* together, but each had his own views. Freckles Li found it easy to accept new ideas, without thinking deeply. His interest grew as he read. He often applied his new ideas to the actual members of their village, classifying landlords, rich peasants and middle peasants, and declaring which should be attacked and which aided. A cheerful smile never left his face, and his unceasing admiration for the Party and for

Chairman Mao made him exclaim: "This is a fine method. This way those rich people can be pushed down and the poor really stand on their feet!" Not a serious thinker, he felt land reform was only too easy to carry out, and was quite confident of success.

Young Cheng, who had joined in the work for fair tax assessment that spring, was well-informed about the land in the village. He looked through the record of households which contained detailed figures as to land owned, and paid special attention to the determination of class-status. "Heavens!" he would say, "Dahai has thirty *mu* of land, but can you call him a rich or middle peasant? Just think what land it is. Nobody would take it as a gift!" Or else, "Don't think Zhendong's hard up for land. A young fellow with three *mu* of good irrigated land!" Or again, "Judging by land, Zengshan is a poor peasant, but he has a trade. He's been able to get married and his wife wears a new padded gown." The distribution of land seemed to him no easy problem. Only if they satisfied the whole village that justice had been done could they be considered to have succeeded. Otherwise there would be disagreement among their own people, and the work would be held up.

Yumin had less to say on the subject than the other two. He was only concerned over the actual extent of their strength, the amount of strength they could muster, and whether they could completely overthrow the old forces in the village. He believed most of the decisions of their superiors would be easy to implement, for with the backing of the Party and the Eighth Route Army no one in the village would publicly oppose them. But to carry the work through conscientiously and overthrow the forces of feudalism once and for all, the people must organize voluntarily to emancipate themselves. And that was no easy matter. He took a poor view of the people's judgement, finding them hard to convince, wavering and easily deceived, only concerned with immediate profit, and accustomed to curse the cadres if they were at all dissatisfied. Yumin knew they must keep close to the masses to have strength, but felt the masses were often unreliable, swinging from one extreme to another. To gain their entire confidence was still impossible. So he looked forward to land reform with a mixture of enthusiasm and anxiety, hoping that capable cadres would be sent early from the district to settle this important business successfully.

Soon after this a mass trial was held at the village of Mengjiagou some two miles away, to try the local despot Chen Wu. He was a notorious scoundrel who beat up anyone who crossed his fields. He thought nothing of abusing people and raping women. It was common knowledge that he sold opium and concealed weapons. On the day of his trial all the cadres of Nuanshui went to watch, as well as some of the peasants. Some forty or fifty people had prepared to accuse him at the trial, but before it was half-way through there was no stopping the peasants rushing up to spit in his face and beat him. Women stood out and cursed him too, waving their braceleted arms and striking him on the head.

The villagers from Nuanshui were staggered, then joined in the shouting. With hearts aflame, they hoped Nuanshui would have its day of reckoning soon, but feared they might not manage things so well. Yumin went again to ask the district authorities to send cadres quickly, and the villagers, realizing that it would not be much longer, could scarcely contain themselves. Sure enough, two days later some men in uniform carrying simple packs on their backs came to the village.

II

IT was late one afternoon in the middle of August that Old Dong and three men from the district entered the village by the wooden gate in the northeast. Old Dong, chairman of the district trade union, went to the co-operative to find Yumin. Dong's companions, comparatively spruce young men who looked like county or provincial cadres, stopped outside the primary school to rest, putting down their packs to wipe their perspiring heads, then strolling about to look at the slogans in the street or glance inside the school where classes were about to be dismissed. The gossips under the trees opposite started discussing them in low tones, devouring them with their eyes as if to take stock of their ability. Peasants just back from the fields looked on from a distance too. A high-spirited youngster of medium build attracted the most attention. He was joking with a child nearby, but the latter was shy of strangers and walked sulkily away. The shortest of the men strolled over to the co-operative, and turned to ask the villagers: "Is Yumin in the co-op, folks?" Only the thin youngster stood still at the gate of the primary school, cheerfully joining in the song being sung inside:

From the red east rises the sun,
There appears in China Mao Zedong.

Old Dong returned preceded by Yumin and followed by Freckles Li and Liuman who walked swiftly over, seized the packs and slung them over their shoulders, then, calling the strangers, set off towards the south street. The thin youngster hurried to take his pack himself, but stumbled on a stone and nearly fell, staggering some distance before he came to a stop. Seeing everybody in the street looking at him, he smiled foolishly, and a roar of laughter went up. He hurried forward again to take his pack, but Freckles Li and Liuman were now some distance ahead. They walked along laughing while he called after them: "Hey! Let me take that myself! Hey! This won't do, this won't do!"

Yumin took them to Old Han's house, the western wing of which was empty. The old man was a poverty-stricken hard worker who had joined the Party that spring, and Yumin had proposed giving him this house which had belonged to Landlord Xu. It was very clean and quiet here. Old Han's son had just returned from Shandong after serving in the army, and there was only one eight-year-old grandson who was at school. Yumin thought it would be a good lodgings for the men from the district, because Old Han could easily make them tea and look after them.

As soon as they had all arrived Freckles Li acting like a host invited everybody to sit on the *kang*, surveying the guests with enthusiastic eyes. He was surprised to see a fiddle strapped to one of the packs.

"This is the chairman of the Resistance Union, Yumin," said Old Dong by way of introduction. He himself had been thirty years a hired labourer. Then pointing to the stout man carrying a pistol, he said, "This is Comrade Wen, this thin one is Comrade Hu, and that is Comrade Yang." Then he handed Yumin a letter of introduction from the secretary of the district Party committee, giving the credentials of the three comrades and explaining that they represented the district Party committee to carry out the work of land reform.

"How many Party members do you have here?" Wen started at once as if conducting an investigation. Yang shot him a warning glance which he failed to notice.

All Yumin said was, "Comrades, you must be hungry, we'll prepare a meal. Young Han, you help your dad. Hurry up and get food ready. Liuman, you go to the co-op for a few catties of noodles." He paid no attention to Yang's request that they should use their meal tickets, but went to Young Han's room to fetch a long-legged oil lamp for them, then told Old Dong: "You rest for a while. I'm going out, but I'll be back soon." Leaving the new arrivals he hurried off.

Freckles Li was loath to leave. He picked up the fiddle and tuned it, asking Hu, "Can you sing Shanxi tunes?"

Wen walked to the door and looked out. The dark courtyard was very quiet. In the kitchen opposite bellows were being used, and steam could be seen rising in the lamplight, while old men, women and children bustled about in busy confusion. He turned round for a few words with Old Dong, eager to efface the impression of slyness Yumin had made on him.

Old Dong, however, was writing on the table on the *kang*. After three years in the Party this ex-labourer had learned to write simple letters. He was delighted when people praised his keenness in study, and he never forgot to carry in his pack his own seal together with stationery bearing the district trade union seal. He seized every chance to write letters and make long, high-sounding speeches.

By the time supper was ready Yumin had come back and sat down quietly beside them smoking. Yang said in the future they must not eat white flour and need not have meals specially prepared for them; but each should use his meal tickets. He criticized Yumin for taking so much trouble. Yumin's jacket was unbuttoned, revealing his hairy chest. Wen was conscious of the smell of sweat and something like liquor too. He remembered the secretary of the district Party committee had told him that the branch secretary at Nuanshui had for a short period fallen into bad habits. His mind kept running on this to the exclusion of the Party secretary's next, more positive statement: "He is a sincere and able cadre from the ranks of the hired labourers."

After the meal Yang and Hu wanted to learn more about conditions in the village, for although the secretary of the district Party committee and Old Dong had given them a general picture, they were still unclear about certain points. Yumin and Freckles Li approved their proposal. Just as they were about to start talking, Comrade Wen said he felt there were too few people present. He decided to call a meeting of all the village cadres, and explained that this would be taking the mass line. Yumin and Freckles Li accordingly had to go out at a moment's notice to search for the cadres.

After a long time Zhao (vice-village head), Zhang (security officer), Guo (captain of the militia), Cheng (chairman of the peasants' association), Qian (chairman of the trade union), Zhao (organization officer of the Party branch), Freckles Li (propaganda officer of the Party branch), and Yumin arrived. This made a total of eight. Only the village head had not come. The village head was no other than Landlord Jiang who had been overthrown the previous year. This spring, acting on Vice-Village Head Zhao's proposal, they had reinstated him, on the grounds that someone was needed to do the leg work, and since he was rich he could afford to put off his own work. As long as they didn't let him have any real power no harm would be done. All the village cadres had felt the force of this argument.

None of the eight men had made any preparations. Although all extremely pleased, they were at a loss for words, and afraid of saying the wrong thing before these strangers. Swarthy Guo, a straightforward fellow, stood shyly and awkwardly by the door, not even willing to sit on the *kang*. He was excited and seething with ideas which he could not express. Since joining Nuanshui's militia he had shown himself completely fearless and ready to risk his life for the cause, but talking was not in his line.

Garrulous Old Dong started expounding to the group the significance of land reform, beginning as usual with the cliché: "Land reform is to do away with the feudalistic landlords who exploit the people...." He declared they must get rid of three fears, and spoke on and on, dragging in the strikes of Canadian workers and Italian sailors, and other stories he had heard. His listeners could not make head or tail of it, but he imagined they must find it very interesting, and if Comrade Wen had not stopped him he would probably have gone on all night.

Comrade Wen wanted to rescue the meeting from boredom, and felt the first thing to do was to see that the cadres' ideology was correct, so he explained point by point the directives for carrying out land reform, most of which he could recite by heart.

They talked very late until it was certain that everyone present understood. Then Comrade Wen decided to call simultaneous meetings of all the people's organizations the next evening to expound this policy. At these meetings the newly-arrived comrades could preside. Notice of this would have to be sent out the next morning before the peasants went to the fields. In Wen's opinion, because of the situation on the Beijing-Suiyuan Railway and the possibility that the Kuomintang might attack at any time, the work must be finished in a week to ten days at the latest.

When the others had gone Yumin lingered behind as if he had something to say, but Comrade Wen did not notice this. Wen just repeated that they must remain close to the masses and not keep everything in their own hands, and that there were too few Party members. Yumin accepted his crit-

icism without a word. Although he still had something on
his mind, Yumin saw they were desperately tired, so he had
to leave. As he left he told them he had set a guard and that
all the inhabitants of the lane outside the rear courtyard,
which led to the west of the village, were their own people.
There was not much chance of trouble in the village.

After his departure Comrade Wen summed him up in these
words: "Timid. Reminds me of a member of one of the old
secret societies."

I 2

YUMIN left the west room with the feeling that something
was amiss. Old Han, who was still sitting at the kitchen door
enjoying the cool of the evening, asked him: "Will you be
coming back?"

"No. Bolt the door."

Old Han followed him out, and said softly: "The whole
village knows, and they've been asking me whether they're
from the district or from the county or provincial government."

"Oh, just say from the district." Without looking back
Yumin went straight to the south street. Seeing Swarthy
Guo standing with a rifle at the top of the street, he thought:
"That's a reliable fellow." He went over to join him.

Inside the room Guo had felt very sleepy, but when he
came out and had taken two turns up and down the cool
quiet street, he grew wide-awake again. Now he went to
meet Yumin, and nudging him with his elbow whispered:
"In the co-op." Yumin scanned his face in the faint light,
and turned north without a word towards the co-operative.

The door of the co-operative was not locked, and opened

at a push. In the courtyard he could hear people talking in the back room, from which came a gust of warm air. Liuman was standing by himself beside the counter in the front room, stripped to the waist, his arms folded and a cigarette in his mouth. He looked sullenly at Yumin as he came in, but Yumin paid no attention to him. He listened to Organization Zhao speaking inside: "You call him a working landlord? True, he doesn't hire long-term labourers, but he hires day labourers. And as for land, he has more than anyone except Li."

"A working landlord?" put in Young Cheng. "What, do you count him as a landlord too? At any rate he's a different type from Landlord Li. Li sits there without lifting a finger, living off the fat of the land, and gambling away. Old Gu has acquired his land by the sweat of his brow, and lives frugally. If we treat him like Landlord Li, people are sure to protest!"

Tian, manager of the co-operative, joined in: "If we take Li's land this time, he'll have to beg for his living. That fellow is as weak as a kitten. The year Yumin quarrelled with him and his cook was ill, he went to the well to fetch two half-buckets of water. He could barely stagger back with them to his gate, and fell down before he could cross the threshold. He was sweating so hard that he caught a chill and was ill for two months."

"Bah! You're always shouting about working for the people, but when it comes to overthrowing landlords you start feeling sorry for them and can't bear to take anyone's land! Cheng! You stink as chairman of the peasants' association! None of you have any guts!"

It was Security Officer Zhang speaking. He had not been active for a long time, but this evening he had stayed in the co-operative and there seemed a good deal of truth in what

56

he said. This made Yumin curious, and he decided not to go in, but sat down beside Liuman on the counter.

In the inner room was the group which had just left Old Han's house. There they had felt drowsy with nothing to say, but as soon as they came out all sorts of questions occurred to them and no one wanted to go home. They had come to the co-operative and woken up Co-op Tian who was asleep. But they were very confused and had no idea how to go about this business of land reform. Moreover, they did not agree among themselves, almost everyone having a different opinion. Vice-Head Zhao in particular was much upset as he sat by himself on a flour case, thinking: "They said letting Jiang be village head was a wrong move. Was it really opportunism?" That had been pointed out by Wen in his criticism, and Zhao felt very bad about it. "It wasn't only my idea. I'd been village head ever since the Japanese were here. For over a year now, I've had no time to work for my living. I'm a poor man with five mouths to feed and only three *mu* of poor land. I have to work as day labourer for others from one end of the year to the other, and the last two times they divided the fruits of struggle I didn't get a thing. Jiang is well off and capable, so why not make him run about? But they say we've given the whip hand to the enemy. That's nonsense, what does Jiang dare do nowadays? Doesn't he have to toe the line? I'm no fool. If anyone is to be fooled, he'll be the one. How can he possibly play tricks on me?" Then he remembered how Jiang, knowing he was hard up and not wanting to embarrass him, had lent him two piculs of grain through a third party. If not for those two piculs of grain his family would have gone hungry.

Trade Union Qian was a straightforward fellow who had worked for other people for more than ten years. After liberation fewer people hired labourers, so he had nothing but day labour. Everybody knew he was a distant cousin of Schemer Qian, and knew too that they didn't get on together. In fact none of Schemer Qian's relatives had a good word for him.

Freckles Li did not approve of Tian's suggestion either, but he resented Security Officer Zhang's cursing them for having no guts, so he called out: "Zhang! It's up to all of us this time. This won't be like last year. Last year you made a lot of noise, but Landlord Xu had gone to Beijing, so nobody was afraid of picking on him. This spring we picked on Old Hou, and got a hundred piculs of grain out of him. Old Hou was ill in bed at the time, and his son is young. People figured it wouldn't matter offending him. But this time — well! Cheng! You're chairman of the peasants' association, who do you think we ought to settle accounts with this year?"

"This year are we just dividing land, or settling scores with the landlords as well?" asked Organization Zhao.

"Land reform is just to divide land, but —" Young Cheng thought of that mass meeting at the next village, and added, "there must be a public trial to settle scores too."

"Of course, without settling accounts how can there be reform?" assented Freckles Li confidently.

"But in Mengjiagou they had a local despot, whereas here we only have landlords, and not even one big landlord. If we had a big landlord like the one in Baihuai with thousands of *mu*, we could set to work with a will. They say although the land hasn't been divided yet, plenty of silk coverlets have already appeared on the cadres' beds." Security Officer Zhang was gradually growing corrupt, and he already loved comfort. If it were only a degree of selfishness, that might be excused. He had once said to Vice-Head Zhao, who was rather uneasy: "We local Communists are quite different from the others. Though the village is liberated, we're not like

58

fish in the sea, free to swim wherever we please. We've all got homes. Leaves fall by the tree, and there's no getting away from Nuanshui. If we offend all the rich people, just suppose a day should come when — well — who can guarantee the Eighth Route Army will remain here? Others can leave at any moment, but we'd have to face the music. We'd be left high and dry like eels in a drained pool."

Zhao despised this kind of cowardly talk. If people were afraid they ought not to join in. He cursed Zhang inwardly for wavering, but not wanting to offend him he kept his thoughts to himself.

Security Officer Zhang knew some people disapproved of his marriage, saying he had been led astray by Schemer Qian. "They're really too unreasonable," he thought. "Qian isn't a reactionary and can't really be considered as a landlord either. If the Eighth Route Army would take his son as a soldier, why shouldn't I take his daughter as my wife? In a couple of years Yi may be promoted and become a prominent Eighth Route Army cadre. Let's see what they have to say then."

He had formerly been respected in the village, and Yumin had thought a lot of him, but during the last half year he had drifted away from the community. Feeling the others were prejudiced against him, he seldom assumed responsibility in public affairs, and his ideas consequently differed from the rest. Sometimes he was afraid the others would attack him, so he pretended to be very "left" wing. At other times he took a negative stand, and would make defeatist remarks.

Freckles Li was still pressing the question: "Whom shall we struggle against this time?"

Nobody had an answer. They mentally reviewed the candidates one by one, feeling at one moment the prospects were too numerous, and the next moment they were not qualified. Or else they thought of someone but felt afraid to speak out.

"Do we have to rack our brains for an answer? Of course we must choose rich ones. Humph! Landlord Li's sweet steamed bread is pretty good! Are you all dumb? Didn't Old Dong say land reform was to do away with the great feudalistic landlords who grind the faces of the poor? In my opinion we should put him under guard tomorrow, and the day after try him." Again Security Officer Zhang assumed an upright and fearless air.

"If we catch racketeers, let's catch the foremost," protested Freckles Li. "Don't think I'm standing up for a rogue like Li. Sure, he had money, but now he's in our power he dares not stir. He's completely under our thumb."

"Do you mean, then, we should leave the landlords alone and not settle accounts?" countered Zhang. "Is Landlord Xu the only one who can be tried? Are we to go to Beijing to fetch him back? You say I'm afraid of him. All right, just you get him back and see if I dare shoot him or not!"

"Don't talk nonsense!" Organization Zhao could not keep quiet either. "All I say is, don't let's shield anybody. Any rich person who's oppressed people and lorded it over the poor can't be let off."

This infuriated the other two. They leapt to their feet to demand an explanation, but he retorted: "If the cap fits, wear it."

To save the situation Vice-Head Zhao asked if they ought to start a temporary mess-hall. They knew there were some villages where this was done, and it had been done the previous year during the trials in Nuanshui. This facilitated the work. The cadres ate with the militiamen, everybody was on the spot if wanted, and it saved going home to eat. Moreover, it made for greater keenness. But opinions were divided again. Zhang said since the cadres were busy and the militiamen were on guard day and night, a mess was essential. In Baihuai, sixty people had eaten together, and very lively it was too. There was no need for special expenditure, they could eat the fruits of victory taken from the landlords which were in hand.

Young Cheng said this was a wasteful proposal. If the cadres had to attend meetings, so did the people. It was the duty of militiamen to stand guard, just as it was their duty to fight. Furthermore, the comrades from the district had already said they had meal tickets and could eat in any family they pleased. There was no need to touch the fruits of victory which belonged to the people. Should the cadres eat them all up? Would they refuse to attend meetings without the fruits of victory?

Cheng's view immediately gained the support of the majority, this infuriating Security Officer Zhang so that he bit his lip and muttered: "You can talk very finely! Let's see if Cheng wants to get land this time or not!"

Freckles Li seized this chance to say: "You're just setting yourself against the group. You won't convince me you aren't sheltering someone."

Yumin had wanted to go in for some time, but felt while they were arguing, especially about the question of whom to struggle against, it would be difficult for him to express any opinion without having decided on a line of action with the comrades from the district. He was not yet on familiar terms with them, not yet really united, and he regretted his lack of learning, feeling he was not up to their standard. He thought of Comrade Pin in the county government who was extraordinarily easy to get on with, the more so since he had come to win over this village and therefore understood conditions here and trusted him implicitly. Now the men inside seemed on the verge of a quarrel, and since disunity was what he dreaded most he jumped down from the counter to go in, but was stopped by Liuman.

Liuman had got wind of the meeting here, and hurried along to stand outside and listen. Now he gripped Yumin with one hand and gesticulated with the other, saying very distinctly in warning tones: "Yumin! Let me tell you frankly, if you seize racketeers you must seize the chief. It's no use catching the small fry! Ha! This time we'll see how you act as chairman of the Resistance Union, eh!" He dilated his eyes fiercely, beating his bare chest with his fists, then without waiting for Yumin to reply, turned and strode off, still muttering to himself in his peculiar southern Chahar accent.

Yumin was taken aback at first, then called out loudly after Liuman: "Every wrong should be righted. If you have courage, speak out. I want to see how you act too."

The men inside heard them talking, and put their heads out to call: "Yumin! Come on in!"

As soon as he went in he became the centre of the group, everybody looking at him, waiting for him to speak.

"All of us here," said Yumin, "including Tian, are Party members, aren't we?"

"Doesn't that go without saying?" they answered.

"No matter whether we started work under the Japanese or joined after liberation, we're all sworn brothers, aren't we?"

"We stick together through thick and thin," they responded. "If we have to jump into the Yellow River we'll do it together."

"In that case, if we have any ideas let's discuss them ourselves, but we shouldn't talk to outsiders."

"Of course!" Freckles Li confirmed. "That's one of the Party rules."

"As to how the .work should be done, there's Old Dong and the comrades from the district to decide. All we Party members have to do is to obey them."

"Of course," Freckles Li expanded the idea again. "That's what you'd call. . . ." While he was still reaching for the notebook in his shirt pocket, he remembered: "Oh, that's a rule of organization."

"Whom should we struggle against this time? Frankly speaking, we can't choose according to our personal likes and dislikes, we must follow the wishes of the masses. People they don't hate we can't try even if we want to. People they hate we can't protect even if we want to." His eyes rested for a second on Security Officer Zhang.

"Right, we're working for the people," said Vice-Head Zhao. He was tempted to reveal the shameless things Zhang had said, but on second thoughts refrained.

"We all took the oath when we joined the Party. If anyone here wants to betray us, we won't spare him. I for one won't stand for it. What do you say?"

"Who'd dare think of such a thing!" they answered. Zhao shot another glance at Zhang, itching to speak.

In the end, though it was not certain whether everyone agreed or not and they had no idea what they would do the next day, their hearts felt lighter, and they had a feeling of solidarity. All were prepared to go through fire and flood for the people.

They began to realize it was late.

"Better go home! Tomorrow there's a meeting to attend!" someone suggested.

"Right, tomorrow there's a meeting, nobody must go out to the land." Yumin walked out first.

The crescent moon was already in mid-sky and the street was very cool and still. Organization Zhao and Trade Union

Qian turned south. All the rest skirted the bean-curd mill and headed west. As they turned into the lane Yumin looked back, feeling there was someone missing, and saw a man at the north side of the street. He grasped the situation at once, but instead of calling out just whispered a few words to Freckles Li.

13

YANG had been instructed to attend the women's meeting, so he went out first thing in the morning to see Gui. He had worked as librarian in the Border Region government library, and although he was only twenty-five or six, and had only had a few years in primary school, during his work as librarian he had read a good deal. In addition to being a bookworm he was painstaking and liked using his brain. Thus although he looked an ordinary, rather quiet cadre, those who were with him for some time realized that he was a youngster who had a mind of his own and was anxious to get on.

In spite of the many advantages derived from his work in the library, he did not want to go on with it. He often thought he would like to work in some district or village. For at the end of the previous year he went to a village to help the peasants settle scores with the landlords, and the experiences of that month had made a deep impression on him. He believed the rural areas were a great living library in which he could study more realistically, which could inspire him, clarify his view of life and help him understand Party policy better. What made him particularly eager to go was that there was a directness about country life which would add warmth to his cold theoretical knowledge, and thereby enrich and strengthen him. He came of a farming family, but the work had taken him away for over ten years, and now that he was coming back to the country he could appreciate still better the simple sentiments which could not be found in his work as librarian. So when he heard that some comrades were to be sent to work in the land reform teams he seized the opportunity eagerly, hoping to do a good job in the country, and learn a great deal. Thus the previous evening when Comrade Wen asked him to attend the women's meeting and find out their conditions, although he felt unsuited to the job, which might prove embarrassing, he nevertheless accepted gladly, since they had no women comrades with them. "Easy does it!" he thought. Now he was going in the cool of the morning to ask where the women's chairman lived.

He turned into the third lane at the west of the village, a narrow lane bounded on either side by mud walls and littered with dirt and refuse. There was a woman standing at one gate, naked from the waist up, with two naked children clinging to her. The children's faces were smeared with eye mucus and snot, and covered with flies. When she saw Yang approaching, instead of going inside she turned to look at him, and the children peeped out stupidly from behind their mother. Yang felt embarrassed to look at her, but could scarcely ignore her, so he asked: "Can you tell me which is Vineyard Li's house?"

The woman was in no hurry to reply, but smiled as if he were an old acquaintance: "Won't you come in?"

"I'll come later to see you. What's your family? What's your name? Right now I have to find Vineyard Li."

Still simpering, the woman answered: "Come in and see our poor house. We're the Zhao family, the vice-village head's family. Have you met Zhao?"

"Oh, so you're the vice-head's family?" Yang could not help staring at this half-naked woman with the matted hair and dirt-streaked arms, while the children looked even more as if they had just crawled out of a dust-heap. He felt a surge of shame, as if he had in some way treated them unfairly, and patting the two children promised to look in later and call on her husband.

After this he hurried off. The woman called out loudly after him: "It's the next house, in the next courtyard."

Vineyard Li had gone to work on the land. Gui, wearing a patched vest, was hoeing the soil under the grape vine. Seeing a stranger in uniform come in she smiled awkwardly as she moved from under the vine.

"Have you eaten?" She did not know what to say.

"Not yet. Are you Gui? I came to see you."

"Oh. . . ." She came out from under the vine.

"Have you heard about tonight's meeting?"

"Yes. But it's not much use our women's association holding a meeting. We've nobody who can speak."

"It doesn't matter if they can't speak. If nobody wants a meeting we needn't necessarily have one. Just exchanging views with a few people will do. What do you think? Let's talk it over now and think of a way, what do you say?" Yang sat down on the mud step outside her door.

"You haven't eaten yet, I'll go and get you something." Ignoring his protests she hurried inside. When she came out again she brought a bowl of kaoliang gruel which she offered Yang, saying: "Our food is very poor. We've nothing good, but have a bowl of gruel." By this time she had changed the patched vest for her one and only white blouse.

Instead of talking about the women's association, he just chatted naturally with her. To begin with she was very shy, confining herself to answering questions, but gradually she began to talk freely. She was from North China and had seen hard times. Her first husband had been conscripted by the Japanese and never been heard of again. She had a son, and after her husband left, it was even harder for her to make ends meet. They were already at their wits' end when there was a famine and her father-in-law had no choice but to sell her to a merchant. She left her home to go with him, but as ill luck would have it he fell sick and died, and she had come here with some famine refugees. Now she had taken up with Vineyard Li, a poor man but a straight one. Her health was not what it had been, but she managed to find time to make shoes to sell. However, she couldn't make much money by it because her customers were poor bachelors in the neighbourhood, who found the shoes sold in the street not strong enough. She often thought of her son who ought to be in his teens now.

She had no one to talk to like this usually. She found this youngster sympathetic, and he listened patiently while she spoke, and asked repeated questions. Presently she asked him if his parents were alive and whether he was homesick or not, and learned his mother had died when he was a child. His father was a peasant with four or five *mu* of land, but he had not heard from him for several years. Having run away with his uncle to join the revolution, wherever he went he considered his home. He was poor himself, so he was at home with poor people and he wanted them to have a better life, for then his father would have a better life too.

When she heard this she was sorry for him and felt drawn to him. She wanted to heat him up something more to eat, and when he refused she brought out a bowl of cold kaoliang which he ate with appetite because he was really hungry. His praise of the little dish of salted turnips pleased her enormously.

Yang got a general picture of the women's association in the village. There was no regular attendance. Before any meeting she had to go from house to house to fetch the women, and most of those who came were members of the literacy class. The association had organization and propaganda chiefs besides two chairmen, but none of them knew what they were supposed to do. Whenever there was any business it was Gui who had to fetch them. The practical work was the literacy class, which had done better than in the neighbouring villages. That spring they had given a dancing performance. But the poor women had no time to attend class and didn't like dancing. Attendance at the literacy class had been compulsory to begin with, but later they were unable to keep that up and had to make it optional, and most of those who attended were from rather well-to-do families. The women did not speak during meetings but liked to come and listen — some because they were young and could accept new ideas easily, and others because they were told by their families to find out what was going on.

Yang learned that the women were not much interested in village affairs but had paid considerable attention to the division of the fruits of victory. They would complain that this family had got too much and that too little, while if someone received one brush more than anyone else it was occasion for her rejoicing. Being shy and afraid of saying the wrong thing, the women dared not talk during meetings for fear of being criticized by the village cadres. But after the meeting they were afraid of nothing and would criticize, squabble and sometimes even come to blows.

"Aunty Gui," said Yang (for so he had begun to call her), "I think you must be a very good speaker, you talk so clearly and consistently. They chose the right person when they elected you as chairman. Especially since you've had a hard time of it yourself, you can understand other people's difficulties. We are all poor. Only the poor are willing to help the poor."

68

He told her it was not necessary to call a meeting. She need only call on the poor families, telling them the principles he had explained to her. By chatting with them and listening to their complaints she would see whom in the village they felt most badly about, and how they thought of the village cadres.

Gui was delighted, and felt he was really a good sort. When he first arrived she had been afraid he would want her to call a meeting and make a speech, which she dreaded. But now he said all she had to do was to make calls and chat with people as he had done with her. She could do this, and knew she would be welcome. When she felt depressed she often called on the shepherd's wife — they had plenty in common. As she agreed to his proposal she felt a faint pink in her sallow and sunken cheeks, and put it down to the unusual heat that day.

The sun really was blazing hot. Even sitting on the steps in the shade they felt it beating in from all sides. He repeated his instructions again, then started on his way. Gui saw him outside the gate and pointed out her neighbours' house to him. Only then did he remember his promise to call on Vice-Head Zhao. Accordingly he walked into the adjoining courtyard which did not even have a gate.

The tiny courtyard was in great disorder. As no one was in sight Yang called Zhao's name, and the half-naked woman he had seen came out from the house and greeted him again eagerly. Yang saw there was another young woman inside, neatly dressed and with glossy hair, who seemed shy and hid herself in a corner, with only her pale face visible as she peeped out. Yang felt he could neither go in nor leave, and asked, "What about the children?"

"They're asleep," said the middle-aged wife of the vice-head with assurance. "Won't you come in and sit down?

69

We've only this tiny room. There's hardly room to turn around. These two rooms in the south belong to our cousin. The place is chock-full of rags and junk. Won't you come in and have a look? My husband will be back soon." Then stepping forward she whispered, "She's the wife of the village head. Doesn't she dress smartly? Ah, I haven't got a thing to wear." She cast a glance over her naked arms and pendulous breasts.

"The village head's wife?" Yang had food for thought, but did not show any surprise, just quietly taking his leave of the good-natured woman. As soon as she was back inside, he could hear her chuckling.

14

BACK in the south street Yang noticed a number of people with a mysterious and apprehensive air come out of another lane, whispering warnings to each other. On reaching the top of the lane they stopped and looked back at one particular house. Yang wondered what they were up to. Joining the crowd he found a young militiaman carrying a local-made rifle, and asked him what had happened. The militiaman was about seventeen or eighteen, and had a white cloth round his head with two corners dangling over his shoulders. He eyed Yang innocently, but only answered with a foolish smile. When Yang pressed him he said with embarrassment: "I'm not sure. People are so superstitious."

At this point another man caught up with them and interrupted to ask: "Did you see it?"

"No," said the youngster regretfully.

"What?" asked Yang again, but the man had already hurried back into the lane.

Yang followed him.

A group of people suddenly burst out of a gate, among them a woman with dishevelled hair and red eyes, carrying a child in her arms. The onlookers held their breath and looked at her sympathetically and fearfully as they followed her out to the street. There some of them watched for a time from a distance, then gradually dispersed. Yang's curiosity was aroused, for all the villagers seemed tongue-tied and unwilling to talk. What could have happened? Looking back he saw that the gate of that house had not been closed, and prompted by curiosity decided to have a look.

The courtyard was so quiet, it was hard to believe there had just been such a crowd there, and there was a strange odour in the air. He quietly walked straight in, pressed his face against the window-pane of the north room, and saw a woman lying on the *kang* dressed in white, her small feet in white slippers crossed. She was facing inward, but seemed to have heard some sound outside the window. However, instead of turning round she called out calmly in a sophisticated voice: "Aunty! Fetch me the fruit that was brought just now."

Yang beat a rapid and stealthy retreat, thoroughly bewildered, while an old woman came out from the west room, from which the heavy odour was emanating. Acting on impulse Yang rushed over and raised the curtain, and the old woman did not stop him, but pursed her lips and motioned with her head towards the north room. Her face was thin and wizened, her eyes red-rimmed and her expression ambiguous. From her winks and pursed lips it was difficult to make out what she wanted. Yang lifted the bamboo curtain and went in. Candles and incense were burning inside, in a brass vessel on the ground some paper money had just burnt out, on the chest of drawers was a shrine with a red silk curtain and white strips of silk embroidered with characters. The pewter

71

candlesticks and incense-burner were polished so that they shone. Yang was about to pull the red silk curtain when the old woman waddled in again and asked sharply: "Whom are you looking for? What are you doing here?" Her back was bent like a bow, and her two feet, not much bigger than a donkey's hooves, tottered backward and forward all the time.

"What's this? What do you do here?" Yang looked piercingly at her.

Just then the sophisticated voice was heard again in the courtyard, calling: "Aunty, who are you talking to?"

Yang came out from behind the old woman. The woman who had been lying on the *kang* was standing on the porch outside, dressed in a snow-white gown which fitted her like a glove. From the bottom of her trousers two diminutive white feet peeped out. Her face was dusted with powder, her arms loaded with silver bracelets, her oiled black hair plastered on her forehead, and her eye-brows plucked in a crescent were blackened too. She stood there frail as a hanged ghost. When Yang came out of the west room she remained as calm as ever, and only asked with a smile: "Whom are you looking for?"

Yang walked quickly out, feeling as if he had unaccountably strayed into an old story book, and hurried to the street as if he had seen a ghost. A pitiless sun burnt overhead. He was hurrying forward, oblivious to everything, mopping his face, when he heard Hu's cheerful laugh behind him.

"Where did you disappear to all morning? I've had a time looking for you."

Yang gripped his hand, smiled uncertainly and was just going to speak when Freckles Li appeared, roaring with laughter, and said: "Well, comrade, how did you come to visit a place like that?"

"Who lives there? What do they do?" asked Yang rapidly. "They have Buddhas inside!"

"That's the famous White Snake!" Freckles Li winked and went on: "She's a widow who can cure sickness. That aunt of hers is an old widow who could cure sickness too when she was young, and she taught her niece. Ho, ho!" He couldn't stop laughing, and putting his head close to Yang whispered: "People say she can cure love sickness too! Ha ha!"

Hu burst out laughing too, and slapped Yang on the back.

"It's all nonsense," went on Freckles Li, as the three of them started towards Old Han's house. "But it really is strange. There was a snake in her house this morning under the eaves, so she threw a fit. She's a witch, and she said it was Lord White reverting to his original form — the Lord, you understand, is the god she has in the shrine. The god said the emperor born of the real dragon is holding court in Beijing, all China will be unified and have peace. Only the people must behave themselves in order to be rewarded by Heaven. . . . She often makes up nonsense like that to deceive people. Today a lot of people went to her house to see Lord White. Liu Guisheng's wife took her sick baby for her to see, but she said Lord White told her the villagers were wicked and the world was going to the dogs, so she refused to go into a trance or prescribe medicine, and the woman was dreadfully upset."

They had now reached Old Han's house. As Wen was still writing at the table, they went on talking about White Snake. Yang asked about her past, Freckles Li told them a number of jokes and Hu kept chortling with laughter. Later Wen, wearing a serious look, warned Yang that he should not run off wherever he pleased, because it would give people a bad impression. But Yang had his own ideas, and was not in the least repentant.

COMRADE Wen had quite an air and seemed a good scholar — at least he succeeded in impressing others with his learning. He had also acquired some of the characteristics of the leisured class and was trying hard to do away with these undesirable traits. He wanted to become more revolutionary and behave like a cultured, responsible cadre or, to put it bluntly — a high-ranking Communist.

He often told people he was a university graduate or even a university professor, without making clear of which university. Probably only his Party branch knew the truth. When doing educational work he hinted that he had formerly studied education. At one period he had seen a good deal of certain writers, and he liked to discuss different fields of literature as if he were well versed in them all. At present he was ostensibly a student of political economy who had published an article in a leading magazine.

Wen was widely read and liked to discuss books. Once he held forth enthusiastically on Mao Dun's *Midnight* and *Before and After Qingming Festival* and the handicaps to China's industry and its future. When asked why the able and shrewd heroines of these two novels while hating their surroundings still entertained people like prostitutes, he spoke at random, saying this showed the author's view of love and represented the most recent aesthetic thought. At this his listeners grew indignant at what they considered an insult to Mao Dun, and thinking they were going to hit him he admitted he had not read either book, only a review of *Midnight,* the preface of *Before and After Qingming Festival* and the news that a play had been made of it.

Another time when he was dining in the house of a committee member of the county Party branch, to make conversation he said: "Your plump face is very like your father's."

Much surprised, his host asked: "Did you know him?"

Wen pointed to a woodcut hanging on the wall, and said, "Isn't that he? Look how alike your eyes are."

At this everybody in the room burst out laughing, the man opposite him who had his mouth full nearly choked. "Heavens! Liu Yuhou! Don't you know him, Comrade? Didn't you say you'd lived in Yan'an?"

"I've seen many portraits of Liu Yuhou. This isn't he. Is it really not your father?" Wen made himself appear quite indifferent, and tried to pass it off by saying that this woodcut was not a good likeness, the only good woodcuts were by Gu Yuan who had stayed with him for a long time. Then people pointed out the artist's name at the bottom of the woodcut, and when he looked he read "Gu Yuan". Momentarily taken aback he soon started expatiating on Gu Yuan's fame abroad, and how even Americans knew that among the Chinese Communists was a woodcut artist of genius, Comrade Gu Yuan. The others were not certain whether he knew Gu Yuan or not, but it was a fact that he liked to visit famous people. Anyone with the least reputation he seemed to know, or at least the story of his life. And he liked to recount his associations with such people to those who had no opportunity or desire to hobnob with the famous.

This was all past now. He had spent a year in Yan'an studying, during which he had analysed himself many times, in some respects very profoundly, and tried to change some of his unrealistic bad habits. He wanted sincerely to go to the masses and learn from them, but after leaving Yan'an he still liked to hold forth, to display his learning, dogma and second-hand information. Sometimes he realized this could not help him get close to the masses, but it gained the respect of the less cultured, and that was enough for him.

75

Now he was joining in land reform, claiming to be study-ing China's land problem and rural economy. The Party considered more experience would be good for him, and there-fore wanted him to take part in the work. But after he reached the district the authorities there, not knowing him and impressed by his fine talk and apparent learning, were exceptionally polite to him, and trusted him enough to make him leader of a work team sent by the district Party com-mittee to take charge of the land reform in Nuanshui with its two hundred-odd families.

From the very start Wen realized it would not be plain sailing, not because he understood the work in the village but because he found to his dismay that he had not yet established his prestige in the group. He regarded Hu as an ordinary propaganda worker of low cultural level but very conceited, and Yang as a pig-headed youngster. In tackling any prob-lem his chief concern was how to impress them. Without any clear understanding of women's or youth associations he ordered them off to attend meetings of these groups, while he decided to preside over the peasants' association himself. He even spent a whole morning drafting the notes for his speech that evening. This speech was to be rich in content and profound in its views, so that if printed in the Party paper it would make an elegant essay.

Old Dong had been sent to Liyu, about a mile away, where there were only fifty families. The district authorities thought it unnecessary to send anyone else, since the team in Nuanshui could supervise the work there too. As it hap-pened, Old Dong's elder brother lived at Liyu, so he was more than willing to go. Thus the evening's meetings would depend mainly on Comrade Wen.

In the afternoon the two younger comrades went off on their own. Yumin put in an appearance, but left on seeing there was nothing to do. Left to himself Wen felt tired out, and since it was a hot day lay down listlessly on the *kang* to practise his speech. He very soon fell asleep, no doubt to appreciate his own eloquence in his dreams.

16

THAT evening many families ate earlier than usual, and after the meal, since there was nothing to do, strolled about the streets. There was an atmosphere of expectancy, and a smile on every face just as at a festival, and people greeted each other with: "Had your supper?" "There's going to be a meeting when it's dark!" They went to the compound which had once been Landlord Xu's, but not a cadre was to be seen there. A militiaman, with a local-made rifle slung across his back and a white towel on his head to keep off the heat, took up his post at the gate, pacing up and down.

"When's the meeting?" he was asked.

"Who knows?" said he. "Many people haven't eaten yet, and some are still in the fields."

So the villagers went out again, some to the orchards to pick fruit and others to sit at the gate of the primary school eating slices of water-melon, the juice of which trickled onto their chests. Some cracked melon seeds or smoked. When they saw a cadre coming they called out loudly: "Mr. Zhao! Isn't the meeting starting yet? Ask old Red-nosed Wu to sound the gong again and sing something!"

Vice-Head Zhao was only a little over thirty, but since he belonged to an older generation everybody called him Mr. Zhao. He always looked busy and wore an old white jacket. Now he answered smiling: "Just wait a little longer, we'll start as soon as it's dark."

As soon as Yumin came in sight, someone asked him: "Can I join the meeting this evening?"

"Are you trying to be funny? You ought to know yourself whether you can join or not. Are you a member of the peasants' association? The meeting is for all poor peasants!" All who heard laughed, for only a fool could fail to know whether he belonged to the peasants' association or not.

Some children came over on seeing a crowd, but when they had stared for a time and seen there was nothing happening, they found it dull and went into the school. School being over, it was very quiet in there too. Both the teachers had disappeared, leaving the cook — the same Red-nosed Wu — washing dishes by the door of the out-house. He was the one who sounded the gong when occasion arose. The children went out again to the fields where some of them started singing the song they had learned that day from Comrade Hu, and the rest joined in: "Unite together — hey! Tillers of the land!" Their singing attracted several old men who came to sit under the locust tree, their foot-long pipes between their lips, gazing round in silence.

The women were out too. Sheng's mother was sitting on a stone bench on the street leading south. She knew there was to be a meeting that night — nobody had told her to attend but she was inquisitive — and no matter what the meeting was she meant to go and listen. Since Sheng had joined the army the village authorities had only given her twenty catties of grain, and everybody called her middle peasant. She didn't care a fig to what class she belonged, but since her son had enlisted the cadres ought to treat her with special consideration. They had promised two piculs of grain but only given one-tenth that amount. Yumin and Zhao and that lot were selfish and on the make. They pushed an old widow like her to one side, even though she was an "army dependent". Sitting on the stone bench, ignored by all, she drummed her cheek as if angry at her own silence.

Just then a merry group of chattering girls and young wives passed by, some of them throwing down fruit cores as they walked. Sheng's mother called to one of them: "Heini! Are you having a meeting tonight? I'm an army dependent too, can I come and listen?"

"If there's a meeting you can listen, why ever not? But I'm not sure if there will be one. We're going to ask the women's chairman!" Heini was wearing a cotton gown with white flowers on a blue ground, her short hair carelessly fastened. Without waiting for further questions she tossed her head and went along with her friends.

Sheng's mother spat angrily in the direction of the pink-stockinged legs, cursing: "How cocky you are! Who hasn't been young once! Bah, you're just too free for words!"

The group Heini was with went to the western quarters to see Gui.

These girls were all of them members of the literacy class. They were young and lively and enjoyed meetings. Although they came from comfortable or even well-to-do homes they were very eager to hear new ideas, and thoroughly approved of communist principles and practice. Early that morning they were delighted to hear there was to be a women's meeting, for the literacy class always took part in the women's association meetings. However, nobody had notified them. During class they told each other to attend the meeting and after supper they reminded each other again. It was nearly dark now yet still no one was clear about the situation, so after discussing it for some time they decided to ask their chairman. They laughed and chatted as they went. Before they realized it they had come to Gui's gate, but nobody wanted to be the first to go in. Each pushed someone else forward, until the whole group poured into the court. Then they all giggled, and it was Heini who called out: "Gui!"

Without waiting for Gui to answer, the group pushed its way up to her door. Inside they saw seven or eight women and several children, chattering away nineteen to the dozen, who stopped talking and turned to stare as they appeared.

"What is it?" Gui did not ask them to come in and sit down, but spoke coldly.

"Gui!" Heini was still in a cheerful mood. "Gui, we've come to ask you if we're having a meeting tonight or not."

"What meeting!" Yue, the shepherd's wife, turned her narrow slits of eyes at them. "Other people are holding the peasants' association meeting this evening! For *poor* peasants!" She emphasized the word "poor," and glanced sideways at each of them in turn.

"We're not asking about the peasants' association." Heini felt somewhat put out, but still smiled with goodwill. "We're asking about our women's association."

"*Our* women's association?" sneered a short woman in the corner.

"Heini, let's go! What's the point of staying here to be snubbed!" said one of the girls.

But now Gui had come forward and gripped Heini's hand. She was thinking how enthusiastic and conscientious Heini was in teaching the literacy class, how she never had to go to fetch her, how Heini had always greeted her warmly and come to see her and make rice gruel for her when she was ill. Heini had also given her dyes, embroidery thread and cloth for her shoes, and Freckles Li thought highly of her. Gui went over to soothe her, saying: "Heini, don't take offence. We're not having a meeting this evening. Whenever we do I'll let you know. It's good to want a meeting. There are so

80

many unwilling to come. Most of us women are so muddle-headed."

"Oh. . . ." Heini looked like a discomfited hen. With her head on one side she walked out.

"Won't you stay a little, Heini? I shan't see you out!" Standing at the door to watch the retreating backs of the group and of Heini, Gui could not help thinking: "She really is a good girl. Her uncle is no good, but you can't blame her for that."

But someone inside the room shouted: "Those creatures . . . Bah! As if we couldn't see through them, coming here to spy on us."

"Come on, let's go to the meeting," said Gui hurriedly. "This evening we'll attend the peasants' association meeting and hear how they mean to go about things. We can't stay away this time. They want to divide the land up for the poor, and we women have our share too. If the poor people don't go, and aren't clear about the business, it will be difficult to go about it. Come on."

"Let's go." The shepherd's wife was the first to stand up, and her face broadened in a smile as she said, "I can't stand those bitches. They don't do a stroke of work, just strolling about all day long."

She was a thin woman with a long face, fine eye-brows and narrow eyes, who sometimes smiled very sweetly but could also show herself a shrew. The shepherd only came home once every four or five days or sometimes not for two weeks at a time. Living by herself she was lonely, and because she had a hard time and was unhappy she often greeted him with sneers. She would not light the fire or clean the pan, hiding the little food that was left, so that the shepherd had to take out two catties of buckwheat flour or a pint of beans from his bag. He would tell her whose ewe had lambed

81

again, but not how a wolf had again stolen two of the flock, just saying their dog was too old and they ought to find a better one. Next year instead of looking after sheep he intended to rent a piece of land and plant wheat. Then if there were a good harvest they would have enough to eat and need not buy food with prices rising so fearfully. He was nearly fifty but had no land at all, and had become a shepherd through force of necessity. When his pretty young wife nagged or flared up at him he would light the fire himself, while she would stand in the courtyard and abuse him shrilly: "It's because I behaved badly in my last existence that now I'm married to an old pauper who is away from one end of the year to the other! How much longer must I put up with this!"

She would go on cursing till the old shepherd lost his temper, and as if catching a sheep he would pull her inside and give her a beating, scolding: "Devil take you, what good are you anyway? By working hard all my life I managed to get together twenty sheep, and sold them all to buy you — how dare you resent my poverty or my age! You bitch, who knows how you carry on when I'm away from home. . . ."

When beaten his wife cried bitterly to think how he wronged her. But she would gradually calm down, and go meekly to knead the buckwheat flour and prepare food for him. Then he would sit in front of the *kang* stove, smoking and stroking his goatee. Glancing at him from time to time she felt great compassion for him. In the summer it was not so bad, but in winter he still had to lead the flock through wind and rain, looking for a mountain valley where they could find pasture and a flat place out of the wind to pitch his tent, with only some herbs for pillow and a thin quilt for cover. Every year he only earned a little grain and a few bolts of cloth, or a couple of lambs. Now he was no longer young and wanted to take to farming again, but where was the land to come from? Each time he came back she would start a quarrel with him, then come to feel she had treated him badly, and look at him tenderly once more. He also would become his usual self again, and after one night they would seem like a newly-married couple, grown quite inseparable. She would accompany him to the outskirts of the village to see him off, sitting down at the top of the road and watching till he was out of sight before coming back. Such was the hard and lonely life she led.

This thin woman apparently had no cause for fear except her husband's fist, and no source of comfort. Hence she was often bitter and impatient. Of all the village women she was least afraid of trouble. She had quarrelled and even fought with people, and during the campaigns to struggle against the landlords the previous year and that spring, had been the most outspoken of the women. Once her temper was up she feared neither man nor devil, and at such times people would gather round her and unite under her passionate leadership.

As they got down from the *kang*, the children started clamouring, and one old woman said she dared not go.

Gui tugged at her, saying: "Aunty! If you don't go to the meeting you won't understand anything, and can't stand on your feet!"

"Ah," sighed the old woman. "But I don't dare go. You know how pig-headed your uncle is. He's going to the meeting this evening, and if I go he'll see me. He goes without saying a word, and doesn't tell us a thing when he gets home. It's not that he wants to go, only he's afraid they'll fetch his son otherwise. He said good or bad he'd shoulder it himself. If he saw me there, there'd be the devil to pay. Ah! What can you do with a man like that. . . ."

This old woman was the wife of Tenant Hou who was

notorious in the village because he had secretly returned to Landlord Hou the one and a half *mu* of land given him that spring. When his son stamped with rage and cursed him for a stubborn old fool he took a broom to beat him. The peasants' association learning of it tried to intervene, but since he denied the business they could do nothing about it.

"Well, can't you scold him and tell him things have changed nowadays?" said the shepherd's wife, perking up like a sparrow again. "How can anyone be such an old slave, clinging to poverty for dear life!"

But the old woman stuck to her guns and went home by herself, while the others started off towards the meeting place in Landlord Xu's courtyard.

By now it was nearly dark and impossible to distinguish anyone at a distance. Militiamen were patrolling the street and some dozen people were standing outside Landlord Xu's gate, while militiamen carrying rifles inspected all comers. Sheng's mother was standing outside the gate too, but they would not let her in, and advised her: "Go home, old woman, it's dark."

"If you want anything, go to see the village cadres tomorrow," said someone. "Don't keep standing here."

"Suppose I like standing?" she muttered. "Can't a person even stand in the street? If my Sheng were at home you'd — well! You talk about special consideration for army dependents, yet you won't even let me stand in the main street!"

"All right," they were forced to say. "If you want to stand there, do."

The courtyard was already packed. It was supposed to be a meeting of poor peasants, but actually most families had only sent one representative, and there were a good many middle peasants too. They were sitting in groups on the steps on all sides, raising a hubbub. The stars were so bright that

84

the militiamen on the roof could be seen. Swarthy Guo was busy examining all comers. The militiamen thought highly of their captain, though they complained of his strictness. Freckles Li was busy too, running in and out calling various people. Vice-Head Zhao, still in his short white jacket, had lit a lamp and put it on the table on the steps of the north side.

When Gui and the other women arrived, Sheng's mother went in with them. The women stood in one corner, and Gui saw Comrade Yang talking in the middle of a crowd of men, and heard occasional roars of laughter from that group.

Hu had appeared on the steps too, and Freckles Li said loudly: "How about learning a song?" Several young peasants agreed, whereupon Hu struck up the song the children had sung: "Unite together — hey! Tillers of the land...."

Many people, however, had their eyes anxiously on the gate, watching for Yumin and the chairman of the peasants' association. They were looking forward eagerly to this evening's meeting, for they had much to say, although they did not know how to express themselves or even if they dared speak out. They had faith in the Communists, knowing the Communist Party was a party for the poor, but they still had too little understanding of it and too many reservations.

17

COMRADE Wen's entry into the courtyard was greeted with a burst of applause from the dark crowd. Everybody made way for him, closing in again as soon as he had passed, and pressing towards the table in front where the cadres had placed a bench. Wen made a gesture as if to decline, and then sat down. All eyes were fastened on him, and he smiled slightly at them all.

Young Cheng, the peasants' association chairman, wearing a short white jacket, his chest exposed and his head bear, stood in front of the table in the dim lamplight which lit up his thick eyebrows and sparkling eyes. Rather nervous, he looked at the crowd and said: "Elders!"

All the audience laughed, and someone said: "Don't laugh!"

He went on: "Today! This meeting today is for discussion of land reform, understand? Is it clear?"

"Quite clear," they all answered.

Red-nosed Wu who was standing by the table stretched his neck and said loudly: "What's not clear about it? We take the rich people's land and divide it up among the peasants, so that those who till the soil have land of their own, and everybody has to work and nobody can live by exploiting others!" Glancing at Wen he sketched a gesture with his hand. "Last year we dealt with one family. We tackled Landlord Xu, and took over eight hundred piculs of grain which, in terms of land, houses and livestock, were divided among the poor. This compound's his, Mr. Chairman! Doesn't that count as land reform as far as he is concerned? Isn't that what you mean?" This was Red-nosed Wu who sounded the gong.

Somebody at the back shouted, "Don't talk out of turn! Listen to the chairman."

"I only said a few words, if we mustn't speak I won't." Red-nosed Wu smiled awkwardly at Comrade Wen.

"There are a lot of principles involved in land reform. Let's get them clear today. Now shall we ask Comrade Wen to speak to us?" When Young Cheng had finished, without waiting for the crowd to say anything, he started clapping.

There was a burst of applause.

As Wen stood up, whispering sounded from the audience. All pressed a little closer.

"Folks!" Wen's northern accent was very easy to follow, and he had a clear voice. "Today is the first time we've met. Possibly —" Feeling the word "possibly" was too literary he searched frantically for another word, but unable to think of one for the moment he had to go on: "Possibly you feel rather strange, rather unfamiliar. But the Eighth Route Army and the people are one family, we'll soon know each other well, won't we?"

"Yes," answered someone in the crowd.

"Now we're agitating for land reform. What is land reform? It's 'Land to the tiller'. That is to say, the man with the plough has his own land, those who don't work won't have. . . ."

Some of the audience were whispering again.

"Silence!" shouted Cheng.

Wen then proceeded to speak according to the draft he had prepared.

First he explained why land reform was necessary, beginning with the history of man and explaining who are the makers of history. He also analysed the situation in China and abroad, proving the timeliness of this policy. To begin with, Wen paid great attention to his vocabulary. But all the modern terms it had taken him so long to learn, all the beautiful descriptions phrased in rhetoric, were entirely lost on this audience. Nobody could understand them. And although he tried hard to find words in common use he did not know many such. Then he spoke of how land reform should be carried out, repeating "mass line" again and again and dividing his speech into numerous headings: firstly, secondly . . . fifthly, and then firstly again, until finally he forgot to pay attention to his vocabulary, carried away by his own eloquence.

The audience listened as hard as they could. They had hoped for something short and simple, a few sentences which would resolve their doubts. They wanted something decisive. They were well able to figure out questions concerning grain, obligations to the government and settling scores with landlords, but they were not interested in historical stages and all the rest of it. They lost interest in the talk, unable to see what connection it had with their life.

Some of them, although they could not understand most of his speech, had to admit: "That's a clever chap, how well he speaks!" But gradually they felt too tired to concentrate. Because of their labours during the day and the fact that they were unusually excited, their eyelids grew heavy and they found it hard to keep their eyes open. Someone nudged his neighbour. Then people started stealthily leaving the crowd to sit on the steps at the back, where they put their heads on their knees and went to sleep with their mouths open.

Yang wrote a note and handed it to Wen. After looking at it the latter crumpled it up and stuffed it into his pocket.

Sheng's mother had long ago grown tired of listening and wanted to leave, but the shepherd's wife would not let her. When a baby started crying and its mother insisted on taking it home, Sheng's mother backed her up, saying: "In a meeting they should consider folks' feelings, not force people. This is simply killing! If an old woman over fifty like me gets her clothes wet with dew and falls ill, who'll look after me? My Sheng isn't at home. . . ."

"You old silly, who asked you to come! Whoever has come will have to sit it out. Just try going, that's all, there are still guards at the gate."

"My, how cross you are! Now that you're chairman of the

women you look down on everyone! I'm not a traitor, why should I be afraid of you?"

Many people were feeling sleepy standing there, and hearing the women quarrelling they turned round and stood on tiptoe to watch. At the same time a young militiaman called out: "Anyone who makes a noise will be tied up."

More people joined in the talking, until there was such an uproar that Comrade Wen had to stop. He eyed this unruly audience with annoyance.

"Don't make such a noise! Keep quiet please!" a cadre standing behind Wen shouted at the top of his voice.

Several people had to hurry over to act as peacemakers before the two women who wanted to leave were allowed out, and Sheng's mother could be heard exclaiming loudly outside the courtyard: "Tie people up indeed! You talk of tying up to frighten people. Go ahead and tie me up if you dare!"

The cadres hurriedly tried to restore order. Yumin stepped forward and said: "We'll go on with the meeting. Today we're listening to Chairman Wen, and must listen carefully. If there's anything we don't understand we can ask him tomorrow. We must get this business straight in our heads. We're the peasants' association and this is our business, so we must listen patiently."

Some people straggled back to their places, but others stayed at the back, and as the steps were already crowded they lolled against the pillars.

The meeting dragged on. Swarthy Guo, captain of the militia, always found it hard to sit still, and when he could not understand he went out to inspect the guards, then after a few turns returned to the courtyard. But seeing Wen still talking he went up onto the roof which was bathed in moonlight. There was a breeze, and wearing thin clothes one felt quite cool. He strained his eyes to look all around. On three sides of the village was dark, dense forest over which floated a grey-white layer of moonlight merging in the far distance with the clear sky. The Sanggan River was hidden behind the forest from some points in which thin smoke drifted up and spread fanwise over the surrounding trees, and the moonlight piercing it seemed even more soft and hazy. The smoke was caused by watchers in the orchards who were burning artemesia herbs and moxa leaves to keep off mosquitoes and insects. Amid the bright, thinly-scattered stars the Milky Way showed as a smudge of white, the North Star was sloping down and somebody's donkey nearby was braying for all it was worth.

Swarthy Guo turned to look at the three guards sitting just below the ridge of the roof, holding their rifles upright or horizontal. One of them approached him softly and called quietly: "Captain! Captain!" Coming closer he whispered: "Folk are tired out, nobody understands a word, the chief's talk is too long and way over their heads. Can you remember what he's said, Captain?"

"They're working for us," replied Swarthy Guo, "so we must take pains. We must keep a good watch."

The courtyard was pitch dark and the oil in the lamp was nearly exhausted. Young Cheng had mended the wick several times and Hu had whispered something into Wen's ear before the latter finally brought his speech to a conclusion. Thereupon a great many people woke up and, without waiting for Cheng to announce that the meeting was over, pushed and jostled their way out, while Cheng shouted after them: "Tomorrow everybody come a little earlier!"

Some cadres emerged from the literacy class classroom rubbing their eyes, and Freckles Li asked sleepily: "Is the meeting over?"

Yumin accompanied Wen and the others back, but on the road no one said a word. Two members of the peasants' association walking in front were in low spirits too, yawning loudly, and one of them made the wry remark: "Our bottoms are going to be sore from sitting before we 'stand on our feet'."

The other glanced back at Yumin and the rest, then nudged the man who had spoken, so the latter laughed and said no more. They put on speed and drew ahead.

"Who was that?" asked Yang.

"Just two mischief-makers," said Yumin. "Demobbed soldiers, you know. One of them is Old Han's son."

When they got home Old Han was still up, and hurried over, eager to hear what had happened. Hu said solemnly: "Let's have a good talk tonight to decide just how the work should be done!"

All the way back Wen had been in a tired but excited state, believing the meeting had not gone off badly, hence Hu's dissatisfied tones surprised and upset him. He wanted to put him in his place, but on second thoughts decided people would know which of them was right and he had better not appear petty. Still in a good humour, he asked Yumin: "What's your opinion of the meeting this evening? Don't you think it was necessary to explain things to the peasants, and carry out ideological mobilization first?"

Before Yumin had thought how to answer, Hu burst out: "What ideological mobilization! The meeting lasted nearly six hours and all the time it was one person talking. It's a wonder everybody didn't go to sleep! Excuse my frankness, Comrade Wen, but didn't you see a lot of them sleeping? And on top of that your language — why — it was quite over their heads."

A few remarks like this were not enough to destroy Wen's

self-confidence, only serving to convince him that Hu was shallow. Taking up a copy of *Northern Culture* which was lying on the table, he said coldly: "Peasants are backward, you know. They aren't interested in anything except immediate gains. We can't hurry things. The first step is to get their thinking clear. It's impossible to expect quick results, only the petty bourgeoisie think like that. As a matter of fact I'm quite satisfied with this evening's meeting, although I admit my language is lacking in folk flavour." With this he opened the book to find an essay he wanted to read.

"You shouldn't underestimate the peasants," said Hu. "Of course their cultural level is low and they can't theorize, but they learned long ago how to fight and how to get land." For confirmation he turned to Yumin: "You belong to the village and know more about conditions here than anyone else, and you've had experience in struggling against the landlords. What do you say? Is it any use holding any more meetings like this?"

Without giving Yumin a chance to speak, Yang broke in: "There must be meetings, and it is necessary to explain to the people just what land reform means. Today's meeting had its uses of course, but — it's too late today, let's say what we have to say tomorrow."

"What does it matter if we talk this evening?" said Hu, still boiling with indignation. "It isn't as if Yumin were an outsider."

"On the contrary, Yumin plays the leading role. Of course the village cadres understand the village affairs best, I just meant that we're too tired this evening, so even if we discuss things we won't come to any conclusion. Won't it be better if everybody sleeps on it and we have a discussion tomorrow? What do you think, Yumin?" Yang looked at him confidently.

"Right, Old Yang. We'll do as you say. Comrade Wen, sleep well, I'm going." And Yumin started out very considerately.

"Wait a bit, I'll come and bolt the gate after you." Yang followed him out, slapping him on the back and speaking in a low voice, and as the two of them reached the gate he said: "There are always obstacles in the work. I know the meeting this evening was a little too long, and the speech was over people's heads, but it doesn't really matter. It is the first day and one has to talk about the nature of land reform. You joined the Party before liberation and started life as a hired farmhand, tell us more of what you think. Don't talk carelessly in front of the masses, but listen to their views while taking a firm stand. You must take more responsibility in village business. We've only just come and have to consult you about everything. Don't be discouraged if there are difficulties. We'll think of a way out together. Tomorrow we can talk things over at length. We've got to make a good job of this, right?"

Although Yumin was reserved himself, he liked forthrightness, and answered: "Right, Old Yang, we'll talk again tomorrow. Although this is such a small village it isn't going to be an easy business. There are all sorts of people here. Luckily we have you to figure out ways and means, and we'll do as you say. Now that you've come we must learn as much as we can from you."

Last of all, Yang said: "So long as we follow Chairman Mao's instructions, take the mass line, enlighten and help the masses, discussing everything with them and making plans for them, success is assured. We must all have this faith, and work harder!"

18

WHEN the meeting was over Gui started home with some other women. The moon shone on the foot of the low walls, the middle of the road was sunken and stony. It was hard to walk carrying children, but all the men had gone on ahead, leaving the women to stumble along as best they could behind. One child was crying. His mother had a baby in one arm and was leading the child with her other hand, scolding: "Crying, crying, you are the limit! Mother isn't dead yet. Wait till Mother dies to cry!"

"Don't cry, Little San, we're nearly home. Tomorrow I'll buy you a cake," said Gui, taking his other hand.

"Ah, dragging your child and carrying your baby!" said another woman. "We got up at the crack of dawn and we've been up half the night! What did we do to deserve this! Sister, why didn't you let Little San's father carry him?"

"Oh, never mind, his father's worse. He didn't even want to come to the meeting. When the peasants' association chairman came to fetch him he said I could take his place, he was really too sleepy, because for two nights he was up at midnight to go to Shacheng to sell fruit. It's twenty miles there and back, with two rivers to cross."

"Whose fruit did you buy?" asked the shepherd's wife. "The fruit isn't really ripe yet."

"Do you suppose we can afford to buy fruit? We were selling it for Landlord Li. Li said he was short of money, so he had some of the riper fruit picked first and sent it to be sold. You little wretch, don't cry."

"It must be nice to have a little orchard land," sighed the shepherd's wife. "Just to look at it would make you happy."

"There are so many orchards in the village, yet not one belongs to us poor folk," said Gui enviously. "If the poor people stand up and each family gets one *mu* that will be fine."

"Yes, and save the children's mouths watering at the sight."

Hearing the grown-ups talk about fruit the child cried even more bitterly.

"Heavens! Stand up, stand up, all this talk about standing up! I think we'll stay this way the rest of our lives. Tomorrow I'm not coming, not on your life."

"Gui," said the shepherd's wife, as if the thought had suddenly struck her, "if we want to rise to our feet we must catch those rascals. Just talking about principles people don't understand and can't remember is no use at all."

Gui grunted non-committally. She did not like to say she agreed, thinking that would be letting Comrade Yang down.

When they were nearly at the turning to the lane they heard the sound of a woman mourning from the fields in the west: "Little Bao! Come back!"[1]

A man's deep voice followed: "Come back!"

Then the woman chimed in again tearfully: "Little Bao! Come back!"

"Come back!" echoed the other.

"It's really too bad about Little Bao. It doesn't look as if he will get better. Even Lord White wouldn't answer prayers." The woman hugged the baby in her arms more tightly. "Oh, hush, Little San, in another minute we'll be home."

"Lord White said people are wicked, that the real Dragon Emperor has gone to Beijing, his capital since ancient times!" said someone else.

---

[1] There was a superstitious belief in the old days that the soul of an ill child was being lured off by an evil spirit. The parents would go out at night to "look" for the soul and "call" it back.

"Oh, who believes that nonsense! I don't!" But no one echoed the shepherd's wife.

As they turned into the lane they could still hear the faint, trembling cries of "Little Bao, come back!" wailing in the infinite empty night.

By the time Gui got home her husband had already lit the lamp and was sitting on the *kang* smoking. "Aren't you going to bed yet?" she asked. "It's nearly cockcrow." Taking a brush she gently brushed the bed, and from the top of the roll of bedding took down a square pillow stuffed with buckwheat husks. "Better sleep. It's cooler now. The room is too hot in summer after cooking here all day. I wish we could afford to build an additional stove in the courtyard." She got down, changed her white blouse for a ragged vest, then said: "I'm afraid Little Bao won't last long, his father and mother are calling his soul in the fields. Lord White wouldn't answer prayers. What's the matter, are you asleep? Look at you, scowling again. Who's offended you? There's a piece of water-melon in the cupboard, would you like it?"

"Bah, you're in high spirits," said Vineyard Li sullenly. Nobody had crossed him, yet he felt put out and wanted to scold his wife, but could think of no pretext. "In future you may have meetings all day."

"Well, didn't you go too? And it's not as if I liked going, the cadres made me."

"Bah, you're one of the cadres too! I'm waiting to see how long you can count on the Communists, and who you'll count on once they've gone. But when that time comes don't drag me into it."

"Oh, when I agreed to be the women's chairman Yumin spoke to you about it, and you didn't disapprove, but now you blame me! I'm only a woman after all, I follow my husband. I've been poor so long. I begged my way here and if the worst happens I can start begging again. What is there for me to be afraid of? It was for your sake I went to the meeting. You were always saying how you would like to have a little land, but if not for Yumin do you suppose you could have borrowed those ten piculs of grain this spring? Now that we've got a plot to cultivate you forget the debt we have to pay back this autumn. I shan't get anything under the land reform. For better or worse I have to be dependent on you, and now for no reason at all you lose your temper with me." She blew out the light and lay down angrily on the other end of the *kang* without another word.

Honest Li did not say any more either. He knocked out the red ashes from his pipe onto the window sill, then refilled and relit it to puff away energetically. Blame his wife? He didn't blame her, he knew how she felt. Still he thought of what his cousin, Shou, had told him during the day. His cousin was poor too. When they happened to meet during the noon siesta he had told Vineyard Li with an air of secrecy: "They say Landlord Xu is coming back, have you heard?"

"Really?" Any possibility of Xu's return made Vineyard Li uneasy, because the vineyard he had bought through Yumin had been Xu's, and he had paid only half the market price.

"I don't know whether it's true or not, but that's what they say. They say too the Eighth Route Army won't be here long. What do you think?" Then bringing his mouth even closer to Li's ear: "It seems Schemer Qian had a letter from Xu. They want to attack from within and without."

This took Li back.

"He's got a foot in each camp," the cousin went on. "Don't be deceived by his son's joining the Eighth Route Army. A radish is red outside and white on the inside."

The two of them talked for some time, but could not think what to do. Qian was chief of the eight village racketeers, hated and feared by all the villagers. Since even the cadres dared not offend him, everybody else had better keep quiet. Qian would be sure to have his spies, and would deal with anyone who was against him. Shou had bought three *mu* of vineyard too. The longer the cousins talked the more at a loss they felt. Nobody could guarantee that the Eighth Route Army would remain. The Kuomintang troops had good weapons and the Americans were helping them. However, Vineyard Li had not lost faith in the Eighth Route Army. He felt they were on the side of the poor and would do what was best for the poor. They always knew what to do, and might even now have arrested Schemer Qian. As for Landlord Xu, he couldn't come back. Accordingly Vineyard Li went to the meeting.

What he understood of Wen's long speech he found interesting, but later he understood less and less, and muttered irritably to himself: "Ah, what are you gassing about! You enjoy talking, but no one enjoys listening. If you don't arrest Schemer Qian and seize that gang and their running dogs, even if you give people land no one will dare take it. Let's see how you cope with their attacking from within and without when Landlord Xu comes back." He did not want to stay, but the guards at the gate would not let anyone out, which increased his exasperation.

At last the meeting was adjourned and he could go home. The house was pitch black and while feeling for the lamp he got his hand covered with oil, and could not help feeling annoyed with his wife: "Meetings, meetings all the time, while she neglects the home." Gui lying on the other end of the *kang* waited a long time for him to speak, and then said: "Better sleep. Tomorrow you have to help uncle's family cut

98

flax. If you don't want me to attend meetings in future, I won't."

Then he told her: "It's always best not to take the lead, but to leave ourselves a loophole. If we've to be poor, it was decided in an earlier life. If by any chance the Eighth Route Army can't beat the Kuomintang troops and we go back to the old life, that will be hard enough. How can the village racketeers be overthrown so easily?"

Gui was a woman after all, and when her husband spoke like this she started worrying too. She thought again of Little Bao and how Lord White had refused to answer prayers because everybody was wicked. And he had said the real Dragon Emperor was in Beijing. She hoped this was not really the case. She wanted everything to be as Comrade Yang had said, but her husband's anxiety was justified. They were straightforward people who had had a hard life and couldn't afford to offend anyone! She felt thoroughly upset, being tortured by the anxiety of hope as well as despair. In vain she racked her brains. The memory of her past misfortunes made her feel that all her life she had been like a rotten branch floating on the water, submerging and rising but destined to sink at last. She shed tears secretly, looking in the dark at her good man. Exhaustion had already closed his eyes as he enjoyed his only pleasure in life.

Gradually, it began to grow light.

19

VINEYARD Li did not wake till it was broad daylight. He could hear subdued voices outside, and when he looked through a rent in the paper window he heard his wife saying softly: "Does your father-in-law agree?"

"No, the old man didn't say a word, he just took his hoe and went off." Li's younger sister, Old Gu's daughter-in-law, was standing with her back to the house. "He didn't come back all night," she went on. "My mother-in-law cried."

"He bought that land bit by bit, how can he bear parting with it in big slices now? What does your eldest brother-in-law say?"

"He doesn't dare say anything to his father, but behind his back he's all for dividing up." Then she dropped her voice to a whisper to say: "What's really going on, sister-in-law? What was said in your meeting last night?"

"I'm not going to any more meetings. There's no point." Gui remembered how unpleasant the previous evening had been.

"You didn't talk about making trouble for my father-in-law last night? My brother-in-law says all the villagers suspect us and we'll probably be attacked."

"Oh no! Nothing was said last night about making trouble for your father-in-law. And Chairman Wen said that people who work themselves, even if they're rich, won't have their land taken away. How could anyone suspect you? There aren't many folk in the village. Everybody knows everybody else's affairs well enough. The last few days there has been all sorts of talk in the village. One doesn't know what to believe. Who was it Young Gu heard?"

"I don't know where he heard it. They didn't want him to go to the meeting yesterday, although he always went to meetings before as vice-chairman of the youth association. And we heard we've been labelled — now what was it — working landlords! Really, who knows what it all means! Suppose we do have a little more land than most, there are a lot of us. . . ."

"Your family does have a lot of land! Only you act fairly,

not like those overbearing bullies. I'm sure no one will make trouble for you. Don't you worry about it."

"Our family's worked up into such a state, Gui. You go to see them and tell them what Comrade Wen said at the meeting yesterday evening, so that the old man can relax. Giving up land would be bad enough, you know, but mass trial would finish him. If it didn't kill him it would leave him as good as dead."

"I'll come over presently. Your brother isn't up yet."

"What, not up yet?"

At this point Vineyard Li called out to them. Both his sister and wife had dishevelled hair, pale cheeks and swollen eyelids. He asked them what they had just been talking about.

It had started when Old Gu and his elder brother were in the courtyard discussing whether they should send Hutai's cart back. Old Gu said since the cart had been entrusted to them they must wait for its owners to fetch it. But his elder brother said: "Our own safety is at stake, better send it back." It so happened that Er, Schemer Qian's daughter-in-law, had come home for a chat, and hearing this conversation she asked her father if he were going to sell his sheep or not, because the Qian family was selling sheep. If they didn't sell they'd just have to give them away. Qian had said this reform could only make everybody in the village poor, that anybody who had any property was out of luck, this being the golden age for the poor.

The women had come and stood uneasily in the courtyard, but the two old men did not say a word. They had slaved all their lives — it had been no joke acquiring their present wealth. Now if property was to be "communized", there was nothing they could do about it, but they couldn't bring themselves to sell any land, nor yet divide it between their sons. They had only five or six sheep, not worth worrying about, but this rumour made them anxious and, even more, indignant. They felt fate was too unkind. Later when the gong sounded for the meeting, Young Gu had gone to pick up news, hurrying along with other members of the youth association, but the militiamen on guard would not let him in. When he said he was one of the cadres someone nearby had laughed: "Your family has so much land, you're the very people we're going to reform, yet here you show up yourself."

Another bystander said: "What if you are a village cadre! Even the village head isn't allowed in. How can you come and listen?" And turning to someone beside him he added: "This is a spy."

Young Gu was thin-skinned, and feeling he could not stand there any longer he stole away, wounded to the quick. He was a primary school graduate, a well-behaved youngster who had always been highly thought of in the village. He had proved an enthusiastic member of the youth association and sometimes when he wrote slogans would buy paper, pen and ink from the co-operative at his own expense. He admired the Eighth Route Army enormously and often wrote to his elder brother urging him to win glory and not be homesick. He felt it most unjust and humiliating to be excluded from the meeting. What had he done wrong? Wanting to put the blame on someone else he gradually began to feel a grudge against his father, believing this had happened because folk identified him with his old man. Why was his father so fond of buying land, so greedy? It would have been better to have bought less and owned only a little, like Freckles Li. What rankled most was to have been dubbed a spy, going to the meeting only to ferret out information. He was no reactionary, people had no right to consider him as such. Puzzled, he walked home angrily, and arrived just as his sister was talking about working landlords. She hated her father-in-law, but this time she acted as a faithful messenger for Schemer Qian who had said that if there were a mass trial in the village this time, it would be Old Gu's turn. This had thrown her into a panic, and she thought it her duty to report it to her family.

What his sister said struck a chord in Young Gu's mind, and he said: "Go back to your husband's family and don't keep coming here. If you keep coming over every day or so, even if we fall into the Yellow River we shan't be able to wash ourselves clean. With relatives like them we really are out of luck. It's only your father-in-law who likes to snoop about. Go on, if you don't go I'll take my case to the comrades and ask your in-laws to pay damages for our pear tree."

Bursting into tears, his sister protested: "It's not my fault that you have such relatives. It was you who were afraid of their power and threw me away! If the Communists want your land now, it serves you right. Who asked you to get so much land! If you won't give any away, go and tell the village cadres. Why pick on me!..."

Then Young Gu said to his father: "Don't take things so hard, Dad. Better give up something yourself rather than be tried in public. If we've enough to eat we should be satisfied. If you and uncle will just say the word I'll go and find Yumin. It'll look much better this way."

Old Gu did not scold his son, but neither did he answer him. Taking up his hoe he went out. Their uncle was a simple soul and he kept silent too. Young Gu's eldest brother, however, said: "Divide it up. There are a lot of us, and divided up it doesn't amount to anything. Anybody who wants to give his away can."

Young Gu stamped his foot and fumed: "The whole family is so pig-headed and backward, if there's a trial it'll serve you right! But I'm not going to keep you company when you all parade the streets in dunce's caps and get beaten. If

103

you insist on being so pig-headed I'll go and join our brother in the Eighth Route Army and get myself an army uniform, without asking for anything else. These few *mu* of land can go with you to your graves!..."

Young Gu's outburst upset everybody even more. His mother cried, at the same time trying to comfort her daughter who was in a rage. The house appeared as if someone had just died there, with all the rooms looking big and empty and all the inmates bottling up their feelings as if bearing a grudge against each other.

After they had passed an uneasy night, Mother Gu thought of Gui who was chairman of the women's association and a relative of theirs, who must know what was happening. She told her daughter-in-law to go and make enquiries and find out what was really going on, so that they could plan accordingly. At a time like this one really felt like a bride in the decorated sedan-chair, unable to see out and entirely in other people's hands.

When his sister had finished Vineyard Li had no solution to suggest, although he thought it would be good if they were really willing to give up some land. Their family couldn't cultivate it all by themselves in any case, but had to hire day labourers. A man should have just enough to eat. What did they want all that land for? As for the talk of bringing the Gu family to trial, that wouldn't be right. All he said, however, was: "Young Gu really is bright, he uses his brains. One has to change with the times. This is no time for rich and powerful people to lord it over the rest. If your father-in-law would listen to him, that would be fine. But everybody can distinguish between good people and bad. They won't harm good people! If you treat everyone fairly you needn't be afraid of a trial. Tell your father-in-law and uncle not to worry. Every road has a turning, this business is bound to be cleared up sooner or later. Your husband has joined the army, so you've nothing to be afraid of. Nothing can happen to you, so keep calm. You go back now. After the meal I'll send Gui over."

When Li's sister had gone, Gui started lighting the fire. She said nothing to her husband because she was depressed, thinking that if Old Gu's family were to be tried that would be going too far.

20

AFTER the meal Gui went to the Gu family. Vineyard Li felt so limp that although he had promised to help his uncle harvest flax, he was loath to go. Yet lying there he felt on tenterhooks. So he walked to the end of the lane, where several people were standing in the shade of a tree watching a pig being slaughtered. When Li went over they said to him, smiling: "Take a catty home to make meat dumplings. It's cheaper than at the market: 160 dollars a catty."

"Sick?" asked Li, not much interested.

"No, it's good pork."

"Whose is it? Killing pigs in the hottest part of summer — if it's not sold in one day it'll go bad."

Nobody said anything. Only after a long pause a youngster explained: "It's my elder brother's. My brother heard property would be divided up, so he decided to kill this pig — the only thing he owns. He said we don't taste meat from one end of the year to the other, let everybody have a treat. Sell what can be sold, and what isn't sold we'll eat ourselves. If it's well salted it doesn't matter. He wouldn't even carry it to the market, saying it wasn't worth the trouble."

At this everybody laughed, and one said: "It'll be a long

time before your brother's considered one of the rich villagers. He's nothing to worry about."

"How stingy your brother is," said another. "Suppose they did take your pig, what would it matter? There are only two hundred-odd families in the village, all related in some way or another. Why couldn't he treat the rest?"

Not thinking to ask these people why they were not working on the land, Vineyard Li walked off. In the main street he met Freckles Li who was still in high spirits and who called out: "So you aren't out working! There's another poor peasants' meeting tonight! Come in good time!"

Vineyard Li grunted apathetically.

"We've got to struggle harder. This is the time for us poor folk to rise to our feet. Don't you listen to that nonsense about the Communists not going to be here long. . . ."

"Hmm." Vineyard Li thought of what his cousin had told him the previous day. But instead of telling Freckles Li what was on his mind, he just said: "The Kuomintang troops have American backing. Just take our village, for instance. Well, poor folks are foolish. We're all simple folk while they have a clever schemer. . . ."

"Let's do away with the schemer," broke in Freckles Li. "What's there to be afraid of? As long as we're united there's nothing to fear. I don't think your attitude is good."

While Vineyard Li was wondering whether to speak out or not, Freckles Li walked off, saying: "If you're afraid, you can't rise to your feet. Be in good time at the meeting this evening. You need to change your ideas."

Vineyard Li did not say any more, but thought: "Yes, I do want to change my ideas, only I can't. We shall never rise to our feet. Ah, once you rise, mind you stand firm. It's no good if you fall again."

All his uncle's family had gone to pick flax. The women

had disappeared too, and the door was padlocked. People who lived in the same courtyard asked in surprise: "Are you ill? You look very pale."

From there he went to his aunt's home. His aunt's husband was a wizened old man who had just finished plastering his roof with mud and come down from the roof, covered from head to foot in dust. But as soon as he saw his nephew he stretched out both arms, urging him to go inside and saying: "Hullo, aren't you working today? I have to spend quite a bit every year on repairing this house, it's so tumbledown. Last time there was rain it leaked like anything. There was heavy rain in the court and light rain in the house, and when it had stopped outside it still fell pit-pat-pit-pat inside for a long time. I've always been meaning to move house. If I used the money I spend on repairs to rent a place, we'd certainly have more space. Only, although I'm so old I'm still soft. I can't bring myself to speak. This house belongs to Landlord Hou too. I've worked on his land for scores of years and we're the same family. Now that he's having a spell of bad luck, I'm not the one to kick a fellow when he's down. Well, come in and sit down. See what your aunt is up to." He went in himself, took a mouthful of water from the dipper, spat it on his hands and rubbed them together, washing off half the mud and wiping off the rest on his old blue cotton vest. This was Tenant Hou. Forty-odd years before he had been nicknamed "Sticky Rice", but now he was as dried up as a buckwheat bun, only his twinkling bright eyes remaining unchanged.

His wife got down from the *kang* smiling: "Well, year in year out I'm busy with the same wretched work. I never finish with these rags." She piled a bundle of old cloth of indeterminable colours onto the head of the *kang*, and went on: "Your wife is doing well now, running right and left, busy on proper business."

107

"Sit down on the *kang*. It's not often you're free. First have a smoke." The old man took the pipe from his belt and offered it to his nephew. But seeing the latter looked in no mood for talking and declined the pipe, he lit it himself, and said jokingly: "Ah, this is the one luxury I have. I can't break myself of the habit."

"Last night your wife went to the meeting. Did you go? What did they talk about? I hear there's going to be more settling accounts. The land will be shared out equally. Whoever works a piece of land will own it. It sounds too good to be true." Li's aunt, who had been forbidden by her husband to attend the meeting, could not help questioning him.

But the old man put in hastily: "Ha, a woman like you, and old too, you're still so inquisitive! I tell you this is none of your business. Clamouring all the time to go to the meeting without caring whether you would understand or not, or what use it would be. Better remember your place, and not poke your nose into everything."

"My wife acts like a queen, as if she could really manage affairs. I can't make up my mind whether to let her go or not. Tell me, Uncle, what do you think will come of all this? There's all kinds of talk in the village." Finding someone he could talk things over with, Li's heart grew a little lighter.

"Why ask me?" The old man stroked his short, thin beard, glanced at both their faces, then started laughing: "Ha, it's no use. I'm not keeping up with the times. This is a new world with new ways. Yesterday evening that comrade gave a very fine talk! Everything is for the poor — yes, but — well, my life is finished. Your aunt and cousins are all against me. If not for me they'd have risen to their feet already and become rich. Ha-ha . . . you'd better let your wife have her way, she's a capable woman. Nowadays hens can crow as well as cocks, men and women are equal." He chuckled.

"This is like asking the way from a blind man. Everybody in the village knows your uncle. He gave Landlord Hou's land back to him. If you ask him he'll say: 'You're destined to be a slave. If you've nothing to eat just tighten your belt.' Oh, what a man, afraid a falling leaf will kill him! Ugh!" His aunt who usually could not stand up to the old man, was emboldened by her nephew's presence to complain, and brought up her greatest grievance.

The old couple's talk disturbed Vineyard Li again He remembered Tenant Hou's obstinacy and how little patience the villagers had with him, all condemning him for his lack of spirit. Vineyard Li told him the villagers had said that if he were willing to stick up for his rights Landlord Hou would have had to give him at least ten *mu* of land and a house.

"There you are!" the old woman echoed, and searched her husband's face for signs of hatred or at least recollection. But she was disappointed. The old man's face was completely expressionless as he cut Li short with: "Oh, that's an old tale. Don't bring that up again."

With an obvious lack of interest in the conversation he got down from the *kang* to put together the tools with which he had just mended the roof. Hence Li had to get up too. The old woman was much upset and whispered to her nephew as she saw him out that she meant to go and see Gui that evening, and that he should pay no attention to his uncle, the old fellow was no good.

2 I

AS a young man Hou had been totally different. Old people in the village could still remember him as a clever and lively youngster in his twenties. His family was quite well off then, with nineteen and a half *mu* of land and a tile-roof house, and he had attended a private school for two years and learned a good many characters. He had been influenced by the plays and operas he read with their stories of loyalty, filial piety and purity, and was carried away by the high-sounding sentiments of those heroes, chaste women, loyal ministers and faithful servants. He often retold these to the friends who flocked round him, and he learned to sing and was a good actor. At New Year he was in great demand and his father could not forbid him to perform. He also picked the prettiest girl in the village to marry. They had a plump baby, and his parents were very pleased. That year, however, there was a famine and they had to borrow three piculs of grain from his grand-uncle, to tide them over the hard times. The following year when they were unable to pay the interest, the grand-uncle sent for Hou's wife to help with sewing for a few days, and since this was between relatives there was nothing they could say. So they let her go. Unfortunately she was fickle, and became involved with Diancai, the eldest son. Hou fetched her home and gave her a beating, threatening to divorce her, and during the night she jumped into the well. Diancai, enraged at the death of his mistress, persuaded the girl's family to bring a lawsuit against Hou who had to spend two months in gaol and give up six *mu* of land before a settlement was reached.

His father fell ill of rage and died towards the end of the year. There was no money to buy a coffin and his mother wanted him to go to his grand-uncle's family again to borrow, but he refused, and spent the New Year sulking while his mother had to go herself to borrow ten thousand cash for the funeral. Staying in the village he could not master his bitterness, so he left to work with a camel caravan outside the Pass. All year long he travelled in the desert. At first he still dreamed of making a fresh start, saving money and returning home. But under the stretching white clouds on the interminable sandy dunes the moon waxed and then waned, the wild geese flew south and then north again. Five whole years passed. Hou's blue cloth jacket was worn out and his old short sheepskin coat had lost its sleeves when a letter came from home saying his mother was dying and waiting for him to breathe her last. There was nothing for it but to go home.

Their house was already occupied by another family. His mother had moved into a mud hut at the back of the tumbledown temple and his plump baby had grown into a thin, wizened little monkey. In her pleasure at seeing him back his mother began to recover, but by the time she was able to leave her bed he fell ill himself. His mother nursed him, interceded with spirits, questioned the oracles and found a doctor for him. He did not know where the money had come from, and only after his recovery did he discover that the little land left to them had all been made over to his granduncle. But this time he could not leave, and had to stay in the village to work as a hired hand.

By now both the grand-uncle and Diancai were dead, and the second son, Landlord Hou, was head of the family. Landlord Hou sent for him and said: "We are still uncle and nephew. What my brother did is past and done with. Let bygones be bygones. It's simply your bad luck that your land was mortgaged to my father. You have to support your mother and son all the same, so you may still cultivate that land that used to be yours. Just give me a few piculs each year as rent as you think fit." Tenant Hou bent his head in silent acquiescence and moved into two wretched rooms belonging to Landlord Hou. After all they were the same family, and his uncle did not ask for any money.

From that time onward Tenant Hou stopped singing operas

or telling stories. For years he avoided the villagers, putting all his energy into his work, hoping by dint of hard toil to forget the past and numb his faculties. Many times during the year Landlord Hou came to fetch him for odd jobs, and not wanting to make much of trifles he did whatever he could. His mother also often went to help cook and sew. And after the harvest he took the good grain to his uncle, keeping the poorer to eat himself. His uncle did allow him arrears in rent, and sometimes gave them old clothes so that they would feel under an obligation. Landlord Hou was a Buddhist and often urged his poor relation to put his trust in the Heavenly King, while whenever Buddhist sutras were read in his house he would send for him. Sometimes Tenant Hou drew a little comfort from these, at others he felt even more embittered by the injustice of Providence. Just at that time, however, as if to punish his resentment, his child caught smallpox and died, so his life became even more colourless until his existence was virtually forgotten in the village. Only when his mother found another wife for him did he begin to have anything to do with people again.

This wife was plain and rather tongue-tied. He was not particularly fond of her, but by her industry and kindliness the poor woman acquired a hold on him. He had children again and gradually resumed his old peaceful life, no longer avoiding people and sometimes even telling stories. But instead of the tales of the Yang family generals or Su Wu tending his flocks among the Huns, he simply retold the stories he had heard in Landlord Hou's house about the reward of good and evil, using the most superstitious and fatalistic arguments to urge men to do good. Resigning himself to fate he pardoned all past injuries, considering all his sufferings as due to fate and welcoming the future in a spirit of atonement. Whatever his life he would not fret. For years now they had lived like this. All his family worked hard, and although they could not eat their fill neither did they starve. Not only was his labour exploited, even his heart and soul had been enslaved by those blood-suckers. He became a likeable old man, but at the same time a laughable fool.

At the trial of Landlord Hou that spring many people urged Tenant Hou to settle old scores, but he refused. He said he must have owed his uncle's family something from a former existence, and if he took back what he had paid, in his next existence he would become a horse or an ox. Thus later he insisted on returning to Hou the one and a half *mu* of land given him. Now his outlook was unchanged. The Eighth Route Army talked very well, but he knew from all he had read and heard that never once in thousands of years had the poor been masters. Zhu Hongwu was born poor, and set himself up as champion of the poor in the 14th century. But after he became the first emperor of the Ming dynasty, although he was all right for the first few years, he changed. He became champion of his own gang while the common people remained as before. Tenant Hou saw that many youngsters in the village took a short view, thinking only of the immediate future and echoing the Eighth Route Army, hence he feared for them. He did not allow his son to mix with such people. If his family had to take part in any activities, he attended himself, thinking it would not matter if anything happened to him. An old man over sixty, who had never injured anyone in his life, need not fear to face the Judge of the Dead. But he kept his thoughts to himself. When others expressed approval he simply tugged his beard and smiled. He knew, of course, one hand could not stop the flood destroying the bank, but he had no idea that the flood would reach his threshold and that he himself would be carried away by it.

113

22

THE unhappy evening passed. After Yumin left, the three comrades of the work team had an argument, but it was not a heated one. Wen accepted their outspokenness calmly. Because of his experience in dealing with people he did not defend his own opinions, but for the sake of the work and mutual solidarity showed himself unprecedentedly tolerant. Thus although the others could not convince him and his prejudice against them remained unchanged, still on the surface they appeared to have reached agreement.

After breakfast the courtyard became lively again. Freckles Li brought along his manuscript for the blackboard news together with the script of a folk opera they had prepared in the spring, and while Yang corrected the manuscript, Hu played his two-string fiddle and Freckles Li started singing the opera. Presently all the village cadres foregathered there. Wen asked for their views in the belief that all problems could be settled by discussion among the cadres, but he could not tell whether their views were right or wrong, because there was no reliable material to serve as a basis for judgement. He asked them to discuss whom to struggle against. This led to argument and laughter. When they disagreed they argued just as on the previous evening in the co-operative when Security Officer Zhang and Freckles Li fell out over Landlord Li, and Zhang and Young Cheng over Old Gu. But when Landlord Hou's brindled cow was mentioned the whole group burst out laughing — Hou had used public funds to buy a brindled cow which he swore was his own.

They also described how Hou had introduced religion into the village, and Organization Zhao said he had gone to kowtow before the shrine. Hou told people: "In a time of desolation and confusion all men are bound to suffer. But once you become adepts in this religion, you can ride a swift horse to the Western Paradise!" Organization Zhao's account put them all in high spirits, and they asked him to repeat the incantation. Accordingly he chanted: "The connecting link, I am the primal Buddha Maitreya, enfolding the connecting link within myself, Amida Buddha! . . ."

Then Freckles Li told Wen and the others how Landlord Hou, when he was about to be tried that spring, said he was ill and would not appear. But later they insisted on his coming, and Zhao had given him a slap in the face for injuring him by converting him to his religion.

They went on to speak of Landlord Jiang, who had already stood trial once, and some even praised his present attitude. Landlord Xu's "running dog", Rong, was mentioned. The previous year they had wanted to try him but had not done so. This spring the comrades from the district had told them not to try too many at once, so they had let him off again. When Xu was *xiang* head, Rong had run all his errands for him, and later helped him when he went to Xinbao'an to do business in coal. Rong had eyes like a dog, fawning on superiors and bullying inferiors. Since his brother was disabled he had taken over his property, but he neglected him and had never found a wife for him. They discussed Rong for a long time, but finally when questioned about his property admitted he was only a poor man now, who could by no stretch of the imagination be classed as a middle peasant. Besides he had to support his disabled brother who had only three and a half *mu* of hilly land which he could not cultivate himself. Thus it was out of the question to make him the principal target for attack. Nevertheless they felt they ought to try him properly and settle old scores.

This meeting lasted a long time, and many names were brought up. All who rented out land or owned much land, as well as all former ward chiefs, were mentioned. A great deal was said, but no conclusion reached. All these people deserved punishment, some heavy, some light, but it appeared impossible to find among them a single outstanding case, guilty of great crimes, to kindle the anger of the masses. The village cadres mentioned various likely-sounding candidates, but a closer examination left them in a dilemma again.

"There's nobody in our village like Chen Wu of Mengjiagou," they said. "Chen Wu used to oppress and beat people, and rape women, and later he killed one of the cadres from the district. He had several rifles hidden in his house with hundreds of rounds of bullets, and he held meetings in the fields with spies from Fanbao to plot against the security officer. There was evidence of all his crimes, which were common knowledge. As soon as the people realized he deserved a death sentence, they cast fear to the winds and started trying him for his life. Our village doesn't have any local despot like that. We don't have any big landlords either like the one in Baihuai, who had over a thousand *mu* and who built that big kitchen. If Nuanshui had such a big landlord we could all become middle peasants after division of land. With that incentive the people would be willing to rise."

They discussed the matter backward and forward, but for all their efforts failed to hit on any outstanding evil-doers, and in the afternoon dispersed. Wen told them to sound out the masses and postpone making any decision for the time being. If there were really no one, there might be no need for a trial. When the cadres heard this their enthusiasm was even more damped, but there was no more to be said, and they went away to prepare for the meeting of the peasants' association that evening.

After they had gone Wen wrote a report to the district

116

asking for advice. But instead of showing it to the others he tucked it inside his notebook, waiting for a chance to ask one of the militiamen to deliver it. Then he set about preparing his talk on current events for that evening. He felt Hu's disapproval of his speech was simply ridiculous. The peasants were completely ignorant and unless things were explained to them they could not understand, and would be unwilling to rise. All Hu wanted was a sensational trial — that was the superficiality typical of the petty-bourgeois mentality. Although acknowledging his own lack of experience Wen could not believe their views might be sounder than his own or their meagre experiences have any value. Their experiences had not been summed up and analysed or raised to the theoretical level, therefore they were one-sided and unreliable. Hu and Yang could, he admitted, get closer to the masses than he — they were out all day long, but this by no means meant their views were correct. Steering a movement required skill to guide the thought of the masses, regulate their emotions and satisfy their desires, instead of simply spending the whole day with a few peasants. Chairman Mao thoroughly understood the Chinese people and had proposed all manner of timely measures, but he could never spend the whole day with the people. As for the mass line, the main thing was to understand its spirit, rather than plunge about blindly. Only callow youngsters like Hu and Yang would pick up a smattering of knowledge and regard it as gospel. However, he forgave them. He considered them both as half intellectual and half peasant, and the fact that they were neither one thing nor the other made the work difficult. Wen decided to take good care of them, co-operate with them and help them. And the thought of his concession to them increased his complacency.

Left by himself Wen presently grew lonely. He wondered where the others had gone and what they were up to, also what the village cadres were doing and what they really thought. So he put down his pen and went out.

23

IN the quiet street two women were sitting gossiping at the entrance to a lane. At the sight of Wen they fell silent and fixed their eyes on him. "Women are great talkers," thought Wen, "but why should they come out in the day-time to the top of the lane to gossip? Why aren't they working?" The two women waited till he had passed, then started chattering again. Although Wen could not hear clearly what they were saying, and could not understand what he heard, he imagined they were discussing him. Passing the top of the lane he walked northwards, ignoring them.

When he reached the street he could see no one he knew. Under the locust tree in front of the stage was a water-melon stall where four or five old men were squatting, not buying water-melon but apparently waiting for someone. A young woman stuck her head out of the beancurd mill to look at him, then turned to speak to someone inside. Wen did not know which way to go and buying water-melon was pointless. He walked over to the blackboard news, and although he had seen the articles in it that morning he read them over again. The characters were well and even elegantly written. To be sure, Freckles Li had told them the teacher named Liu was not bad and wrote characters well. As Wen was reading he felt the old men's eyes boring into his back and suspected there were two heads sticking out of the beancurd mill now. He was not afraid of being looked at or discussed by these people, but still it made him uncomfortable. He walked to-

118

wards the primary school to see whether Hu was there teaching songs or organizing a folk dance. Young Hu had been in a dramatic troupe and could not hide where his interest lay. Wen felt if he could find him all would be well.

He crossed the threshold of the school into a quiet courtyard. As he was looking round a man in a short jacket came out from a small building beside the gate, and greeted the unexpected visitor most obsequiously: "Come in and sit down! Ah, do come in, do come in! . . ."

"Are classes still going on?" Wen had to ask.

"Yes, yes, the pupils aren't out yet. They will soon be out."

Wen followed him in to a kind of reception room. On a square table by the window was a musical clock under a glass case, on each side a hatstand, and on the opposite wall a lithographed portrait of Sun Yat-sen and a painted portrait of Chairman Mao. Beside these portraits were pasted two slogans in shiny paper: "Serve the people!" and "Develop the culture and education of New Democracy!" Essays and drawings by the students pasted on different coloured paper underneath made a brave show. On the left was a long, low chest with a roll of bedding on it. On the right wall hung two rows of whips used in folk dances, decorated with red and pink paper flowers. The host hastily invited Wen to be seated, and poured him a cup of tea from the table by the chest.

"Have some tea, have some tea! We're very shabby here, ah, very shabby!"

"You belong to this school?" Wen asked.

"Yes, yes, I work here. Well. . . ."

"What's your name?" Wen had to ask.

"My name's Liu."

Wen realized this must be the school teacher, and asked: "Are you the one who writes the blackboard news?"

"Don't mention it, don't mention it. My writing is so abominable."

Wen took another look at him. He was a man of nearly forty, with a long face and narrow, short-sighted eyes. His nose was big, his hair long, his white cloth jacket exceedingly dirty, and his excessive formality did not please Wen at all, who thought: "Must you act like that?" He asked a few more questions, all of which Liu answered most humbly and respectfully, till Wen lost patience and said: "Are either of our comrades here? I came to look for them."

"Just gone. Comrade Hu has just gone. But if you like I'll go and find him for you."

"No need, no need." Wen went out again. By now classes were over and a crowd of children swarmed out, shouting and singing at the top of their voices. Some pushed forward to look at him, and others crowded behind him, imitating in fun his style of speaking: "Do you understand, folks? Is it clear or not?" Wen was not accustomed to such disorder, but all he could do was to feign indifference and walk out slowly. Teacher Liu anxiously saw him out, muttering as he followed him: "Please favour us with some instruction. . . ."

Wen emerged from the school with a sense of relief and held his head higher as he started walking back. Suddenly someone called out from the window of the co-operative: "Chairman Wen!"

It was Security Officer Zhang, who for some reason always gave him this title.

As Wen hurried over Zhang shouted: "Come and have a look at our co-op!"

Through the window could be seen two counters of mixed

goods, all daily necessities, besides a counter for flour, a rolling board and an oven. Zhang's face was red as if he had just been drinking, and he introduced a short man who hurried out to greet Wen: "This is the chairman of our co-op, Tian, a good businessman, very able."

Thinking he ought to discuss the co-operative with him, Wen asked a few questions. Co-op Tian did not look in the least like a businessman. He seemed straightforward and answered sentence by sentence. Wen remembered Yumin had told him to look in the co-op if he needed him, so he asked: "Is Yumin here much?"

"Yes, he's often here."

Looking from Zhang's face to a pot of wine on the counter, Wen felt he knew how things stood.

Seeing that Wen was unwilling to come in, Security Officer Zhang vaulted out through the window, and said: "Are you looking for Yumin, Chairman? His home is near here, just over on the west side."

"No, I just asked."

"Yumin is busy with public business and private affairs. People keep calling on him at all hours." He laughed shortly.

"What?" Wen divined some hidden significance in this.

"Chairman, when the fruits of victory are divided up this time, make over three good northern rooms to Yumin. That eastern room he's living in now is too poor, and there's his brother. . . ." He laughed again.

"What is it? Do you mean — ?"

"Yes, it's just that! You must drink some wine at his wedding, Chairman, before you go!"

"What family is the girl? How is it going?"

"Is there any need to ask? She's a widow! She has a lot of land, but no house. . . . Ha-ha. . . ."

Talk like this irritated Wen very much, but at the same

121

time he felt proud to think that after all his sense of discernment was not at fault. So he walked northwards, meaning to talk further with Zhang.

Zhang accompanied him and told him that he had joined the Party before liberation. Only because he was simple and lacked ability he was just given the title of security officer, while Yumin actually kept everything in his own hands. Zhang gave it as his opinion that they could not work up any struggle to settle accounts this time. When Wen insisted on knowing his reasons, he said after much hesitation: "See here, Chairman, why don't the peasants dare settle scores with the feudal landlords? It's all the fault of the cadres. Think for yourself. We all grew up together in the village. If people aren't related by marriage, then they're neighbours. Ah — when people act selfishly it's hard to get anything done. Don't you understand, Chairman?" But who it was that was swayed by selfish considerations he would not say. So they walked all the way to the end of the village.

When they returned Wen saw a swarthy young man standing by the side of the road with clenched fists, looking at them coldly. His face was familiar and Wen asked him: "Didn't you go to the fields today?"

Before the other could answer, Zhang said: "I'm off, Chairman. See you later." And passing behind him he vanished.

The dark young man cocked his head and said to the people across the road: "One sees ghosts in broad daylight. Ah, after all, evil can't overcome good. See . . . he's made off."

Someone across the street said: "Go on home, Liuman, your wife's been looking for you for a long time to go home and eat. What's happened to you these last two days! You'd better settle down to work properly!"

The dark youngster flung out an arm: "Work — eh? Aren't

122

we working on land reform now!" Then he turned to ask
Wen: "Isn't that right, comrade?"

But Wen, thinking the fellow must be wrong in the head,
said nothing and started back, while Liuman stood with
clenched fists watching him walk away.

By the time Wen got back there was still no one in. Old
Han was plying his bellows to prepare supper while his
grandson was sitting at the threshold playing with a locust
whose wings he had torn off.

24

AT this time Yumin and Yang were still in the orchard,
where more and more fruit was ripening. The two of them
walked slowly. Faint sunlight filtering through the leaves
chequered the ground and their bodies, and they had sampled
the fruit as they filled a basket chock-full. This land belonged to Yumin's uncle, Quan, who had been given half a *mu*
of Landlord Xu's orchard after the settling of scores the previous year. Yang had never seen a sight so beautiful as these
great fruit trees stretching as far as eye could see. In the
distance voices could be heard, but not a soul was in sight.
The branches of sweet-apple spread out to form a magnificent
awning, and the spread of one tree could have covered a
small house. Above hung big juicy fruit, dark red, pale red,
dark green and pale green. Sometimes they could pick the
fruit by stretching out their hands, sometimes they had to
stoop and bend their heads as they passed under the trees for
fear of knocking the thickly clustered fruit. Here was a feast
for the eyes: you had no sooner discovered the biggest apple
you had ever seen in your life than you caught sight of one
that was rounder, redder and brighter than all the rest. And

all the time you were inhaling and distinguishing between different scents, so that simply to draw breath was a delight. There were more sweet-apple here than other fruit trees. Here and there were a few apple and crabapple trees. The crabapples hanging down in clusters were more red and fascinating than flowers. Yang could not resist picking a small cluster and toying with it. There were quite a few pear trees too, the pears heavy and juicy, weighing down the branches.

Whenever Yang passed a tree he felt like asking to whom it belonged, and when he learned that they belonged to the poor he could not contain his delight. The fruit seemed more radiant with the rosy colour of victory. He started calculating for the owners of the trees, and asked: "I suppose a tree like this must yield at least two hundred catties of fruit?"

"Nothing of the kind. In a bumper year like this, every tree yields at least eight or nine hundred, sometimes over a thousand catties. If the railway isn't cut the price will be higher. If one *mu* of orchard isn't worth ten *mu* of paddy fields, at least it's worth seven or eight *mu*. With hilly land there's even less comparison."

Yang was surprised at this figure and his eyes opened wide. Yumin went on to explain: "Really poor people still prefer the irrigated land which isn't such a risk as orchard land. This year the fruit has ripened wonderfully, but last year not a single tree ripened, not even the village children got any to eat. Even when the fruit ripens well, it still isn't like rice that you can eat. See how beautifully this sweet-apple has ripened and how sweet it smells. But it doesn't keep well, not as well as other fruits. It has to be sent off without a moment's delay. Yet if we are too anxious to get rid of it, the fruit dealers will only give a miserable price. It may be true that it costs two or three hundred dollars a catty in Zhangjiakou, but the fruit-growers only get a hundred a catty. A little later it'll only fetch seventy or eighty dollars a catty, with transport costs to come off that, while damaged fruit can only be kept to dry for the children to eat."

Yang calculated again how much the income from this orchard would be. These ten *mu* which had previously belonged to Landlord Xu, had been divided among twenty poor families the previous year. If the yield was at least thirty thousand catties, that would be worth three million dollars, a hundred and fifty thousand for each family, equal to about seven hundred and fifty catties of millet at the market price. If a small family of three could find a little additional work that would be just about enough to live on, while if they had another small piece of land of course that would be so much the better. Yang's interest in the orchard was thoroughly aroused. He went on to ask details about the number of trees in the whole village and the names of the owners, all of whom were landlords or rich peasants.

After they had walked for some time they found the orchard very quiet. No one was about but Old Quan hoeing the soil under the trees, breaking the earth up and smoothing it down, so that if anyone were to come and pick fruit from these trees his footprints would betray him.

When they had figured out the probable proceeds from the fruit, Yumin reverted to the subject they had been discussing on the road. "Of course I can't bring it up at the meeting. He has his spies among the cadres. Before matters came to a head he would take fright and make off. Another thing, if I brought it up and it wasn't passed, that would be worse than useless. Everybody has in mind 'The rafters that jut out rot first'. Do you suppose they really don't understand?"

"Haven't you already posted the militia to keep a secret lookout?"

"I don't dare tell everything even to the militia! If they

were all like Swarthy Guo that would be another matter. He's a stout fellow. He wouldn't care if the enemy belonged to his own family. Living or dying he'll be true to the Party."

"Zhao is a former vil'age head, but he seems to me a sensible man. His family is so poor his wife hasn't even a vest to wear. Is he unreliable too?"

"He knows what's what, but he's soft. This year he borrowed two piculs of grain from Landlord Jiang, and is still carrying on as if no one knew. Because he's in debt to Jiang he can't stand firm. Oh, all these people have their own connections. Whoever we attack, there's always someone against it!"

"Judging by what you say, if the village is to get rid of the bullies, it's got to be Schemer Qian. But if you attack him the cadres to begin with aren't to be relied on, is that it?"

"Exactly! I'm not saying they're a'l of them no good, but if half of them don't say anything do you suppose the others won't watch which way the wind blows? Some things can only be said among ourselves. Just take the case of Young Cheng. He used to work for Schemer Qian as a hired hand, then became his tenant. Now he's the chairman of the peasants' association and ought to be very keen. Well, that fellow takes the lead in everything else, only in this business he pretends to be stupid. He's not as straightforward as he appears, still he's one of the good cadres. Oh, people are only human after all, and he can't forget the feeling that man's niece has for him! O'd Yang, when you've been here a little longer you'll understand it all. The people are watching the cadres, but the cadres aren't willing to give a lead. You tell me, what are we to do about it?"

"Isn't there a single person in the village willing to take the lead? Let's try to find one. There must be someone cruelly wronged, who's willing to speak out. If the cadres won't take the lead let's look first among the masses. If the masses are willing to make a move the cadres' private feelings won't matter."

Yumin cited the example of Tenant Hou, and said that before the people's outlook had changed no matter what you told them it was no use. Yumin had led two trials. Both times had been smooth sailing, making him feel that the people would do just as he said. But he realized this time it would be extremely difficult. He knew that it was not enough to get land for the poor peasants. During the process of getting land they must unite in order to stand up properly, and understand that they were now the masters. So he was treading very warily. In addition, a number of difficulties had cropped up, and sometimes he felt thoroughly depressed. Still he was a dogged fellow who could never be content to let things drift. And after explaining the situation to Yang his heart felt lighter, for Yang gave him fresh courage. In particular he felt Yang was not a helpless individual, and that now he had real support. He agreed to Yang's suggestion that after the meeting of the peasants' association that evening he should explain the situation again to Wen. Then they could think out some plan of action together.

It was growing late. Yumin left first with the basket of fruit, while Yang went back to the hut where Quan lived as watchman of the orchard.

The old man with his drooping moustache was rather a taciturn old fellow. He was leaning complacently against a tree outside the hut.

Yang noticed some rotten fruit in the basket by his knees, and asked: "What use are they?"

The old fellow smiled and muttered: "They're all rotten . . . but still parts of them are all right. If they're dried they'll be good to put in tea. . . ." Then opening his eyes wider to look at Yang he said: "Comrade, in the old days we couldn't even pick up one of these rotten ones! Fifty or sixty years I've just looked at these trees, and now I've got a few of my own. How can I chuck the rotten fruit away? Not me, not me!"

Yang thought of Quan's generosity when his nephew had come just now to pick fruit. How he had pointed out his trees and told them to take all they wanted, and that when these were eaten he would send over some more. How he told Yumin not to trouble to come because he knew he was busy. "You're really a good sort," Yang could not help saying. "Look how many of yours we picked just now."

"Many? Not a bit of it." And the old fellow went on seriously: "Didn't I get all this from you? You're good people. You divide up rich people's things for us poor folk. Now you're here to do the same thing again. Everybody in the village knows that."

"What sort of people are we? Why do we want to do this kind of thing?" Yang was intrigued by the old fellow.

"You," the old man laughed heartily, "you're the Eighth Route Army. You're Communists. Your leader Chairman Mao tells you to do it!"

"And what does Chairman Mao do it for? Let's see what you say to that, Uncle."

"He does it for us! For the poor! He's the poor people's friend." The old man smiled broadly again.

Yang leant against the tree trunk too and laughed. Then he quietly asked the old man: "Are there any Communists in your village?"

"No, we don't have any."

"How do you know there aren't any?"

128

"I know everybody in the village. They're all ordinary people. We don't have any."

"Uncle, if there were Communists in the village, would you join or not?" Yang questioned him.

"Why not? If there were any I'd join. But since there aren't I can't join all by myself."

"What are you afraid of by yourself?"

"I'm not afraid of anything, only one old fellow can't get anything done."

"Ah." Yang felt unexpectedly happy, and went on to tell him there had been Party members in the village for some time, only because he was not one no one had told him. He urged him to join the Party. After joining the Party everyone could unite more closely and be even stronger against those rascals. The old man listened chuckling, and finally told Yang that before joining the Party he must first talk it over with someone. "How can you talk over things like this?" asked Yang. "This is something you have to decide yourself! Just suppose you told a bad man!"

The old fellow looked embarrassed and finally Yang had to ask him with whom he proposed to discuss it. He answered in a low voice: "With my nephew Yumin! Do you think that's all right?"

At that Yang roared with laughter. Nodding his head again and again, he said: "All right, quite all right."

It was growing dark. Yang found the orchard an enchanting place. He gripped the old man's hand several times, and told him he would come to see him again. The old man too smiled innocently and happily, and wanted to keep him to a meal. But Yang had to leave. On his way back he kept turning back to look at the fruit trees gradually merging into the darkness, and at Quan deep in the orchard.

25

COMING out of the north street Yang had just reached the wall of the primary school when he heard people talking at the top of their voices in the co-operative opposite. He hurried over and saw that it was quite dark inside. There was a crowd there, many of whom were talking at the same time. Squeezing up to Young Cheng he heard the latter say: "You people! When we had to assess our taxes, you refused to register, but now you come one after another. Look here, what do you say to this: a widower father and an unmarried son can count as two households. There are over a thousand people in the whole village, but does that mean over a thousand households? You want to have infants in arms counted as separate households in order to get a bit of irrigated land. You don't use your brains to think how much land there is in the village! Isn't that just making unnecessary trouble!"

A young peasant of eighteen or nineteen who was standing by the corner of the *kang* went right on complaining: "The land my dad cultivates is Landlord Li's, the land I cultivate is Landlord Jiang's. Don't you know that? We sleep on one *kang* but work for two different families. Long ago we started each managing his own affairs."

"Hurry up and choose a wife, and get a son. Won't that be three households then?" joked someone standing by the door.

"That's right. This morning Zhendong's mother was saying their family ought to be counted as five, because her daughter-in-law is seven months pregnant, and the baby ought to be counted in. I said: 'What if she gives birth to a wild cat?' The old woman was hopping mad." This was Bugao, organization officer of the peasants' association. The last day or two group after group of people had come to see him about registration of newly divided households.

There was a roar of laughter.

"Isn't your peasants' association going to do anything about it?" The young peasant refused to be crushed, and stayed angrily on.

"Our peasants' association has got too much to do. Is it our business whether you're impotent or not?" retorted Bugao complacently. Although his face could not be seen clearly in the darkness, there was a decided note of vengeance in his voice. His last remark set the whole room resounding with shouts of laughter.

The youngster felt he was being made to look a fool. Unable to restrain himself any longer he headed furiously for Bugao: "You bully, taking advantage of the fact you're organizer of the peasants' association to bully people. . . ."

Yang felt this joke had gone too far and was just going to interfere when Hu stepped out of the group. Hu grasped the youngster with one hand, restraining Bugao with the other, and said: "Don't be angry, my friend. Old Bugao shouldn't have said what he did. Of course the peasants' association ought to mind whether you and your father are counted as one family or two. The peasants' association must decide according to what's right, and not shrink from trouble. Mr. Chairman, shouldn't your peasants' association discuss and make a set of regulations and act according to them?"

"Right, what Comrade Hu says is right." Young Cheng too felt that the squabble had taken an ugly turn. Wanting to help keep peace, he turned to the young man and said: "You go back. When we've discussed this business of you and your father in the peasants' association, we'll let you know."

Bugao had taken the opportunity to slip outside, so there

was nothing for the youngster to say. But instead of going out at once, he remained standing there.

"What's your name?" asked Hu.

"Guo. My father's Guo Boren."

"Are you both tenants?"

"Yes, they both work other people's land. His father works eight *mu* of Li's irrigated land, and he works ten *mu* of Jiang's land, one in the south, the other in the east, about three miles apart."

"If you work Jiang's land, you ought to settle scores with him, while if your father cultivates Li's land he ought to settle scores with him. It doesn't matter whether you're one household or two, do you understand?"

The onlookers endorsed what Hu said: "Yes! You've each got different grudges and a different landlord to settle scores with. Each of you settle his own, isn't that right?"

"I can't settle anything. I'm a member of the association, and the peasants' association doesn't help us. My dad's even more hopeless."

"To settle scores is easy. If you can't, I'll help you. You just have to dare go. All the peasants' association can do is to help you, but it can't do the job for you, understand?"

"Go by myself?"

"What are you afraid of?"

"I can't explain things by myself."

"Well then, get some people to go with you. . . ." Hu was just going to ask what other tenants Landlord Jiang had, when Cheng walked over and cut him short, saying: "What are you all crowding in here for? Those who don't want to buy anything go out. This is a co-op!" As he was shouting this, Cheng nudged Yang secretly and made a sign to the young man. When some men had gone slowly out Co-op Tian brought in an oil lamp, and Yang saw a man of over thirty standing by the door, with eyes wide open drinking in everything, and a forced smile on his face. He seemed to want to come in but hesitated. Hu noticed him too, and asked: "Who are you looking for?"

"Er . . . I'm not looking for anyone, Chairman, you. . . ."

"This is our village head, Jiang," said Freckles Li, who was standing next to Hu.

"Er . . . I'm Jiang. Since the year before last Comrade Pin often came to my house and sometimes stayed with us. . . ." He spoke in a small voice.

There were still seven or eight people left in the inner and outer rooms but no one said anything.

Yang cast a meaningful glance at Hu and said: "Let's go back." He led the way out.

"Right." Hu immediately followed him out, and once in the courtyard said in a low voice: "Well! Those bastards certainly get about. That teacher Ren in the primary school isn't up to any good either."

When they reached the street it was already pitch dark, so they hurried towards Old Han's house. At the turning to the house there seemed to be a man squatting, and Hu called out: "Who's there?"

"The sentry," the other answered softly. Yang went over to see, and sure enough it was one of the militiamen who had already stood up. "Have you had your meal?" Yang asked.

"Yes. Yumin is at your place now, and Old Dong."

They had already reached home, when Yang said again softly: "It's not going to be plain sailing here. We'd better tell Wen and Old Dong, and plan carefully what action to take. Now Old Dong's back, that's all to the good. He's more experienced than we are."

26

IT was very lively inside, several peasants who had come with Old Dong from Liyu were looking eagerly at Wen, while Old Dong, seated on the other side of the *kang*, looked flushed as if he had been talking for a long time. "That's a small village, and it's no good," he was saying. "They can't fill in forms or use the abacus. There are no landlords there, only a few rich peasants, and rich peasants aren't anything special. There's one rich peasant called Yang who's a bad lot, who might be tried, but no one dares to speak out. They all say if there aren't enough people it's difficult to have a mass trial. We held a meeting of cadres and they all lacked confidence, and at a meeting of the peasants' association I was the only one to speak. When poor clay's put in the kiln nothing good will come out. It's just a waste of effort. Nobody said a word, just like so many deaf mutes. . . ."

Wen was sitting on the near end of the *kang,* laughing heartily, while the cadres with Old Dong nodded from time to time and said, "Yes, that's right," to confirm his statements. Now Hu who was also standing there listening interrupted to ask: "Haven't you anyone in your place who can use an abacus? Can't the teacher in your school use one?"

"There's nobody who uses it well — of course the teacher can!"

"That'll do, as long as you can add and subtract that's all right. That problem can be solved, can't it?" The cadres just smiled doubtfully.

"We'll make up a specimen form for you. Then with the registration for assessing taxes as the basis you make another investigation, and put down separately the self-cultivated land, land rent out, rented land, mortgaged land, land rented from other villages, and land rented to other villages. You must distinguish between the irrigated land, hillside irrigated land, hilly land, dry land, orchard, vineyards and vegetable gardens. All you need is to make a thorough investigation, not leaving anything out. There are only forty or fifty families, so just the few of you can do it. What's the difficulty? It doesn't matter if you write badly, so long as you know what you write and other people can understand. That's the main thing, don't you agree?"

Catching some of Hu's enthusiasm the cadres took heart a little and said: "You're quite right, comrade. It's just that we've never done this before. If only you'll come and show us how to manage, it will be all right. Won't you come and stay in our village, comrade?" Again they looked eagerly at Wen, waiting for him to speak.

Yumin reminded Wen again that he should go to the meeting, and just as he was leaving he accepted the invitation to Liyu, saying he would go the next day and look round himself. This made them overjoyed. They pressed behind Wen, and followed him out, saying: "Come early! Come and have breakfast in our village."

When only three of them were left in the room Yang asked Old Dong whether he had had a meal or not. Old Dong said he had eaten at Liyu. Then they started talking about affairs in the village again.

Old Dong was fifty that year. He was clean shaven, with a red face and a powerful chest and shoulders. As soon as the Communists had come from Nanshan to the Third District he had joined them as a guerrilla. Some people thought he was too old, but he said: "Don't just think I'm older than you, let's see who's stronger, let's see whose legs are strongest. I don't let myself get left behind in farming, and still less in guerrilla fighting." At that time Comrade Pin was in charge in the Third District and he kept him on. At first he just kept up with the others. He could not shoot and when he saw the enemy he jumped for fright, unable to advance, while his mouth grew dry, so that all the others laughed at him. However, after a few encounters he said, "Dead or alive it's all the same," and stopped being afraid. They gave him a pistol with no bullets. He had to use the wrong-size bullets and after each shot he had to clean the barrel. All this area was then occupied by enemy garrisons which had established many strong points, so that when guerrilla warfare was first started it was no joke. Once some twenty of them were holding a meeting with Comrade Pin in a village. Enemy spies learned of it and sent thirty or forty men over with a machine gun. Then all they said was, "We'll be revolutionaries to the end. If we have to jump into the Yellow River we'll jump together!" They left the village and laid an ambush. The enemy who had caught up with them knew exactly what their strength was. They had only six rifles, two pistols and two Hubei rifles. They had all only just put down their hoes and taken up guns. Their aim was poor and they were panicky. The enemy made fun of them, shouting: "Guerrillas of the Third District, we'll give up our guns. Look . . . these are all good rifles, do you want them?" The guerrillas were furious. "Don't be afraid," said Pin. "Keep calm and we'll each aim at the same man, the one with the leather cap. When I give the word all fire together, got that?" They did as he said, ten rifles sounded together, and the enemy was wounded, whereupon they all jumped for joy. They continued in the same way and wounded three or four one after another, until the enemy beat a hasty retreat. Immediately the country people prepared noodles, and the district office bought five chickens for them. Later the county office gave them a rifle as a prize. After that Old Dong grew even more resolute. He spent three years that were a hundred times harder than working as a hired hand on the farm, often sleeping without even a mud *kang*, simply digging a trench in the ground and lining it with a little grass, eating dumplings that had frozen hard. He learned how to fire a gun, and became a loyal Party member, braving death to carry out orders. Later they sent him to work in the district trade union, and after the chairman of the trade union was transferred he was made chairman.

He was an energetic Communist cadre, but had never got used to using his head. He liked a cut and dried job, not caring if it were hard, only afraid of being on his own and having to make decisions. The district authority had sent him to Nuanshui this time partly because he came from Liyu himself and was familiar with conditions there, but largely because Wen and the others were coming, and he could act as a guide and also learn something. The district office respected and trusted Wen implicitly, and Old Dong with his reliance on others came with him. When Wen sent him to Liyu it was a chance to go home and see his brother whom he had not seen for many years. He had made no attempt to understand conditions in Nuanshui, and had not even explained to the others what he had known of the village in the past.

When Yang and Hu told him all they had found out during the last two days, and analysed it, he did not feel it worth studying, and wondered if he should tell them a piece of business of his own. On his return to Liyu he had found his brother suffering from stomach-ache. His brother urged him to come back to the village and get a little land. He was no longer young and had had a rough enough time of it. He should spend a few years peacefully with his brother. Old Dong rejected this proposal, saying that as long as he lived he was a Communist, and he would die a Communist too. He must still work for the people. But his brother said his health was no longer good. Both of them were still bachelors. They'd never had a woman, and even if he was working for the people he ought to leave a descendant for their ancestors. His brother said there was a widow in the village, and although she was already forty she still looked strong enough to bear children, and would do as a wife. He himself was incapable of marrying, but he wanted to fix up a marriage for his younger brother. Now his brother was a cadre, he need not worry the woman's family would refuse. Old Dong's face turned red with embarrassment. "You're joking," he said; but it unsettled him. The village cadres too said he had worked hard for the revolution, and wanted to give him three *mu* of vineyard. He said nothing. He had worked several dozen years as a hired hand and never even in his dreams hoped to have three *mu* of vineyard. He was very tempted, thinking he could find time to come home to work, and his elder brother could help him to look after it. But suppose by any chance the comrades in the district did not approve? Suppose they said he was selfish and self-seeking, or called him backward? At the same time he felt he could not spend all his life at public expense. If he had a little land he could support himself. As for selfishness and self-interest, he had not made money, but he could have some land to work on. Chairman Mao said they should carry out the policy of "land to the tiller". Since he had worked on the land dozens of years why shouldn't he have some? Finally he decided if only he would not be condemned for it he would ask for the land. As for a wife, that could wait for a bit. But he did not know whether he would be criticized or not. He wanted badly to talk it over with the other two, but they had not the slightest inkling of his feelings and did not give him any opening, absorbed as they were in their own business, talking on and on about the working styles of certain cadres, putting people's thinking straight, extending the organization and strengthening the armed forces. Finally seeing that Old Dong looked dispirited, they said he had worked too hard the last two days and had better rest. Then they themselves left for the meeting.

Although there were not as many people at the meeting that evening as the previous day, it still ended very late. Because Wen wanted to overcome the peasants' fear that the Kuomintang would come back he felt he had to make a minute analysis of the situation, and spoke of the democratic movement in Kuomintang-held territory, the hatred of the soldiers for the war, and the mighty strength of the Soviet Union. Then he spoke of Gao Shuxun and Liu Shanben, described the progressive American writer Agnes Smedley and the assassination by Kuomintang agents of the progressive professors Wen Yiduo and Li Gongpu. Finally he talked about the defence of Sipingjie and the fighting outside Datong. He said the Eighth Route Army had already surrounded Datong and it would be taken in two weeks at the latest. All this talk had its significance, and some of the audience found it interesting. Unfortunately it was rather academic. There were too many terms the peasants could not understand, and it was far too long. The audience felt tired, and by the end many of them were asleep again. But Comrade Wen, in his enthusiasm to lay bare his heart to them so that they would understand everything, could not compress his speech. After the meeting broke up he was exhausted and his head reeled, and as soon as he reached home he lay down and went to sleep. Yang and Hu had to postpone their plan to the next day. But the next day Wen had no time. He had promised to go to Liyu, and without leaving even the simplest plan of work he left hastily with Old Dong. He stayed at Liyu two whole days and one night, holding two meetings at which he repeated all he had said at Nuanshui. Meanwhile Yang and Hu discussed how to go forward with their investigation, in particular how to find evidence of the facts of which Yumin had told them, and how to find people from among the masses to start the struggle.

27

EVER since the land reform team's arrival in the village, the primary school had become a hive of activity. There were more fights and accusations. You could often hear shouting inside: "Down with the little feudal landlords!" And then a child would cry. Once Hu had taught them a song which the poor children liked particularly. As soon as they left class they would start singing cheerfully: *"Landlords have oppressed us, oppressed us all these years. . . . Now we must unite to settle our old scores."* The clear childish treble echoed on every side. When they gathered in groups to play, one or two mischief-makers would deliberately bump into the children of landlords' families, who usually dressed better than the rest, and tease them. Then those children would start shrieking, and the teachers often had to settle these disputes. Teacher Liu never scolded the poor children, at the most he would say: "It's no use picking on them, they aren't responsible." And he would comfort those children now so vulnerable: "You must work in the future and earn your own living. Be good citizens and tell your parents to be so too, otherwise sooner or later you'll all be attacked. . . ."

But not so Teacher Ren. He turned threatening eyes on those children who had no socks to wear and, not daring scold them out loud, would whisper fiercely: "Don't start rejoicing too soon. Wait till the Kuomintang government troops come and punish you creatures!" Some of the children were afraid and dared not make trouble again, but others went and told Teacher Liu who made a mental note of it, but said nothing for the time being. Ren also expressed sympathy to the children who had been teased, hoping they would repeat his remarks to their parents. He not only busied himself in the school, out of school hours he would make calls too. He called on several landlord families, dropping a few ambiguous remarks to increase their anxiety, and then giving them some hope and courage. Things couldn't go on like this, rich people would have endless suffering in the hands of the Communists. But the Communists couldn't beat Chiang Kaishek, or even if they did they couldn't beat America. Sooner or later they would be swept clean.

He himself was not at all rich. He was one of the middleclass impoverished intelligentsia, but still he sympathized with the rich and was willing to run their errands, hoping to pick up crumbs from their tables and grow fat. He did not like poor people, and hated the cadres who worked for the poor. He hoped the land reform would be a failure and cause trouble. Or at least that it would not turn out well.

The evening that Old Dong came back from Liyu, Teacher Ren went to Landlord Li's house. This was the only house Li had left. The gate was very high, with two or three steps up to it, the big iron-plated door was half closed. He pushed straight in, and as he rounded the corner two dogs started barking fiercely at him from the empty porch, but luckily they were fastened by an iron chain to a pillar. Hurrying into the courtyard he called, "Mr. Li!" but no one answered. Only after a long time Li's elder daughter Lanying came out. She was a girl of eleven who had just got back from school and still had a smudge of ink on her face. When she saw that it

141

was one of the teachers she stood to attention and said: "Are you looking for Father? Father isn't at home."

"Your mother?" Ren looked around. All he could see were a few children's clothes hanging on a wire in the court-yard with a woman's red silk brassiere. Outside the east room two big baskets of dried fruit were being sunned.

The girl hesitated a moment, then said: "Mother's in the back yard."

Ren understood, but he wanted to see for himself. By now the girl had run down the steps and was hurrying off to the left, saying as she passed him: "Mother's busy." Seeing there was no way of stopping him, she called out loudly: "Ma! Ma! Someone to see you! Teacher Ren's here!"

A plump woman in her thirties hurried out of the shed where hay was kept, still showing traces of alarm, but said smiling: "It's you! Do go back to the north room and sit down." Hay was sticking to her flowered blouse and hair.

"Mrs. Li, it's no use hiding your title deeds in the hay," said Ren maliciously.

Mrs. Li belonged to the richest family at Wujia Village. Since childhood she had been waited on, and she was known for her fine white complexion. At Ren's remark she involun-tarily started, but immediately steadied herself again, and answered smiling: "We took out our title deeds long ago and put them in the drawer. Did you come for the deeds? All right! Just as long as the peasants' association agrees."

"I haven't come for the deeds, but sooner or later some-one will." Ren darted an unfathomable look at her.

She did not show him into the north room, but took him into the east room where there was a big *kang*, in front of it two large pans, and opposite it two dressers covered like the counters in a grocery shop with jars of oil, salt, soya and vinegar, all polished till they shone. Taking a bright copper dipper she ladled water from the water barrel and poured it into a flowered basin to wash her hands which were covered with mud. Ren said again, laughing: "Well, look how you rich wives have been dragged down!"

Li's wife was an enterprising woman. In her mother's house she had never done a stroke of work, only able to embroider grasses and flowers as a pastime. The first few years after she married Landlord Li passed quite comfortably, but Li was an opium addict and a gambler. Although he had a good income from rents he was always short of cash, and every year had to sell a little land. One year Schemer Qian persuaded him to be the puppet ward chief. Everybody else made money as ward chief, but he was a fool and got cheated by others, so that he had to sell another hundred *mu* of land and a house before he could settle his debts, and asked people to plead hard for him besides giving a good deal of money to Schemer Qian before he could get rid of the job. These last two years his income had not been too little. They could afford a labourer, and if they hired someone to cook, carry water and run errands to town they could have been more comfortable, but his wife did not approve. She saw things were shaping unfavourably for them, and advised him: "Just that bit of land is left, and you can't keep money. All the villagers are watching you. Don't put on too much of a show." She decided to do the cooking herself. At first she only thought of the few traitors in the village. Afraid they would cheat Li of the little money he had left she worked very hard, doing everything herself. When rents were collected she came forward and would not let all the money fall into her husband's hands, but took some herself to save for a rainy day. After liberation when Yumin and the others were in control she knew things were going to be even worse. She pretended to be even poorer, and was still less willing

143

to hire a servant, eating and dressing simply, smiling when-ever she saw the village cadres, saying Li had already stop-ped smoking opium but was in poor health, their four children were all young, her husband was not reliable and she didn't know what would become of them in future. She had taught her children to be clever too. They never offended people and did well at school, but they understood quite well, and when they came home they never sang the songs they learned in school or talked about their meetings. She hated Schemer Qian and his group because they had cheated her husband, but she was even more afraid of Yumin and the rest. Some-times, however, she asked Yumin to eat something she had specially prepared. She knew he liked to drink, but he who had been their hired hand now put on airs. He would not give her any face but always left without drinking a drop. A couple of weeks previously she had gone home to her own family. Wujia was in a state of ferment. Her elder brother had fled but had been fetched back by the peasants, and the property that had been in the family for a hundred years had all been confiscated. All her relatives were sharing the same fate. The river water was flowing east, and its course could not be changed.

As soon as she got home she told Li to go to Zhangjiakou to lie low for a time while she stayed at home. She was a woman, and Yumin and the rest would hardly make trouble for her. Then if she talked nicely and begged people to help, they might get by. But Li felt it was useless for him to go. He could not shift for himself long away from home, he was not a resourceful man. He believed he had not too many enemies in the village, so he stayed, waiting to see which way the wind blew. He spent the day in the orchard, sometimes coming home for a while in the evening. His wife tried all day long to hide here a suitcase filled with jewels and clothes, there a barrel of grain, with the idea of burying everything they had under the ground. All the time her heart was in her mouth, but sometimes she went out to take a few turns and find out some news for her husband.

After she had washed her hands she took a key and unlocked the door to the south rooms. The three south rooms were packed with utensils and containers holding grain, besides various baskets of different sizes packed with things. The rooms had been varnished spick and span, even the boards on the *kang* were carved. But now they were thick with dust and crammed with things. Reed mats were nailed to the windows for fear people should see the treasures hidden here. During the day not a ray of light got in and the whole room smelt musty. Mrs. Li hastily measured out half a basin of flour, then hurried back to the kitchen to keep her guest company. She knew Teacher Ren was only a double-dealing opportunist, but one could always hear some news from him.

"Oh, all that white flour! You eat only good things. If they don't divide up your property, whose will they divide!" said Ren deliberately, following her to the kitchen.

"Let them divide it if they must. There's only this little bit. It'll all be finished sooner or later. What are you so pleased about? You won't get a share! What have you heard at the school?"

"Nothing, except that they're going to settle accounts again. The people who weren't tried last year will have their turn this year. This year they specially want to do away with the big exploiting, feudalistic landlords."

Mrs. Li gave another start, but her hands mixing the flour did not pause, and she asked: "What do you mean by big exploiting, feudalistic landlords?"

"It's written up very clearly on the blackboard news. It

means you people who live on rents! You're to be wiped out."

Mrs. Li felt afraid and her hands stopped moving. She was just going to ask how they would be wiped out when she heard the dogs barking again on the porch of the south room and someone shouting at the dogs. She realized that the men who sold fruit for them had come for their evening meal. She put her head out and said: "Oh, you've come just in time. You've been busy these last two days. We'll eat pancakes this evening. Ha, ha, just now Mr. Ren here said we had a lot of flour, and was jealous, wanting to divide up our property. All right. Food comes out of the ground, does it matter who eats it? We're all friends, ha, ha. . . ." Three tall, stout fellows came in as she was laughing. Their faces could not be seen clearly, but they all seemed to have unbuttoned their jackets.

"Sit down on the *kang*, while I light a lamp." A hand which had once been very delicate carried a lamp to the table on the *kang*, struck a match and lit it. The rosy lamplight danced on her plump face, making her eyes look even more like bright, transparent drops of water.

A man sitting on the end of the *kang* took up the bellows, but she said politely: "You rest, you've been on the move all day. Let me do it. There's water in the pan. Have a drink first."

Ren had no desire to watch this woman flatter these three labouring fools, so he asked: "Where's Mr. Li? When will he be back?"

"I can't say when he'll be back." But after a pause she added: "Did you want to see him about that fruit sale? If so, go into the orchard and you'll find him."

"What fruit sale?" Ren wondered. Immediately he understood. Glancing at the three men he answered hurriedly:

146

"Yes, it's about the fruit. But it doesn't matter if I don't see him. You can tell him when he comes home. It's getting late. I'll be going!" Before the woman could say any more he had hurried out. At the door he met several children who had just come home, each one with fruit in his hand, so he asked: "Is your father still in the orchard?"

Without looking at him the children answered: "Yes, he's still there."

28

IT was beginning to grow dark now in the street, but Teacher Ren walked softly on out of the little alley on the west side. Some people were talking in their doorways and it seemed unusually quiet because all the dogs in the village were tied up. One heard only the chirr of insects from the fields, the distant croaking of frogs and the buzzing of the mosquitoes that swarmed round. Ren approached an orchard. There was not a glimmer of light there, all was black. He bent his head to look at the ground and groped with his hands to avoid bumping into the fruit trees. But after walking for a while his eyes became slightly more accustomed to the gloom. He saw a bonfire ahead which served as a guide. He could already hear the drip of water in the well and knew that he had not gone astray, so he walked noisily humming a tune.

He grew increasingly cheerful as he approached the fire, all the time marvelling to himself: "How cowardly he is, not even daring to go home! I'm going to give him a fright!"

Fallen leaves and wild mugwort were piled in a heap. A fire smouldered slowly beneath. Dense smoke billowed out till blocked by the thick foliage, then spread horizontally, like a very thin transparent canopy. However just then none of this was visible. Only the acrid smoke could be smelt. The fire threw a faint circle of light to illumine one or two tree trunks in the vicinity, and a small hut at one side. Reaching the fire without having seen a soul, Ren groped his way to the hut and called out. No one answered, so he retraced his steps. But there was still not a sound to be heard, only an axe cutting wood in a distant part of the forest. Even the bonfire was screened by the trees so that all was darkness. Ren began to feel a little panicky, and was just considering finding his way home when he suddenly saw the red glow of a cigarette not far off. He called out eagerly: "Who's there?" But there was no answer and the red glow disappeared. Growing impatient again he hurried forward, but tripped and fell over something. When he got to his feet again he saw there were some dozen fruit baskets here barring the way. But now a man's voice sounded from the darkness: "Devil take you, what are you crashing about here for? You've crushed the fruit." Ren recognized the voice of Landlord Li's hired hand, Orchard-keeper Li. He was rather angry at having fallen, but had to control himself, and called out: "You hide under the trees and watch people fall down, then have the heart to blame them for crushing the fruit! I've come to find Mr. Li. Has he gone home again?"

The old man did not answer, just came out to examine the crushed fruit, and put the baskets in order. Ren had to ask again: "Where's Mr. Li?"

The old man still did not answer, just raising his head to stare over Ren's shoulder. The firelight shone on his vacant and stubborn eyes. He remained motionless and expressionless, causing Ren considerable alarm. He was just going to repeat his question when a tall figure stepped out from behind him, and said slowly: "Is it Old Ren?"

Ren gave a start and gripped the tall thin man, exclaim-

148

ing loudly: "Oh! I had such a time finding you. Where were you hiding?"

"Don't shout! What's your business?" Li took out cigarettes and offered him one.

"Oh, there's no business. I haven't seen you for several days and came to see you, knowing you don't feel easy —" Li poked him in the back to stop him going on.

"Have you had your meal? I haven't eaten yet, I'm not going back this evening." Turning to his hired hand, he said: "Uncle, you go back to the village now and fetch me something to eat together with my bedding. It's much cooler here than at home, much more comfortable!" Landlord Li leant against a tree, and reached down for a piece of fruit which he passed to Ren. "Here you are. See how big this sweet-apple is!"

"There are a lot of mosquitoes." Ren slapped his forehead hard. "Everybody says your fruit has done very well this year. This orchard is quite a size."

"A lot of fruit's not necessarily so good. Nowadays I sell seven or eight loads a day, getting fifty or sixty thousand dollars. But after deducting the labourers' expenses only thirty or forty thousand are left, not enough to pay back the spring wages."

The old man had already gone quietly off.

"You'd better sell this fruit at once, better sell at cut prices rather than have to give it away. Get what you can for it."

They had both squatted down. Li looked around in the dark, then asked softly: "What news is there? Living out here I feel like a dead man. I don't know what's going on."

"Mr. Li, why don't you go away to hide? In the village you've got the most land, and you were once ward chief. It's always best to be on the safe side."

"Um!" Li lifted his hand to support his drooping head.

Even in the faint firelight one could see how pale he was. He remained silent for a time, then sighed and said: "Ah! As for being ward chief, heaven knows, Xu and Qian and their group tricked me into it!"

Ren had heard this too. When Li was ward chief he had had to pay out subsidies to the big shots in the village, sending grain to each family. When the *xiang* office demanded fifty thousand dollars the village racketeers added twenty per cent. The villagers couldn't pay and the racketeers cursed him as incompetent, and if he failed to hand over the grain they put pressure on him by threatening to report him to the *xiang* office. Group after group of people asked him to gamble and they conspired to swindle money out of him. These people were connected with the Japanese and puppets, so he dared not refuse them. However, Teacher Ren had not the least sympathy for him, and said: "Nowadays it's no use blaming other people. Mr. Qian's an army dependent. Jiang made his money as ward chief, and he's now village head. Nobody will touch them. You're different. You have money but no power, so I'm worried about you. You try all the time not to offend people, yet you still have all these enemies. Why don't you think of a way out? Just now your worst enemies are Yumin and that group. He was once your hired hand. Is it possible you never offended him?"

Li could not think of a reply. He lit another cigarette and puffed at it furiously. He was completely at a loss and stared all around as if there were people hidden in the depth of the blackness, just waiting to come out and seize him. Involuntarily he sighed.

Ren too started straining his eyes through the darkness. A cool breeze was blowing in their direction, he leant more closely against the tree, and whispered: "Nowadays it's a lawless society! This is what's called pulling up turnips. Last year they pulled up Xu. After all he was an able man. He saw what was coming and moved his whole family away. Well, who knows whether he won't come back some day to take his revenge? This spring they pulled out Old Hou, and Old Hou's Buddha couldn't save him. He had to pay up a hundred piculs of grain. And now, mark my words, it's going to be worse than last year. Three of them at once have come from the provincial capital. Chen Wu of Mengjiagou has been put to death. Last year at least no one in our village was killed, but who knows what will happen this year?"

The night breeze ruffled the leaves, and Li's heart was going pit-a-pat too. He was a nervous man to begin with, and listening to Ren he felt even more agitated, and could not help crying from his heart: "Heavens! What can I do! I've a few *mu* of land, but I didn't steal them or seize them by force. They were left by my ancestors, and now I'm to be punished for it! Old Ren! Tell me what I should do!"

"Keep a grip on yourself. Don't talk so loudly." Ren stood up and walked round the fire, but could see nothing amiss. The night was very quiet, so he walked back and whispered comfort to the young landlord who was doubled up with fright: "There's nothing to be afraid of. You're not the only rich man in the village. You should all get together and think of a way out. Take the case of your tenants. There are a lot of people with the same surname as yours, and when all's said and done you're all of the same family. Even if they don't respond to friendship they've got to think of the future — will the Eighth Route Army be here forever? There's bound to be a day when the Kuomintang army comes. You ought to try to win them over. What's the use of hiding here all the time?"

Li sighed. It was easy to increase his fear, but very difficult to dispel his anxiety. He was crouching on the ground,

151

his two hands spread out, looking the picture of despair. After a pause he said: "Oh! Old Ren, what d'you mean by family ties and friendship? They can't be counted on. I'm afraid it's no use now for me to bow right and left and speak respectfully."

"Then just speak to them frankly. Ask them if they want to keep alive in future or not! Mr. Li, the Beijing-Suiyuan Railway's cut again, the Eighth Route Army has surrounded Datong. Do you suppose the Kuomintang won't come? Hush!"

Suddenly hearing footsteps on the left both men were startled. They stopped talking, Ren recoiling a step to stand in an even darker place. Holding their breath they listened to the approaching steps. It was Orchard-keeper Li, carrying a roll of bedding and a basket, who emerged from the darkness. Without a word he put the basket down in front of Landlord Li, then withdrew to the little hut. Landlord Li put on a solicitous air and said: "It's not easy walking on a dark night like this. Come and eat some pancakes, Uncle." He had already uncovered the basket.

"The road's all right. There are militiamen patrolling. They're patrolling outside this orchard as well as others. They say they're afraid some families may have forgotten to tie up their dogs and may let them out to trample the fruit."

The two men exchanged glances in the dark. Ren stood there a little longer until he heard the old man go into the hut, apparently to sleep, then he quietly nudged Li, turned away and was swallowed up in the darkness.

29

ON his way back Teacher Ren did not see a single militia-man. He re-entered the village by the same road he had come, and returned to the primary school. Teacher Liu was sitting by the lamp correcting students' compositions. Ren looked at the big pile of exercise books on his own desk, but did not take the trouble to read them, and went to look for Red-nosed Wu, the cook. However, the old fellow had gone to the south end of the village to the poor peasants' meeting. It was stifling hot inside, and he ladled himself some cold water to drink in the kitchen. He went back to the room which he and Teacher Liu shared. The latter was still sitting bolt upright, with his whole mind on his corrections. Ren felt even less like correcting his own pile of compositions, and lay down on the *kang* to think. Mosquitoes, as if deliberately to antagonize him, immediately swarmed humming about, from time to time launching surprise attacks. He felt complacent and even happy to think he had just done a good deed, sympathizing with, comforting and helping someone in distress. He and Landlord Li had formerly been very friendly. Now Li was out of luck. All the villagers wanted to vent their anger on him because he had over a hundred *mu* of land which made many of the poor envious, and now he was scared out of his wits, not even daring to go home. The rich had oppressed him and were now avoiding him. Landlord Li had not a friend in the world, but he, Ren, a primary school teacher, had at this time stretched out his hand to him — how grateful Li must be! Ren felt he had just accomplished some heroic deed and wished people knew of it so that they could praise him. But now that he was back in the school there was no one there but Teacher Liu whom he heartily despised.

Teacher Liu was not a graduate of the rural normal school. When he corrected compositions he often wrote the wrong words and had to keep thumbing through his dictionary. But because he played up to Freckles Li, the latter thought highly of him and always consulted him in difficulties. Liu was a native of the village too, so of course he had an advantage there. He was nearly forty, his son would soon be marrying. Yet he still showed such enthusiasm in learning folk dances, and danced so badly it made you want to laugh. He also played the guitar and flute. Ren often thought of leaving and seeing what would happen to Liu then. It was only because Ren could not find a job right away that he had to stay on. Sometimes he had to talk to Liu about their daily life or work, but apart from this they had nothing to say to each other. Occasionally Ren felt so lonely he would forget the old fellow's stubbornness and address a few remarks to him, but invariably he gave up after a few words, which proved they had nothing in common. Now Ren was feeling again that he must find someone to talk to, but he could not confide in Liu, for if the latter knew what was in his mind he might tell the village cadres. This being so, Ren hated him all the more, especially when he saw Liu always in high spirits, as if he could never be depressed.

Ren was isolated in the village like floating duckweed without roots, with nothing to support him. But he could not leave yet or his livelihood would become precarious. That was undoubtedly one reason why he could not tear himself away. Another reason was that although Nuanshui fell short of his expectations in every other respect, it nevertheless contained a great attraction. He was twenty-five, and had read a number of sentimental novels, but was still a bachelor. He hoped very much to marry in Nuanshui, but the object of his affections had made no response. He would not give up hope, believing that a certain social force was on his side, and this encouraged his dreams.

He tossed and turned on the *kang*, smoking one cigarette after another, while Teacher Liu kept on writing, sometimes reading aloud. Finally Ren could contain himself no longer. He got down from the *kang*, and went to stroll in the courtyard, passing out through the gate. The street was refreshingly cool, the leaves of the locust tree rustling in the breeze. He caught sight of a figure in motion, hesitated, then asked: "Who is it?" A man turned to confront him, and asked very politely: "Are you still up, Mr. Ren?" It was one of the militiamen, carrying a local-made rifle, who went on with a smile: "Ho! The meetings have gone on pretty late the last two days." Ren knew him, and said: "It must be rather hard on you men."

"It's for our own sake," said the other, "and we can't complain. We just have to do our part. Why don't you go to bed, Mr. Ren?" Saying this he turned south. Ren stood there for a second, then hurried off to the east and turned the corner in a northerly direction.

He had not gone far before he came to a gate which was already bolted. After giving two light raps he heard someone coming to open it. The porch was very dark, and a woman's voice said softly: "Is it Mr. Ren?" He recognized Mrs. Qian's voice and answered quietly: "Is Mr. Qian at home?" Without waiting for her reply he walked straight in.

Lamplight shone through the windows of the north room, the courtyard was grey. Schemer Qian, wearing a pongee jacket, stepped out from under the shadow of the oleander tree to greet him, and motioned him into the darkness, saying: "Come and sit here, it's cool."

There were two stools here and cold tea on a *kang* table. Ren saw there was only a light in the north room on the right, while all the rest were pitch dark. He looked carefully towards the room that was lit up, and hearing sounds of crying there felt misgiving and uneasiness.

Mrs. Qian came over to make tea, and fetched another

stool, then sat down beside them and whispered: "Have you heard anything, Mr. Ren? How has the village decided to conduct the trials this time?"

"Do you suppose they'd tell us their plans? You've got a security officer as son-in-law, you ought to know all about it. And the chairman of the peasants' association is a relative of yours —" He stopped to listen carefully again for any sound from the room with the light.

"Our son-in-law says —" began Mrs. Qian, but Qian cut her short to answer: "Old Ren, we two see eye to eye, I can say what I like to you. We two are out of luck, so we have to watch our steps."

Ren thought of all the villagers who hated Qian in silence, and said: "I'm concerned for you too, Mr. Qian! Some people in the village are talking about you." He was struck by Qian's uneasiness. He had never seen him in such a mood before.

"Well, of course I'm not afraid." Qian narrowed his eyes to two slits again while his glance darted right and left from behind lowered lids in a way he had whenever he wanted to appear master of the situation. "Well!" he went on after a pause. "Let's see what that little Yumin can do to me!" Twisting his thin moustache ends, he started chuckling.

Then Ren used Qian's usual arguments: "Of course you're not afraid, you're an army dependent. Don't mind about them. Let them do their worst."

"Right!" Qian immediately regained his normal manner, and paused for a moment to consider this young man who was sitting opposite in the darkness. He had had this primary school teacher under his thumb for a long time. "I've long wanted to persuade you," he said more solicitously, "not to show too much interest in other people's affairs. I heard you went to White Snake's again today. That's a centre of mischief. In difficult times like these other people are trying their best to avoid being involved. Another thing, Jiang is a slippery customer, and if you don't look out he may stab you in the back. Look at all the money he made, starting with nothing. Who helped him get that far? Now he forgets the source of benefits and is like the weed on the wall leaning both ways. White Snake is only a woman after all. What can she have to tell you?"

"White Snake says Jiang still owes her several tens of thousands of dollars, and if he doesn't hurry up and pay, a day will come when she'll tell everything. She'll dissociate herself from him, and not act as a medium to spread rumours for him any more."

Qian's heart missed a beat, but hiding his feelings he said: "Just as I say, how can women like that be taken into one's confidence? What is Jiang really planning to do?"

Ren knew that Qian liked him to keep in touch with the landlords, although pretending to dissuade him from going, and he thought: "Do you still distrust me? You really are cautious. I know how to be loyal."

Ren knew how many enemies Schemer Qian had, but thought they could not harm him. Qian's son-in-law and relatives could help him. He knew too that Qian was afraid, although feigning complete indifference. This suited him. He wanted Qian to be desperate so that he could prove his loyalty and win an unexpected prize. Sometimes he realized that Qian was not a good man to trifle with. No one could expect anything from him. But Ren could find no other friend, to say nothing of his other hopes.

He also told Qian about Landlord Li, and Qian alarmed him by saying that if Li really went to his tenants and tried to win them over, and it was discovered, Ren might be involved. Qian said that Ren ought to think of a way to sever relations with Li. He hinted to him that he might write some short articles for the blackboard news informing against Li. He also said a great many bad things about Li. He said that Li, a graduate of normal school, looked down on other people, and had denounced Ren as not up to normal school standard. He claimed Li did not value friendship in the least. In the past many police and secret service bullies from the *xiang* had gambled with him, winning his money. They had taken him to the club at Zhuolu and done all sorts of bad things, but Li treated them as if they were his parents. When all his money was spent he sold houses and land, but had no regard for the village. During his period of office as ward chief he had even asked Qian to do some manual labour for the government. Qian said he was busy and didn't want to go, whereupon Li said he could send his hired man. Qian flatly refused, and asked how much money he wanted. Only then did Li realize how foolish he had been, and hurry over to apologize. Qian declared Li was growing very miserly now, pretending to be poor. When he kept people to a meal they only ate millet, while the flour and white rice were kept for him and his wife. Ren remembered how the few times he had eaten at their house they had just served a few vegetable dishes with the wine, not even any fried eggs, although they kept hens themselves.

By now the sound of quarrelling could be heard from the house, and Ren longed to go and see what was happening. Qian knew what he was thinking, and explained to him: "It's nothing. It's just that niece of mine who's growing up and isn't married yet. We can't find anyone suitable in the village, but can't keep her quiet at home. I've always said, as long as a man is good, it doesn't matter if he has no property. It's not too late now, but she's not young either.

158

You're one of us so I don't mind telling you: someone came and mentioned the chairman of the peasants' association. But that would never do. My own daughter's married a security officer, and I'm already regretting it. This is a vital matter. He may be one of the village cadres now, but one must think of the past — what sort of people were they before? And one must take thought for the future, one day the Kuomintang troops will come, and who knows what will happen to this lot then? When that time comes my niece will come crying home and I as her uncle will feel very bad. If you can think of someone, of the right age and up to standard, simple and honest, then tell me, and we'll settle the business." After saying this Qian deliberately sighed, then screwed up his eyes again to watch the embarrassed primary school teacher in the dark.

Ren was at a loss for an answer. Not finding anything suitable to say at once, he sipped his tea. He felt unbearably hot, while the mosquitoes under the trees were attacking them still more savagely. They were both quiet for a time. Then Ren got up to take his leave. Qian did not ask him to stay and Mrs. Qian saw him out. The street was absolutely silent, and the door closed behind him as soon as he crossed the threshold.

30

AFTER meeting with such a rebuff in Gui's house, Heini felt a discontent which she could not put into words. She had always behaved very well to everyone. Her Uncle Wenfu was always warning her to be on her guard, saying: "Heini, your uncle Qian's done many bad things in the village. We've got to be extra straightforward to make people forget that we belong to the same family, and to avoid being involved in future!" Heini did her best to get on with Gui. There had been some opposition when she was asked to teach the literacy class. But her hard work and conscientiousness in teaching had won the confidence of Gui and Freckles Li, and the latter praised her sense of responsibility. Still she could not altogether avoid cold stares, envy and hatred. Even the instinctive hatred which her youth and beauty aroused was considered reasonable by those to whom she was a temptress or monster or something despicable. Whenever she was snubbed and had no way of working off her feelings, she would run to the vegetable garden and under the melon trellis would complain tearfully of the injustice to her hard-working old uncle. Wenfu would stop his work, sit down beside her and sigh. Or he might say: "Ah! It's too bad! This is all your uncle Qian's fault! You'd better come and live with me." Sometimes Wenfu was very tempted to urge her to hurry up and get married, but one could scarcely talk like that to a girl. And she was not free to do as she liked. Although Schemer Qian was not really fond of her he insisted on taking charge of her, knowing that she was not bad-looking and would serve as a bait. Thus he was not willing for her to be married off so simply. Wenfu understood something of Heini's problem, and felt she was too loyal to Young Cheng. But if he so much as hinted at this, she would start crying bitterly. Her old uncle did not know what to do or how to help her.

Unable to attend the meeting, Heini went home. Her uncle and aunt were talking again. Dani had come back several times, hiding in her father's room each time she returned, as if something portentous were about to happen. When Heini went in they always stopped talking, and her aunt would tell her to boil some water or else to go to her sister-in-law's room in the western courtyard to fetch a pair of scissors or some sewing. Sometimes she felt curious to discover what they were discussing all this time. Sometimes she spitefully paid no attention to them, leaving them to their underhand doings. Gradually, however, she began to understand that because land reform was going to start in the village her uncle was afraid in some way. At the same time he had some kind of scheme. These surmises made her very uneasy. She had no idea what the upshot would be. All she could do was to confide her simple conjecture to her Uncle Wenfu. Honest Wenfu could not solve or explain Heini's problems either, and their vauge premonitions of disaster made both of them a prey to anxious fears.

When Er came back from her home, she was crying bitterly and demanding to have the family split up. She did not dare broach the subject to Qian, but found his elder daughter-in-law and passed on her fears to her. They had both been given twenty-five *mu* of land apiece and registered as separate households, but the title deeds were still in Qian's hands. All they had was the name of owner without real possession. Now if in the coming trial all the land were confiscated, they would be in trouble. They vented their anger on the bowls and pans they were washing in the kitchen and spoke bitterly, adding fuel to each other's indignation, and even looked askance at Heini because she was his niece. Qianli was a simple fellow and did not say a word. Seeing the state his wife and sister-in-law were in he left for the orchard. He had three *mu* of vineyard of his own to cultivate. Later on he moved to the orchard altogether. He was afraid of his father, but unable to control his wife. Then the elder daughter-in-law went to find Trade Union Qian to announce that they had divided up the family's property that spring. Trade Union Qian had never been on friendly terms with them, so he said: "This business of yours has nothing to do with me." Then she went to see Young Cheng, but he kept out of her way and she could not find him, which made her feel even more alarmed. But she dared not ask her father-in-law for the deeds. Schemer Qian found out what they were thinking, but instead of scolding them, said: "You really have no conscience. This land wasn't left me by my ancestors. I earned it inch by inch myself and I shall do what I like with it. In the spring I said I'd give it to you, because I want you to have separate households and settle down. But Qianli is a fool and can't manage property, while Yi has gone to join the army — what can you women do? I hold the property merely to take care of your interests. Now that the village wants to divide up property, you're the first to raise a howl. You're starting the fight at home. Who would have thought you would be the ones to take the lead and strike the first blow! Very well, if you think your wings are strong enough and you don't need rely on the old man any more, that's all right. The deeds are here. If you want them, take them. Only if there's trouble in the future, don't come running to me for help!"

When the women heard this they dared not take the deeds, for fear their father-in-law would injure them later if they did. They were both so afraid of him. Later it was Qian who reassured them saying there could not be any trouble, they could not possibly be involved, they had registered long ago as separate households, and shared out the land. There was nothing to worry about. The deeds could be left in his place for a few days. Whenever they wanted them he would let them have them. Meanwhile, in order that people might know they were really separate households, he told them to prepare their meals separately. They could take some of the store of grain, oil, salt and fuel to use. The women were delighted. Er took this opportunity to move into the western courtyard where she would be a little further away from her father-in-law. They got busy with small stoves and small pans, thinking they had triumphed, not realizing that this was just a plan arranged by their father-in-law for a safe way out.

After the two young women had moved out, the courtyard was much quieter. While Qian considered this rather fitting, Heini found it lonely. In the past the cordial chatter and laughter of her sisters-in-law could often be heard in the courtyard along with the innocent crying and shouting of children, whereas now all that could be heard was the old people's dry coughs and furtive whispers.

Dani had always been down on Heini, but now she suddenly became very friendly. She showed great interest in the women's literacy class and praised her cousin, urging her to keep up the good work. She said Heini was the only capable one in the family, because she was in touch with the village cadres, and more useful than her own husband, Security Officer Zhang. Dani also spoke well of Young Cheng, saying how reliable and promising he was, claiming to have thought well of him while he was their hired man, as if she had never made fun of Heini's friendship with him. In addition, she recalled many past incidents in her life with Heini to evoke pleasant memories. However, Heini did not enjoy these conversations. She remembered too well how her cousin's family had always been against their marriage. She had sometimes even hated them for it. Moreover, Young Cheng's fickleness had changed her hope to bewilderment, her bewilderment to bitterness. The more disillusioned and wretched she felt, the more reserved she became and the more unwilling she was to talk of anything connected with marriage. Dani did not understand this, and when Heini

163

was silent or said "Don't talk about it, I'm not interested," she felt this was simply due to girlish shyness. All girls liked to hear people talking about their future marriages, at the same time pretending to be indifferent. Accordingly she went a step further, and put straightforward questions to Heini. This had happened when Teacher Ren was in the courtyard, and accounted for the crying and sound of remonstrance he had heard from the north room.

Heini's cousin wanted her to go and find Young Cheng, and said: "You used to be on such good terms with him. He must have had some understanding with you. You fell in love with him when you were seventeen. You're a woman now. You've lost four whole years. How can he be so heartless as to jilt you? You ought to remember what was said between you. You go and ask him and see what he says. He'll have to give you an answer. This is the most important thing in your life. You've got to decide it for yourself!"

Heini gritted her teeth and answered: "I could never do a thing like that. I'm not going."

Dani goaded her, saying: "Then you just let him take advantage of you?" In order to worm out of her whether there had been anything between them that she was ashamed of mentioning, Dani added: "A woman only has one body. Whoever she goes with she ought to stay with to the end. You've studied — doesn't it say in books a woman can't have two husbands?"

Heini was so upset by the injustice of these improper remarks, she started crying. She wanted to reproach her cousin, but an unmarried girl can scarcely quarrel about such things. Angry and humiliated, stamping with rage she thought: "Oh! Even if I jump into the Yellow River I can't wash clean. It would be better to die!" Then she started crying even more bitterly.

At last when she saw Heini was adamant, Dani urged her again: "Heini! If you don't think of yourself, won't you think of the old man? Ever since your mother married again you've lived with my father, and he's treated you like his own daughter and brought you up. He likes to poke his nose into other people's affairs, so he can't help offending people. Now there's going to be a day of reckoning in the village. Don't you suppose those bastards will take advantage of the excitement to hit back in the name of public welfare? Luckily Young Cheng's chairman of the peasants' association. If he wants to make things hot for us the others will have to follow his lead. If he sees our side of things the others won't dare say anything. You may not care about paying your debt of gratitude, but we're all one family. How can you stand by, watching the crowd trample on us? If things go badly they'll have all our family up for trial. What shall we do then!"

At this point Heini's aunt came in and sat down beside her to soothe her, patting her body and limbs which were soft and numb after crying. The old woman did not say anything, only stared despairingly at the dimming oil lamp and heaved sigh after sigh. Heini was exhausted and her head ached. All she wanted was to stop thinking and forget everything. Yet this new problem troubled her. She did not like her uncle Qian. Sometimes she hated him and was even willing to let him suffer a little. But now that Dani had raised this point and her aunt had come to her, entreating her sadly: "Heini! Save us old folk!" She really did not know what to reply. How could she possibly go to see Young Cheng, asking him to take her? She was a girl, how could she ever say anything like that? Besides, she did not know what his feelings actually were.

Since Young Cheng had started playing a leading part in the village Schemer Qian had decided to use his niece to win

165

him over. He had often given Heini hints, encouraging her to go boldly forward, but he had taken no proper steps to settle this matter which had been dragging on for several years. He had not suspected that this hope would fail him. Young Cheng was very scrupulous, while Heini was only a girl and helpless. Now Qian had to bring stronger pressure to bear on her, using family relationships to play on her feelings. If he could win over Young Cheng it would mean the loss of a niece, but the gain of a strong ally.

After a whole day and night of crying and recriminations, Heini finally resorted to delaying tactics. She postponed making her decision until the next day when she could go to her Uncle Wenfu for advice.

3 1

GETTING up in the morning Teacher Liu paced to and fro in the cool courtyard. In another corner Red-nosed Wu was sweeping the ground which was littered with bits of paper, shuttlecock feathers, fruit stones and dust. This cheerful old man who beat the gong cocked a mischievous eye at Liu, and said as if to himself: "Ah, dancing *yangge* folk dances makes people young again. . . ." His red nose was pointed in Liu's direction, and with an exaggerated drawl he started singing softly:

In the middle of the night the door opens wide,
Full of emotion he creeps inside! Heigh ho!

Teacher Liu had no idea what he was driving at, so he laughed and said: "Old Wu, what was said at the meeting yesterday evening? You seem to be out of your senses again."

The old fellow did not answer, but replied as if giving a

formal warning: "In future if you have to go home, you must tell me, I'm the school janitor. You keep strutting about and muttering, and even creep home at night to your wife, thinking I don't know about it. Studying books has spoiled you people."

"Nonsense, you're simply talking nonsense."

The old man's eyes flickered again, as he said: "Have I wronged you? When I got up this morning I found the gate open. I thought to myself: why opened so early? But when I came back from the latrine the gate was closed again, and presently you appeared like a crazy fellow. Seeing you like this I gussed what you'd been up to. Humph, did you think you could keep me in the dark?"

"How could that have happened? Could Mr. Ren have gone out?"

"He's sleeping soundly. I just went to have a look. Listen, like a fat pig in a sty."

"Could such a queer thing really have happened? Maybe you forgot to close the gate when you came back last night." Liu rubbed his head of bristling hair, "We'll have to be more careful in future, Old Wu, this is the time for land reform!"

"That's just it! Just what I think! When I came back last night I fastened the gate carefully. If you didn't go home, somebody else must have opened it. But what are you walking about here for? Composing an essay?"

"See here," said Liu, brightening suddenly, "Old Wu, you've got your head screwed on the right way. You tell me — bombs, bombs, what does that mean? Yesterday Comrade Hu said to me the blackboard news ought to be like a bomb. What did he mean?"

"A bomb?" The old man took a small tobacco pouch out of his pocket. "Why did Comrade Hu say that? Um, when you educated people talk, it's never clear, as if you didn't want other people to understand. He said the blackboard news should be like a bomb? Well, let's think. A bomb... bombs are to kill people. Can't be that. How could the blackboard news kill people? That's not the meaning. Bombs explode... aha, the blackboard news ought to be like a burst of flame, setting fire to people's hearts. What do you say to this wild guess of mine?"

"Um, there seems some sense in it, only how can it be like a flame?"

"People say our blackboard news is like the 'heavenly gospel' — nobody understands it. How can it be like a bomb, setting fire to our hearts, since it has nothing to do with us?"

"All the articles on it are explaining what land reform is. Writing just those few words was some job, I can tell you. You see, there's nobody in the village to write. It all falls on my shoulders. I gave it all to Freckles Li and Comrade Hu to read. I was afraid Comrade Hu would say it was badly written."

Red-nosed Wu shook his head and said: "If you want to write a composition, I'm like a rolling pin used as a bellows — no good at all. If the blackboard news is to be like a bomb, like a fire, well, then all that classical language of yours is like cold water. I've got an idea here. You think it over and see if I'm right. If the blackboard news is to make people want to read it, you should write a few songs expressing what's in folks' hearts. Take my sounding the gong for instance. If I just shouted: 'Meeting, meeting!' that would be no fun. So I make up a few lines and sing at the same time. When people hear the singing they like it and listen. Then they know what's happening."

"Yes, whenever you make up new rhymes and sound the

gong all down the street, there are always people following behind, laughing away. To tell the truth, to make up a few lines out of the daily conversation of the country folk is easier than writing a composition. Only I'm afraid the cadres wouldn't approve."

Looking rather concerned, Red-nosed Wu said: "Oh, if Freckles Li told you to write, that means he thinks you're all right, and wants you to decide things for yourself. Why be afraid of this, that and the other? If he were dissatisfied he could write himself. I say you're a good sort, but a bookworm. If you'll listen to me, I'm not afraid of being laughed at. I'll make up a few lines for you, and while I say it you write. I know all that goes on in the village. We'll make one about Third Zhang exploiting Fourth Li, and put in something about Fifth Wang going hungry. When they hear that they're in the news, everybody'll want to read it. If only you can express what's in their mind, you'll stir them up, and once they're angry they'll hate their enemies. Don't you think that's a good idea? Another thing, when the Japanese were here, we peasants were treated like dirt. We'll settle all those old scores and make those running-dog traitors make it up to us. Wouldn't that be good? All right, I'll say a piece. You listen, and see if it's all right." He paused a second to swallow a mouthful of water, then started chanting:

> *The Communist Party has won men's praise,*
> *Land reform's starting one of these days!*
> *Poor country peasants stand on their feet;*
> *Soon our vengeance will be complete!*
> *We were conscripted, we were oppressed,*
> *While each traitor landlord feathered his nest;*
> *Taxes and levies were no end of bother,*

After one land tax we paid out another.
On public expenses, poll tax and all that,
Our eight chief families soon grew fat.
Old Li to death was cruelly done,
Zhang Zhen at Hongshan lost his son.
Religion made our Old Hou blind,
Liuqian was driven out of his mind. . . .

"What do you say to that?" The old man squatted there complacently, struck a light with his flint and started smoking. Then, putting his head on one side, he screwed up his eyes, and started guffawing.

Teacher Liu screwed up his short-sighted eyes too and started laughing, then squatted down next to him and said, gesticulating: "Old Wu! You're really it! Now I see my way, I'll write the blackboard news for the people! Not for those few cadres! That business of writing a composition in fits and starts really made my head ache. Never mind what we write, whether it can be sung or not, it must be the language we talk, and express what the villagers are thinking. We must state our grievances and recall the injustices done to us. Thirty years the river flows east, then thirty west. Every pebble will come up to the top some time. We must unite to overthrow the gods and break up the temples, uprooting the bullies so that we can live in peace! — Ho, ho, Old Wu! You've been my teacher today! Come on, we'll work along those lines. These damn compositions can go to the devil!" He took some manuscripts from his pocket, tore them into shreds and started roaring with laughter, happy laughter that seemed incongruous with the face ravaged by long years of hardship.

Just then Freckles Li hurried in, and Teacher Liu looked up cheerfully and greeted him.

Not waiting for him to go on, Freckles Li, mopping the sweat from his head, said: "What d'you think you're up to? Look what you've written in the blackboard news!"

"Those confounded compositions, those 'heavenly gospels', really are pointless. I was just going to rub them out. Hmm. Today you say they're bad too, but yesterday you were nodding your head and praising them."

"I didn't mean that one," shouted Freckles Li.

Teacher Ren, who had just got up, appeared in the doorway.

"If it wasn't that, did you mean this?" Looking very distressed he indicated the scraps of paper he had torn up.

"Anyone who didn't know you would start feeling suspicious! You say the village cadres are covering up for criminals. What proof do you have of that?"

"What?" Liu looked completely bewildered and opened wide his short-sighted eyes.

"You say Landlord Li is bribing his tenants in order to have land reform in name but not in deed — that doesn't matter much. But then you say the cadres are covering up for people, they've all been bought by the landlords. What did you mean by writing such a thing? Were you quite out of your mind?" Freckles Li took a towel from his shoulder to fan his bare chest, and went on, shaking his head: "Comrade Hu says if the cadres aren't good the peasants should criticize them. But there must be evidence. The blackboard news can't just make up things. He also says this is in line with the rumours spread by those rogues, that the Eighth Route Army won't be here long. It has the same bad effect."

"Ai! My god! What are you talking about! I swear by all that's sacred I showed you every single sentence I wrote and got you to pass it before writing it up on the blackboard news. I've made a living by teaching for over twenty years.

I'm supposed to be a scholar, but all my life I've always had to bow to the rich people. When spies and traitors came to the school, I had to stand like a servant listening respectfully to their instructions. At long last we have the Communists who treat the intelligentsia well. This spring they sent me on a trip to Zhangjiakou and I saw many high officials and leaders, all of whom treated us well. For the first time I felt that I too was a man, a useful member of society, and I determined to listen to their good advice and reform myself to serve the people. How could I write attacking the cadres, and undermining land reform? Oh, you're wronging me badly! You've got to look into this."

Red-nosed Wu had been standing by all this time listening, and now he put in a word: "I think maybe, first thing in the morning, someone may have gone and written there secretly. There is more than just the one teacher in the village who can write."

"Yes! I'm not the only teacher."

"Old Liu, don't bite indiscriminately just because you're driven to the wall. You'd better be careful what you say." Ren put on an indignant air.

"I think we must get to the bottom of this. If a needle's disappeared, it must have been taken by grandmother or grandchild. The people who can write in our village can be counted on two hands. Get their writing to compare it, then won't we know at once? What do you say, Mr. Ren?" Red-nosed Wu shot another glance at him.

"Right," Ren was forced to say. However, he immediately contradicted himself: "But not necessarily. It's difficult to distinguish writing in chalk."

"I can't read, so I can't say. But I often clean your writing and Mr. Liu's off the blackboard, and I can see they're quite different. His writing looks square and straight cut like dried beancurd, while yours is crooked just like yourself. Do you say they can't be distinguished? I don't believe it. Get some students here and ask them."

"Old Wu's right. There are just a few who can write in our village. Primary school graduates don't count. Take my case, I've studied for a couple of years, but I sometimes can't even read what I write. Don't worry, Old Liu. We'll easily settle this." Freckles Li had calmed down a little.

"Well then, let's go, we'll look at the writing. I'd know the writing of anyone in the village, even if it were burnt to ashes," said Liu confidently, pushing Freckles Li towards the door.

"Let's go," Ren could do nothing but follow them.

"Damn!" Freckles Li stopped suddenly, stamping his foot. "Aren't I a fool! As soon as I'd read it I wiped it off. I didn't want everybody to see it and spread it, so I just wiped it off. Ai! What a fool I am! I didn't think of finding out who wrote it."

Ren covertly mopped his forehead.

"Oh! Then I shall still be unjustly suspected," said Liu on the verge of tears.

"Don't worry, Old Liu, I'm going to follow this up."

"I don't think you need make any search," said Red-nosed Wu. "I understand quite well, and presently I'm going to see Yumin to tell him all about it. Ha, I've seen this coming. Someone's been so busy recently, getting up early and going to bed late, sneaking about up to no good." He nodded his head and flickered his eyes triumphantly.

"Who do you mean?" Freckles Li still did not understand.

"You still don't get it?" said the old man mischievously. "If you'll only agree to have these persons arrested, I'll promise to tell you. What do you say?" He laughed as he saw Ren making off. Liu looked significantly at Freckles

Li too. The latter did not ask any more questions, only said: "Better go and write it again. Do you have any manuscripts ready?"

"Yes, oh yes." Teacher Liu had recovered his spirits. "Our Old Wu is full of ideas, he can make impromptu verses as well as Cao Zijian.[1] Ha.... If you want compositions, that's difficult, but if you want bombs, that's easy. We manufacture them here. As soon as they're let off they'll explode!" He chuckled.

32

TEACHER Ren, acting on Schemer Qian's advice, had used the blackboard news to accuse Landlord Li, but his plan had miscarried. However, Li's sudden flight set many tongues wagging. It was when Lanying took food for her father to the orchard that his disappearance was noticed. Orchard-keeper Li said: "He was here all right at dawn. I didn't see him after the fruit-sellers left, but I took it for granted he had gone home. Hasn't he gone back, Lanying?"

The child shook her head vehemently, and ran home like a mad creature.

When Orchard-keeper Li went back to the village he told his nephew, his nephew told the neighbours, and soon the story spread. Some of Li's tenants grew anxious and went secretly to tell the cadres. Groups of idlers gathered in the street or at the door of the co-operative, but not to buy things.

---

[1] Cao Zijian (192-232) was a great poet. His brother, founder of the Dynasty of Wei, jealous of his talent, once forced him to make an impromptu verse within the space of a few seconds. The request was complied with successfully.

One would say: "All the landlords have fled, so what kind of land reform can there be?" Another would say: "Every day we have meetings, but it's all thunder and no rain. How can there be a revolution without violence?" Others would laugh at Swarthy Guo: "Old Guo, have your militiamen been going after women?" Some, however, said covertly: "Li's a weak-kneed coward. Someone must have frightened him, saying that this time he'd be the first to have his land divided. When he heard that, he was scared stiff."

Others answered: "We've heard that too, that he'd be the first to be tried." And so it came about that popular anger against him increased: "The dirty dog! Who said he was straightforward? Huh! As soon as he heard there'd be land reform, he hid himself every day in the orchard selling fruit. He used not to mind giving great packets of money to spies and traitors, and to those rich people. But now he hears there's to be land reform he makes off! Well, if you go, don't hope to come back again! The run-away monk can't take the monastery. Let's see if you're smart enough to keep your land. Now you've gone, d'you think we don't dare touch you?" And people went to the peasants' association and said: "He may have taken all his title deeds with him."

At this the peasants' association began to be alarmed, and wanted to send tenants at once to ask for the deeds. Young Guo's father had been called too, but he was sitting quite helplessly on the *kang* in the inner room of the co-operative while Young Cheng paced up and down, from time to time pouring himself a drink of water from a porcelain jug, and asked: "Uncle Guo, how long have you cultivated those eight *mu* of his?" Some tenants were still unwilling to go and ask for the title deeds. When the peasants' association ordered them they agreed, but then they went back to work on their land. The association had to talk them round individually.

Tenant Guo crooked his fingers and reckoned for a time, then answered: "Twelve years."

"How much rent do you pay a year?"

"It's hilly irrigated land I cultivate, so the rent isn't high. It used to be three pecks a *mu*, but the last few years it's been increased to four and a half pecks."

"Why was the rent increased?"

"The land's better than before. It's a plot by the hill. When I first rented it it was full of stones and the ground was hard, but after I cultivated it I turned over the soil twice a year and put down plenty of manure, often carrying up rich soil to spread over it and weeding it well, so it yields more than before."

Bugao walked in from the outer room and, looking at the simple old fellow, couldn't help saying: "Then I suppose you'd say it was right to increase the rent!"

Tenant Guo just looked at him.

But Young Cheng went on asking patiently: "How much grain does each *mu* yield?"

"Don't you understand, you can't say for certain. In a good year each *mu* yields six or seven pecks, but if there's a drought one gets only four to five."

"Uncle Guo, what kind of life do you lead?"

"Oh, so so." He forced a slight smile.

Just then his son came in. Young Guo stood in the doorway looking at his father, and said: "Dad! What year have we ever had enough to eat? You don't taste proper grain from one end of the year to the other, just husks of beans, husks of wheat, husks of rice all the time. That tattered matting of ours is only enough for one side of the bed, yet you can say 'So so.' Why, cattle live better than we do!"

"Ummm . . . there you go again. . . ." He seemed about to reprove his son, but stopped, his lips trembling.

"Uncle, think it over. You go to work with stars overhead and come home with stars overhead. Where does the grain you grow go to? They sit in the shade without having to stir hand or foot, eating good rice and flour. Do you really think it's right?"

"Well, it's his land." With damp eyes he looked at Young Cheng.

"You say it's his land? If we didn't work like beasts how could grain come from his land? — Dad's such a clod. When you wanted him to go to a poor peasants' meeting he complained of backache. — Now that Li is gone what more are you afraid of?"

"Well, but the land's his."

"His, his! Wouldn't the rent you've paid for the last twelve years buy those few fields!" somebody else put in from the outer room. By now several of Li's tenants were standing outside. They had heard long ago that land reform was to give the land to whoever cultivated it, and had been waiting all this time for the cadres to give them land. Now hearing that Landlord Li had run away, they were afraid he had taken the title deeds and nothing could be done about it. They had crowded outside to await orders from the peasants' association. When Young Cheng saw them he asked: "Are you all here?"

"Not all," they answered. "Some of them are afraid of trouble, and some are related to him, so they won't come."

"Related to him? What use is it being related to him? Does that entitle them not to pay any rent?" said Bugao, the organization officer of the peasants' association. He often worked himself up into a state of indignation over the people's backwardness, and he had a quick temper.

"All right, just the few of you will do. You go and ask for the deeds and bring back the deeds for the land each of you cultivate. If she won't give them, then work out the account for her. Be sure to say you were sent by the peasants' association." Young Cheng made this decision, speaking for the association.

"If the deeds aren't there, don't leave, but tell her to produce Li, do you understand?" put in Bugao.

"Right, we'll do that. Uncle Guo, let's go."

"Uh. . . ."

"You're not the only one, Dad. What's there to be afraid of? It's the peasants' association that told us to go!" Young Guo raised his father to his feet.

"Well, it's a woman. . . ."

"And hasn't the woman sucked your blood too?" Now they were all talking at once. The courtyard was filled with people who had come to watch, who were standing on tiptoe staring. When they saw the tenants come out they hastily made way for them. "Don't be afraid of that woman's sharpness," called out Bugao. And added in a whisper to Young Cheng: "The title deeds are certain to have been taken to Zhuolu County. We'll send people to the county government to fetch him back."

"The peasants' association tells you to go, you've got to go. Bring back the title deeds and those eight *mu* of land will be ours," said Young Guo pushing his father into the group of tenants.

A band of people marched to Li's gate. Those who had come to see the fun stopped some distance off, while the tenants began to confer with one another. Someone behind shouted: "Don't you dare go in? She's only a woman. What's there to be afraid of?"

They walked quickly in. Tenant Guo was pushed through the door too by his son.

Three children playing under the archway of the gate

178

stopped to stare at the newcomers. Lanying, who was older than the other children, realized what was happening. She turned and hurried in, calling out shrilly: "Ma! They've come! They've come!"

The dogs tied up on the porch started barking.

The few tenants stood in the empty courtyard exchanging glances, not knowing what to say. The bamboo curtain of the north room rattled and Mrs. Li came out. She was wearing a blue cotton jacket and trousers, her hair was uncombed, hanging limply. Red rims round her eyes, caused by crying, were conspicuous on her plump white face. In her arms she was carrying a red lacquered box. One of the tenants called out: "Mrs. Li!"

She hurried down the steps to kneel by the side of a porcelain tub holding an evergreen shrub, tears streaming down her face. "Masters," she said, sobbing, "please be kind to us and have pity on a poor woman and children. This is my husband's . . . please take it, it's a hundred and thirty-six *mu* and a half of land altogether and one house. You all know that quite well, good friends and neighbours. My husband's no good, the children and I can't depend on him. Now we're counting on you who've all been our friends for so many years. We're feudalistic landlords and ought to have our land divided. I've nothing to say against that. Only please, masters, remember I'm only a woman, and have pity on the children. I'll kowtow to you! . . ." Then she kowtowed to them all repeatedly and took up the box again, her face streaming with tears. Lanying also knelt at her side, while the two younger children standing among the crowd started howling.

All the tenants who had entered so boldly seemed struck dumb at the sight of the woman kneeling before them. They thought how she had been born into a rich family and never known hardship, and they began to remember her little acts of charity, until some of them pitied her present plight. No one moved to take the box. They forgot what they had come for, completely taken in by the act she had put on. Tenant Guo sighed, then turned round and retreated to the very back of the court.

"Mrs. Li, get up to talk," said the man who had first addressed her, probably some relative who had perhaps never had any intention of taking the title deeds.

The woman made as if to get up, but pretended she had not the strength and sat on the ground, just slapping her daughter and saying: "Why don't you pass it to the gentlemen." The child took the box, stood up and started towards the men, and they all fell back a step.

"This is all your father's fault," Mrs. Li started crying again.

One of the tenants slipped out, followed by another. The whole group gradually retreated in disorder till only Tenant Guo was left standing there dazed, wanting to say something, but not knowing how to say it. The woman stood up and said, crying: "Uncle, sit down a little before you go. You've known us for a long time. Please forgive us for the wrongs we've done you. Please, Uncle, be generous! Although I'm only a woman with children I'll repay you bit by bit. My husband ought to be blamed. See how he's gone off without caring what happens to us, going off like that! It must be my fate to be unlucky! Please, Uncle, take these title deeds to the peasants' association, and do put in a few good words for me and the children. Our life is in your hands!"

Tenant Guo looked distressed too, and said: "Don't cry, we're all old tenants. We can talk things over. It was the peasants' association that told us to come. As for the

180

title deeds, you keep them. You'd better have a rest. I'll be going too."

The tenants who had beaten a retreat did not go back to the co-operative, but one by one slipped back to the fields or to their homes. Young Cheng and the others waited for a while, and when no one came back they sent to find out what had happened. Outside Li's gate and inside the courtyard all was quiet. The children were sitting by the sieve for drying fruit, eating fresh red fruit as if nothing at all had happened. Greatly surprised, the cadre went to make further enquiries, but when he went to the tenants' houses to ask, they just answered quietly: "If Landlord Li were at home it would be all right, but one woman, with her children, crying and pleading, how could we? How could we look her in the face again? As for the title deeds, better let the peasants' association fetch them."

33

WHEN Young Cheng heard this, Yumin was also in the co-operative. The latter's calm reaction to the news surprised Cheng, who thought: "We're like brothers. We've worked all this time together, both trusting each other absolutely. Why should he behave now as if there were a mountain between us?" He could see that Yumin had something on his mind, but could not guess what it was. He suspected that Yumin disapproved of him, but was unwilling to examine his own shortcomings. He often felt himself surrounded by a special atmosphere. Yumin was not the only one to avoid him. Whenever everybody discussed which landlord to attack, he felt he was being covertly scrutinized. These cold looks made him uneasy, but he had not the courage to force his way out of this miasma. Sometimes he thought: "If you want to have that trial, go ahead. I won't oppose it. I still stand for the peasants' association." Sometimes he thought of mentioning this to Yumin, but when it came to the point he never spoke. He had not seen Heini for a long time. He did not want to see her, yet her eyes, so appealing, passionate and resentful, especially of late, made him unable to forget her. He felt he had let her down, and tried to avoid thinking of anything connected with her.

The co-operative was a scene of confusion. There was no office in the village, and the cadres liked to meet here. Now they started discussing this business and Young Cheng asked Yumin straight out what he thought of it, while others asked too: "How did it happen that none of the peasants wanted the title deeds!"

"The peasants still haven't stood up," said Yumin. "They were afraid and didn't dare take them."

"Afraid of that woman?" they exclaimed.

"Ah, women don't fight with guns but they're full of tricks. The proverb says, 'Beautiful women make heroes falter' — well . . . this time she fooled them with her crying and snivelling. That wife of Li's is not so simple as she looks. She's a smiling tiger, much smarter than her husband. In a word, they lost and turned tail! The peasants' association has been too impatient. Before we're united ourselves we send our men out to fight!" He followed this up with another glance at Young Cheng. Cheng sensed a double meaning in Yumin's remarks, but because there were so many people present he did not say anything, and merely made a calculation on the abacus in front of him. Yumin set his jaw, stood up and went off to find Vice-Head Zhao.

Yumin knew the people hoped to get land but were unwilling to take any initiative. They still had their doubts.

Unless the old powers were overthrown, they were afraid to show enthusiasm. There were several racketeers in the village, and to suppress them thoroughly would not be easy. That spring they had chosen a comparatively weak opponent to try: Landlord Hou, a bed-ridden old man. The cadres felt nobody ought to be afraid of him, but to their surprise only a few enthusiasts got worked up and shook their fists. Members of the peasants' association in the crowd shouted: "Speak up! Just one word!" Then people shook their fists and shouted with them, but at the same time looked furtively to where Schemer Qian was squatting at the back. Hou was fined a hundred piculs of grain, payable in terms of forty *mu* of his land which was divided among some score of families. Some people were pleased, others were afraid after the land was taken and dared not even walk past Landlord Hou's gate, while Tenant Hou secretly returned the land thus received. The trial had taken place and representatives from the district government had made favourable comments on it. But in this play, as Yumin knew perfectly well, it was the same few characters coming in and going out all the time. And now the cadres still had not made up their mind, while in addition they had a traitor among them. To begin with, Yumin had wavered too. Schemer Qian was an army dependent and presumably should not be tried, or even if he deserved trial, he could not possibly be held guilty enough for a death sentence — such, very naturally, was Yumin's view based on long experience. That spring the higher authorities had corrected a wrong trend in land reform. A number of landlords whom the people wanted to execute had been sent to the county court. After being imprisoned for two months they were sent back for re-trial with the explanation that the policy was to be lenient, because the previous year it had been implemented too radically. The people were still afraid there might be a change in the political situation. They felt that if a man were tried it must be for his life, lest he take vengeance in the future. Accordingly people like Schemer Qian, under existing conditions, presented quite a problem. However, Yumin's mind was made up. He saw that since Wen and the others had come, although the demand for land reform had raised all manner of expectations in the people, still the doubt as to which landlord to choose and the various rumours going about the village had reduced this interest. He felt inexpressibly worried, and had made a clean breast of his anxieties to Yang. Their talk in the orchard had not only strengthened his resolve but also increased his enthusiasm. If they still acted as they had in the spring, land reform could not be carried out. Although owing to Wen's absence the matter had not been discussed and decided upon, he had started persuading and winning over the cadres and had come to an agreement with Freckles Li and Swarthy Guo. Organization Zhao would probably not oppose them. He always followed the majority. Their outlook was gradually becoming more uniform. Moreover, noticing how Yang and Hu spent all their time in peasants' homes or on the land, he was sure they must have gained a good deal of material which would increase their understanding and make them all the more inclined to accept his view. Now only two important cadres were left with whom he had not had a heart-to-heart talk — Young Cheng and Vice-Head Zhao. Not sure enough of Cheng, who had given no indication of his attitude, he decided to leave him to the last, for fear of not reaching a satisfactory conclusion. Or else he might ignore him, leaving him and Security Officer Zhang out of it.

When he went into the lane he saw a crowd of people round Vice-Head Zhao's door, and heard shouting, so he hurried over. Some people who saw him coming wanted to tell him something, but he could not stop to listen. The rest made way for him, and he rushed to the open space in front of the house where he heard Zhao cursing furiously: "... You've really lost face for good and all! How can I ever hold up my head again in the village!..." Yumin was just about to go in when a woman burst out of the house. When she saw all the people standing outside, she gave a start, then turned round, pointed to the window and cursed Zhao: "You beast! Do you think you can spit blood on people — making false accusations! You shan't slander people without paying for it, damn you!"

Yumin recognized her as Landlord Jiang's wife, a slim little elf-like creature, with dreamy eyes and long hair streaming down her back, who had been a loose woman in a neighbouring village and had moved over when Jiang was ward chief. She was not married to him, and all day long she gossiped from house to house, acting as go-between for illicit lovers, always up to no good. She went on gesticulating and shouting wildly, but Yumin did not care. In two strides he confronted her, and asked sternly: "What are you up to?"

The woman wanted to go on cursing, but seeing it was Yumin standing in front of her she stopped at once, and turning her head started crying. As she walked out she complained to the onlookers: "The good are never rewarded! We're terribly wronged! How can we live? Heavens!..." However, she quickened her pace, crying as she went out, and was soon out of sight.

Crashes were heard from the house, and a woman's shrill voice called out: "He's beating me to death, help, help!" Before Yumin could reach the door Mrs. Zhao burst out, looking like a ghost with dishevelled hair, flying as if for her life, still shouting: "Help! Help!" Before anyone had time to intervene, Zhao came out in pursuit, his chest bare,

185

and kicked her over. Yumin put out a hand to stop him, but he paid no attention and lunged forward again. There was a tearing sound, and the flower-printed jacket his wife was wearing split from top to bottom, disclosing her dingy breasts. Seeing that some men had hold of him, his wife sat on the ground and started weeping bitterly, pulling the tight pretty jacket round her. But try as she would she could not cover her breasts. Held by others Zhao exclaimed furiously: "Look at the shameless whore! She's spoilt my good name. After all I'm still vice-village head!"

Several neighbouring women crowded round to comfort his wife, with whom they sympathized: Mr. Zhao was so fierce — as if he couldn't settle any trouble by talking! Although he was a cadre, he still beat people! She was already the mother of several children. But they could not help laughing when they looked at the flowered jacket fitting her so tightly. This jacket had been given her by Landlord Jiang's wife. Jiang had sent his cunning wife every day to bribe her with presents of food for the children and a flowered jacket for herself, until Mrs. Zhao thought they were good people. She had put on the jacket and felt very pleased, and praised Jiang in the presence of her husband. Now she had been beaten. Looking sadly at her torn jacket she complained naively and tearfully: "Oh . . . all summer I've had nothing to wear. He wouldn't let me make a dress, just kept saying he was vice-village head. What if he is vice-head? His wife hasn't even a gown to wear. Isn't it a shame!"

Zhao went with Yumin to the latter's home. This was an east room which he had rented. It was not big but looked roomy. The *kang* was empty except for two grimy pillows and a heap of bedding and clothes piled in one corner. At the head of the *kang* were a little stove and a pan. Against the wall a dilapidated chest with bowls, chopsticks and the like on top, and in front of the chest a small water container. Zhao went to the water container and drank a dipperful of water, then used his bare arm to wipe the sweat from his head. Yumin sitting on the edge of the *kang* said: "Men don't quarrel with women. A fight between husband and wife who have been married a long time doesn't look good. People laugh at you."

"Oh, what's there to say! When people are poor they lack will power. My silly wife is so damn backward, if you don't beat her she won't behave! And this is the only way to stop that witch from coming any more." Zhao sat on the *kang* too, his legs stretched straight out. He accepted a cigarette from Yumin, made sure there was no one outside the window, and said: "Yumin, I won't deceive you. This spring I borrowed two piculs of grain from Landlord Jiang. Who knew this land reform would crop up again? Wen says we were wrong to let him be village head. Jiang saw us hold meetings without sending for him. He can put two and two together. He invited me to a meal, but I didn't go — does he imagine I can be bought with two piculs of grain? As a matter of fact, if I could be bought so easily my wife needn't be jealous of other people's fancy clothes. I think I've sacrificed quite a bit so far. When we were fighting the Japanese I became village head, but my family never gained anything apart from these few brats. I've got nothing to lose. I say we haven't put in enough effort this time. The people may not say anything, but they feel dissatisfied. Don't you agree?"

"Right, Old Zhao, I came to see you about this very thing." Yumin jumped up and started walking up and down, unable to conceal his delight. He was just going to say why he had come, when Zhao went on.

"You've come just at the right time. I was going to find you. Ah, so many people have said to me, this is a serious

187

business! Do you understand? Have you thought of that? There is a big harvest this year in our village. Just think, there are over a hundred *mu* of orchard in the village. If you walk by you'll see all the fruit. Now that we're starting land reform people can't sleep at night for thinking of it. But the land can't be divided at once, and things are dragging on. By the time the land is divided there'll be nothing but leaves left on the trees! Now the rich people are selling fruit for all they're worth, and it's making the poor frantic! They keep coming to see me about it, wanting us to do something. What do you think we should do? I think from tomorrow onwards we should forbid the rich people to sell, and have all the orchards watched. This is an important business! Think of all the money involved!"

Yumin had thought of this some days before, but having so much to do had forgotten about it again. The last few days he had been busy talking to people, and so it had slipped his memory entirely. Now that Zhao reminded him he felt the urgency of the situation, and jumping up said: "Right! This is an important business! But just watching them won't do. These perishable fruits won't wait for us to carry out our land reform slowly! So what's to be done?"

"Let's go and find Young Cheng. I think it would be better if the peasants' association took responsibility in this. Just a few people can't make a good job of it. What do you think?" Seeing Yumin nod, Zhao added: "We must find some people who can keep accounts. I think the peasants' association had better take charge of selling all the fruit, then later whoever gets the land will get the money."

"Better find quite a few, and we'll have to let the group know," said Yumin as he was going out. "And I think we'd better go and talk it over with Yang first."

34

ON their way back the two of them met Sheng's mother, with her glistening coils of hair. She was hobbling on her bound feet from house to house to tell everybody: "Well, what do you think of Yumin! Those men really are hard! When my Sheng joined the army, they made it sound all very fine, but once he'd gone they changed their tune. They'd promised me two piculs of grain, but only gave me two pecks, and kept calling us middle peasants. Middle peasants, indeed! In that case why ask middle peasants to join the army! ..." She had this off by heart, in fact most of the others knew it by heart too. When she had said this she laughed: "Oho, but now there's justice. The men who've come this time know what they're about! Comrade Yang said: 'Middle peasants are on our side. Haven't they suffered just the same? If there's anything good going, the middle peasants must have some share in it too. She's sent a son to the army. She's an army dependent. How can they keep back one picul and eight pecks of her grain?' Ah, Vice-Head Zhao still wasn't pleased. He told me to go to the co-op to fetch it, but I said: 'Mr. Zhao, I'll wait till Sheng comes home to carry it for me.' Yumin said furiously: 'All right, we'll tell someone to send it to you!' Aha, it's going to be my turn now!"

People in the street knew the old woman had a sharp tongue and could make things hot for people. Although they were perfectly aware the village cadres ought not to have kept back some of her grain they had all held their tongues, thinking it was none of their business. They were glad for her sake that her problem was solved, and advised her: "Now they've given you the grain, better not go on scolding them."

"Comrade Yang talks sense," she replied, "for all he's so short and young. He told me: 'If you've anything to say, speak out boldly. That's good. Nowadays we want people to speak out. Yumin is working for the people. If the people aren't satisfied they should criticize him. Only we're all friends. Don't scold and be prejudiced. Isn't that right?' Ah! That silenced me, I could only say: 'Oh, I'm only a woman. Sometimes I don't know what's right.' 'It doesn't matter,' he said, 'If you've any other complaints, speak out.' I thought: he's come for land reform and it would be wrong to go on being on bad terms with the cadres, so I said: 'Nothing, nothing else!' This time I really feel good. It's not so much the picul and eight pecks of grain, but now Yumin can't keep saying things against middle peasants all the time. I asked someone to take a letter to Sheng, telling him not to worry, because the people sent by the district are looking after me. Even though I'm a middle peasant I'm not afraid of anyone!"

There were two other people in the village who were a thorn in the side of the cadres. One was Old Han's son, the other was Ex-soldier Zhang, brother of Bugao, organization officer of the peasants' association. They had both been in the army and were rather troublesome. They often criticized the village cadres, despising them. At the same time they felt that the cadres did not appreciate them or look after them properly. The cadres said these two did not do productive work, just fooled around. But they were afraid of the ex-soldier's biting remarks and could not talk them down. The cadres' records were not so good as those of these two men who were able to claim they had shed blood for the revolution. Since it was out of the question to do anything against them, it seemed best to have as little to do with them as possible. Now it had suddenly come about that Young Han and

Yang had become good friends, and Young Han had come meekly to the peasants' association to help sort out the census record, carefully checking up on each family in turn, registering the amount of land and other property they had. He did not smoke a single cigarette belonging to the association, but took his own pipe and flint. At first Young Cheng was not too willing to have Young Han join the work, afraid that the latter would take advantage of his ignorance. But later Cheng was pleased to find he had got a good helper.

Ex-soldier Zhang had been even more active and liked to gossip. Now Swarthy Guo, captain of the militia, came to see him and said: "You give our militia a class every day, I'll get them together at the right time. You're an old soldier. You know more about fighting than we do!" Ex-soldier Zhang wanted to show his skill so that all could see that his claim of being an old Party member was not an empty boast. (His Party records had not been transferred to the village and Yumin had said there was not enough proof of his membership to include him in the local branch of the Party, which annoyed him exceedingly.) Accordingly he said: "Fine! If I don't teach well, please point out my faults!" After that he lectured to the militiamen every day about warfare and his experience as a guerrilla, giving a very graphic account of the battles he had participated in, and the men listened spellbound. Even Swarthy Guo said: "When we've time we must have more exercises. I was really a fool not to ask you to speak before. If it came to actual fighting you'd be much better than me even though I'm captain!" Swarthy Guo was open-hearted, and at once started being friendly with him, saying: "With the same surname we're like one family. Let's call each other brother."

So the villagers spread the news that the men sent this time knew what they were doing. People came to Yang and Hu

191

to settle disputes about money, land, marriage or property. They solved some of the simpler cases and started investigating the more complex ones. These disputes brought them in touch with many people. They learned more about conditions in the village, and entered into a new relation with everybody. A few days before, whatever house they visited the host would greet them politely: "How are you?" Or say: "I don't know whether I've understood land reform, but everything you said is right: the poor have got to stand up!" They might say smiling: "Welcome. If we poor people don't support the Communists, who should we support!" Formerly they limited themselves to some such simple remarks, without going deeper. Now, however, there was less formality. People would say: "Old Yang, we've got a problem for you to solve!" Or else edge up to him and whisper: "Come to my house for a meal, I've got a secret to tell you."

This day Yang had gone into the fields to help hoe the grass. He had just got back to the village and barely rounded the mud wall when he felt a heavy slap on his shoulder. Looking round he saw it was the dark youngster Liuman, his hair unkempt, his eyes wide open and flashing. Liuman was wearing a pair of black trousers, and was stripped to the waist. "Old Yang!" he said, "I'm the only one you won't see, but I've been waiting for you!"

"That's right," Yang answered, "I've never found your house. Do you live here?" At once he remembered someone had told him Liuman's brother had once been ward chief.

"Come on, come with me. My house is rather dirty, but that won't kill you." He practically pushed Yang into a small alley.

"Why didn't you come to find me?" Yang asked.

"Ah," Liuman fetched a deep sigh and was silent for a

long time, then said: "Here's my house. My brother's out. Come in for a while."

Yang entered the courtyard with him. It was like a long alley, the east and west rooms crowded together. Liuman stood in the middle of the yard and looked all round, not knowing where to ask Yang to go.

A woman with infected eyes came out from the east room carrying a child whose eyes were so filled with mucus it could not open them, while flies swarmed round its head. "Where have you been all day?" she asked. "Your rice is still kept for you. Do you want to eat?"

Liuman paid no attention to her, as if unaware of her existence, and said impatiently: "It's hotter inside, let's sit here, Old Yang."

"Is this your house?" Yang walked to the door of the east room and looked in, then added: "Do you still cook inside?"

Flapping at the flies on the child's head the woman said with a sigh: "Oh, he never pays any attention to his family, out all day long and never coming back. I've too much to do. It's terribly hot inside. When he does come home he just looks grim. Well, won't you have something to eat?"

Just then a young woman came out of the west room, walked over and said timidly: "Brother, go and sit in my room."

Yang followed him into the west room. It was cleaner here. On the wall were pasted a faded pair of scrolls and a picture of a woman. The cover on the *kang* was folded, the matting looked fairly new. There was a pair of not too old blue embroidered pillows, and on the chest of drawers a mirror and two vases. Yang could not help looking surprised and pleased, and was just going to praise the room, when Liuman spoke: "Old Yang, don't think too little of me. I wasn't always so poor. It doesn't matter if people have made me poorer, but I have a grievance which is eating me alive!"

Liuman opened wide his round eyes again and fixed them on Yang, who sat on the *kang* and answered: "Take it easy. Tell me all about it. We're the same kind. I won't give away any secrets. You can say what you like to me."

But Liuman fell silent again, not knowing how to start his story, walking up and down the room, clenching his fists, sometimes rumpling his thick dishevelled hair.

His wife brought in a bowl of millet gruel and a dish of salted vegetables, and gave Yang a cigarette and a light. She stood in the doorway, rubbing her inflamed eyes, paying no attention to anyone else, just waiting for her husband to eat.

"Liuman, go on with your meal," said Yang.

But Liuman planted himself in front of Yang and said quickly: "To tell you the truth, ever since the day Nuanshui was liberated, I've been waiting, waiting for the sky to clear. Ah, who could have thought those bad people would get their roots into the Eighth Route Army? Now I'm waiting to see what you're going to do, Old Yang! To see whether you're only picking on the soft ones."

"Take your time if you've something to say. You must excuse him, Chairman. Our second brother was driven mad. . . . Ah, eat this bowl of millet now." Although his wife looked rather afraid of him, she could be stubborn too.

"That's right, Liuman, when you've finished your meal we can talk."

"If you don't take it away, I'll break the bowl." Liuman walked over again and glowered at his wife. She did not falter, but looking at him steadily said with unspeakable bitterness and regret: "You just won't think how hard it is for people!" Then she turned and went out, and could be heard sighing again outside.

"Liuman!" said Yang again. "Now is the time when we peasants come up on top. In the past people exploited us and oppressed us, but now we're settling old scores one by one. The worse a man is, the more harshly we must thrust him down — why should we pick on soft ones? Don't be afraid. If you've any grievance you shall have your revenge. The Communists will back you up."

"Hm, that sounds very fine, Old Yang, but things are not like that. Frankly, it's no good your just listening to what the cadres say. The cadres are men of straw, they daren't offend anyone. Just think, you come and make things hot for a while. You don't need to be afraid of anyone. You'll be going away again. But the cadres can't look at it like that. They have to stay in the village. They have to figure out whether they'll get the better of those people or not. They've got to think of the future. Yumin isn't a bad chap, but just now he's keeping out of my way, and I know why. He's afraid I'll expose him. Whenever I see him I call out: 'Chairman of the Resistance Union, whose boot are you really going to lick?' One day he wanted to hit me, but he was afraid of what you'd think, so just said: 'Liuman, I've treated you all right. Why are you trying to do me in?' He did treat me all right, even introducing me to join the Party!"

"Join the Party?" Yang felt even more astonished. Since coming to the village he had met all the eighteen Party members, but had never heard Liuman was a Communist, so he questioned him further.

"Oh, I date from long ago. I joined before the liberation. For a time I had a hand in things too; but this spring they expelled me. It was Yumin who spoke up for me and made them change it to suspended membership. Since then I've been left out of the affairs of the village. I've become a non-existent Party member. That's why I feel wronged, because they are on the racketeers' side and apart from losing my lawsuit I was criticized by the district government. Now, Old Yang! I want to take up the lawsuit again and win, not for the sake of that bit of land, but to settle my grudge, to overthrow Schemer Qian! That Qian — do you know him?"

Liuman had poured all this out in a rush, not caring whether the other understood or not, as if others must understand such things naturally, taking advantage of this opportunity to get his grievances off his chest. After saying all this, however, he did not seem relaxed, but rather like a soldier who has just joined battle, standing there in a state of extreme excitement, looking at Yang, not knowing what to do.

Yang breathed a sigh.

Liuman came over again, pouring out another torrent of words. Several times his wife, hearing the din he made and afraid he would get into trouble, hurried over to the door to look. She saw him gesticulating frantically, while Yang watched him quietly, saying from time to time: "Take it easy. And what else?" Finally she saw her husband lie down panting on the *kang*, while Yang said: "I understand, I understand, Liuman! You lie down and rest now. Don't get worked up. We'll gradually think of a way."

Then the woman went in, and standing in the doorway said: "Ah, if only you can help him to win the lawsuit, we'll be able to live properly again! His second brother is mad. Now look at him, he's nearly mad too. Oh, this old grudge is deep-rooted!"

Yang sat with him for a long time, and when he saw Liuman was gradually quietening down, he asked his wife to bring some gruel. Liuman got up to see him off, his eyes as red as his wife's inflamed eyes, the rims even moister, but he was very calm. He put his hand on Yang's shoulder and said clearly: "You said rightly, when it rains the ground is slippery, but anyone who falls down must get up himself. We can't stand on our feet except by our own efforts. And you said even more rightly, all the peasants in the world are one family. If they don't unite they have no strength and can't stand up. You've shown me the way, Old Yang, and now I won't let you down!"

35

YANG had no sooner left Liuman's house than he met a peasant who told him Wen had returned and was looking for him everywhere. He hurried back, and as soon as he reached the courtyard he heard Wen describing in cheerful tones the success of his work in Liyu. When Yang went in Wen just nodded to him, and went on with what he was saying: "It's very simple. Tomorrow evening we hold a trial, forty-nine families attacking one family. Nothing could be easier. There's only one family of rich peasants. It really is a poor village."

"How much land is involved?" Hu, sitting on the chest of drawers, was listening eagerly.

"He has over thirty *mu* altogether, so he ranks as a rich peasant in Liyu. It's intended to leave him twenty *mu*. Old Dong's been given three *mu* of vineyard. Old Dong, now you've got that land, who will cultivate it for you?"

Old Dong sitting in front of the *kang* table polishing his pistol looked rather flushed, but it might have been the reflection of the red silk round his pistol. And then Wen cracked another joke at his expense, saying they must be sure to attend Old Dong's wedding feast before their return to the district. Old Dong hastily protested there would be nothing of the kind.

Judging by these brief remarks, Yang felt that his view of conditions in Liyu could not be the same as Wen's. But there was not much he could say, so he just asked: "Then forty-nine families are dividing a dozen of land, and Old Dong is getting three *mu*?"

"No," said Wen, still very complacently, "don't get excited, Comrade. Of course that's not the case. Some of the land they cultivate belongs to people of other villages — there are some fifty *mu* belonging to Nuanshui landlords, and ten *mu* to Longwang landlords. In this way, with the exception of a few middle peasants, each family will get on the average two *mu* of land. They're very pleased, aren't they, Old Dong?"

"Yes, those village cadres are enthusiastic," agreed Old Dong.

"I think their Party branch is better than Nuanshui's. What do you say, Old Dong?"

"About the same. It's a small village there, and easier to manage. Yumin's not bad. Only Nuanshui's affairs are difficult to manage." Old Dong put away his pistol and went to turn over his portfolio.

"I suppose this will only solve matters for tenant farmers," said Yang again. "The poor peasants still won't have their problems solved. When the cadres are enthusiastic it doesn't necessarily mean all the people are pleased. Are forty-nine families attacking one family simply because he's the only rich farmer there?"

Wen felt Yang always liked to find fault. Rather displeased, he answered coldly: "If he didn't qualify, would they attack him? If you're interested you go to their meeting tomorrow evening. We've got everything arranged in advance."

Yang thought of saying: "Relying on advance arrangements is not necessarily going to get things done." But before he could speak Wen went on to ask about conditions in Nuanshui during his absence. Hu and Yang made a detailed report. And Hu described how Yumin and Vice-Head Zhao had come to discuss the question of selling fruit.

Wen sat there patiently listening, looking as if he were the only one who could decide a policy. He much disliked the way these two had of bluntly displaying their little knowledge and upholding certain views. He thought to himself: "You two can do investigation work, but you've not the ability to decide a far-reaching policy." He always posed as being very experienced and having a thorough understanding of policy, often quoting from books. As a matter of fact, he was not particularly able. In his heart of hearts he considered himself a prudent man who could not go far wrong. He often felt he saw the truth of things, and had a way of analysing events after they had happened. In addition, he was very skilled in expressing his views.

Clever people are not easily stumped. Even in mass activity they can often dodge, or come down heavily on others. When things go wrong they tend to make jokes and shift the responsibility to others, and on all occasions pose as infallible. Such people, who often appear very enthusiastic, quick and competent, can for a short time deceive a few people into thinking them comparatively able. But in the eyes of the masses they are hardly better than the opportunists concealed in the revolutionary ranks.

"Oh, that Liuman, I know him!" Wen remembered the circumstances under which he had met him in the road. "He seems completely crazy. Since his elder brother is mad, it's quite possible it runs in the family. Old Dong, who else in his family is mad?"

"No one that I know of," replied Old Dong. "I heard of

199

his lawsuit this spring. It's possible the village cadres were rather careless in their investigation. Maybe Schemer Qian and Landlord Jiang were behind it. He really was a Party member before, but as to when he was suspended, not even the people in the district are clear about that."

Wen felt that anyone who had been a ward chief must have squeezed money and been a traitor. Now when he heard that a man only became ward chief because he was forced into it by his enemies and that he had become an impoverished peasant and been driven mad, Wen simply did not believe it. He had little faith in talk of this kind. That Schemer Qian stirred up lawsuits in the village and involved others in intrigues he considered highly probable. But from the economic standpoint, Qian had only a dozen *mu* of land after deducting the fifty *mu* he had divided between his sons. He could at most be counted a middle peasant. Even if he rented out his land, that was not a heinous offence. From the political standpoint, he was an army dependent. Not to improve the social status of a dependent of a revolutionary soldier was already bad enough. How could they attack him? Because of this he felt the cadres were absolutely right not to suggest attacking him. On the other hand he disapproved of the way Yumin neglected to bring this up in meetings but was so voluble outside. What kind of a way was this to go on! It only served to confuse our aim and throw our camp into confusion. And these two workers in his unit, although they did seem able to get close to the masses, had insufficient power of analysis, so that it was easy for them to be deceived. Wen had specially pointed out to them that the business of the blackboard news clearly expressed the voice of the masses, yet they persisted in believing Freckles Li's account of it as subversive activity on the part of reactionaries — wasn't Freckles Li of the same family as Landlord Li? All these cadres were activated to a certain extent by personal feelings! But still these two inexperienced comrades insisted on believing them.

Old Dong, with his understanding of the village and his peasant's intuition, felt that dividing up the land of either Li or Old Gu would make everyone happy. But if there was to be a trial very few people would speak up. In fact there might be some who sympathized with Old Gu, while Li's little acts of charity in the past might make people feel he was being treated too harshly. Old Dong's way of thinking was unconsciously much like Yumin's, only he was even more cautious than Yumin, more of a prey to doubt. In face of Wen's profound knowledge of political theory he dared not maintain any definite attitude, and therefore just expressed vague opinions, although this was quite alien to his nature.

The discussion dragged on. The empty references to the mass line and the baseless generalizations made Hu unable to contain himself, and jumping to his feet he said: "If we go on quarrelling over our work like this, there can only be one outcome — failure! I've taken part in the work of reducing rents and rates of interest in the past, but never seen work done like this!"

"Yes, I feel too that the views of the work team are not sufficiently in harmony," replied Wen slowly and deliberately. "Too many side issues and being too democratic make it difficult to centralize. The main reason is still that our understanding of policy and principles is not the same. But, as for the work, I don't think it will turn out as you hope — or shall I say as you fear — it won't be as bad as that." He laughed.

Yang felt only the word "bitterness" could describe his feelings. A feudalistic landlord like Li ought to be dealt

201

with, and that thoroughly, but before the peasants acquired class consciousness they could not understand the relation between the bullies and the landlords. They hated the bullies even more than the landlords. Until the former were overthrown they would not dare arise. He felt if things remained so confused, it would be better to go back to the district or the county government, and ask them to decide about the work. But he controlled himself, reproaching himself for not being resourceful and being poor at co-operating with others, and thought: "I suppose this is a very good trial for me." And again: "Why quarrel over a matter of procedure? First do something, and let the facts prove that we are right. Let reality decide our action." So he suggested that since they had failed to obtain the title deeds, they should start an attack in which they might be confident of success, then use that minor victory to stir up fighting spirit, for before a big decisive battle a small victory had its uses.

This proposal was immediately accepted by all since it injured no one's self-esteem and obstructed no other plans. Tired of quarrelling they found it comparatively easy to reach agreement on this new question and on the concrete work of preparation. The atmosphere in the room changed, and they discussed the problem very cordially together.

The image of Young Guo in the co-operative kept recurring to Hu. He said smiling: "The father was defeated, now tell the son to go in and win."

"Right, there's nothing soft about him. He can put up a fight!" The others agreed.

Old Dong said Landlord Jiang was a slippery customer, they should first tell his tenants how to settle accounts with him, and the reason why. This suggestion was quite correct too. The last time they had not made it clear to the tenants why they should take the title deeds, and that it was not robbing Landlord Li but just recovering what had been extorted from them.

On the question of dividing what they would confiscate from Jiang, Wen also made proposals which the others approved, with amendments. In short, on the matter of getting the title deeds they were all in complete accord. This gave them a delightful feeling of regained confidence, and they decided to reach this objective before going on to anything else. They set out at once to the co-operative to look for Yumin, Young Cheng and the others to discuss starting this work.

36

A GREAT many people were standing in the street outside the co-operative, close to the wall and in the shade, and a good few others were squatting in the shade of the trees by the platform. They all had their heads together. Yang saw Gui's husband Vineyard Li there too. He knew that Vineyard Li had something on his mind and would not be enthusiastic until it was settled, so he went over and asked him what he had been doing the last few days, and how soon his grapes would be picked. Vineyard Li replied that he had found a widowed aunt to look after his vineyard. During the day his wife helped there, he said, and the grapes were nearly ripe and would be picked in a couple of weeks. Because they had nothing to eat for the time being, he was doing odd jobs, making trips to Shacheng to sell fruit.

"Are all of you selling fruit?" asked Yang, including the others in his glance.

"No," answered an old man at their side: "I'm a watchman in an orchard."

"Whose orchard?"

"He's Orchard-keeper Li. He's watchman in Landlord Li's orchard," Vineyard Li answered for him.

"Oh!" Yang looked carefully at the old man, and asked again: "Why did Li run away? Did he say anything?"

"No, he didn't say anything, just sold fruit. After you came he started selling fruit. That was before it was all ripe. Each day seven or eight hundred or even over a thousand catties were sold."

"The night before he left someone from the village went to see him," added Vineyard Li.

But the old man just nudged him, and said: "His is not the only family selling fruit. If the village cadres don't do something about it, more than half the fruits of victory in the village will be gone. This is a bumper year. There hasn't been anything like it for over ten years."

"If Datong is taken, fruit will go up in price at once," said someone else who was squatting nearby. "In the old days we didn't only go west, but east too. Every train carried a few carloads of fruit."

"Do you sell fruit too?" Yang saw he was a youngster.

"No, my elder brother has one and a half *mu* of vineyard. They say the peasants' association is going to have all the fruit confiscated. My brother's afraid they'll confiscate his vineyard, and is half frantic. He doesn't dare come and ask himself so he sent me to find out. Comrade Yang, my brother only has five *mu* of land altogether, three and a half *mu* of irrigated land. With three in the family we manage all right, but can't be considered well off. Do you think they could take his land?" The youngster seized this opportunity to question Yang.

"Has your brother done anything bad in the village?"

"No, nothing bad or good, he's too busy with his bit of

land for anything else. His brother's a straightforward fellow too." Again it was Vineyard Li who answered.

"Then what's he afraid of? If he's not a landlord or a bully, there's nothing to worry about. If a peasant who is on the same side as the masses doesn't get a little share of land or some movable property, what good does it do him when the poor seize power? You tell your elder brother not to be afraid, and if anybody ill-treated him before he can even have his revenge. Don't you all think that's how it should be?"

"Yes, a few *mu* of land can't count as anything, and it's not as if the land produced crops itself. A man lives by the sweat of his brow," they said smiling.

"His brother was scared stiff. People frightened him by saying he was a middle peasant, saying after the landlords were overthrown it would be the turn of the rich peasants, and after the rich peasants were overthrown it would be the turn of the middle peasants. They said nowadays only the poor people without stick or stone of their own can prosper, that the poor people even if they don't work, just by attacking others and eating the fruits of victory, can have good things to eat. His brother couldn't bear the idea of this and killed a pig, saying he'd rather enjoy it himself than wait to be upset by seeing other people eat it later." Somebody else had squeezed in to speak.

"Will they really not sell his fruit?" the youngster asked again to make sure.

"Oh, listen to him! Didn't the comrade just say it depends on the opinion of the masses?"

"What opinion do the masses have? If the peasants' association says they will sell it then the masses don't dare protest. If the comrade puts in a word, that's the only thing that will be any use. Comrade Yang, will you please speak to the peasants' association about it?" The youngster pressed further forward.

"The peasants' association belongs to the community, not to a few people, so it has to follow the wishes of the majority. If not, then you shouldn't let it have its way. Speak out. The Communist Party is here to back you. Don't you know that?" This remark of Yang's delighted them all. Some did not altogether believe him, others agreed, saying: "With you comrades here we aren't afraid of anything. If you weren't here, how could we sell other people's fruit?"

By now Old Dong, Wen and Hu were surrounded too, all discussing the sale of fruit. "Aren't all the owners of orchards afraid?" Wen asked. "How many people have orchards?"

"Yes, they're all frightened," the crowd answered.

Hu told him that the eleven landlords and fifteen rich peasants all had orchard land, besides five middle peasants and twenty poor peasants. Vineyards were not included, because grapes were not worth much.

"How can they sell poor people's fruit too?" said someone in the crowd. "They must only sell the landlords' and rich peasants'."

"Not all the rich peasants will be dealt with. To control their fruit wouldn't be very good. That way those five middle peasants would be frightened too. Did you think of this, or was it the idea of the peasants' association?" Wen felt that it was not good to be so indiscriminate.

Everybody looked at everybody else, and no one said anything.

"What does it matter?" After a pause someone stepped forward to speak. It was Tenant Hou's son. "We're not robbing anyone. Those who oughtn't to have their fruit

206

confiscated can be given their money back. They can come and weigh out their fruit. If we're fair it's all right."

"If we have the fruit watched, surely a few days' delay in selling won't matter?" Wen asked again. "By that time, whoever the land belongs to can go and sell it. Won't that save trouble?" He spoke naturally in an authoritative tone. When nobody answered he repeated the question.

An old man in the crowd answered: "Of course that would do. We're just waiting for your orders, Chairman. We'll do just what you tell us."

But Old Dong said: "If the land could be divided up very quickly that would be all right. It doesn't matter if fruit is left for a few days. The only danger is prices may drop, if the days drag on. Apples and pears are all right, but there'll be trouble with the sweet-apple. . . ."

"Right!" Without waiting for him to finish the crowd started shouting. "Chairman Dong understands the difficulty. You can see he's a native here!"

Wen could not well say any more, so turned to Hu: "Let's rush the work of dividing land. Let's go and find Young Cheng and the others. If we can rush this work, better postpone selling fruit. Because if this isn't done well, there may be big trouble."

"We can't hurry it. But if even the rich peasants' fruit is controlled that won't look good. I agree with you on that." Hu followed him out of the crowd. Yang joined them, and they could hear Young Hou saying to Old Dong: "As soon as they heard there was to be land reform, the poor people started eyeing the fruit. Everybody hopes to get a few hundred or even a thousand catties. If all the fruit is gone the bare branches aren't so jolly. Chairman Dong, you put yourself in our place. Even that old die-hard, my dad, when he heard they were going to sell fruit, didn't protest, but found out what he could on the sly from my mother."

37

ALL the villagers were saying to each other: "Aha, the orchards of the eleven landlords are being watched. Members of the poor peasants' association are standing guard there."

"Ah, who are these eleven landlords? It looks as if they're all going to be dealt with!"

"I hear they're only taking fruit from those who rent out land. Rich peasants can still sell their own."

"That won't do! Aren't we going to deal with the rich peasants?"

"They say they can't all be tried. Some families will be, but by that time it'll be all right if they just pay up. There should be no trouble."

"That's right, if the fruit of the whole village were confiscated, the peasants' association would have all its time taken up selling fruit, and couldn't do anything for land reform. The land still has to be divided, hasn't it?"

Presently old Red-nosed Wu came along sounding his gong again and singing. He announced the members of the fruit-selling committee, and the decisions reached by the committee.

"Fine! If Co-op Tian's on it, it'll be all right! He's a clever chap. He can look after our interests. Look how well he runs the co-op. Every peasant can buy on credit and yet the co-op makes money."

"Oho, Orchard-keeper Li's on the committee too. He's all right. He knows all about the orchard land. He's walked over it for twenty years and knows exactly how many trees each family has. He can figure out the number of catties of fruit on each tree, good and bad alike, he's got them all in his head."

"It looks as if this time the poor are going to get complete control. Tenant Hou's son has come out too. Won't that make his father mad!"

They did not confine themselves merely to talking in the lanes and neighbours' houses, calling on relatives to find out what was happening, or crowding to the door of the co-operative to spread news, but went to the orchards to have a look. Some of them were assigned work, and women and girls went to watch the fun.

The fifteen rich peasants who had heard that all the fruit in the village would be confiscated, now smiled and encouraged each other, saying: "I always said the Communists wouldn't drive people to death! They wouldn't be unreasonable!" Their whole families went into the orchards to pick all the ripe fruit. They must not delay, but must get the fruit off as soon as possible.

The eleven landlord families who had their fruit under surveillance came to the orchards too to ask the crowd to leave a part and to see if the peasants would give false figures for the amount of their fruit or remove any secretly. The landlords sent their children to take advantage of the general confusion to pick some up and carry it home. Even one apple or pear was good and shouldn't be given away just anyhow!

When the earth was awakening in the thin clear beams of the dawn, gusts of laughter could be heard in the cool, quiet orchards. The merrily chirping sparrows flew off, and the scaly insects that love to flutter in the morning breeze darted in all directions. The thick leaves on the spreading branches rustled slightly, but could not hide from sight the rich profusion of fruit. Sparkling dewdrops could still be seen, like stars twinkling on a frosty night. And the bloom on the red fruit, or perhaps a film of dew, made it look even softer and more moist. Scarlet-tinted clouds mounted into the sky and through gaps in the thick foliage cloudy golden motes appeared, until the orchard reflected innumerable vivid violet and golden rays. Ladders leant against the trees. Men climbed the ladders and fruit dropped into their broad, work-roughened palms, thence into the baskets, while a fresh fragrance was wafted through the translucent rays. Whose orchard was this? Orchard-keeper Li was directing the work. For twenty years he had watched other people picking fruit or picked fruit himself for other people. He was taciturn and continued to work as silently as a statue amid all this activity. Judging by his joyless expression he did not know how fragrant and sweet the fruit was, as if what they were picking were clods of earth or stones. Yet today his sense of smell had woken with the earth, as if aware for the first time of this verdant and luxuriant atmosphere. As when a beggar suddenly finds a hoard of gold coins, the gleaming fruit dazzled his eyes. As Orchard-keeper Li directed the work, he said: "There were twenty-eight *mu* to this orchard, seventy sweet-apple trees, fifty pear, nine apple, three crab-apple, thirty date and one walnut. In the time of Li's father there were even more sweet-apple, but when it came into his son's hands there were some trees which hadn't been well grafted, and he had them cut down and planted pears in their place. Li isn't good for anything else, but he knows how to grow pears. He told us how to manure them and prune them. He read it in a book. It's a pity only these eleven and a half *mu* are left now. Five *mu* in the northwest corner were sold to Landlord Jiang, half a *mu* in the south was given to Rong, and he didn't get a cent for it. The three and a half *mu* by the well were sold at a good price to Old Gu, and another seven and a half *mu* were sold bit by bit to four or five different families. Those people don't know how to look after them, and since they only have such a little they leave everything to luck. But this year I must say they haven't done badly."

Some men's work was to carry the filled baskets to the place where the fruit was being collected. The pickers moved from branch to branch, and as the fruit gradually diminished the leaves seemed to grow more dense. Some of the pickers could not restrain their delight and threw fruit to the men working on the next tree, and if it was caught roared with laughter, while if it fell to the ground the people below raced to pick it up. If anyone bit into it a bystander was sure to shout: "You're breaking the rules. We're not allowed to eat any. This fruit already belongs to us poor people!" "Oh, crushed from falling, can't it be eaten? It doesn't matter eating one of Li's."

Some people teased Orchard-keeper Li, saying: "What makes you so cheerful, Uncle? Once Li's orchard is divided up you'll lose your job as watchman, won't you? So why are you so happy?"

"Watching the orchard is a good job, quiet and cool. An old fellow can sit here all day smoking, and if you're thirsty you just put out your hand to eat whatever you want. Uncle Li won't be able to have such a soft time any more."

"Oho!" Orchard-keeper Li seemed to have become a talkative old man, and answered smiling: "Quite right, I've had a soft time of it long enough. They ought to let me have two *mu* of land this time, and set me working hard too. An old bachelor like me — I've been without a care for dozens of years. If they give me a wife too, and if I have to put up with her nagging, that would be even better. Ho ho. . . ."

"We always said you'd been sleeping with the orchard wood fairies. If not for that why should you despise all the pretty girls in the village, and never ask a go-between to call on one of them? The wood fairies must have bewitched you. Everyone says they like old men!"

There was a roar of laughter and then another, the laughter spreading to all sides. Everybody was in high spirits.

Basket after basket of fruit piled up. The sun shone on the tree tops. Not a breath of wind could penetrate. Some men took off their jackets and hurried about with bare arms, wiping the sweat from their faces with towels. But no one complained of the heat.

Comparatively the most serious were the fruit weighers led by Co-op Tian. They recorded the fruit that had been weighed, at the same time packing it into baskets.

After the meal Mrs. Li came over. Her hair was combed and shining. She was wearing a clean gown and, smiling broadly, she approached timidly.

Nobody paid any attention to her. Even Orchard-keeper Li pretended not to notice her presence, his face resuming its original dull expression.

She went over to where Co-op Tian was, and said with a smile: "Our orchard isn't too big now, only eleven and a half *mu*. Uncle Li knows more about it than I do. Every year my husband sold a piece."

"Go away," said the bean-mill worker, who held the scales. "If the poor people trust us, why don't you? You've already sold quite a lot of fruit."

"Let her stay," said Co-op Tian.

"Ah, we're still in arrears," she complained, "the spring wages haven't been paid yet. . . ."

One of the pickers said to the men on the next tree: "Well, who said Landlord Li could only raise pears, not sweet-apple? Look what a big sweet-apple he's raised, really white and soft and plump and fragrant!"

A bellow of laughter sounded from the next tree.

The woman went to sit down a little further off. She looked at the trees, at the red jewels hanging in the green boughs. This was their property; in the past if anyone walked under the trees, she had only to look at him and he would come smiling to explain. Now how had it happened that none of these people knew her? They had crowded into her orchard and were deliberately climbing her trees and trampling her ground, while she seemed like a beggar woman with no business there, to whom nobody would give any fruit as alms. Concealing her humiliation she looked one by one at the men who were gaily showing her contempt. She could not help thinking sadly: "Fine, even that old rogue Li is against me. We might just as well have fed a dog all these years! How true it is that people only show their true colours when you're in trouble!"

But not a single person sympathized with her.

She was not a weak character. Since her own family had been dealt with the previous year she had seen the writing on the wall, and the danger impending, and had tried to think out a scheme to escape it. She did not believe things would remain like this forever, so she became generous, often giving away old clothes or lending people grain. She would talk with the hired labourers, and cook them good things to eat. She had suddenly grown sociable. She went out frequently, and whenever she met the cadres she would start talking to them, inviting them to her house for a drink. Even more, she became hard working, doing everything in the house herself, often taking food into the fields, helping with weeding or threshing. The villagers said she was not bad, that Landlord Li was no use, and some even believed her when she said that they were hard up, claiming that if they did not sell more land that year they simply could not make ends meet! However, there was no way out of this trouble. She had to show a stiff upper lip, and dodge and suffer through this storm. Not for a moment did she show her implacable hatred for these people, or how she was suffering! Instead, she employed all her feminine wiles to put them off their guard and appeal to their generosity.

Seeing them extending their field of work, she walked a little farther off, looking round everywhere, reluctant to leave her land, hiding the pain she felt at the sight of these "brigands".

At midday the peasants went home for their meal and the orchard seemed much quieter. Mrs. Li walked over again and looked at the green leaves which had lost their lustre, since even the fruit which was not thoroughly ripe had all been picked. She passed the red pile of fruit. In the past such a sight would have gladdened her eyes, but now she looked at it with hate. "Hm! There's someone sitting under that tree watching!"

She walked from her orchard to the well, where the plash of water could be heard against an earthenware container that had been set upside-down at the place where the spring gushed out of the earth. The water sounded very clear and a small stream ran out from under the container. Li's family had made this well, later selling it together with the land to Old Gu. But Old Gu had never changed the course of the water, that is to say, he had never stopped their supply of water. The brook ran right round the orchard, and watered twenty-odd *mu* of land. She thought: "Ah, before I always felt it a pity to have sold this land, but now I feel it was just as well!"

There was no one in Old Gu's orchard. The trees were

214

laden with fruit, and some windfalls had fallen to the ground. He had not many pears, but his red sweet-apples were exceptionally large. He did not grudge manuring the trees or working on them, but it had only amounted to working for the benefit of others. She imagined his three and a half *mu* of orchard had been taken under control too, and the thought gave her pleasure. If they must sell fruit, then let everyone's be sold. If they must divide land, let them mismanage the division.

Just as she was thinking this she heard the sound of girlish laughter, and saw a figure in light blue flit past. Who was it? Reflecting, she went to the side of a ditch, where a willow tree from the other side of the ditch had fallen on top of a pear tree on this side. Most of the pear was dead, only one branch was left, but that bore an astonishing number of pears. She knew whose orchard it was over there. "Oh, so it's her!"

She could see Heini in her light blue dress hanging on a tree like a woodpecker, nodding to someone below. The orchard seemed like a big cage around her. The fruit beyond her looked like bright stars, and these brilliant stars kept falling from her hands into a basket hung on the branch. Suddenly she slid down the ladder, her white trousers flashing. Qian's daughter-in-law popped up like a wild rabbit to take the basket, while Dani could be heard calling: "Heini! You're just playing about!"

Heini had only just been liberated. Her Uncle Wenfu had warned her: "Everybody in the village hates my brother. Better not go out much, keep out of trouble. You're a girl, you mustn't listen to him. Be on your guard. You mustn't give people any cause for gossip."

Heini had done as he said, refusing to go to see Young Cheng, telling her family: "If you keep on forcing me, I'll go and tell Yumin." But whatever she did they would not relax their pressure on her. They kept her close, not letting her take a breath of fresh air. Suddenly, however, the clouds parted. Today the whole family was smiling. When Red-nosed Wu beat his gong and made the announcement about the eleven orchards to be taken under control, their ears were glued to the door, but none of them heard Qian's name. They exchanged glances and smiled significantly. Her uncle had stopped pacing the courtyard and was lying on the *kang*, blissfully waving a black paper fan. Her aunt ran from the east wing to the west, not knowing how to occupy herself, and when all the women had been sent to the orchard, Qianli sent the workman to hire beasts. Heini felt most light-hearted. She thought now they would stop pressing her. It was not for nothing after all that cousin Yi had joined the Eighth Route Army! And she said privately to Er: "Don't be afraid of my uncle! Right now it's thanks to Yi he's got off."

Landlord Li's wife could not help cursing them to herself: "Whore's filly, man-crazy bitch! That devil Qian ought to be slowly hacked to pieces! He makes his girls play up to the cadres, and those bastards think our Li family easy to bully! What kind of Communists are these? Hell! Talking big all the time, agitating every day to settle old scores and take vengeance, yet protecting a bully and traitor and treating him with honour. Nobody dares lift a finger against him! Our family has a few *mu* of land more than most, but because none of us have joined the army or played the whore we're in trouble. That little stinker Yumin! Some day I'm going to tell him off!"

She could not bear to look any longer and started running home like a demented thing, but saw coming toward her a number of men who had finished their midday meal, and were driving in beasts. Thereupon she turned her head and darted off to one side, unwilling to face them again. She hated them and was afraid she could no longer conceal her hatred, yet she must on no account show her real feelings. So, like a whipped dog, tail between its legs, veiling the hatred and fear in her eyes, she fled.

People were foregathering again. Young Hou headed the transport corps. Two big iron-wheeled carts were waiting on the road to be loaded. Even Hutai's rubber-tyred cart and mule were there. Old Gu himself would not accompany the cart, and had not come. Vineyard Li was here grasping the reins and holding a long whip. A smile had taken the place of his previous anxious frown, for he felt things were hopeful. A procession of men carrying baskets had emerged here from the depth of the orchard. Young Hou standing at the head of the cart shouted: "Old fellow, you get down! Go and pick fruit in the orchard or find something easy to do! Who told you to come here!"

This remark was addressed to Quan who was in one of the iron-wheeled carts at the back. The old man was wearing a broken straw hat and an old blue jacket, and without turning he answered: "Nobody told me to come, I came because I wanted to. I've two and a half fruit trees myself I haven't picked yet. What if I am old, isn't an old man any use?" He suddenly caught sight of Yang's short figure carrying a basket of fruit over, and fingering his drooping moustache said loudly: "Can an old man lag behind, Yang? Come over here! There's skill needed in packing a cart, not just brute strength. Isn't that right?"

"Oh! It's you! Have you sold your fruit yet?" Yang rested a moment beside the cart, wiping his face with his sleeve, before looking round.

"No, I haven't much. It can wait a few days." Quan bent down to take the basket Yang was raising.

Remembering their last conversation Yang asked: "Have you talked things over with your nephew yet? Have you come to a decision or not?"

"About what?" Quan gazed at him for a minute then, understanding, began to smile. "Oh, that business! Ah, he's busy all day long! Look, the youngsters all think I'm too old to be any use! Well, it doesn't matter. I'm old, I'll do less, but each should do what he can!"

Yang saw a young woman had come to his side. She slowly lowered the heavy basket on her shoulder to the ground, calling out urgently: "Uncle Quan, hurry up and take it!"

She was a thin woman with a dark ruddy complexion and fine arched eyebrows. Her hair was combed back neatly into a bun on the top of her head. She was wearing a man's white vest, stretching out her long arms. On one wrist she wore several red artificial pearl bracelets which caught the eye.

"You make my head spin!" A young peasant had come over laughing: "You're really special-— like a donkey turd in a sheep-fold!"

The woman showed no sign of weakness, but tossed her head and retorted: "You were born with a dirty mouth!"

"Right! My mouth is no good. I can't even sing 'From the red east rises the sun. . . .' Aha. . . ." They were not watching the face he made, but everyone burst out laughing. And someone said slyly: "Do sing for us!"

"Oh, you people are the limit! If you're good for anything, go and speak up at the mass trial! But don't let the devil run away with you! I'm not afraid of anyone!" She turned and left with a quick, light step.

"Who's that? She's quite something!" Yang felt he had seen her before, but could not remember her name, and asked Quan.

Quan screwed up his eyes in a smile, and said: "That's Yue, the shepherd's wife, famed for her sharp tongue, prickly as a hedgehog, not afraid of heaven or earth. She shouts louder than the men at meetings. She's vice-chairman of the women's association. All their members are here today."

"Carrying a basket of fruit, staggering and shrieking under the weight, she still thinks she's cock of the walk!"

"She cock of the walk? Not a chance! She's minus the cock's most important part!"

They all started laughing again.

Presently the carts were piled high with fruit, tied firmly on. Young Hou bursting with pride called to the beasts, Vineyard Li cracked his long whip and the carts started slowly off. Three carts rolled off, one after the other. Behind the carts came some dozen mules and donkeys which had been loaded in the orchard, forming a long procession. On both sides walked peasants following the carts and leading the beasts. Others stood close to the mud walls at the side of the road, stretching their necks, following the lively troop with their eyes. Some were unwilling to return directly to the orchard, and crowded in the gateway, gesticulating and talking enthusiastically. It was more lively than the lantern festival at the first moon and more novel and welcome than a bridal procession. Quan was standing by the wall too, twisting his drooping moustache. When he had watched the procession out of sight he asked Yang softly: "Is it all really for the poor?"

Wen had come to the orchard too, but his feelings were entirely different from those of his last visit. Last time he was here he had been enchanted by this dense wood, and

219

felt it would be an ideal place for study. He also thought it would make an excellent location for a convalescent home. Wandering among the endless greenery, the fruit had seemed like so many scattered blossoms. Listening to the breeze in the branches and the merry chirping of birds he had been filled with content, reluctant to tear himself away from such a scene. Today, however, he had been attracted by the happy peasants. They were nimble and skilful, light-hearted and humorous, busy yet orderly, careful yet at ease. Usually he found them slow, stupid and dull, but today such epithets applied only to himself. At his approach they greeted him, but he could not say anything to raise a laugh or even to attract attention. He saw Co-op Tian, their commander-in-chief, assigning jobs, inspecting the work, calculating, checking and making a record. Everybody went to him for advice. He attended to each in turn, and each one left him looking satisfied. But he still looked just as he did behind the counter in the co-operative, not putting on any airs at all, quite cheerful and unflustered.

Hu put it even more explicitly, saying: "We couldn't do this in his place, could we?"

Of course Wen was able to console himself with the thought that this was only a kind of administrative technique. They were only peasants, after all, unable to direct policy. However, this scene forced him to acknowledge the people's ability which he had never previously suspected, and even more to acknowledge the gulf that still existed between him and the masses. As to the reason, whether it was because he was more capable than the masses or unfamiliar with them, he was not at all clear, and was not willing to inquire into it more deeply.

They went back before long to busy themselves in arranging the business agreed upon the previous day.

The orchard continued as lively as ever, especially when the sun was sinking in the west, when even the old women came hobbling along with their sticks to look. This was something absolutely unheard-of, that poor people should take control of rich people's fruit and take it to the city to sell. As numbers increased, those who had been rather afraid to begin with overcame their reservations. Some who had just come to watch the fun now joined in the work too. Since the river had risen so high, what did it matter if they got a little wet? If everybody joined in, all would share the responsibility. There was nothing to be afraid of. The only thing to worry about now was that one might get left out, and other people get all the benefit! This business stirred up all the poor villagers, as well as Yumin, Vice-Head Zhao and the others. The cadres were pleased with the peasants' determination, pleased that their own prestige was growing, and that the villagers praised their good management. Of course they hoped the work would continue as smoothly as this. At any rate this was a good omen. They hoped there would be no complications or troubles ahead.

38

AFTER breakfast when Young Guo went to Old Han's house, he found only three of Landlord Jiang's tenants in the courtyard. There were nine of them altogether, and the previous day they had attended a small meeting here at which Wen had given them many explanations of principles, which they all appeared to understand, and they had agreed to meet today to go together to ask for the title deeds. But now the others had failed to show up. They separated to search for the missing tenants.

Young Guo was very excited. He cultivated ten *mu* of

arid land belonging to Jiang, for which he had to give four piculs as rent each year. Every year he quarrelled vainly with Jiang over these four piculs, and burned with frustration. The land was poor. It only yielded four to five piculs altogether, and unless he did odd jobs on the side he could not make enough from one end of the year to the other even for drinking water. He had thought several times of giving up the land, but it would not be easy to find any elsewhere. He thought that if he were given this land after land reform he would have a solid basis. Besides having enough to eat, if he tightened his belt, being young and strong he might earn enough to buy one or two more *mu* of land, and with this property he need not be afraid. He longed for land, he was headstrong and not afraid of difficulties. He strode off energetically to look for the others. He wanted to get his hands on a title deed at once. He had never seen this thing which so vitally affected his entire life.

Gradually all the tenants arrived, including a youngster of seventeen named Wang and three old men who seemed less timid with the young men to lend them courage, but who remained comparatively quiet. After the previous day's meeting they were willing to go to ask for the deeds, but they told Wen that Landlord Jiang as a former ward chief was a good talker and experienced, and probably would not give them up!

Yumin said too that Jiang had told White Snake to spread rumours that the emperor born of the real dragon was in Beijing. Jiang had sent his wife every day to work on Vice-Head Zhao's feelings. The landlord was a slippery customer. Probably these few tenants would be no match for him. To make sure, Wen therefore asked them: "Are you still afraid?"

They all answered together: "With you comrades here we're not afraid!"

Young Cheng told the story of how Tenant Hou, when Landlord Hou was dealt with the previous year and his land divided, had been forced by the cadres to go too and settle scores with him. Tenant Hou had no way out, but had to go. The landlord who was lying in bed had asked: "Who's that in the yard?"

"It's me, Uncle," Tenant Hou had said.

"Oh, you, what do you want?"

"Nothing," said Tenant Hou. "I just came to see you, Uncle." Having said this he found a broom and started sweeping the yard.

"Oh! You really are a good sort after all, I thought you'd come to settle scores too. If you want to settle them you'll have to go to the King of Hell, and let him decide whose things these are destined to be! By the way, nephew, you can forget about that ten thousand dollars you owe me. We're the same family. After all these years we can count on each other's friendship."

"Oh, that won't do, that won't do. . . ."

When Tenant Hou went out and people outside asked him if he had settled accounts, he said: "Yes, it's all settled. I still owe him ten thousand dollars!" Later the peasants' association gave him one and a half *mu* of land, and he actually returned it secretly.

"You people won't copy Tenant Hou, will you?" asked Young Cheng. "He is the kind of man who would rather die than rise to his feet."

"We aren't such weaklings," they answered, smiling, "to want to make a laughing-stock of ourselves!"

Although they had recalled their past sufferings and made pledges, Wen did not feel altogether assured. Since he could think of nothing else just then, he imitated a landlord asking fiercely: "What are you doing here?"

Young Guo caught on at once, and answered: "We've come to settle accounts with you."

"Settle accounts? Very good!" Wen went on: "You've cultivated ten *mu* of arid land of mine. Was it you who asked to cultivate it, or was it I who forced you? It was put quite clearly then, set down in black and white, the rent would be four piculs a year. Have you never owed me rent? Now you want to settle accounts, fine! First pay me what you owe, and then we'll settle! If you don't want to farm the land, all right! I can find plenty of people who do. Let me ask you, is it your land or mine?"

"Can the land grow crops for you by itself?" asked Young Wang.

And Young Guo went on: "Jiang! Let me tell you! When you were ward chief you used Japanese backing to swallow our rationed cloth, everybody knows that. And that year I repaired your house for you, you agreed to one pint of rice a day. I worked for you one month and three days, and you only gave me ten pints of rice. Think back, am I telling the truth or not?"

"It's true," replied Wen still playing the part of the land-lord. "Wasn't the rationed cloth used for an awning when we had a play? I didn't take it! When you worked on my house, I didn't underpay you. Wasn't the food you ate for one month and three days to be counted? Another thing, the year before last, before the Japanese left, you accused me, and I paid you then all there was to pay. Is there no end to your extortions? I worked for the Eighth Route Army too."

This made them all furious, and they started shouting: "Good! You say we extort. If we hadn't sweated, you couldn't have had such a soft time of it! How much land did you have before? How much land do you have now?

Would you have grown so fat without our blood and sweat? If you don't produce the title deeds today we'll beat you to death...." As they shouted they saw Wen and the rest laughing, and started laughing themselves. One of them said: "Chairman Wen, you really make a good landlord!" Someone else said: "Just like Jiang, he's difficult to deal with!"

Then Wen asked them what they would do if Jiang's wife took a leaf out of Mrs. Li's book, and came out crying and snivelling. They all said they would pay no attention to the whore. And Young Guo said: "The year that bitch came, she asked me one day to help them turn their millstone. I didn't dare refuse. After the wheat was ground, I ground millet until evening. Then I cleaned up the stone for them, and stabled the mule and fed it hay. Only when I was leaving did she say: 'Have a bowl of gruel before you go.' But just then, Landlord Jiang returned, and as soon as he came in he said: 'What do you mean by coming here while I'm out? Carrying on with my wife! Fine! I'll have you sent to the ward office and punished with hard labour!' That woman just sat inside not saying a word. Whatever I said Jiang wouldn't believe it, and finally I had to go to Xiahuayuan twice to fetch coal for him before he would let me off. If not for that bitch I wouldn't have got into that trouble. I want to settle accounts with her too. If she cries I'll hit her! I certainly shan't act like my old man!"

Wen asked them some more questions, to which they made satisfactory answers. He wanted to give them more encouragement, but they could not contain themselves any longer, and someone said: "We've got it all straight now, let's go." "We're bound to come off victorious," said Yound Wang. "Don't you worry!" Wen saw them to the street and watched them go, while again some villagers followed behind.

Young Cheng also followed them to see how they would make out.

The nine of them swept like a gust of wind to Landlord Jiang's door. Young Guo was the first through the big gate, the rest followed at his heels. There was no one in the courtyard. From the north room could be heard the sound of furniture being moved. Young Guo hurried up the steps and pushed his way in. Jiang was standing in the middle of the room. Seeing these poor tenants come in he guessed they had come for the title deeds, but he was not afraid of them, and said: "Did the peasants' association tell you to come? You can ask for anything you want. I've been with the Eighth Route Army too. Of course I understand the situation. Only you must get things clear yourselves. Don't let other people cheat you! Young Wang, are you here too?"

The others had nothing to say, only Young Guo said loudly: "We understand everything, Jiang! We've come to settle accounts for all these years!"

"Settle what accounts?" Jiang started indignantly, but noticing the expression on their faces and hearing steps in the courtyard he immediately changed his tune, and went on: "There's going to be land reform in the village, as if I didn't know that! This is a good business. I have a fair amount of land, more than I can cultivate myself. I told the cadres long ago I'd decided to make a present of the land. Let everyone have land to farm and food to eat. That's only fair!"

Hearing that he was going to make a present of the land Young Wang lost his head, and asked impatiently: "What about the title deeds?"

Jiang promptly opened a drawer and took out a package, saying: "I got it ready long ago. I was just thinking of sending this to the peasants' association but now you've come just at the right time. There are twelve sheets here, fifty-three point three *mu* of land. It's all pretty good land too. I'm young and can stand hard work, so it doesn't matter my giving so much. Your five *mu* are included, Wang. You take it to the peasants' association. If you still think it's too little, tell them Jiang says he can give some more. After all I'm village head. I ought to set an example for others!"

"Jiang! What game are you up to!" Before Young Guo could finish, Young Wang had snatched the package and run out, and the others, seeing him run, taking the title deeds with him, followed at his heels. When the people in the court, by the gate-house and outside the gate, saw Wang rushing out helter-skelter, they could not imagine what had happened. They crowded out too, some of them asking in frightened tones: "What happened?"

As they were rushing pell-mell out of the gate, Young Cheng hurried over and asked: "What are you doing! What's the idea?"

Wang raised his hand high, unable to restrain his excitement, restless as a cock after a fight, unable to speak.

Another tenant next to him said: "We've got them! We've got the title deeds! As soon as we went in he gave them up!" There was nervousness rather than delight in his voice.

By now Wen, Yang and the others had arrived. They thought that the tenants had been frightened and turned back, and asked at once how things had gone.

Young Wang was gripping the package firmly, in naive excitement. "Didn't you say anything?" asked Wen. "Did you just take his title deeds and leave without saying anything?"

They looked doubtfully at him, wondering what was wrong.

"We want to settle accounts with him. We don't want

him to give away land. The land is ours. What right has he to say he'll give it away? We don't want his land. What we want is our own land. For you to run off with the title deeds without settling accounts is no good. He'll say we're unreasonable, won't he?"

When the inexperienced tenants heard this, they said: "Right! We went to ask for what he owes us! How did he manage to stop our mouths so quickly? It was all the fault of that good-for-nothing boy, Wang. As soon as he ran, everyone followed. Let's go back! Come on!"

"What about Young Guo? Has he gone home?"

"No." They suddenly realized he was still there alone in Landlord Jiang's house. Nobody had seen him come out. "Come on!" With renewed courage the group wheeled round and hurried back.

When Wang and the others had rushed out, Young Guo had become anxious, and called after them: "We haven't settled scores yet, what are you running off for?" But nobody heard him, and just as he was at his wits' end Jiang's woman darted in from the inner room, threw him a disdainful glance, taking stock of him, then said to her husband in her syrupy voice: "Really, what a gang of brigands! Did they take all the title deeds away?" Young Guo halted and glared at her, asking: "Who are you cursing? Who are brigands?"

The woman's hair was long and dishevelled, framing a small pale face. The bridge of her nose was pinched a purple red, her upper lip was very short, revealing a row of irregular teeth which attracted all the more attention since two of them had gold crowns. Still ignoring Young Guo, she walked wide around him as if he were so much dirt, and scolded Jiang: "You dolt! You let them take the lot, but didn't you buy the land? It wasn't stolen, was it? Couldn't you reason with them? Communizing, communizing. Your property has all been communized now. If they say share wives, you'll share your wife. See how you like being a cuckold tomorrow!"

"Dammit! Shut your stinking mouth!" Jiang knew it was no use tipping her a wink. He turned impatiently towards Young Guo: "What are you still hanging round here for? Your ten *mu* of land have been given too. Why don't you go home?"

"We haven't settled scores yet." Young Guo remembered they had said they'd come to settle accounts, but now that he was left all alone he felt tongue-tied. He detested that woman. Hit her? He could not raise his hand. Leave? He did not like to show weakness. He was not afraid of Landlord Jiang, only he felt awkward. But just then he caught sight of Young Wang and the rest coming back, and was as pleased as a released prisoner. He could not help shouting: "Wang!"

Wang marched straight into the room, ignoring him, threw the title deeds on a table, and bellowed: "Who wants you to give land! It's our own that we want today!" Then he winked at Young Guo, looking very confident.

At once Young Guo knew what to do. Drawing himself up he said: "You, Jiang, we won't count earlier scores. Just since the Japanese came, you say how much that land of yours has yielded. We won't trouble with the reduction of rents we are supposed to have. Just say I should take half the yield. In that case each year you made me pay about a picul and a half more than I should. Then there was the grain tax I paid for you, for nine years, interest piled up on interest. How much do you think you ought to repay me! And then there's the wages you owe me. You kept making me do this, that and the other for you. That's got to be counted too."

229

A shout came from behind: "You, Jiang, I'm not going to have farmed your land five or six years for nothing!"

By this time many other villagers, knowing they were settling scores with Landlord Jiang over his rent, had come to watch the excitement. Finding Jiang floundering inside they joined in the attack from outside the window: "The bastard! When he was ward chief he made us pay taxes and act as army porters just as he pleased, sending our men to Tangshan and Hongshan, so that some of them never came back. We want his life in exchange!"

When the tenants saw the crowd outside, they grew bolder. The three old tenants who had come had not meant to say anything originally, but now they joined in the shouting too. One of them cursed: "You rogue, Jiang, do you remember New Year's Eve the year before last when you brought guards to my house and took away all my pots and pans just because I was three pecks of rent in arrears? On what charge was my property confiscated? On New Year's Day we didn't even have a mouthful of gruel to eat at home. Old and young were crying. You heartless brute!"

Outside the shouting grew even more menacing: "Beat the dog to death! Shoot him!"

Seeing things were going badly his woman hid herself inside, afraid of being beaten. Jiang was in a towering rage, but dared not act tough any more, thinking: "Damn! Now I'm in for it! Discretion is the better part of valour." He was afraid to think — all right, let them shoot! But his mind was in a turmoil. He thought of Landlord Chen Wu who had been beaten by the peasants. Making up his mind he ran inside, brought out another red package, bowed to the ground before them all and with a glum look entreated them: "Good masters, I've let all my neighbours down. Please be generous. I really owe each of you too much. I can't possibly repay. The only thing is to take the land as payment. These are my title deeds. They're all here, a hundred and twenty-seven *mu*. If you'll all be generous I'll be a good citizen in future. . . ."

Now that he was humbled and all the title deeds had been produced, the crowd began to subside, for they had not planned any further settlement. Reluctantly they took the title deeds, saying: "All right, we'll work it out and see. If there's too much we'll give you some back, and if there's not enough you will have to think of a way to make it up."

"Let's go." Those inside and those in the yard all started leaving together. The trampling of feet could be heard, interspersed with some curses, which, however, were filled with satisfaction. Jiang went into the courtyard to look dejectedly after their retreating figures. He gazed at the grey sky and sighed involuntarily. Inside, his woman burst into bitter wailing.

39

THE disposition of Landlord Jiang's land was entrusted to the nine tenants who had taken his title deeds to the peasants' association. This was something they had never hoped for even in their wildest dreams. The nine of them crowded into Young Guo's house, and the peasants' association sent Young Han to help them write an account. They did not know how to begin, simply feeling they must find a vent for the emotions with which they were overcharged. Their life during the last three days had changed too drastically, especially in the case of the three old men. One of the latter said: "Ah, the day before yesterday when the peasants' association asked me to describe all the hardships I've had in my life, I thought, in all these scores of years has one single good thing ever happened to me? Happiness no sooner reached me than it turned to sorrow. That year when my wife was lying in and people came to congratulate me on being a father, I thought: 'Eh, why make this fuss! She's lying in bed waiting for me to go and borrow some millet to make gruel.' All day I tried in vain to borrow some, so the next day I took some bedding to pawn for three pints of rice.... Another year I owed Landlord Jiang one picul eight pecks for rent and he was pressing me for it. We didn't even have husks at home, but I was afraid of him — if he grew angry he could send you off as a porter for the army. There was nothing I could do, so I sold my eldest girl. Ai, why worry about her, at least she got a way to live. I didn't cry, in fact I felt pleased for her sake — anyhow, I had nothing to say. I'd already stopped being human, I couldn't feel like a man. So I didn't say a word. When the association told me to go for the title deeds, I was afraid to go. I'm old, why make enemies for the young folk? But I didn't dare say I wouldn't go, so I followed along with the rest. My, who could have believed that the world really has changed! Fine, Jiang's hundred and twenty-seven *mu* of land are in our hands now! The power's changed hands! The poor are masters now! Who could have imagined it! Ah, we ought to be pleased, but strangely enough I actually feel sad! I'm remembering all my past troubles!"

Another said: "I always used to think that I was indebted to Landlord Jiang, that I must have owed him something in an earlier life as well as in this life, so that I could never pay it all back. But yesterday when everybody reckoned things up like that, why, I've cultivated his land for him for six years, paying eight piculs rent a year, while he didn't lift a finger except to use his abacus. Six eights are forty-eight piculs, plus interest upon interest. With that, I could have bought fifty *mu*, not fifteen! We were poor, too poor ever to rise to our feet. Our children and grand-children had to work like beasts just because the landlords lived on our rent. The more we provided them with, the tighter they clutched us. But we're not beasts after all, we're men! Why should we live like horses in harness, working without stopping till our hair is white! Now at last we see things clearly. Ah, our sons and grandsons won't be ground down like our generation!"

"We've got Jiang's land in our hands," said the third old man, "but he's still village head. There are still people who're afraid of him, who have to obey him. This time we've got to take that job away from him! Another thing, he's not the only rich person to have exploited us. It's no good unless we overthrow them all together. So I say this is only the beginning."

"Jiang usually gives himself airs," said another. "Look how he tried to browbeat us when we went in, and then how suddenly he went soft, like wax by the fire, cringing and scraping. I think it was just because there were so many of us. There's strength in numbers, and he knows we've got powerful support with the Eighth Route Army and Communists backing us up!"

Young Han was an ex-soldier, so now he encouraged them by saying how good the Eighth Route Army was, always working only for the poor. When Young Wang heard this he became very enthusiastic, and leapt to his feet saying: "Tomorrow I'm going to tell the comrades everything you've said. If we don't rise up to attack Schemer Qian properly, I shan't be satisfied. The year I was fourteen he forced me to go to the garrison at Guangan to help build defence works, then accused me of shirking work, and wanted to send me to

Zhuolu to join the Youth Corps.[1] My dad was nearly frantic, because joining the Youth Corps meant joining the puppet army! He went to find Liuqian who was ward chief then. My dad was always hot-tempered and he cursed Liuqian saying he had no heart. Liuqian didn't say a word but the next day he brought two guards to tie me up, and they beat my dad. Dad wanted to have it out with Liuqian but Liuqian knelt down before him and said: 'Even if you kill me, there's nothing I can do. You don't look for the King of Hell, you only come to one of his little imps. How can I cross your son's name off the list of dead?' Later other people told my dad to go to Schemer Qian. Qian hemmed and hawed. Finally we had to mortgage our house for six piculs of grain and send that to the ward office before the trouble was at an end. But my dad kept bearing Liuqian a grudge for bullying us out of six piculs of grain. Only after Liuqian had sold land to repay his debt and then gone mad did my dad understand who was behind it all, and then he didn't dare say any more. Qian's not a person you can cross! Ah! If we attack him, if only the group's willing, my dad can settle accounts with him, and get that house of ours back!"

Most of them started recalling their past sufferings, and Young Guo had a good deal to say. He felt it was better to divide up Jiang's land at once, remembering how Wen had said by this means they could stir up other tenants and make them go themselves to settle scores with their landlords. It was easy to rouse them this way. So he urged them all, saying: "Now that we've come into the open, don't let's collapse. The comrades and cadres all say this is serving the poor. I don't mean to ask for this land myself. Let's divide it up among the very poorest. Let the villagers see how fair

---

[1] An organization for training young fascists.

234

and unselfish we are, and everything will be all right. I'm young and I've no wife or children, I shall manage somehow. I don't want this land. You who've got old folk and children at home ought to keep some, but don't keep too much. We'll keep not too much nor too little. There are so many people he injured in the village, we've got to think of their suffering too. The association said most of the land is cultivated by us. We'll have to see what can be spared, then take our proposal to the meeting to be discussed. It'll have to be approved by everybody."

On returning to the peasants' association the previous day, Wen, Yang, Yumin and the others had talked things over and decided to divide up Landlord Jiang's land first, and since at the moment it was not possible to hold a mass meeting to elect a committee for dividing up the land, it was decided that the tenants should make a preliminary division, to be discussed by the masses, in order to heighten the villagers' enthusiasm and increase their confidence. Accordingly these nine men had been chosen as a temporary land-division committee.

When this news spread, many villagers grew very excited. Group after group went to the co-operative to lodge complaints with the peasants' association against Jiang, demanding to go and settle scores with him too. They asked for his property to be confiscated, saying he had no right to go on living in such a good house. It was a house he'd built when he was ward chief, built out of the people's sweat and blood! Why should he be allowed to store so much grain? He had a double wall full of grain. Everybody knew there was a narrow lane at the back of his house, where he stored his grain. Why should he be allowed to keep so many clothes in his wardrobe, now that so many people had nothing to wear? They raised pandemonium, and some pushed their way into Landlord Jiang's house, just as he was busy pulling all the strings he could, calling on the cadres, hoping they would leave him a little more land. When the villagers saw he was out they were afraid the cadres would be deceived by him and listen to him. Then even more of them went to find Yang and Wen, asking to have all his property moved out. Wen, who was afraid of going too far and mechanically clung fast to a few "policies", felt that such a proceeding would be beyond the scope of land reform. He wanted to have nothing to do with it, even urging the villagers to hold off. But the people refused to leave, some wanting to move the things themselves. When the militia came over they said sarcastically: "What are you doing here? Have you come to keep a watch on us?"

Yang had a long talk with Wen, and finally won his consent to have all Jiang's movable property confiscated for the time being by the peasants' association. Wen realized that as matters stood some action must be taken, so he turned the matter over to the peasants' association.

Young Cheng headed the militia to paste up notices of the property being sealed, and to seal up all chests, containers and unoccupied rooms, leaving only one bedroom and kitchen for Jiang to use for the time being. But crowds of people, still not believing, followed to look, and shouted: "We won't lift a finger, only watch. It's all right now that the association is taking charge of this! As long as you are not keeping these things for Jiang, that'll do!" Standing at the side they made suggestions and supervised the work, until finally even the containers of oil and salt for daily use were all sealed up. Jiang had returned by now, and bowing repeatedly to them all he begged them not to seal up so much. The woman, her eyes red from weeping, sat sullenly on the millstone in the courtyard. Seeing her, someone said: "This millstone should be sealed up too." But another answered: "They can't move it away. No need to seal it!"

That afternoon White Snake had also gone to the co-operative to the association to accuse Jiang of forcing her to deceive people. Since her husband had died she had no way of making a living. She wanted to marry again but Jiang would not allow it, only letting her claim to be a medium. He often took people to her house to gamble, who would give her a certain percentage from their winnings. But sometimes he pocketed the money himself, and now he owed her seventy to eighty thousand dollars. The members of the peasants' association were up to their ears in work. Nobody would pay any attention to her, and people who were looking on said: "Go home. Your scores are so many, better settle them on the bed." White Snake said too it was Jiang who had made her spread rumours that Lord White had told her in a vision that the real Dragon Emperor was in Beijing, to keep the villagers from agitating. Then they all laughed at her and cursed: "You people killed Little Bao! Just because you said people were wicked and god was punishing them, Liu's wife nearly cried herself sick and Little Bao's illness was neglected. Otherwise by going to Xinbao'an or Zhuolu to consult the doctor the child could have been saved. 'People are wicked' indeed! It's you people who are wicked!"

Seeing they would pay no attention to her, White Snake, who was afraid her seventy to eighty thousand dollars would melt away, and even more afraid she might be involved, sat some distance outside the door, and whenever she saw a cadre coming she went over to make a garrulous complaint. Finally they had to say: "You can say all this at the mass meeting, and if the people believe you, you may be given two *mu* of victory land. Don't hang around now complaining in the street."

Although these events were not enough to prove that the masses had risen, they were none the less evidence that some had shown initial political consciousness. They had begun to realize why they had suffered. Without urging they wanted to settle accounts. This was something which had never happened before in the village. Wen with his limited experience naturally felt this was already a great deal, and that in certain respects they were even going too far. He derived great satisfaction from the victory which he considered was all thanks to his planning.

Even Yumin found himself out in his calculations. Although they had held public trials before, they had never been disorderly like this, but conducted according to instructions. Now everybody was shouting at once, the cadres were ordered about by the people, and even Wen had to follow the masses. If they had not sent immediately to seal up Landlord Jiang's property, the people might possibly have taken matters into their own hands. Sparks can start a conflagration, and although their light is small, it may foreshadow the brightness of the future. In the prevailing excitement the team was doubly anxious to press forward with the work, and to reach agreement over the issues which they had temporarily shelved. Accordingly, the conflict became keener.

Yang acted on knowledge derived from his intimacy with the masses, most of whom were poor peasants. They had all made suggestions regarding Schemer Qian, who was regarded as the most dangerous leader of the landlord class. In order for the people to rise to their feet the most important thing was to overthrow him. Yumin had started life as a hired labourer. Even now he did not know where his next meal was coming from. He was still close to the poorest of the poor among whom he had his prestige. How could he be regarded as being in opposition to the masses? The relation between the cadres and the masses could not be interpreted mechanically, any more than what constituted an army dependent. Yet Wen felt that Yang had surrendered to the cadres. For no reason whatsoever Wen mistrusted Yumin still more, but he would not go deep into the masses to get to know the facts. He only listened to gossip like that told him by Security Officer Zhang, and paid exaggerated attention to it. Because Yumin had formerly gone once or twice to White Snake's to gamble, he considered him a rogue or Landlord Jiang's hireling. Hence it was impossible for him, with his way of looking at things, to distinguish between black and white. Although Yang, too, lacked experience, he could look at things comparatively objectively. Because he had drawn close to some of the poor peasants he had an intimate understanding of the masses, and was thus better able to grasp their problems. But because he was young he had not yet acquired sufficient drive or keenness of analysis with which to convince people. And because Wen was in charge here, he could not decide questions. He found Wen very difficult to deal with and sometimes even regretted having to work with such a man. His original intention had been to take every opportunity of going to the masses and learning from them, little thinking that working with his own team would be much more involved and difficult than arousing the masses.

Wen was patting himself on the back for the victory over Landlord Jiang. He failed, however, to realize this was just a sign that the people were stirred, but that it could not yet be said that the masses were all politically conscious and had launched into a movement. So he misjudged their progress. He was already fearing that once the movement started it was bound to go to extremes, persuaded that at a time like this the leaders must be very prudent in handling affairs, and very careful, while listening to all sorts of opinions from the masses. They must at all costs avoid jumping down into the tide themselves and letting the water blind their eyes. Because of this he was more obstinate in refusing to accept suggestions, only trying to arrange struggles along the old lines. He was searching eagerly for those who had acted as hired labourers to Old Gu, because the latter had no tenants, only short-time labourers. Although there were many of these, at the moment it was not easy to find strong ones. A good many of the village cadres had worked for Old Gu, but even they lacked enthusiasm. Wen believed they had been deceived by little favours and flattery from the rich. They had actually chosen Gu's son to be vice-chairman of the youth association. From this fact alone he judged that the cadres' class consciousness was defective and required careful study. Yumin said very impressively that he and the other cadres had not shared in the fruits of victory. Yet they did not go into the fields all day. What were they living on? Hadn't Zhao borrowed grain from Landlord Jiang? Wen longed to call a mass meeting right away to give a good lecture to these selfish, self-seeking cadres, these childish political workers. He felt the time had come and there should be no further delay.

Of course Hu took Yang's side, but he could not settle anything either. They argued until evening, and in the evening something unexpected happened. Although the desire to settle scores with Landlord Jiang had reached a high pitch, in the busy orchard excitement ebbed, and many people went home. The happy excitement which the control of the orchards and sale of fruit had aroused now seemed to have palled. It was said that Liuman and Security Officer Zhang had quarrelled over some personal trifle and even come to blows. Nobody had tried to mediate or take sides, just quietly watching the security officer's attitude, waiting to see what the outcome would be. This seemed on the face of it a very commonplace incident, but it was clear that the effort of several days was now virtually undone, and unless they quickly regained the ground lost still more people would be influenced. This was an immediate warning to their shallow complacence. Victory was still far off, and the road was fraught with difficulties.

40

SECURITY Officer Zhang had two *mu* of irrigated land by the river, and Liuman had one and a half *mu* there too, downstream on the ditch which watered the plots of both. Zhang had wanted to exchange three *mu* of hilly land he had for this plot of Liuman's, so that all his land would be in one place. When he went to talk it over with Liuman, Liuman calculated that the two pieces of land yielded about the same amount, in fact the three *mu* yielded two or three pecks more than his present plot. But it meant harder work and a higher tax, so he refused. After this when Liuman went to irrigate his fields, Zhang often diverted the water for his own use. Zhang did not irrigate his own fields at the proper time, and would use the water when it was Liuman's turn. As a result, the two were always quarrelling.

Security Officer Zhang passed the word that he still wanted this piece of land, and some people advised Liuman to let it go. He would not lose out by the exchange, and there was no point in antagonizing the security officer. After thinking it over for some time Liuman was convinced his best course would be to agree. However at this point Zhang suddenly showed himself unwilling to exchange, saying Liuman wanted to take advantage of him, exchanging a small plot for three *mu*, and he would not be such a fool. When Liuman heard this he flew into a rage and made some biting remarks, whereupon Zhang cut off his water, intending that Liuman should find the situation intolerable and give up the land more cheaply in exchange for one and a half or two *mu*.

Liuman's fury knew no bounds. He took the matter to the cadres, saying he was willing to exchange the land. Not knowing the inside story the cadres said if Security Officer Zhang was not willing to exchange they could not compel him, this was none of their business. Liuman in desperation started a scene and made certain scathing remarks, at which some people said he was a troublemaker and wanted to tie him up, while others, who had only heard Zhang's side of the story, thought Liuman wanted to force an exchange of the land. Unable to get the better of Zhang, Liuman felt very injured. One day in the fields he started cursing again about the water. Zhang came over and the two of them had a fight. Zhang reported that Liuman had assaulted him. The village cadres reprimanded Liuman again and even suspended him from membership of the Party.

After this Liuman kept quiet, but resentment smouldered in his heart. Later people told him that originally Zhang had wanted quite honestly to exchange his three *mu* of land for Liuman's one and a half. But later he listened to his father-in-law and thought he would try to drive a bargain, taking advantage of his position as security officer to bully Liuman. This made Liuman even more disheartened. Because he could not irrigate his land properly, the crops were not growing well. Other people's kaoliang stood over ten feet high, with thick, heavy ears, while his kaoliang looked like his wife who was always falling ill, thin and weak as if a high wind would blow it down. The sight of his land made him angry as if people were bullying a child he had brought up, so sometimes he kept away. His feud with Zhang dated from this incident, and he kept hoping that some day there could be a fair judgement.

At first Security Officer Zhang did not take Liuman seriously. But when the cadres came from the district government to start land reform he felt Liuman was a bad enemy to have. He was often conscious of being followed, often felt Liuman's revengeful eyes boring into him, or was goaded by his cutting remarks. He began to be afraid that he would be dragged into the whirlpool of struggle, knowing that on account of his marriage and various differences of opinion he had lost the support of a number of the cadres, and the peasants were not satisfied with him. At first he had unconsciously sympathized with Schemer Qian simply because the latter was his father-in-law; and because he was young and inexperienced and lacked class consciousness he was deceived by him. However, now for his own safety he felt he must find some means of crushing Liuman. The question was what support could he find? Hence he grew increasingly anxious, and pulled all the strings he could to maintain his father-in-law's power in the village. So he had to betray Yumin and be cautious in his dealings with the cadres, reporting all he knew or surmised to Schemer Qian, discussing the implications with him, and then carrying out his instructions.

Security Officer Zhang was not rich. He had just enough land to support himself, and he was used to eating and dressing poorly and being ill-treated like the others by the rich people, running dogs, and traitor ward chiefs. He had been to school for two years, was strong and could stand hardships, but was hot-tempered and could not tolerate being crossed. He dared raise his hand against the rich, and soon after a Party branch was organized in the village Yumin recruited him. He was enthusiastic and a better speaker than Yumin. In public he always took more of a leading part than Yumin. Soon he became security officer. The previous year when Nuanshui was liberated their group had become even more powerful.

When Schemer Qian saw that power was changing hands, he became quieter. But he hated this group, and tried to think of a way to bring it under his control. As a first step he sent his son to join the army. With him in the Eighth Route Army, Qian had someone to lean on, making it difficult for the village cadres to do anything to him. In fact Yi, when he left, said he'd shoot anyone who offended his father. Yumin and the others regretted having asked Schemer Qian's son to go, but there was nothing they could do about it, and the villagers certainly became more hesitant about attacking Qian. Qian also utilized his daughter to gain a foothold in village politics. Thanks to his ready tongue the dowry he gave Tani and the fact that she was quite ready to fall in with his plan, the security officer was captured. Of course this had its effect, since the cadres, for fear of offending Zhang, could not very well say anything, while the peasants were even more afraid. But Schemer Qian was not entirely satisfied. The security officer had lost the confidence of the cadres and become estranged from them. Although during the present land reform Zhang was active again and did his best to protect his father-in-law, Qian saw that he was still isolated, and therefore he had to make plans regarding Young Cheng. If Young Cheng were to show the least sign of wavering, he could use the security officer to stir up the masses to overthrow the chairman of the peasants' association. This would throw things into confusion, of which the security officer might take advantage to win over the masses and the cadres. But he found himself up

244

against an unexpectedly obstinate girl who could be moved neither by kindness nor sternness. Schemer Qian was really worried for a few days, until the disposition of the fruit set his mind at rest a little. The fact that his name was not among those of the eleven families, seemed to indicate clearly enough what the cadres' attitude to him was.

However he had not foreseen Security Officer Zhang's quarrel with Liuman, which arose precisely out of the fact that Schemer Qian's orchard had not been taken into custody. Liuman remarked loudly and scathingly in the orchard that the cadres were all hiding behind their wives' skirts and had become dogs' tails, and added that the security officer had been recruited by the traitors' camp. Nobody dared agree openly but some people gave him secret encouragement, so he spoke out more boldly. Pointing to Qian's orchard he started cursing, making sure Zhang should hear every word he said. Zhang was not a good person to offend. Because he was afraid of being involved himself he had done his best to keep quiet, but he could not stand these insults in front of practically the whole village. Emboldened by the fact that Qian's name was not among those of the landlords, he started cursing back. Liuman seemed to be fully prepared, confident that plenty of people would back him up, so he let himself go. Zhang's answer to his curses was just what he had been hoping for and he heaped abuse on him till Zhang tried to stop him by force. Liuman was glad of a chance to start a bigger row, but Co-op Tian and others managed to persuade Zhang to leave. Besides, the latter was afraid of coming off worst, and wanted to enlist the help of the cadres again to suppress Liuman. This quarrel not only attracted the attention of the peasants, but made Schemer Qian start worrying again. The more so since the ominous quiet in the orchard made him fear there was some plot against him afoot. He waited restlessly for Zhang's return, planning to make a redisposition of his forces. This time he was forced to utilize his wife, which showed that he was at the end of his resources.

Now Security Officer Zhang was cursing away in the cooperative where he had found Yumin, Young Cheng and the rest of the cadres. He declared that he would have Liuman arrested, saying this was his duty as security officer, because Liuman was sabotaging the land reform. He spoke very loudly as if the other cadres were in some way to blame. But the others answered him coolly and sternly, until gradually he lowered his voice. Nobody sympathized with him, nobody opposed him, however he saw they all disagreed with him. At last Yumin said: "You go home now. No need to arrest anyone. We won't make any arrests. The association will look into this business. Let the association take complete charge of it."

Zhang wanted to protest, to argue that he was security officer, but everyone advised him to go home, so he had to leave, thoroughly exasperated and with nowhere to go. Without thinking he turned in the direction of Schemer Qian's house. Now that he was acutely aware of his isolation from the masses, he had to stick closer to his father-in-law, so he went there to find out what to do.

4 I

THOUGH nobody said anything during this quarrel, all understood its nature, and did not want to discuss the rights and wrongs of the squabble itself. They felt that Liuman was in the right. Day after day he neither ate nor worked, restless as an ant on a hot griddle. All the villagers knew why, and assumed the village cadres must know too. And since they

246

all understood it there was no need to talk about it, just wait and see how the cadres would deal with the situation. When they went home they exchanged knowing glances as they chatted. But they were unwilling to discuss the orchard any further, just making sarcastic remarks to dispel their feeling of unhappiness and injustice. Outwardly nothing seemed to have happened in the village, but things were not really so peaceful. Whispered arguments had started in a number of households, quarrels without words. Many people were torn between two conflicting feelings. Their hopes were high, but they had to control them, perhaps even pour cold water on them. However there were others who could never stand quietly as bystanders again, who could no longer worry about themselves but went urgently to find Yumin and Freckles Li. Then the militiamen told their captain they would undertake to keep a stricter watch, for fear anyone else should run away. They felt badly about Landlord Li's case.

Prompted by his wife, Vineyard Li persuaded his cousin Shou to go along with him to Freckles Li and tell him all he had heard about Security Officer Zhang's intention to co-operate with the Kuomintang. "It's not fair not to confiscate Schemer Qian's fruit!" he said reproachfully. "How can you count him as a middle peasant? Aren't you afraid the peasants will call you his running dogs? Are you really going to listen to the security officer and arrest Liuman? Don't you realize everybody's on Liuman's side? . . ."

Freckles Li, that cheerful young Communist, jumped up, stamped his foot and exclaimed impatiently: "Why didn't you say this before? You hear such important things and don't tell us. Heavens! This won't do, I must go and find Yumin!"

Young Hou's father locked him up, but the youngster threatened him saying: "If you don't let me out I'll set fire to your house, and see how you like that." Tenant Hou walked up and down the courtyard with a hunched back, sighing, his daughter following behind, asking for the key of the door, while his wife sat pursing her lips on a stool outside the door, not knowing with whom to sympathize.

"I'm not going out to kill anyone. What are you afraid of! You're such a die-hard, Dad! We've only just risen to our feet, and must still make an effort. We can't lie down to let people trample on us again. You're so pig-headed, you'll never see things straight. If you still won't open the door, I'm really going to set fire to the room!"

The old man stubbornly ignored him. He felt he saw things much more clearly than his son. He was a fatalist. No matter what happened now, he believed that in a few days, once the cadres from the district left, the village would go its old way again, while very soon, if Datong were not retaken and the Kuomintang troops advanced towards Huailai in this direction, all would be up. Even Yumin would have to fly. Young Hou was his only son. He had never done a wrong thing all his life. He must look after him and control him at all costs. But his son seemed to have changed: he would not keep quiet. He was a young man, it was easy for him to accept new ideas, and since he had acted as transport chief and felt the power of the masses, his outlook had changed. He had held the whip and shouted orders, moving the landlords' treasures of fruit, which normally they scarcely dared look at. No one had dared stop him. The poor along the road had asked him where he was going, and when he told them he was taking away the fruits of victory they had all smiled broadly, following him and the procession he led with envious looks. Then he had laughed like a triumphant warrior. He felt he had power, as long as the masses were united there was nothing they could not do, nothing they need fear. He was very concerned too about the cadres' treatment of Liuman, but he did not want to wait. He wanted to go and state his own views and describe the dissatisfaction and reservations of the masses. He wanted to see Yang and the others, and thought anxiously: "These cadres have only been here a dozen days or so. How can they be clear about everything in the village?" But his father had taken him by surprise and locked him inside the house. Actually his father had been in the orchard too, and had smiled, but he was timid. After the quarrel he had reverted to his old position. Young Hou was furious with his father, and true to his word went to the stove, took some wood and started a fire in the middle of the room to frighten the old man. When his mother and sister saw the light of the fire they shouted wildly, laid hold of Tenant Hou, snatched the key from his pocket and opened the door. Then the youngster bounded joyfully off, his father pursuing him like a madman, until he stumbled and fell, panting with rage.

Teacher Ren hurried right and left in search of news. He walked to the top of the street and stood there. When he heard voices he edged over, but people stopped talking as soon as they saw him. He dared not call on Schemer Qian or Landlord Jiang now. The only thing was to see White Snake. However, White Snake was doing all she could to sever connections with Landlord Jiang. When she saw him she shouted: "Mr. Ren! If you've no business don't come. I'm only a woman with no husband to rely on. I can't afford to be involved. People say I'm lazy and want to reform me. In future I'm even going to send away Lord White. I daren't call the spirits. You're a troublemaker too, so better not come here!"

Ren felt like cursing her angrily: "You've grown very particular all of a sudden. Let's see how you manage to live!" But he restrained himself and went back to the street. He had no intention of going home. Red-nosed Wu kept making biting remarks in his hearing, and Teacher Liu did not use the articles he wrote, asking Red-nosed Wu to make up verses for him instead. He detested the pair of them, and longed for a day of reckoning.

Then he met Young Gu, vice-chairman of the youth association. In the past Young Gu had often come to the school to write slogans, so they knew each other, but Ren had not seen him for a long time. He knew their fruit had all been picked by the villagers, so he tried to provoke him: "Liuman was attacking the unfairness of your treatment. It's a pity he'll get into trouble. Cadres always back each other up! I bet you a feast your vice-chairmanship will be taken away and you'll be given a tall white hat to parade the streets. Don't you think so?"

Recently Young Gu had been at loggerheads with his father. Smouldering with rage, he could not put up with such remarks. He turned on Ren fiercely, quite unlike his usual gentle self: "We can look after our own affairs. No need for you to butt in. If you say another word I swear I'll knock you down!" Saying this he glared at him, and Ren had to make off as fast as he could, muttering to himself: "All right, let's see! You'll be tried, sure as fate. Let's see if you're still so fierce then."

Rejected on all sides Ren could not find a single person to talk to. He wanted to do something but found no opening. He knew Red-nosed Wu had said many bad things about him to the village cadres. A number of people were eyeing him askance and avoiding him like the plague. This only frightened him more. Schemer Qian was still trying to encourage him with Heini, but his ambiguous remarks made Ren feel hope was slight and sometimes he could not take much interest. Now he felt inexpressibly bitter, hating the whole of Nuanshui, and, feeling there was nowhere to spend his time, he walked outside the village. On either side of the road were low mud walls. The orchards were not entirely quiet, from time to time could be heard the loud calling of cicadas. The sun fell on him, and although it was no longer very hot it increased his exasperation. Passing this section he reached the plain by the river where at least forty *mu* were planted with kaoliang. The tall stems, big leaves and thick heavy ears, looked from a distance like a sea, dazzling the eyes under the sun, and the bright red ears clustered so close together swayed slightly in the breeze like ocean waves. He knew this land had belonged to a landlord in Baihuai, and had been allotted to Nuanshui — what cause for rejoicing! But this rich scene gave Ren no pleasure, only a feeling of resentment and contempt. This poor teacher who was the friend of landlords constantly tried to bolster up his self-esteem, even if behind was nothing but emptiness.

"Ren!" He suddenly heard his name called, and apprehensively looking round saw, coming from the field opposite, a man in a white shirt with bare head, a blue cloth jacket thrown over his shoulders and trousers rolled high up his leg, who had just waded across the Sanggan River. Ren recognized him, hesitated a moment, then called back: "Oh! Comrade Pin! So you've come. Where have you been?"

Comrade Pin had already come over. His young face was always smiling, his long almond eyes did not impress you as small, only as intelligent and shrewd. Giving Ren a friendly pat on the shoulder he asked: "Been busy at the school recently? Tell me what's been happening in the village, how is the land reform going?" He spoke with a good southern Chahar accent, only the natives could tell it was not the true Zhuolu accent.

251

Ren had to walk back with him, and said listlessly: "I'm not very clear about things." He sighed. But suddenly a happy thought struck him. Looking at that young innocent face and feeling it would be easy to deceive him, he said: "Things aren't going well. They've let off the chief landlord, and all the peasants are saying he must have bribed the village cadres. They've made up a song: 'You only hold meetings, you don't divide the land. . . .' I hear now they're going to attack army dependents! Tell me, can army dependents be attacked or not?"

Comrade Pin did not express any opinion, only encouraged him to go on. Then the foolish teacher at once forgot his past worries, confident his lies would bear fruit, as happy as if he had found a treasure, and tried to ingratiate himself with Pin while blowing his own trumpet. However, just then they came to the top of the street. The youngster wanted to see Yumin and as they were separating he said to the teacher: "Old Ren! Don't go talking so carelessly in future. Just stick to your teaching. The intelligentsia ought to have brains. Oh, you wait for me in the school this evening. I have something to say to you!"

Ren lowered his head and cooled down. Comrade Pin was head of the county propaganda work.

42

COMRADE Pin had worked on land reform in the Sixth District which formed a triangle between the north bank of the Sanggan and the south bank of the Yang, comprising about a dozen villages with some comparatively big landlords besides Roman Catholic power, so there were various problems. Now that the work of land reform had to be speeded up on account of the military situation, the county government had decided it must be completed by the end of August or the beginning of September. A meeting of all the peasants' associations in the county was to be held early in September, so Pin was very busy going from one village to another, making a thorough investigation of each and urging a speed-up of the work. The secretary of the county Party branch had told him time and again: "Look how quickly it's been done in Huailai. They've already finished two-thirds, and are getting ready to hold the overall peasants' association meeting. We must remedy the cautious methods of the past and have a free hand in rousing the masses. The authorities have directed us to finish as quickly as possible. The Beiping-Suiyuan Railway can't remain quiet forever. . . ." Pin had been a political worker among the youth and had come to southern Chahar three years before. Now he was taller than when he first came, grown to a considerable height, with long legs and a quick silent stride. Each time he reappeared suddenly, the villagers found it hard to believe that he had been away, and would ask: "Old Pin! Where are you going?"

He was very good at his job. Although he had not been in any village long he was quick at solving problems. He realized that this distirct had not been well equipped with cadres, many of whom were new at their jobs. He had certain misgivings about the comrades of the work teams, and often disagreed with them. Sometimes he felt they left too much land to the landlords, and then he would shout: "This won't do! At the most leave him an 'upper poor peasant'!" The work team cadres might say: "The central committee sent a telegram, instructing us to leave enlightened landlords land equal to the share of two middle peasants or even four."

Then he would grow more impatient and rub his cropped head, shaking his head repeatedly and saying: "What, two middle peasants! You're talking nonsense, comrade! Don't go taking the name of the central committee to scare people! Where did you hear that rumour — the central committee, the central committee of the Communist Party! Impossible, I'm not going to believe your rumour! I can only work according to the conditions of the people!" If anyone else demurred he would say decisively: "Never mind, if there's any mistake I'll take the blame. The one rule in land reform is to satisfy the peasants who have little or no land, so that they can really rise to their feet. If we can't satisfy them, what the hell is land reform for!" Sometimes a rich peasant came to make a present of land and someone might say that this rich peasant wasn't bad, they mustn't take too much for fear of frightening the middle peasants; but he would always retort: "We will take it, why not? And we'll take good land too." He was a very firm character, although this firmness did not match his youthful appearance.

Those who worked with him often joked with him and parodied his way of rubbing his head or the nape of his neck, his long thin neck projecting from a collarless shirt. They mimicked his voice which was rather impatient but at the same time firm. They imitated his laugh, his innocent laugh, his laugh of satisfaction when a problem had been solved. But no one could look down on him, not because he was a responsible cadre but because of his understanding of the masses and experience in solving problems.

His experience and skill had been acquired the hard way. When he left his work among the youth to come to southern Chahar he was still not nineteen. To begin with he did not even have a rifle, often only two hand grenades. The puppet ward chief despised him, thinking it would be easy to deal with a boy like this, and often cross-examined him as to whether he had attended school, how many characters he knew, whether he could shoot or not. He had to learn how to deal with people, to avoid traps. He had to keep all his wits about him. Before he went into a village, he had to sense the conditions there. At that time there were traps everywhere — a heavier step, a louder cough or a sounder sleep might cost him his life. He had been here three years. At first he had worked under others, later he had been responsible himself for several villages, and then by degrees for a district. His work was to extend the Party, build up armed forces and cover the areas unreached by communist influence. He had suffered such hardships that he was reluctant to speak of the past. Several times he went without cooked food for over a month, living on raw pumpkin and raw maize. Sometimes people who worked with him were killed. At other times guerrillas who had come over from the enemy turned traitors again and tried to catch him. He had escaped over walls — if he had not had eyes like a hawk and the speed of a deer the enemy would have caught him easily.

Once he went to a village near a Japanese garrison. It was his first visit, and he did not know a soul in the village. He asked the way to the house of a puppet ward chief who was a big landlord. As soon as Pin went in he seized the ward chief. Just then the enemy entered the village, looking for the ward chief. The puppet hastily took Pin to the back door and said, "You clear out. I won't hurt you!"

But Pin refused to go, saying, "I don't care if I die here. There'll be people coming to avenge me. First call your son here as hostage, and then you go. I warn you that the moment the enemy come into the courtyard I'll kill him." Then he took hold of the boy and crouched behind the window of the room, holding his rifle, waiting. The ward chief did not dare do anything. After some time he got rid of the Japanese and came back. Pin had not turned a hair, but the boy had wet the whole *kang*.

Later when this became known the people said "Good for him!" and all wanted to see him. If all the Eighth Route Army were so bold, why be afraid of the Japanese? China wasn't finished by a long chalk. And so amid these difficulties he learned the only thing was to struggle, only the firm could succeed. He learned how to get the upper hand of the enemy, and understood still better on whom to rely for everything, how only among the people could he find absolutely reliable friends — the poor!

From Honggu near the county of Laishui he had worked north until he came to the south bank of the lower reaches of the Sanggan. He opened up one village after another. At that time the old Third District was the scene of his greatest activity and the guerrillas of the Third District became famous. Even now the militiamen in this area were comparatively better organized, and could be responsible for their own work.

Naturally he was the first of the Eighth Route Army to come to Nuanshui. He often made his home in the row of vineyards by the mountain. On winter nights he slept in the vineyard watcher's hut or in a pit in the ground, in his left hand a frozen muffin, in his right a frozen salted turnip. He would sleep for a while then jump for a while to prevent his feet becoming frozen stiff. Then as the work in the village attained a sounder footing he often went to the mud houses in the western end. At first not many people knew him although many knew of his existence, and whenever they heard Comrade Pin had come to the village they would spontaneously keep guard for him. Later he showed himself in the village and more people came to know him. They had called him Captain Pin, District Head Pin, sometimes Old Pin. Now he was Commissar Pin. But no matter what they called him, they remained on the same friendly footing, because they had come through trouble together. It was only since his arrival that the peasants had resisted the forces of darkness and hoped for light, beginning to struggle against tyranny, and gaining victory. They saw clearly the difficulties and dangers of his work, and knew that he was working for the people and only for the sake of the poor he was taking his life in his hands and risking death. Their struggle and survival had depended on mutual help, so they had greater understanding and more feeling for each other than most people.

Two days before, Pin had received a letter from the secretary of the county Party branch, enclosing a report from Nuanshui. The county secretary told him that the district had sent an intellectual who lacked experience there to do the work. Now after more than two weeks they had not started the struggle. There were also some inside problems. The comrades of the district did not know how to deal with these rather better educated people, and hoped the county would send someone to help settle matters. They wanted him to cross the river to have a look. He knew more than anyone else about the situation there.

After receiving this letter Pin could not leave at once. He availed himself of the opportunity to make inquiries in the neighbourhood, but everybody said: "Nuanshui is getting on fine. Perhaps this year it is the best in land reform. The peasants there all go in groups to Shacheng and Zhuolu to sell the fruits of victory. The fruit this year has grown well. Each family will be able to get several hundreds of thousands. Our Sixth District's soil is rich, but we don't have a single fruit tree. There are big landlords, and when land is concentrated things should be easy to handle. But most of the land is outside the village. That makes it hard to settle accounts, and when the land is divided it may not fall to our share...."

This news delighted him, so he delayed another day before crossing the river, planning to return the same evening to the Sixth District. He felt the cadres in the village were comparatively reliable and had a fairly good mass foundation. Although it was a newly liberated area they had worked there during the war against Japan building up political power in the village, and there had never been any trouble. He had no idea as he went there of the confusion the village was in, especially where the cadres were concerned. They had had all kinds of talks, but these talks were merely whispering behind other people's backs, which increased the mutual suspicion and made it difficult to reach a decision. Because of this, Pin's arrival was easily seen to be most opportune.

4 3

PIN was standing in the street looking to see if there was anyone he knew, when suddenly a man came up from behind, slapped him on the shoulder, and said laughing: "Where are your eyes since you went to work in the county! Here I've been following you all this time, and you didn't recognize me." This was Swarthy Guo, who was carrying a rifle. He laughed cheerfully, and went on: "Do you still travel by yourself now you're a county cadre? You should be escorted by a man with a Mauser to lend you an air." Swarthy Guo was usually too shy to speak in front of people, but he was not afraid of the young commissar, thinking his collarless shirt and shaved head a good joke.

The young commissar punched him and said: "Look here, what's the idea, frightening people like that!"

But Guo said seriously: "I saw you a long time ago from the fields, and saw that rascal muttering away to you, so I didn't call out. Let me tell you, you can't believe what he says." Drawing close he whispered, "I'm not worrying about anything else, only that *that* wily bird may fly away."

"Old Pin! When did you get here! Why sneak in without letting anyone know? Oh! Yesterday the village was in a hubbub, you've come too late." Several people came over, and Pin greeted them.

And they said smiling: "Look how high you've rolled up your trousers. After going to the county town you still look so countrified. You must at least have learned to smoke. Here, have a cigarette."

When they saw there were no outsiders, one said very softly: "Old Pin! There was a fight here yesterday. It's not settled yet. They say there'll be a meeting of the peasants' association tonight to settle it. Do you think Liuman will win?" Not stopping to think whether Pin understood or not, he brought up their problem.

"Whether he wins or not depends on whether we dare speak or not. Old Pin! Let's go and find Yumin." Swarthy Guo hastily led the way.

Pin, standing to one side, was saying to the others: "One man's strength is small, but the strength of the group is great. One handful of wheat straw is no use, but a pile of wheat stalks is. Liuman's struck the first blow. It's for you to follow up. You elected the cadres. It was you who gave them power. If any of them don't want to work for you and won't follow your advice, you can have a new election!..."

Rounding the corner they came to the gate of the primary school. Red-nosed Wu rushed out, greeted Pin and said:

"How I've been waiting for you to come! You don't even wear a hat, look how sunburnt you are! Come in and have a drink." Pin went over and said something to him in a low voice which made Red-nosed Wu nod his head repeatedly; but in the presence of so many people he made no comment. Only when Pin was going he said, "Old Pin! Take a look at the blackboard news."

"Read the rhymes our Old Wu's written," said one of the bystanders with a chuckle. "Every other day he has a piece in the news. It's very interesting. He knows everything that's going on in the village."

Pin went over and had a look.

More and more people gathered round. In the distance an old man was sitting at the foot of a wall, sunning himself. Swarthy Guo nudged Pin who saw it was Landlord Hou, and asked, "Is he better yet?"

"Long ago. He came to the peasants' association today to ask if we still want to deal with him or not. Says he's only got about forty-two *mu* of land, but if there isn't enough land to go round he can give a little more. The peasants' association is urging Young Hou to go and ask him for the title deeds. He sits here all day long sunning himself, watching what's in the wind, while everybody laughs at him behind his back, saying 'Aren't you going to heaven?' . . ." As Swarthy Guo was speaking, bystanders who heard started laughing. The old man pretended not to have noticed, sitting motionless there like an old monk engaged in contemplation.

Tian stuck his head out from the co-operative window. He had just returned from the orchard where everything was very quiet; there were only a dozen old men there packing the fruit which was piled on the ground into baskets. Tian had looked everywhere for helpers, doing his best to get the job finished as soon as possible. He had made time too to hurry back and write up the account for the fruit for the last two days, planning to make a report that evening at the meeting of the peasants' association.

"Old Tian! Who's in the co-op?" asked Guo.

"Only me," answered Tian, and called out, "Comrade Pin! Come in and have some tea. I'll send someone to find them for you."

"I'll be back presently." Then Pin asked where Wen and the others were.

A child of twelve or thirteen who was standing nearby said: "I know where Yumin is. I'll take you there."

"Good. Better find Yumin first." Swarthy Guo pushed the child forward, and then pushed Pin, who said, "All right, let's go and see him first. If you've got something to do, you go back." Guo went with him part of the way, then turned off, saying, "We have to be on our guard."

Pin and the child chatted all the way. When he met people he knew on the road he greeted them, and even those he did not know called his name. Realizing he was busy, they did not stop him. After some time the two of them reached Vineyard Li's house next to Zhao's. "This is the woman chairman's house," said the child.

Gui, wearing an old cotton jacket, was sitting on the doorstep sewing. She got up at once, and called into the house: "Freckles Li! Here's Comrade Pin from the county."

Several faces appeared behind a small pane of glass, the people could be heard jumping off the *kang* and running outside. Gui went on: "Come in. Yumin's inside." But she herself went and stood at the courtyard gate.

They met him at the door and hurriedly pulled him inside, all saying, "Ah! You've come just in the nick of time!"

Pin saw that in addition to Yumin and Freckles Li there were two men he did not know well, but Freckles Li said:

"These are two elder cousins of mine. They're both straight-forward people. This is Vineyard Li, husband of the chairman of the women's association, and this is his cousin Shou."

"Go on with your business, I'll just listen." Pin asked them to sit on the *kang* again, while he sat down by the wall.

The two men were timid by nature, and now looked even more awkward. Vineyard Li said: "This morning I told Freckles Li, because my wife said that we must report it. Whether it really happened or not, I can't say, only that's what he told me."

And Shou said: "Really, that's all, but it's still pretty important. I wouldn't dare add anything. But if you question Schemer Qian, don't say I told you. I heard a child in the school say it, and what children say isn't always reliable. . . ."

"How many racketeers in your village?" asked Pin.

"I don't know," said Vineyard Li. "Everybody says eight big ones."

"Of the eight there are only a few tough ones," said Freckles Li.

"Right!" And Pin went on: "Last year Landlord Xu ran away, this spring you tackled Landlord Hou. Now Hou sits sunning himself every day in front of the stage and nobody pays any attention to him. When Landlord Li learned that his land was to be divided, he ran away. Does it look as if they're afraid of us, or we're afraid of them?"

"They're scared stiff. The death of Chen Wu of Mengjiagou frightened the life out of them. They're afraid of the Eighth Route Army and the Communists," said Shou.

"Aren't they afraid of you?" asked Pin.

"Afraid of us? Ha ha. . . . No, they're not afraid of us."

"Of course they're not afraid of any one of you, but if all

the poor people in the village get together, aren't they afraid? If you don't say they're bad, how can the Eighth Route Army know? There's strength in numbers, do you understand that?"

"Yes, I understand. Only the people won't get together. Even the cadres don't get together. If you don't believe me, ask Yumin. All the peasants curse the security officer for marrying that man's daughter. It's blinded him, otherwise wouldn't he be working for us instead of his father-in-law? Didn't he quarrel with Liuman yesterday just for this?" Vineyard Li brought it all out.

At once Yumin argued: "That's just the business of the security officer. Aren't we going to settle it this evening at the meeting of the peasants' association? If you say he's wrong, how can we say he's right? We're not covering up for him!"

"Those bad eggs aren't afraid of a few cadres," explained Pin. "They're only afraid of the poor people uniting. Cadres can always be changed. If anybody's spineless and can't take the lead, don't have him as cadre. When the Japanese were here, we could manage to elect Jiang. How's it that our hands are tied now? Whoever serves as a running dog of the rich, we'll pull down together with the rich. If all the poor people in the village are united, there's nothing the rich people can do. The poor are masters now, if they dare speak out. Not to mention these few racketeers, if Chiang Kai-shek came we'd tell him to get out."

The two cousins laughed again, and Vineyard Li said: "That's what Comrade Yang said too. Ah, we're so set in our ideas, it's impossible to change all at once. I keep thinking: a poor man can't afford to offend anyone. That's what my uncle says too. Actually it's my wife who's the more enlightened one. I understand all right, only I'm afraid. I'm not man enough to shoulder the responsibility."

"His uncle's Tenant Hou," put in Freckles Li.

"If there was someone to give the lead that would be good, don't you agree? If someone else led the way you wouldn't be afraid, would you?"

"Now nobody will lead the way."

"If only the masses would rise, nobody would be afraid." Shou looked more alert. His eyes flashed and his colour was heightened.

"Why isn't there anyone? There's Liuman to begin with, those who went to get the title deeds from Landlord Jiang, those who wanted to divide up his houses and sealed up his chests — aren't they all leaders? Now all that's needed is for the group to follow up. The cadres shouldn't just make arrangements and give orders. They should play the leading role among the masses. You've had to put up with a lot in your time. Settle your scores with the landlords in front of the whole village, don't just rely on the old way of doing things. Are you afraid of exposing yourselves? Our work in Zhuolu County since last year has suffered from this. We're always afraid of going too far. A few cadres think things over again and again, afraid they won't be able to control the situation or that the people will make mistakes, so they don't dare stir them up. This means they don't trust the people. Now the people are criticizing us, and quite rightly, saying we won't strike when the iron's hot. Isn't that so?"

"Yes, that's how it is. We're not clear what the higher-ups want. On the one hand we're afraid the lower-downs won't agitate and on the other that they may go off the tracks. It's not that we don't understand affairs in the village, it's that we're afraid of making mistakes! Another thing, there are the comrades from the district too; everything has to be decided by them." Hearing Pin's criticism, Yumin immediately realized that he too was lacking in courage. He had found such a simple matter so difficult.

"Don't be afraid!" said Pin, patting Vineyard Li's shoulder. "This time we're going to get started and do away once for all with those rogues. See if they can still co-operate with the Kuomintang! He who makes the first move gets the upper hand. Let's weed them out, then nobody'll be afraid."

The two cousins were so pleased they jumped up, and shouted with laughter, "How right you are! If we stand up we must stand up properly: we won't eat half-cooked rice."

"If we haven't stood up properly, we must make greater efforts. If the food is half-cooked we must add fuel to the fire. Can we afford not to rise, not to eat? Dealing with problems we've got to take a long view. Just now we're like a small tree with green branches and green leaves, which have still to grow big, blossom and bear fruit. The rich people's sun is setting. It'll only be red a little longer. Never mind if some people are still afraid of them. The world's already a different place, and it's going to get better still. What we must do now is make everyone think back to the sufferings the rich caused us in the past, the injustice and cruelty of the old feudal society. That's the only way to fight successfully. And we must think too how to make sure of keeping the rich under, so that they won't dare try to take revenge again. You go and tell people what we've been talking about and reason with your uncle again."

Pin got up too, and said to Yumin: "Come on, there's not much time. Let's go and find the comrades of the work team. Difficulties should be discussed together."

Freckles Li and Yumin followed him out to Old Han's house. They dared not criticize Wen, only on the way told

Pin how Wen failed to get on with Yang and Hu. Yang insisted on holding a meeting of the peasants' association that night to settle the quarrel, intending to propose an attack on Schemer Qian, and had already arranged for a good many people to speak. Only Wen did not know yet. He said it was all right to hold a meeting to discover the attitude of the masses. They said he was a cultured man, not easy to get intimate with. Yumin, who felt very wronged, said Wen had believed Security Officer Zhang's lies about his having an affair with a loose woman, and had questioned several of the cadres about it.

44

WEN had spent the last few days quite leisurely as usual. He often told people that all creative work, all gems of thought, were the product of an orderly and tranquil life. He had consented to the proposal of Yang and the others for holding a meeting that evening, but knew nothing of their preparations, still confident that by his speech, his air, his status, he could beat Yang. The peasants would sympathize with him, that is to say they would sympathize with the argument that Schemer Qian was a middle peasant and an army dependent, they would sympathize with the way the cadres had dealt with the orchards and sympathize with Security Officer Zhang. He felt, in fact, that only the weight of public opinion could stop Yang's mouth. This being so, he was very optimistic, intoxicated by his own wishful thinking, actually avoiding the issue, and so he looked on the young commissar's visit as just so much more trouble. However he was pleased to think that the achievements in Nuanshui should satisfy Pin.

Wen had met Pin in the county seat, and his impression

of him then was that he was like many other youngsters who had grown up in the revolutionary ranks, possessing a lovable simplicity and loyalty. They could bear hardship and were brave, but always retained a kind of countrified shyness together with a certain complacency — not that they were proud, but just because they did not yet understand the wider world. Wen was very fond of such youngsters and often envied them. He would clap their shoulders and say: "You were produced from the struggle of the masses, from practical experience. You have richer knowledge than we have, we ought to learn from you." This was what he said. He did not really think such experience had much value so he could not really respect them, much less learn from them.

Now the few of them had finished talking over conditions in the village, and were discussing their next steps. First Pin made some encouraging remarks: "This time we started late in Zhuolu. It was lucky you people came down to help. You're more resourceful than we are. All the people in the Sixth District praised your fruit-selling. This is the first time in Zhuolu the masses have spontaneously wanted to seal up a house and furniture. I shall report this when I go back to the county government as an experience in giving free rein to the people."

Naturally Wen was delighted, and said without thinking: "Our meetings now are not on the old model. You always used to make preparations first and fix on definite people to speak, whereas now we let the people speak as they choose. Thus it's difficult to say beforehand which problems a meeting will clear up. The sealing up of Landlord Jiang's house was a spontaneous act of the masses. Now the masses are aroused. All we have to do is keep some restraint, and not let them go to extremes." He had completely forgotten that only the previous day he had been against sealing up the house and confiscating all movable property.

Yang and Hu did not say anything about their plans for the meeting that evening. They felt they were forced into being secretive but that their motives were good. They only asked to review the work of the past two weeks, convinced that if they did not see eye to eye on the past and distinguish right from wrong, future problems would be difficult to deal with.

However Wen preferred to let bygones be bygones, and said magnanimously: "I don't think we need stress any differences of principle. The only real disagreements are about the order of the work. Comrade Pin has said too that everything should be in keeping with the level of political consciousness of the masses and we need not keep blindly to rules. This is very true. As for any differences between ourselves, we can talk of those later."

Pin approved of postponing the discussion too. He casually asked Yang and the others about their preparations, and was fairly satisfied with what he heard. Yumin added that all the members of the peasants' association were poor peasants, with a few middle peasants who did not have much land; only one member of each household came to meetings. In the past sometimes all the members of the youth association and the women's association had attended meetings, including all the literacy class, so they could not avoid having some landlords and rich peasants. But this time they had restricted it more severely. Young men and women from landlords' or rich peasants' families were not allowed in. The people were beginning to wake up. Ever since Liuman's quarrel with Security Officer Zhang in the orchard, a number of peasants had felt disturbed, fearing the cadres were prejudiced, saying they had become the running dogs of the old powers. Others said what was even worse, that the Eighth Route Army wasn't really much better than the Japanese, otherwise why should those who did so well under the Japanese be on such friendly and intimate terms with the Communists. Only when these things were explained today did those peasants feel relieved and convinced that the cadres were really on the side of the poor. This cleared the way to struggle. If this had not been done, they still would be sleeping with their tails between their legs and wouldn't be able to struggle at all!

When Wen heard this he was very surprised. Without so much as looking at them he thought: "Some sense of Party discipline! And these are supposed to be Party members!" However he did not want to enter into an argument. He felt none of these problems could be settled in front of the young commissar, moreover he began to suspect that Pin and Yumin had already had a talk. "Ah! They're in league. He's the cadre put up by Pin; of course he listens to him." Thereupon he had to adopt a passive attitude, doing his best to carry out the decisions of Pin, his Party superior.

Sure enough, in a moment Pin had reached a decision: he inclined to agree with Yang. However, Pin realized that it would not be proper to leave the cadres aside and not educate them. Believing that most of the cadres had been tested and were more or less sound, he called off the meeting of the peasants' association that evening to have a meeting of Party members and cadres. Young Cheng would still be invited, although he had taken a rather ambiguous stand, and Security Officer Zhang too, even though he was working with all his might for Schemer Qian. Pin really had not yet learned how to discuss questions patiently or in detail with everyone. Past conditions of work were responsible for this, as well as the limited time he had at his disposal that day.

This decision really disappointed Wen, destroying all his previous complacency. He remained quite silent, coldly observing Yang's and Hu's pleasure and Pin's youthful forcefulness. His opinion of Yumin naturally sank even lower than before.

Old Dong came back from Liyu. He had worked under the young commissar before. He agreed entirely with his decision, and said: "I said all along if Nuanshui didn't attack Schemer Qian, we wouldn't get anywhere. He's the one the people hate most." But he added naively: "I've no brain. I can't remember clearly that book of directions Comrade Wen brought. I'm only good for a follower. I can't do anything on my own! I daren't make proposals. I'd like to go back to the guerrilla days when I dared go anywhere."

After this question was settled, the conversation became more animated. Freckles Li told many stories about happenings in the village, imitating White Snake and Mrs. Li to the life. White Snake no longer dared rouge and powder herself and had invited Lord White into a chest. If people complained of stomach-ache she would reply: "I'm not superstitious any more, you go and see the doctor. They bullied me into it before." . . . Mrs. Li spent more time than ever at the top of the street, pretending to be looking for her children. Whenever she saw the cadres coming she would go over and greet them, making eyes at them, calling Yumin and Freckles Li "elder brother". Freckles Li was no relation of hers, but if she insisted on recognizing a relationship he was two generations her junior.

Pin roared with laughter, and said: "Shameless dogs! That parasite Landlord Li, gambling and drinking, up to no good, has sucked the people's blood all these years. Then there's his brother Ying. Don't let either of them off! When I return to Zhuolu tomorrow I'll have him sent back. Let him taste a little hardship. Yumin! You were his hired man. Why don't you go to settle scores with him — don't let him off!"

Yumin told how he had done all kinds of jobs for Landlord

Li. They wanted him to empty Mrs. Li's chamber pot but Yumin said, "I'm a man after all, and I don't want to be unlucky. I'm not going to do jobs like that." "So emptying my chamber pot is unlucky, is it?" said Mrs. Li. "I was afraid you were pouring out good luck with it. Let's see if you can get rich without emptying it." . . . Another time she was washing her feet, and called Yumin in, wanting him to pass her the soap box. Devil take her! He was angry and walked out, tossing his head, saying: "I'm not a slave girl you've bought." Other things he didn't mind, but these he couldn't stomach, so he had quarrelled with them, and would not work for them even if it meant starving.

However, later Pin explained that in newly liberated areas like this the people hated most were the petty tyrants, traitors and running dogs. But it was impossible for them to gain a deep insight into the landlords' exploitation all at once. They did not see that landlords and tyrants were the same class, all partners in oppressing the people, even though they sometimes quarrelled among themselves. The first step was still to weed out the racketeers, and after that go for the landlords. Only they must enlighten the masses by showing them the facts and making them recognize their own power before the peasants could finally rid themselves of the idea that things might change again. Otherwise it would be a case of wanting to eat but not daring to.

Still Wen said nothing, thinking this was a lecture to him, and reflecting irritably: "Bah! All right, let's see how you get on. Nowadays young people are so lacking in knowledge, yet look down on everyone!"

"The work here wasn't well done in the past," continued Pin, looking at Yumin. "It wasn't your fault. I take the chief blame and the district government didn't give constant guidance and enough help, either. Just think, even in the

271

Sixth District, the peasants told me that the worst person in your village was Schemer Qian. They said Landlord Xu was not such a Schemer nor half so cunning as he, yet we've never attacked Qian. You told me this spring, but unfortunately I didn't go into it carefully then. I gathered several cadres for a talk, but nobody brought his name up. Somehow or other we decided on Landlord Hou and made arrangements accordingly. Hou is a bad man too, but because we didn't attack Schemer Qian the people didn't dare speak out. At that meeting only a few Party members spoke, calling out slogans and raising their fists, so that things looked lively, but actually, thinking back, that was all there was to it. You're always cursing Tenant Hou for a die-hard, but the fact of the matter is we didn't do a good job. Yumin! Everything else about you is fine; you don't mind poverty, you're really disinterested and you can unite the cadres. You weren't timid to begin with, but in this business you've been over-cautious. You ought to analyse the reason for it! What devil's got into you! Ha ha!"

His laughter was so frank it set a good many others chuckling too, and started Yumin roaring with happy laughter. Unconsciously stroking the back of his neck like Pin he said: "One reason was ideological confusion. I wasn't really thinking of the people. Fear was the first principle. I kept being afraid we wouldn't bring it off, worrying about this and that, worrying about the result if we didn't agitate successfully and failed to overthrow him. Wouldn't I be losing face for nothing, and get criticized? Bah! I really had no guts. I looked at things from a personal point of view, not taking a firm stand. It was lucky Comrade Yang kept planning things with me all the time. But frankly, I didn't mean to do wrong!"

Old Dong too said he had disclaimed responsibility and

let things slide, giving all his attention to Liyu, just because the cadres had said they'd given him three *mu* of vineyard. He really had the backward peasant mentality....

Hu asked him slyly if his marriage were fixed up or not. Old Dong turned red and denied it emphatically: "How could it be? That would be too much of a joke...."

In this cheerful atmosphere Wen relaxed a little. Hu asked Yumin again whether he were looking for a wife. Yumin stoutly denied it, and Freckles Li explained that once in the past Security Officer Zhang had suggested introducing a widowed cousin to him, but Yumin had refused, saying he was a poor bachelor and could not support a wife. Zhang had asked Freckles Li to persuade him, but when Freckles Li spoke to Yumin the latter cursed him. He'd heard that after the woman's husband died she had not behaved too properly. Then Zhang spread rumours about him, deliberately trying to make trouble.

Hu teased him, saying that he couldn't see anything wrong about it. For it would mean getting both the woman and her property. Surely now that he was secretary of the local Party branch he must look for a wife; Hu would certainly help to find him one, and wouldn't leave the village until he'd attended the wedding.

At this the fourteen-year-old bride who was being brought up for Freckles Li became subject for laughter. By now the atmosphere had grown cheerful, and Wen joined in too. Pin was a youngster and a bachelor himself, but he declared boldly that once after the chairman of a women's association had held his hand, he had not slept well all night. The next day he had given her a good talking-to, telling her to work hard in future and be careful what impression she made.

Just as they were talking away nineteen to the dozen, Zhao and Young Cheng burst in. They joined in the laughter too, but pressed the others to go to eat. They had to put an end to the long hours of excitement and prepare the meeting for Party members that evening.

45

COMING out of his father-in-law's house Security Officer Zhang planned to go to the co-operative and then to see Wen, meaning to find out what had happened since Pin's arrival. His father-in-law had spoken seriously to him and he felt a little uneasy. However, Wen had said repeatedly that army dependents would be given special treatment. Besides, Wen had come from Zhangjiakou. He was a cadre with some background and Pin might not be a match for him. His wife followed him, urging repeatedly: "Mind you do what father says, be sure you remember! If they really mean — aiya! In that case don't on any account go to my father's house again. Come straight home and tell me! There are times when one has to play safe...."

By now it was dark. A new crescent moon hung in the western sky, its faint beams falling on the low wall in the east. All along the base of the wall crickets were chirruping. There was already a feeling of autumn in the air and people no longer came out to cool off. Zhang quietly told his wife not to worry, and to go home, he would be back very soon. His wife was about to say something more when someone appeared round the corner of the wall and challenged them: "Who's there?" Zhang saw that it was one of the militiamen, and holding his frightened wife with one hand he called out, "Don't you know me? It's I, the security officer. Why do you shout so loudly? If there was anybody bad about he'd be frightened away."

"Oh! It's the security officer. Yumin's been looking for you for hours. He wants you to go to Old Han's house." The militiaman came nearer, still holding his rifle, and looked the woman over from head to foot.

"What's happened? Has Pin from the county left or not? Where is he?" Then he nudged his wife and said: "You go home first."

"Hey! If it isn't the security officer!" Two figures emerged from the dark. "Where have you been? We've had such a search, and all the time you've been here on guard!" These were Freckles Li and Organization Zhao. Chuckling, they took hold of Zhang and led him away.

All Zhang could say was, "What's the joke, where are you taking me?"

The other two laughed again and said: "Were you going to visit relatives? What was your wife tagging along at your heels for! Aren't you afraid of being laughed at?"

Zhang was uneasy, and with a sense of foreboding asked: "So you're not holding a meeting of the peasants' association after all. What does Pin say about our quarrel yesterday? It wasn't my fault. Everybody knows Liuman did it deliberately to make trouble!"

"Pin hasn't said anything. He's talking to Wen and the rest about what happened in Li Gongde's family in Baihuai. They confiscated over three thousand garments, but not a single one that could be worn by ordinary people — all brightly patterned silk gowns and high-heeled shoes. And he says Li's second wife is a devil. She didn't shed a single tear, but with her head high stalked out of the main room filled with glass-ware, to move into a room beside the kitchen, a little room where the cook used to live." Organization Zhao was still as fascinated as when he had just heard the story.

"I've said all along," said Zhang, "we don't have any big landlords like that, no one really worth attacking. Landlord Li is fairly well off, but we let him run away. Do you think in the meeting this evening they'll discuss our quarrel yesterday?"

Freckles Li did not answer, only asked, "What are you afraid of?"

"Afraid?" Zhang did not like the sound of that, and replied, "I'm not afraid of anything. In the first place I'm not a landlord, in the second place I'm not a traitor. It was Pin who approved my joining the Party. What can he do to me?"

There were guards too at the door of Old Han's house. Zhang thought, "Surely in this land reform they're not going to make me the scapegoat? I said yesterday Qian is an army dependent, and that's true. That's what Chairman Wen said too. Last time they classified people I wasn't the one to do the classifying. I'm not afraid."

There were too many people for inside, so they were all sitting in the courtyard where their faces could not be seen clearly because the court was too big. Although there were only about two dozen present, still it seemed very lively.

Most of them had joined the Party before liberation. They were sworn brothers, who had nothing against each other, and the atmosphere in the courtyard was very harmonious. In addition to this Pin's presence made things even more gay, as if there had not been so many people together for a long time.

Only Security Officer Zhang looked as if he had a guilty conscience, and paying no attention to anyone he sat down silently. Zhao sitting next to him did not say anything either.

After Yumin had checked their numbers he opened the meeting, but all his speech was a condemnation of his own conduct. He said during the past two meetings he had not brought up Schemer Qian's name for fear it would be no use, that he was suspicious of various comrades, and although peasants often came to see him to ask what was happening and make suggestions he had not told Comrade Wen, not even trusting the cadres from the district government. He said how bad it was to try and keep everything in his own hands like this, how he had failed to work for the good of the masses. "I've worked two years for the revolution," he said, "but I'm still so short-sighted. I ought to tell the people to beat me up. I've lived twenty-eight years and worked a dozen years as a hired labourer. Other people grew up eating grain, but I ate more husks than grain, working day and night for people like a donkey in a stable, yet not as valued as a donkey. I have been poor all along. Yet now instead of thinking for the masses, I hide things from those above and deceive those below. I'm really beneath contempt! The masses see things clearly. They know quite well if we're acting selfishly or not. If we have a boil on the back of our head we can't see it ourselves, but it's ridiculous to imagine other people can't see it. This evening we'll talk quite frankly, like cadres of two years' standing, like brothers who have sworn to stand or fall together. Haven't we all been afraid of the power changing hands, afraid of offending people, anxious to compromise, taking personal feelings into consideration, held back by selfish considerations? With these faults we've forgotten ourselves. Now all this is from my heart, and if I still tell even a white lie you throw me out of the Party. I have another suggestion which is this: Let everyone say frankly what's on his mind."

During his speech the atmosphere in the courtyard became more and more solemn. Everyone felt conscience-stricken yet delighted. They wanted to say something like Yumin. But because they were taken unaware they were unprepared and did not know what to say, while Yumin's speech stirred up such wonder and admiration that many of them felt bewildered.

There was a pause during which no one spoke. The silence had become almost unendurable when Swarthy Guo jumped up and shouted in a rough voice: "We've all been like that! Haven't we? Every day we call on the people to arise, while we cadres just sit in the co-op drinking tea or stroll about the street. During meetings, although everyone knows who it is in our village that kills people without a knife, we just talk nonsense, all afraid because his cousin and son-in-law are cadres, and we want either not to offend him or else to get some connection with him! Now Yumin wants us to tell the truth, and nobody says anything. Yet we say we aren't acting from personal feelings! It ought to be clear to all." Having said this he walked to one side, breathing angrily.

Trade Union Qian was a straightforward fellow, interested only in his work. He had been made chairman of the trade union, but without understanding what his duties were. He was Schemer Qian's cousin, but they had never had anything to do with each other. He had never proposed attacking Qian, neither had he opposed it. He had no idea that because of him the others had not spoken out, and this gave him a sense of injury. He was a man of few words, but now he stammered: "What d'you mean by cousin? Doesn't everyone know that no one in our family has anything to do with him? Haven't you seen how his elder brother Wenfu, that poor old bachelor who has one *mu* of vegetable garden, doesn't have anything to do with him? He never shared his money or power with anyone. In the past his friends were those people in the puppet government or the rich people in the village, not us poor relations. If he could have changed his name he'd have stopped calling himself Qian long ago. If you want to attack him I've nothing against it. None of us in the Qian family are against it."

"We're not asking whether you're against it or not, but whether you approve or not," said someone.

"I approve, I approve! Only one thing: I can't speak in the mass meeting. Not for any other reason, but I can't get the better of him in argument."

At that everybody laughed, and asked him what he was afraid of.

Following this several others spoke, some at considerable length, some just saying a word or two. Co-op Tian mentioned the quarrel in the orchard, saying since then he had had to run about all day to get a dozen people to work there. The job could not remain half done.

By this time Security Officer Zhang had already made up his mind. He admired his father-in-law's foresight. Evidently the straightforwardness of all these comrades was no match for one Schemer Qian. Not troubling himself about the rights and wrongs of the case he felt quite unmoved, the only idea in his head being to extricate himself from this predicament. Qian had ordered him, if he saw things going badly, to steer a new course. If only Qian could get by this time or go into hiding for a time, he would take his revenge some day. Qian had also told him a day would come when Yi would return to avenge him. Believing him, relying on him and at the same time fearing him, Zhang linked his fate with that of his father-in-law, unconscious that he was leaning on a broken reed. After reflecting for some time and figuring out how to put things, he had a suitable opportunity to speak.

"There's not much I can say. You've all made up your mind that I'm in with Qian, otherwise I couldn't have married his daughter!" He paused a second to see if there were any objections, but the courtyard was absolutely silent as they all listened to him. "Ever since I married his daughter you've all looked on me as an outsider. The proverb says a man doesn't tell the truth to his wife. Do you suppose I could be under the spell of a woman? Doesn't everyone take an oath on entering the Party? If you insist on suspecting me, what can I do about it? Whenever there's any business you all talk about it behind my back. I don't know what you intend to do. I can only go by guesswork. If you say we must find someone sinister to attack in land reform, I don't deny that he's known as the Schemer. He's injured lots of people. I know that. In the past he had connections with the Japanese and with traitors and spies. But you didn't say that. After talking backwards and forwards you only said to do away with the big feudalistic landlords, so I guessed that meant choosing whoever's land was most. Yesterday I quarrelled with Liuman, saying Qian was an army dependent. But that isn't something I made up. The district cadres said the same at the other day's meeting. Another thing, it seemed to me according to your classification of people he was out of it. I don't mind admitting I'm muddle-headed, but I never forget my origin. I'd never oppose the decision of the group. I joined the revolution before liberation too."

"Ha! How well he makes it sound!" they all thought, and were at a loss to answer.

"Zhang's attitude is very good," said Wen. "It was wrong of us to suspect him like that in the past. We can't distrust a revolutionary comrade so easily. This is a lesson for us!"

Silence followed. Zhao who had just been preparing to question Zhang about his activities, sighed and shifted himself, in order to move further away from him.

After a while Zhang got up to ease himself outside, but

Zhao stopped him, and shouted to the chairman: "The meeting's not over, nobody can leave." Zhang had to sit down again, muttering, "Bah! You still don't trust me."

The meeting became lively, with shouts of "Right, before the meeting's over no one must leave!" Others shouted: "Have Schemer Qian arrested!" The rest responded: "If he's arrested, just see how keen the people will be tomorrow!" "Right, have him arrested!"

Young Cheng too was disgusted but could not argue with Zhang. He hadn't the courage. He often wished he were braver, but there was always something dragging him down. He thought, "She's oppressed too, but she lives in his house. Outsiders don't realize; they just think of her as his niece. Ah, I can't very well say it. Why let people trample on her? It's enough for me not to oppose attacking that old rogue." — Young Cheng always considered himself very just and he hated Schemer Qian, so he was very willing to attack him; but he shrank from mentioning Heini for fear of involving her, instead of realizing that this would liberate her. He felt he had already wronged her and now if he mentioned her in order to clear himself it would be even more inexcusable. "Anyway, if I never marry her," he thought, "the matter will clear itself up. No need to explain it."

Not until a number of people had looked at him wanting him to speak did he declare that he had classified Qian as a landlord. But then Security Officer Zhang had protested, saying he had already divided his property with his sons, whereupon Yumin had changed his category. He, Cheng, wasn't responsible for that. He believed Qian ought to be classified as a landlord; his division of property was only a pretence.

That evening everybody was dissatisfied with him. He

was Schemer Qian's old hired man and tenant, besides being chairman of the peasants' association, yet his attitude was irresolute and apathetic. Someone suggested that the next day they should elect a chairman for the association's meeting, and that no one connected with Qian should be eligible, All present agreed to this proposal — Right! Let the masses elect whom they pleased!

Pin said too this was an ideological problem, and there should be no coercion. It was no use talking well but acting badly. In the future they must judge from the facts and let deeds speak for them. He also spoke of their common class origin, urging them to act as a vanguard instead of falling to the rear of the mass movement. This put each man on his mettle. Each one, conscious of his own defects, wanted to do a good job of work.

When the meeting was nearing its conclusion, Swarthy Guo stood up and asked in a low voice: "Can I go first?"

"All right!" said Yumin. "You go first. Have him taken for the time being to the shed in Landlord Xu's back courtyard. We'll put some more men on guard."

Security Officer Zhang gave a start, but realizing it was too late to do anything, he said: "Right! First have him arrested. I'll go myself as security officer. I'll see he doesn't escape." However, the others objected saying, "Just the captain will do."

After Swarthy Guo had gone the feeling of tension still persisted. Although there was nothing more to discuss, nobody wanted to leave. They waited for a time until Guo came back, and only then were they content to go home. All the way they could not resist discussing this happy development in loud voices, so that before the next day a number of the villagers knew what had happened that evening, and all were eager to spread the news.

46

WALKING home with the crowd Young Cheng was unusually silent, while the others talked and joked loudly and indulged in horseplay together. Whenever anyone bumped into him he just gave way quietly. He could not explain himself. To begin with he had felt embarrassed, then wronged, and finally rather timid. It was as if he had committed some crime or injured somebody, so that he could not hold up his head. Such a feeling he had never experienced before. Listening to all that Comrade Pin said it seemed as if every sentence was aimed at him, and he became conscious for the first time of his own vile conduct. Pin had seen it clearly. Young Cheng had been a straightforward fellow who never deceived people, but now he felt he was dishonest, he had deceived himself. He realized it had simply been a pretence when he said he would not marry Heini. It was only because he was afraid of criticism that he had forced himself to avoid her and keep her at a distance. It was only to deceive people, not because he had any hatred for her uncle, the worst man in the village, whom everyone detested. Hitherto he had always had a clear conscience, thinking he had not sided with Schemer Qian, whereas in fact he had never opposed him! For his niece's sake he had forgiven him everything! He had overlooked the injuries Schemer Qian had done to everyone in the past, had forgotten how he himself had suffered and been exploited in his house. He wanted others to go to settle accounts and ask for the title deeds, while he himself was not brave enough to settle accounts. Had he not cultivated eight *mu* of dry and two *mu* of irrigated land of his? Pin said they must not forget their origin, but he had forgotten. In what way had he been thinking of the poor? He had been thinking only of himself, mortally afraid of offending the niece of a landlord, the niece of a rogue. He had looked down on Security Officer Zhang because the latter, for the sake of his wife and some small conveniences, grew every day closer to his father-in-law, drifting away from the comrades in the group who were his brothers, and from the peasants, until all the villagers despised him. But in his own case, although he had not married Schemer Qian's niece or been to their house, only secretly protecting her in his heart, it was equivalent to protecting them all, to upholding the privileges of the land-owning class — how could he claim not to have forgotten his origin or to be better in any way than Zhang?

His steps grew slower and slower as these thoughts flashed through his mind, and he fell behind the crowd. A door in the lane opened with a creak, and he heard someone step outside for a moment, then go in again closing the door behind him. Listlessly Young Cheng gazed blankly into the darkness — what ought he to do?

Presently he reached his home, which was in a courtyard where several families lived together. The door was not bolted and he walked quietly in. Everybody was asleep and he could hear snores from the north room. The hens kept by the family opposite stirred restlessly in their small coop, and gave a few soft squawks.

A faint light showed from his room. He had forgotten that his mother was no longer at home, having gone to stay with her sister to keep her company during her lying-in. So he was not surprised by the light, as he stepped apathetically over the threshold.

A tiny point of flame hovered on the wick of the oil lamp, and the faint light seemed more gloomy than complete darkness. As he went in, a shadow detached itself slowly from the black corner by the *kang*. He paid no attention, feeling

284

as if this shadow had nothing to do with him. It just occurred to him to think, "Hasn't Ma gone to bed yet?" However, still immersed in his own affairs he went and sat down on one end of the *kang*.

Sure enough the black shadow was a woman. She came over to him before he had lain down, and he suddenly remembered that his mother had been away for several days. Besides, this woman did not look like his mother. Involuntarily, in his surprise he asked sharply: "Who are you?"

The woman made a sudden clutch at his arm, and said: "It's me! Aunty."

He withdrew his hand, backed up against the wall, and looked fixedly at this ghostly shadow.

She immediately gave him a cloth bundle, and in a tone meant to be kindly but actually embarrassed, wanting to laugh but unable to do so, said softly: "Here you are. It's a present from Heini. She wanted to come herself because she has something to say to you. She solemnly swears she wants to be your wife. Cheng! Don't let her down!"

He wanted to send this woman with her bundle and her talk packing, but he did not do it. He could not raise his hand. Guilt and shame pinned it down. He wanted to curse her, but his tongue was numb as if he had taken some strange drug.

"Her uncle will do anything for her," Mrs. Qian went on. "You can have her, you can have the land, eighteen *mu* altogether including the vegetable garden. Cheng! Our Heini's counting on you!"

Young Cheng shuddered from head to foot. He felt there were countless eyes in the ceiling and in the cracks of the wall smiling sarcastically at him.

Qian's wife thrust her face closer to his, her mouth by his ear, and said distinctly: "Her uncle says we mustn't put you in an awkward position. You're chairman of the peasants' association. Of course you have to say things. Just so long as you understand at heart. Well, after all we're one family!..." She squawked like an egret and laughed with appalling shamelessness.

Young Cheng could stand it no longer. He shook himself, as if using all his might to dislodge a heavy load from his back. "Go away!" The words burst harshly from his throat. "Get out of here!"

Shaken by his tone, Mrs. Qian recoiled a step. She moved her lips, but for the moment could not speak.

Picking up the cloth bundle he threw it at her, his sense of insult increasing his fury, and shouted: "I don't give a damn for your stinking land! You've come to buy me, but it's no use! Take it back. A day will come when we'll settle accounts."

She seemed to roll outside with the bundle that had been thrown down, her small feet scarcely touching the ground, as she rocked from side to side. Regaining her balance with difficulty, she clutched the door post with one hand and paused, panting, then darted forward again, saying tremulously: "Our Heini...."

"Don't you use that name again. I don't want to hear it!" Young Cheng leapt forward to confront her furiously. Fearing he would strike her she lowered her head but dared not cry out.

The feeble rays of the light lit up her fearful expression, her hair dishevelled, her wild eyes staring wide, her lips awry disclosing the yellow teeth. Young Cheng tasted the gratification of revenge. With a ghastly smile he said: "Are you still not going? Your old man has already been arrested and shut up in Landlord Xu's backyard. You'd better go home to cry. Get some wood ready for the coffin."

286

The shadow contracted, receding slowly from him as she retreated into the courtyard. He followed her to the gate where she suddenly came forward again to look at him, then burst out wailing and hurried outside. The sound of her cries gradually died away in the darkness.

Young Cheng felt as if he had suddenly woken up from a bad dream or as if he were standing on a wild plain. Shaking his head he walked slowly back into the courtyard, looking up at the autumn sky where the stars were twinkling quietly. No more snores were coming from the north room. The lively chirrups of insects could be heard from the four corners of the wall, while the fowls in the hen-coop opposite shook and stretched their wings in the dark narrow coop, and crowed stridently.

"Don't fall behind the mass movement. Don't fall behind the masses. Don't forget your own origin." These words started milling through his head again. But he no longer felt distressed by the invisible bonds that had bound him. He shook himself and went, relaxed and with a light heart, into the house.

47

PEOPLE from different families called on each other, old men sought out their cronies, youngsters their pals, women other women. When people saw each other they exchanged significant glances, then put their heads together. They told each other of what had happened, first speaking rather sceptically or even in a shocked tone, and after questioning each other they would go to ask those who were close to the cadres, or the militia, while some of them went to see the cadres. The news was confirmed, but it grew in the telling. Some people said that by the time Swarthy Guo went to look for Schemer Qian he was not to be found, and finally was dragged out from under the hay in the stable. Others said that he was lying on the *kang* and on Guo's arrival all he said was, "So you've come. I've been expecting this a long time." Still others said the militia dared not lift their hands against him, and it was Guo who tied him up. Others again said that before leaving he put on a new pair of socks as well as a green woollen gown, saying it was cold in the middle of the night. Maybe it was because he was afraid he would have no decent clothes to die in!

Old women were still sitting on the end of the *kang* cooking breakfast, but the young people had lost interest even in food. Group after group made its way to Landlord Xu's gate to have a look. A militiaman on guard at the gate forbade them to go in, but they said they were looking for someone and forced their way in. Pushing their way among the families who lived there they questioned them, but they said they had seen nothing. All they knew was that while it was still dark there had been a commotion, and Qian was shut up in a rather out-of-the-way little courtyard at the back. There was just a big room for firwood there. Now there was no firewood left, only an earthen *kang* and some broken boards. When they still wanted to go in and look they found the gate to the small courtyard firmly fastened. There were militiamen within and without, so they had to leave. But some of them thought they could see Schemer Qian through a crack in the door, fanning himself most unconcernedly.

Those in the know said: "Yesterday Comrade Pin from the county government arrived. He may look soft, but after all he did grow up with a gun in his hand. He's knocked around our district for quite a time, and been through a lot. In a business like this it's no use being cultured and refined."

The streets were filled with people as if it were market-day. There was a crowd in front of the blackboard news, the people in front reading and the ones at the back listening, all of them smiling. Others stood in front of the sales window of the co-operative and craned their necks to look inside, and when they saw cadres moving about inside they strained their ears to hear what was being said.

Sheng's mother could not be bothered to cook. She fastened up her skimpy hair and went out into the street. Her daughter kept coming out to call her home, but she refused to go. Whenever anyone crossed the road she would ask: "Do you know someone was arrested in our village last night?"

Everybody knew she was a gossip, and did not pay much attention, giving a careless answer and passing on. But some, because they were in a good humour, forgot her temper. Then she dashed forward and said: "Ah! At long last the sky is clear! If our village doesn't overthrow that flag-pole, no matter how capable and just the Communists are, the sun won't reach us. In the old days Sheng's dad when he had a little spare time in winter would sometimes sell peanut cakes, but Schemer Qian said we had earned money and didn't give him presents, and at New Year confiscated his basket. There was nothing my man could do except give him ten catties of peanuts and a catty of sugar. But that brought shame on Qian and he threw all the presents on the ground. He said we had taken him wrong and insisted we had broken the law, wanting to send my husband to be tried in the *xiang* court. My husband was a simple fellow. He didn't know what to do, and after kowtowing and paying him money he got off being sent. Later Qian wanted to send my Sheng to Hongshan as a coolie. Everybody knew that people who went to Hongshan never came back, so then we had

289

to sell a pig. Ah! I mean to get that pig back. It was at least seventy or eighty catties. . . ''

Enthusiasts like Young Guo, Wang and Tenant Hou's son all crowded into the co-operative, then hurried after Yumin, Freckles Li and the others to Old Han's house, wanting to find the members of the work team to get more information from them.

There seemed to be an unending stream of militiamen too, sometimes several running in a row as if something tremendous had happened. But if questioned they maintained a wooden silence.

Landlord Hou came out too and sat down stealthily as usual at the foot of the wall. Since it was still early and the sun had only reached the top of the wall he was wearing a lined jacket. As he pretended to be sunning himself, he took advantage of the times they overlooked him to try to catch a few sentences to file in his mind for future reference. Young Hou kept on walking in Landlord Hou's direction, wearing a look of complacence, sometimes saying loudly to bystanders: "We must clean them up!"

Tenant Hou, who only yesterday had locked his son in the house, had heard the shepherd's wife talking to his wife as soon as he woke up. Since he usually despised the woman, thinking her a gossip and busybody, he went out at once. However he could not help hearing what they were talking about and had to go on listening, standing outside the window playing with some thread hanging on the porch, unwilling to leave. He could not believe his ears. After the shepherd's wife had left, his wife went out in high spirits as if she were going to the fair. His son and daughter were out. He could not resist standing in the doorway looking out, and presently his nephew Vineyard Li came over and said:

"Uncle! Seems to me that calendar of yours is out of date. Now we've really changed dynasties."

"What? Really?" was all he said.

"Yes, he's been arrested, everybody's asked to accuse him!"

"What should his punishment be?"

"I should say death!"

The old man said nothing. He could not overcome a feeling of panic, anxious as a boatman who suddenly sees a storm approaching. He was happy too, but this happiness could only be hidden deep in his heart. It was as if he had suddenly seen something he dared not hope for even in his dreams realized, already at hand, but he still wanted to conceal his feelings. He dared not stretch out his hand for fear of frightening it away, for fear that the actuality would once more change into an illusion. He could only ask himself sceptically again, "How did it happen? Can it be true?" However, finally he gave himself a satisfactory answer — bad people must always come to a bad end; men reap what they sow! Finally he went out too, walking to the main street pretending he was not looking for news. He headed for where the crowd was thickest, and presently arrived at the front of the stage. Seeing that there were too many people, he turned round and withdrew to one side to strike his flint. But while he was striking it he saw Landlord Hou sitting like an old beggar at the corner of the wall looking furtively at him. He felt as if he had been whipped. That stealthy glance of reproach made him hang his head, and immediately letting his hands fall he hurried off with bent back.

The school children were not having lessons either, but standing and looking out from the school gate. Some people rushed into the school, but finding nothing came out again, followed by others. The two teachers were both busy, hurrying in and out. Some people seized Teacher Ren to question him. Ren was completely panic-stricken and wanted to go home, but dared not because there were so many militiamen about. He tried to deceive himself: "What are you afraid of? You're not a landlord or a traitor or a spy. You don't even belong to the village. Just teaching, how can you go wrong? Don't be afraid. That bastard Qian has been arrested, and it serves him right. What's it got to do with you?" Still he could not allay his fears. Why had Comrade Pin told him to wait for him yesterday? What the devil did he want to see him about? It couldn't be anything good now! There was no way for him to leave the village. Red-nosed Wu, as if he knew what was in his mind, was always at his heels. Wherever he went he could see that red nose glistening.

Finally Pin appeared, still wearing the same collarless shirt, bare-headed, without socks on, his shoes tied with string. His shirt was thin, and a bulge showed at his waist where he carried a gun. People crowded round him, all talking at once, so that he didn't know whom to listen to.

"Pin! Don't go till you've cleared up our village."

"What are you going to do with Schemer Qian?"

"When's the trial going to be?"

"Should have been arrested long ago."

"Ah, before he was arrested who dared say anything?"

"This time Chairman Mao's answered our wishes. . . ."

Seeing how happy they all were, Pin could not help laughing with pleasure. Rubbing his neck repeatedly he said: "You see who's stronger after all. The people can do whatever they want, only now the thing is to get everyone to unite closely. Only by uniting closely can the old powers be overthrown and we stand on our own feet! The chief racketeer in your village has already been arrested. Those with grievances should speak up, those who want vengeance state their cases. Now that the Number One Racketeer's overthrown, there's no need to be afraid. You can say what you like. Bring your charges against him so that we can deal with him. We in the county are behind you. With our backing don't be afraid!"

A crowd surrounded the school when Pin went there. Yumin followed him in, and a militiaman stood guard at the door. Some people guessed what was happening while some were in the dark, but they all waited outside to see. They saw Red-nosed Wu hurry to and fro. Presently Teacher Liu came over too and looked outside without saying anything. Soon Pin and Yumin came out with Teacher Ren at their side carrying a roll of bedding on his back, mumbling incoherently. Seeing all the people outside Pin said to the militiaman: "You escort Mr. Ren some of the way. Walk slowly, I'll catch up with you presently."

Trying to look unconcerned, Ren walked shakily out. Some villagers followed him out of curiosity, but turned back after a short distance.

Someone in the crowd said: "I said long ago that fellow was no good. All the time sneakily making up to the rich. Wonder what he was up to?"

"Is he being taken to the county?" asked another.

"What's your opinion of him?" asked Pin, smiling.

"Who doesn't know?" they all said. "He's drunk so much ink he's turned black."

"He's young! We must try to reform him and he'll be all right. I'm going to take him back to the county to join the teachers' training class. When his mind's been remoulded you shall have him back. This way he won't spoil your children!" Having said this Pin walked out.

"That's fair enough," said the crowd. "Have him well taught."

Some caught up and said: "Comrade Pin, are you going? If you go how shall we manage?"

"I'll be back in a couple of days," said Pin as he walked on. "I have things to attend to. Comrade Wen and the others are here. If you've any ideas go and see them. Or see Yumin."

Yumin escorted Pin right out of the village, and as they walked they had another long talk. By the village gate Pin said: "You go back. Consult the people's opinion in everything, and it will be easy. Look how things are this morning — everybody's bold, no need to fear they won't attack. Only — well —" He paused for a minute, but did not finish the sentence.

Yumin looked at him and he looked at Yumin, both realizing what the problem was, and after a long interval Pin had to say: "Whatever happens, don't let him be killed."

"In that case we'd better hand him over to you."

Pin started thinking hard again. He could not think of a good solution. He was used to working in villages and understood the psychology of peasants: either don't attack or attack to kill. They did not like going through legal procedure, fearing that, if they did so, someone they thought deserved death might only be imprisoned. They often felt the Eighth Route Army was too lenient. They were not yet able to take a longer view, but clamoured for revenge, for a clean sweep. The peasants in some villages just killed their hated oppressors under a rain of fists. The district and village cadres all put the blame on the masses, but there were so many people it was impossible to say who was responsible. Pin knew too that the village cadres, just like the masses, worried lest the tables should be turned in future, and were therefore eager to do the job thoroughly. To persuade so many people at short notice was far from easy.

"No need to hand him over to us. The county government can't settle so many cases all at once. Better settle it in the village."

"Uh huh." Yumin realized the difficulty too. He was rather at a loss and said: "You understand the whole situation, don't you? Whether the people will be enthusiastic or not depends entirely on this."

"Is that the way you feel too?" asked Pin.

"Most of the cadres feel that way."

"That means you fear the reactionaries may come back. We ought to correct that outlook. Killing people at will isn't good. We can collect statements of his crimes to give the court. Execution ought to be legally carried out. In agitating nowadays we defeat landlords on political grounds, wanting them to bow to the people, not necessarily wanting to kill them. You'll have to talk the villagers round."

"Um." Yumin had to agree.

"See how you get on, and after I've reported the situation at the county government we'll all discuss it again. If the people really want him killed, and his crimes deserve death, then we'll send cadres over. I can't settle the matter by myself, you know that.... Listen, the gong's being sounded. We'll leave it at that for the time being. You must organize the people to be thorough, but have him kept alive. During the struggle we want to see the united strength of the masses, and do away with that fear that the reactionaries may return."

By the time Yumin was back in the village Red-nosed Wu had already sounded the gong down to the south street. The gong was unusually loud, and many people were following him, shouting. All one could hear was "Dong ... dong, dong." When the gong stopped, his hoarse voice started chanting cheerfully: "The Demon's caught alive! We're happy as at New Year! Hurry to the meeting! Accuse him without fear!"

48

PEOPLE streamed into Landlord Xu's courtyard. The earliest arrivals picked good places, but the late comers pushed them aside. They surged this way and that. People were lost in the crowd, and did not know whether the cadres had arrived or not. The militia were unable to keep order. They went several times for advice to Swarthy Guo, and he said: "The peasants' association can't have so many members. We usually only get about a hundred people at a meeting." He stood on the steps and shouted: "Those who don't belong to the peasants' association go away! This is a meeting for members of the peasants' association." But still more people came in while no one went out. Then Swarthy Guo went to ask the advice of the peasants' association and Bugao the organizer said: "This puts us in a fix! At previous meetings just one person came from each family, sometimes the father, sometimes the son. Sometimes they even sent the wife or daughter-in-law. But who should it be today?"

Swarthy Guo with his hot temper flared up, and shouted: "You're in charge of organization! Yet you don't even have a list of your members!"

"Who says I haven't!" Bugao was worked up too. "Only the head of the family appears on the list, but at meetings they ignore the list. If the old man's ill his son represents him, and you can't forbid it; while if the son's out the father comes. It's better to have someone than no one at all. But now they've all come! Which ones can you send away?"

"Devil take it!" Guo grew even angrier. "You manage things so sloppily. I don't know what you think you're doing! How do you expect us to keep order?"

"Why can't you let them all in?" someone asked.

"If they all come in, they'll burst the house!" growled Guo.

Seeing them quarrel, people quietly pushed further in.

In one corner Freckles Li started to lead some youngsters in singing. The volume of singing grew, more and more people joining in, and the sound of the quarrel was drowned. They moved aside and were at once swallowed up in the crowd. The only sound to be heard in the whole courtyard was the roar of the song: "Unite together — hey! Tillers of the land!... Landlords have oppressed us, oppressed us all these years.... Now we ... settle our old scores!"

More and more people filled the porch to overflowing, blocking the doorway. A few small groups out in the road tried to push their way in. They were blocked and withdrew, but after a while came again shouting: "We're members of the peasants' association. Why can't we go in?"

Organization Zhao looked for Vice-Head Zhao, Vice-Head Zhao looked for Yumin, Yumin looked for the comrades of the work team. They squeezed in and out of the crowd, but no sooner caught sight of the one they were looking for than he disappeared again. The work team cadres said they wanted to talk things over with others, whereupon Yumin again looked for Vice-Head Zhao, Vice-Head Zhao for Organization Zhao and Organization Zhao for someone else. Everybody had agreed to assemble in one place, but it was damned difficult to find anyone, although not a soul had left the courtyard!

The singing was a confounded nuisance. There was such a din you couldn't make yourself heard when you called out somebody's name. Yet if they didn't sing the crowd would probably make even more noise.

When the few of them managed to squeeze together to talk things over they found no place to go to, and Yumin took them into a side room. There was an old woman there, a toothless, deaf old crone who could hardly walk, but her face was pressed to the glass window, and she was chuckling gleefully as she watched the masses outside, tears standing in her eyes. When the men burst in she was taken aback for a moment, then suddenly seemed to catch on, crawled over from the other end of the *kang*, shaking her head again and again, holding up her hand and opening her mouth; but instead of saying anything she just laughed, laughed and laughed until tears suddenly started pouring down her cheeks. Hu who was standing by the *kang* hurried over to put an arm round her, and she leant on his shoulder and started sobbing like a child. Hu patted her, and after she'd cried for some time she raised her head to look at them all, wiped her tears with one hand, leaning against the wall with the other, then crawled back to the corner of the *kang*. Once more she flattened her face against the window pane.

They all crowded into a corner of the room to talk, and Wen said: "Things are too out of hand! Things are too out of hand!"

"It's all the fault of the peasants' association," said Swarthy Guo. "They don't even know who their members are."

The people want to attend the meeting, let them all come. Why shouldn't the peasants' association meeting be changed into a mass meeting?" suggested Old Dong.

"Bah!" said Vice-Head Zhao. "Yesterday evening why didn't we decide to hold a big meeting? Now we've gone and changed again."

"It doesn't matter changing," said Yang. "Yesterday we

didn't foresee things clearly enough, and there were reasons for calling a peasants' association meeting. Since there are so many people, we can make a last-moment change. We may as well go to the stage."

"Right, let's go to the stage. Ha, if we hadn't arrested Schemer Qian, the people would never have come like this."

"No one else would have done."

"No more empty talk. Get Red-nosed Wu to sound the gong once more. There are still some people who haven't joined the peasants' association. Let them all come."

"Wait a moment, Yumin. Some things will have to be arranged all over again. Let's discuss that." Yang pulled Yumin back into the room. The others hurried out. The courtyard was still a babel of sound.

Very soon Red-nosed Wu appeared on the steps. He sounded the gong lustily and the singing stopped, while everybody quietened down. Then he bawled out: "This courtyard's too small. We're going to hold a mass meeting by the stage!" But before he had finished, pandemonium broke out again. Everybody pushed towards the gate, jostling each other to crowd through, and shouting. Women and children kept calling out shrilly as they were jammed.

Without knowing what it was all about, the villagers outside followed the stream. As if a fire had broken out, nothing could be heard but the tramp of feet.

Presently they were gathered before the stage. There was more space here, no need to fight for room or jostle each other. Some people moved away to the foot of the wall to sit on the stone benches or wooden boards, talking in twos and threes.

In the meantime Landlord Hou had appeared and slunk into his old place. The people sitting nearby, as soon as they saw him, moved further away.

At the same time Red-nosed Wu could be heard in another lane, beating the gong and calling out: "Women and children, old and young! Come to the meeting, everyone come! Come to the stage, settle old scores! Tillers, you'll have the land that's yours!"

49

RED-NOSED Wu hurried along highways and byways, from this lane, to that. A good many people were already standing at the crossroads, and when they saw others going from the lanes to the main street and thence to the stage, they followed suit. Some of the rather better dressed looked anxious here and there were one or two merchants wearing straw hats like the local gentry, who mixed in with the crowd, cracking jokes. There were women too who had put powder on their faces, with glossy hair and close fitting gowns, who walked in twos and threes, swaying their hips, to stand in a group at the back. There were also some poor old people who had been left at home, but who locked their doors now and came out, as well as some women who really had so many children they could not get away, yet now came out carrying one and leading another, making their way as best they could. People started asking: "Why doesn't the meeting start?"

Standing in the middle of the stage, Yumin directed operations: "Women to the right. Will you people please make way. When you're in place, don't move. You by the wall, come over here."

The crowd did as they were told, but as soon as they were in position they turned round again and some started moving back. Then the primary school students marched out to attend the meeting, with Teacher Liu at their head, singing.

The children behaved as if they were at a sports' contest, intense and in the highest spirits, singing with all their might: "Without the Communist Party there would be no New China." The strains echoed to the sky. Yumin hurried to greet them and had a corner cleared for them in front of the stage; their procession came in through the crowd, and everyone made way for them naturally. Teacher Liu had his work cut out to get them arranged in order, and told them to stop singing.

In the crowd people started whispering: "Has the accused arrived or not?"

"No. He's still locked up."

"Look at old Landlord Hou."

Schemer Qian's wife was standing behind the stage too, with her back to it, and kept wiping her tears with her dress, snivelling. She had just taken her husband food, and whenever she saw any of the cadres she kowtowed to them, and said sobbingly: "What harm has he done you since you became cadres? Have a heart. Remember our Yi's with the Eighth Route Army.'

Someone threatened her: "If you don't keep quiet, we'll have you tied up." But still she would not go.

Someone shouted: "Start the meeting!"

"Yes, start the meeting!" Yumin jumped up again onto the stage. With his shirt unbuttoned and opened, he looked at the crowd and waited for them to be silent.

Freckles Li blew on a whistle.

"Our village has been agitating for land reform now for more than ten days," announced Yumin. "We want to stand on our feet, but it isn't easy. There are lots of landlords in our village who exploited and oppressed us. Today let's catch the racketeers. Yesterday evening we arrested the notorious chief racketeer, whose nickname is the 'schemer'."

The people started clapping and calling out: "Well done! Beat the dog!"

"Another thing," Yumin went on, "that rascal Zhang, our security officer, didn't stand up for the people but for his father-in-law, sabotaging our land reform. The county government has removed him from his job. In the future we'll have to keep an eye on him. . . ."

There was more clapping. People in the crowd said to each other: "Serves him right." And someone shouted: "Down with the renegades!" "Have all those collaborationists tied up!"

"Our meeting today is to settle scores with Schemer Qian," continued Yumin. "Lets add up the score first, and when it's about complete we'll read it out in his presence another day. We peasants are in charge of the meeting ourselves; let's elect chairmen. What do you say?"

"Fine!" "Yumin!" "Or let the peasants' association choose!" Different cries were heard.

"Let the people elect them. You choose yourselves. Choose a few people you can trust," said Old Dong, who was standing behind Yumin.

"All right, then we'll choose some! I propose Young Guo." This was Young Wang speaking.

"Do you agree to Young Guo or not?"

"Yes. And I propose Orchard-keeper Li."

"Orchard-keeper Li, right."

"I propose Yumin too. Without him we won't get anywhere. What do you all say to that?"

"Right, we want him." "Those in favour, raise your hands!" "Ha. . . ."

People pushed Young Guo and Orchard-keeper Li up from the crowd. Li just laughed. Young Guo felt awkward too, and looked as sheepish as a bridegroom.

Yumin pulled Orchard-keeper Li to the centre of the stage and conferred with him for a minute. Then the old man put on a serious expression, stepped forward and started speaking: "I'm a poor man," he said. "I've looked after the orchards these scores of years, but I don't own a single tree. I'm sixty-one this year, and about as withered as the autumn leaves that fall to the ground. Even in my dreams I never imagined a day like this, when I'd be chairman! Well! I'm happy, I'm the poor people's chairman. Today let's attack Schemer Qian properly. Now is the time for revenge, for righting wrongs or paying debts, or taking a life for a life. My outlook's quite simple, I'm a poor man. I've finished what I want to say as chairman, the rest of you speak now."

Nobody laughed at him, they were all satisfied with such a chairman.

A great many people wanted to speak, and the chairman told them to take their turn. But each speaking in turn, nobody could say very much. After a few sentences each one stopped. When the crowd shouted, their feeling ran very high, but after one or two people had spoken incoherently the atmosphere of the meeting relaxed. Freckles Li therefore shouted slogans at the top of his voice, but irrelevant slogans seemed beside the point. Liuman was worked up to fever pitch. He jumped on to the platform, staring, then raised his fists and shouted, "Do you want me to speak?"

"Liuman! Liuman! Speak out! You talk well!"

"If you want me to speak, I must ask the cadres whether I'll be punished for what I say?"

"Go on, Liuman! No one'll punish you! Who dares to punish you! We want to see what there is in you. We're counting on you to give us a lead!" Yumin reassured him with a smile.

"Who dares to punish you! Go on, Liuman! You did a good day's work when you beat that dog of a security officer!" Someone in the crowd encouraged him.

"Talk about Qian's business," Yumin reminded him.

Liuman looked round at them all with eyes that were blood-shot for lack of sleep. He beat his chest, and said: "I've a big score to settle. I'm going to start at the beginning. Some of you know my story, others don't. Ah! But how can you understand my resentment these last dozen years? I've grown big by stuffing myself with injustice." He slapped his chest, as if to show how full it was of resentment. "My father had four sons. We were all good workers, and judging by our strength we ought to have managed pretty well. Before the war against Japan we saved over two hundred dollars. My father wanted to invest in a little property and, as ill luck would have it, hit on Schemer Qian, who told him he could make a good profit out of a mill. Qian persuaded him to start a mill and helped him rent a building for it, also invited a friend of his to come as assistant. Since it was someone from another village, my father wasn't pleased, but he agreed anyhow. That friend started looking after the business in the mill, but in less than two months he made off, taking with him a couple of donkeys and over a thousand catties of wheat. My father complained to Qian, and Qian sympathized with him, cursing his friend for involving him. He took my father to Zhuolu County to take the matter to court. The case was won, but I can tell you nobody should try any lawsuit. We kept putting in more and more money, but still no judgement was handed down. My father fell ill with anger, and the next year he died. The four of us killed a hen and took an oath at New Year that we'd be revenged. Ah! Before we'd done anything my eldest brother was suddenly dragged off to join the army! Goes without saying someone was behind that dirty business! As soon as my eldest brother had left, the Japanese arrived. He was swallowed up like a pebble in the ocean, and year after year went by without any news from him. His wife couldn't stick it, and married again. She left a little girl, who's still with me."

"That's true enough," said people in the crowd.

"The second year the Japanese were here," went on Liuman, "Schemer Qian came to see my second brother. He said he felt he'd let our father down, that he felt bad about the money we'd lost over the mill, and wanted to help us, and advised my brother to become ward chief, saying that way he could get a little of the money back. My second brother didn't want to. He was a straightforward fellow and was needed on the farm. Besides, he wasn't a man of the world. We all hated Schemer Qian, and my brother wouldn't take on the job. We refused Qian and he left, but a couple of weeks later an order came from the *xiang* government appointing my second brother ward chief. There was nothing he could do about it, he couldn't get out of it. The *xiang* government would ask for money one day, for grain the next, for porters the day after; and groups of spies and traitors kept coming to the village who cursed and beat him for not looking after them properly. If ever my brother didn't send Qian the money he squeezed from the people, Qian was ready to say he was disloyal to the Mikado's army, and threatened to send him to the barracks. My brother acted as ward chief for three months, and if he hadn't fallen ill he wouldn't have got out of it even then. Brother! Come up here and let them see what you're like! — Come on, Brother! . . ." His voice broke, and died away. Unable to speak he just beat his breast.

The people below stirred as Liuqian was found and sent

up to the stage. He wore an idiotic smile. They passed him from hand to hand, till he reached the foot of the stage, when Young Guo hurriedly helped him up. The mad former ward chief did not understand what it was all about. He blinked stupidly round. His hair was several inches long, matted all over his head, his face was dirty and streaked with mud, his great eyes were sunken, and the whites kept showing: children meeting him at dusk would cry for fright.

Not a word was said by the crowd, only the old people sighed.

Suddenly Liuman raised his hands and shouted, "I want vengeance!"

"Vengeance!" followed a thunderous roar. Fists were shaken.

Freckles Li led them all in shouting: "Qian is a scheming, murdering devil." The crowd shouted with all their might after him. The women put all their strength into shouting, no longer needing to be urged by Gui.

"I've a score to settle with Qian too." Young Wang jumped on to the stage. A few days had changed him, and he seemed to have grown up overnight. He was no longer scatter-brained but had confidence, and took this struggle for granted as if it were the only thing to do. He had grown more and more enthusiastic, and when he saw people still sitting on the fence or sighing, he flared up. The youngster was full of confidence and hope. He described how in the past when Liuqian was ward chief, Schemer Qian had secretly pulled strings to have him arrested and sent to the Youth Corps. From the stage he asked his father if he wanted Qian to return their house or not. His father answered, "He must return it!" Thereupon the crowd roared out: "Qian arrests people for nothing, and steals their houses and their grain!"

Then an old man emerged from the crowd, pushed up to the stage by others. He could not say a word, just gazing at them all. They all kenw his son had been sent to Hongshan to do hard labour and never returned. After looking round for some time, he suddenly started crying. Everybody urged him: "Speak out! Don't be afraid!" But although he opened his mouth, he could not speak, and started crying again. Then the crowd became quiet; only sighs were heard in the stillness.

After this one after another went up, and after each had spoken the crowd gave a great roar. The more people spoke the angrier they grew. Some speakers were so enraged that after a few sentences the words stuck in their throats, they had to stand aside for a moment and recover their breath before going on.

Wen and the other members of the work team had never seen anything like this before. They could not help feeling excited and disturbed. Old Dong in particular was so exhilarated he kept pacing up and down, saying: "Look! This time the people have stood up!" And from time to time Hu would say to the presidium: "What do you think of this? Have you ever seen the like before?"

"Never!" Orchard-keeper Li answered. "Today we've turned the tables. We're not afraid of anything, we don't care about anything! Well, let them all speak, get everything off their chests! When we deal with Landlord Li I'm going to speak too, see if I don't, and I'm going to start from his grandfather's time."

They felt the opportunity was not to be wasted, and discussed taking advantage of the occasion to have Schemer Qian brought out. It would not matter extending the meeting — in a meeting like this the people would not feel tired.

When Orchard-keeper Li proposed this to the crowd, there

was not one dissenting voice. So he immediately ordered Qian to be brought. Swarthy Guo himself took several of the militiamen to fetch him.

No more people spoke on the stage, only a few people below whispered together. Some children left the meeting to go to the top of the lane and wait there.

The crowd began to fidget, people coughed, babies cried and their mothers coaxed them. The chairman had to announce a three-minute interval.

However, folk didn't go far away, because they wanted to wait for Schemer Qian. Only a number of women slipped off to a distance to sit down, some of those with bound feet chafing their feet. Gui and Yue went to fetch them back one by one, but they no sooner got some back than others slipped off. The presidium and cadres were busy discussing matters and making arrangements.

Presently two buckets of water were carried up, and people crowded round them for a drink.

Then a tall hat made of white paper was brought over, on it written "Stamp out the feudal power".

The militia were drawn up in excellent order, lined up in front of and behind the stage, holding their rifles grimly.

Villagers crowded round to look at the hat and at the militia. These were all their own men, but how dashing they looked.

So they waited for their enemy to come.

50

WHEN they heard the footsteps of the children who had followed the militia out, the men on the stage glanced at each other, knowing what it meant. The crowd stood still, craning their necks for a sight. The militia looked even sterner, and stopped talking. Yumin, Orchard-keeper Li and Young Guo posted themselves in the middle of the stage, and Freckles Li started shouting slogans: "Down with the local despots!" "Down with feudal landlords!" The crowd shouted too, at the same time pressing forward, watching and waiting in an agony of impatience, so that when they were not shouting slogans they were absolutely still.

With a smart movement the militia obeyed the order to cock their rifles, and the crowd's tension increased even more. Then three or four militiamen took Schemer Qian up to the platform. He was wearing a lined gown of grey silk and white trousers, his hands tied behind him. His head was slightly lowered, and his small beady eyes were screwed up, searching the crowd. Those reptilian eyes of his which used to strike fear into people's hearts still cast a blight and quelled many of those present. His pointed moustaches made him look more sinister. Nobody said a word.

Members of the persidium looked at each other anxiously. Old Dong and other members of the work team exchanged anxious glances too and looked expectantly at Freckles Li, who in turn was looking expectantly at the members of the presidium who were looking at the crowd. The crowd was looking at Schemer Qian, and still not a word was said.

For thousands of years the local despots had had power. They had oppressed generation after generation of peasants, and the peasants had bowed their necks under their yoke. Now abruptly they were confronted with this power standing before them with bound hands, and they felt bewildered, at a loss. Some who were particularly intimidated by his malevolent look recalled the days when they could only submit, and now, exposed to this blast, wavered again. So for the time being they were silent.

All this time Schemer Qian, standing on the stage gnawing his lips, was glancing round, wanting to quell these yokels, unwilling to admit defeat. For a moment he really had the mastery. He and his many years of power had become so firmly established in the village it was difficult for anyone to dislodge him. The peasants hated him, and had just been cursing him; but now that he stood before them they held their breath and faltered. It was like the pause before two game-cocks start fighting, each estimating the other's strength. The longer the silence lasted, the greater Qian's power became, until it looked as if he were going to win.

At this point a man suddenly leapt out from the crowd. He had thick eyebrows and sparkling eyes. Rushing up to Schemer Qian he cursed him: "You murderer! You trampled our village under your feet! You killed people from behind the scenes for money. Today we're going to settle all old scores, and do a thorough job of it. Do you hear that? Do you still want to frighten people? It's no use! There's no place for you to stand on this stage! Kneel down! Kneel to all the villagers!" He pushed Qian hard, while the crowd echoed: "Kneel down! Kneel down!" The militiamen forced him to kneel down properly.

Then the masses' rage flared up, they tasted power and stirred indignantly. A child's voice was heard: "Put on the hat! Make him wear the hat!"

Young Guo jumped forward and asked: "Who'll put it on? Whoever'll put it on, come up here!"

While the crowd was shouting, "Make him wear the hat! Put on the hat!" a boy of thirteen or fourteen jumped up, lifted the hat and set it on Schemer Qian's head, at the same time spitting at him and cursing: "Here you are, Qian!" Then he jumped down amid laughter.

By now Qian had lowered his head completely, his malevolent eyes could no longer sweep their faces. The tall paper hat made him look like a clown. Bent basely from the waist, screwing up his eyes, he had lost all his power, had become the people's prisoner, a criminal against the masses.

The man who had cursed Qian turned now to face the crowd, and they all saw that it was Young Cheng, the chairman of the peasants' association.

"Friends!" said Young Cheng. "Look at him and look at me! See how soft and delicate he is: it's not cold yet but he's wearing a lined gown. Then look at me, look at yourselves. Do we look like human beings? Hah, when our mothers bore us, we were all alike! We've poured our blood and sweat to feed him. He's been living on our blood and sweat, oppressing us all these years; but today we want him to give back money for money, life for life, isn't that right?"

"Right! Give back money for money, life for life!"

"Don't let's be afraid of him any longer. Today we poor people are standing up! Let's forget our personal likes and dislikes. I'm chairman of the peasants' association. A few days ago I wasn't keen to struggle. I'm ashamed of myself, I forgot myself! I let all of you down. You can spit at me or beat me if you like and I won't say a word. I've seen light at last, and I want to settle scores with him. Since I was a child my mother and I went hungry. And all for what? In order to toil like a beast for him and become his running dog! It's no go! I must tell you — last night he even sent his wife to bribe me. Look, what do you think this is!" Young Cheng opened the white cloth bundle and shook out one title deed after another. Another roar rose from below, mingled with cries of amazement, rage, sympathy and approval.

"No! I'm not like that! I want to have a thorough settlement with that beast who feeds on human flesh! I've only one thought: I'm a poor man, I'm travelling with the poor, I'll follow Chairman Mao to the end of my way!"

"We peasants must unite! We must wipe out feudalism from the face of the earth!" Freckles Li had rushed to the front of the stage. The crowd shouted after him.

Yumin shook his fist too, and shouted: "Young Cheng is a good example for us all!"

"All peasants are brothers!" "Support Chairman Mao!" "Follow Chairman Mao to the end!" Shouts sounded from the stage and from the crowd.

Then people rushed up to the stage, stumbling over each other to confront Schemer Qian. Mrs. Qian stood with tear-stained cheeks behind her husband, pleading with them all: "Good people, have pity on my old man! Good people!" Her hair was dishevelled, there were no longer flowers in it, but the traces of black varnish could still be seen. She was like a female clown in the theatre, making a fine couple with her husband. She had echoed him all her life, and now she still clung to him, unwilling to separate their fates.

One accusation was brought after another. Liuman kept leading the crowd to shout slogans. Some peasants were so carried away that they climbed onto the stage and struck at Schemer Qian as they questioned him, while the crowd backed them up: "Beat him, beat him to death!"

Qian was helpless. Trying to extricate himself, he said: "Good people, I was guilty in every way. I admit everything, whether I did it or not. I only ask you to be generous!"

His wife too said tearfully: "For the sake of our son in the Eighth Route Army, don't be too hard on him!"

"Damn it!" Liuman jumped up. "Have *I* wronged *you*! Say, did you trick my father into starting that mill or not?"

"Yes, I did," Qian had to admit.

"Did you have my eldest brother conscripted or not?"

"Yes, I did."

"Did you drive my second brother mad or not?"

"Yes, yes."

"Have I condemned you wrongly?"

"No."

"Damn it! Then why should you say 'whether I did it or not'? Let's ask him what injustice there's been! What does he want us to take him for, damn him! Let me tell you, I'm going to thrash this out with you: you give me back my father, give me back my eldest brother. Give me back my second brother!"

"Let him pay with his life!" someone shouted. "Put him to death!"

Peasants surged up to the stage, shouting wildly: "Kill him!" "A life for our lives!"

A group of villagers rushed to beat him. It was not clear who started, but one struck the first blow and others fought to get at him, while those behind who could not reach him shouted: "Throw him down! Throw him down! Let's all beat him!"

One feeling animated them all — vengeance! They wanted vengeance! They wanted to give vent to their hatred, the sufferings of the oppressed since their ancestors' times, the hatred of thousands of years; all this resentment they directed against him. They would have liked to tear him with their teeth.

The cadres could not stop everyone jumping onto the stage. With blows and curses the crowd succeeded in dragging him down from the stage and then more people swarmed towards him. Some crawled over across the heads and shoulders of those in front.

Schemer Qian's silk gown was torn. His shoes had fallen off, the white paper hat had been trampled into pieces underfoot. All semblance of order was gone and it looked as though he was going to be beaten to death, when Yumin remembered Comrade Pin's last instructions and pushed his way into the crowd. Having no other way of stopping them, he shielded Qian with his body, and shouted: "Don't be in such a hurry to beat him to death! We've got to ask the county authorities!" Then the militiamen started checking the people.

The crowd was furious at seeing Yumin shelter Schemer Qian. They pressed forward together. Yumin was considerably knocked about but still he said to them: "I swear, there was a time I was afraid we couldn't get the better of him! Now you want to beat him to death, of course I'm pleased. I've long wanted to beat him to death to clean up our district! Only, there's been no order from our superiors and I don't dare. I daren't take the responsibility. A man can only be executed with the county court's approval. I'm asking you to delay it for a few days. Do it as a favour for me! Don't kill him yet; we'll punish him suitably later."

By now quite a few others had come over to help him keep the crowd back, and they said: "Yumin's quite right. A sudden end is too good for him. Let's make him suffer." A lot of people were persuaded, feeling that it was best to consult the county court before killing anyone, and since it was certain the county would grant the people's request, it did not matter waiting a few days. But still some of them were dissatisfied. "Why can't we kill him? The people want to kill him, what's to stop them?"

Old Dong stepped forward and addressed the crowd:

"Schemer Qian owes you money and lives. Just killing him won't make it up to you, will it?"

"If he died several deaths he couldn't make it up," someone said.

"Well, look," said Old Dong, "can he take any more beating?"

By this time Qian had already been carried back onto the stage. He lay there panting like a dying dog, and someone said: "Kill the dog."

"Bah! Killing's too good for him. Let's make him beg for death. Let's humble him for a few days, how about it?" Old Dong's face was red with excitement. He had started life as a hired labourer. Now that he saw peasants just like himself daring to speak out and act boldly, his heart was racing wildly with happiness.

"Right," someone agreed.

"If you don't pull the roots, a weed will always make trouble," another said.

"Are you still afraid of him? Don't be afraid. As long as we're united like today we can keep him in order. Think of a way to deal with him."

"Yes, I've a proposal. Let's have the whole village spit at him, what about that?"

"I say his property should be divided up among us all."

"Make him write a statement, admitting his crimes, and if he opposes us again, we'll have his life."

"Yes, let him write a statement. Make him write it himself."

Schemer Qian crawled to his feet again and kneeled to kowtow to the crowd. His right eye was swollen after his beating so that the eye looked even smaller. His lip was split and mud was mixed with the blood. His bedraggled moustaches drooped disconsolately. He was a wretched

315

sight, and as he thanked the villagers his voice was no longer clear and strong, but he stammered out: "Good people! I'm kowtowing to you good folks. I was quite wrong in the past. Thank you for your mercy...."

A group of children softly aped his voice: "Good people! ..."

Then he was dragged over to write a statement. He took the brush in his trembling hand and wrote line by line. Then everyone discussed the question of confiscating his property and decided to appropriate all, including that of Qianli. But they could not touch Yi's twenty-four *mu*. The peasants were dissatisfied, but this was an order from above, because Yi was a soldier in the Eighth Route Army! So they had to put up with it.

By now the sun was sinking. Hunger made some of the children so restless, they were kicking pebbles at the back of the meeting, and some of the women went quietly home to prepare a meal. The presidium urged Schemer Qian to hurry up and finish writing, saying everybody was tired of waiting for him, and asking where his usual ability had gone to.

When the chairman started reading the statement the crowd grew tense again, and shouted, "Let him read it himself!"

Qian knelt in the middle of the stage, his lined gown hanging in shreds, shoeless, not daring to meet anyone's eyes. He read: "In the past I committed crimes in the village, oppressing good people ... !"

"That won't do! Just to write 'I' won't do! Write 'local despot, Qian.'"

"Yes, write 'I, the local despot, Qian.'"

"Start again!"

Schemer Qian started reading again: "I, Qian, a local

despot, committed crimes in the village, oppressing good people, and I deserve to die a hundred times over; but my good friends are merciful. . . ."

"Who the devil are you calling your good friends?" An old man rushed forward and spat at him.

"Go on reading! Just say all the people of the village."

"No, why should he call us his people."

"Say all the gentlemen."

"Say all the poor gentlemen. We don't want to be rich gentlemen! Only the rich are called gentlemen."

Qian had to continue: "Thanks to the mercy of all the poor gentlemen in the village. . ."

"That's no good. Don't say poor gentlemen; today we poor people have stood up. Say 'the liberated gentlemen', and it can't be wrong."

"Yes, liberated gentlemen."

Someone chuckled. "Today we're liberated gentlemen!"

"Thanks to the mercy of the liberated gentlemen, my unworthy life has been spared. . . ."

"What? I don't understand." Another voice from the crowd interrupted Qian. "We liberated gentlemen aren't going to pass all this literary stuff. Just put it briefly: say your dog's life has been spared."

"Yes, spare your dog's life!" the rest agreed.

Qian had to go on: "Spare my dog's life. In future I must change my former evil ways completely. If I transgress in the slightest or oppose the masses, I shall be put to death. This statement is made by the local despot Qian, and signed in the presence of the masses. August 3."

The presidium asked the crowd to discuss it, but very few further amendments were proposed, although a few people still felt he was getting off too lightly and they ought to beat him some more.

Schemer Qian was allowed to go back. He was only permitted to live in Yi's house for the time being. All his property apart from his land was to be sealed up immediately by the peasants' association. As to the question of how much should be left him, that was left to the land assessment committee to decide.

Last of all a land assessment committee was elected. Everybody shouted Liuman's name. Young Guo was elected too. Orchard-keeper Li had made quite a good chairman, and he was elected too. Quan was an old peasant who knew more than anyone else about the acreage in the village, so he was also elected. He rubbed his bristling moustaches and said with embarrassment: "If you don't think I'm too old, and want me to do a job, how can I refuse!"

Co-op Tian was elected too, because he was good at using the abacus and quick-witted. Without him they would be in the soup with their accounts. Young Hou could calculate too, and he was young and not afraid of offending people, so he was nominated and elected. Last of all they elected the chairman of the peasants' association, Young Cheng. Cheng had refused Schemer Qian's bribe, staunchly leading them all in the struggle; they all supported such a peasants' association chairman.

By now land reform here could be considered as well under way. Although the peasants still had certain reservations, at least they had passed one large hurdle, and overthrown their greatest enemy. They intended to continue the struggle against the bad powers in the village, settling accounts with each in turn. They meant to stand up properly. They had the strength, as the events of the day made them realize. Their confidence had increased. Nuanshui was no longer the same as the previous day. As the meeting broke up they shouted for joy, a roar like thunder going up into the air. This was an end, it was also a beginning.

5 1

THAT day Old Gu had gone to the meeting like everyone else. At first he had stood in front of the wall, not far from Landlord Hou, but not wanting to be with that old fellow he had moved away to one side. However, he discovered there were several members of landlords' families near him, so moved away again and not wanting to excite attention mingled unobtrusively with the crowd. All around him people were exchanging views; some of them spoke to him too. At first he dared not answer, just listened. He knew they were to attack Schemer Qian today, and was pleased. But at the same time he was afraid of being attacked himself, because they had dubbed him a working landlord. When the meeting started and he saw Orchard-keeper Li was chairman, he felt reassured. Orchard-keeper Li was an honest fellow, and they were on good terms, having worked on the land together since they were children. After Old Gu had bought Li's orchard he often went there because, to begin with, he did not know how to look after it, and often asked Orchard-keeper Li's advice. They spent a good deal of time together, one looking after someone else's orchard, the other tending his own. Their friendship was the same as in their young days. No barrier had come between them because their way of life was approximately the same, both toiling hard. Old Gu felt that Orchard-keeper Li understood him and could never consider him a landlord, could never try to attack him or take vengeance. This being the case he was able to relax a little at the meeting, daring to look at the people round him and answer the questions they put to him. Sometimes he even joined in a discussion of his own accord.

Later, when Liuman went on to the stage, he felt great sympathy with the accusation he made. All Liuman's family had been ruined by Schemer Qian. If he failed to get vengeance there was no justice in the world. So he shook his fist along with the others. Later his son Young Gu suddenly started speaking, demanding that Qian make good the loss of their pear tree, claiming that Qian had forced his sister Er to marry into his family, and then bullied her and tried to seduce her. And this although she was his daughter-in-law! Listening to his son, Old Gu felt as happy as if he himself had spoken to relieve his feelings, and then worried because he felt it was not proper to say all this, it made them lose face. However, no one laughed at them, it only made the crowd angrier, shouting: "Shameless wretch! Old lecher!"

In the end he was completely carried away by the anger of the crowd, like a charging horse on the battlefield he followed along with the rest, shouting slogans, shaking his fist, his face crimson, forgetting his worries of the past fortnight, forgetting the odious name of working landlord. When Schemer Qian was pleading on the stage with averted face, calling out again and again: "Good people! Good people!" he laughed too, marvelling how times had changed. How had it come about? Had the world turned topsyturvy?... So he backed up everyone who went on to the stage, backed up every accusation and protest. He supported the Communist Party, for without the Communists this could never have happened. The Communists had done right!

When he went home after the meeting, all his family was there, still behaving as at the meeting, speaking one after the other. And the children in the middle were re-enacting the scenes they had enjoyed most, one cursing loudly: "There's no place for you to stand on this stage! Kneel down! Kneel to all the villagers!" Then another repeated tearfully: "Good people!" Meanwhile Young Gu was demanding loudly from the middle of the group: "Mum, Dad! All of you say: should we give up some of our land or not?" When Old Gu heard this, it was like a blow. All his excitement and pleasure melted away, leaving him standing speechless in the doorway, without the courage to go in.

And then Young Gu went on: "You tell me what's wrong with the Communists? They help poor people overthrow the local despots. Even we were able to get something off our chests. Our family has much more land than Schemer Qian but they haven't had a meeting to attack us, they haven't sent people to get our title deeds. You don't think it's because they're afraid of us, do you? We're so stubborn, hanging on to a few *mu* of land for dear life. I say it won't do! We'd better go while there's still time to see Yumin and the others. That'd look better than waiting for them to come here! What do you all say? Uncle! Dad! Where's Dad? Why isn't he back yet?"

"Brother's quite right. It doesn't matter having a little less land. Besides, it'll be divided between poor friends. What's the objection to that? That's my opinion," said Old Gu's elder daughter-in-law.

Some of the women started squabbling, and feeling ran high. Old Gu had no desire to discuss this question which he did not know how to answer, and hearing the others asking for him, he quietly made off. The street was empty. He strolled slowly back to the empty space in front of the stage. The ground was scattered with dusty melon-seed shells, fruit stones and a torn white paper hat, shreds of which were fluttering on the ground. Only the frame of the hat was left, with a few wisps of paper still sticking to it, blown here and there by the wind, but never flying far before falling to roll on the ground again. The place seemed the more desolate on account of its recent animation. Old Gu, feeling as unsettled as the broken paper hat, sat down on a piece of wood in front of the wall, looking round dubiously, wanting to rid himself of a little of his unhappiness. He did not oppose his son's proposal, but he had to think it over, and would have liked to ask: "Why should someone like me, who's worked hard all his life, be classified with Landlord Li and the rest? I count as a landlord because I've a lot of land, but I earned my land by the sweat of my brow, by my life's blood!" The name working landlord he had been given made him both uneasy and indignant, and he kept thinking: "I'm not going to give up the land. If you want it, come and take it; if you want to attack me, do."

Dusk was gathering. Flight after flight of crows flew overhead. But the old man kept sitting there, smoking pipe after pipe, looking round with his bleary eyes as if in search of something to comfort him.

After a while a rather stooped figure approached from the turning at the northeast corner, advancing slowly step by step, looking around too, but without catching sight of Old Gu. Old Gu saw it was not one of the villagers, but he recognized the man although he could not put a name to him. He got up and walked over to accost him. The stranger suddenly realized Old Gu's presence, and stood stockstill for a second, before calling out cheerfully: "Old Gu! How are you?"

At once Old Gu realized who it was, and seized his hand, saying in a voice shaking with emotion: "Oh, it's you, Old Hutai!" However at the same time he gripped him fearfully as if he had seen a ghost, looking round furtively as if to spy out the land, and went on softly: "Come home for a talk. How have things been going in your village?"

"The business at our village is over," answered Hutai calmly. "I've come for my cart. They know it's here. They say it's used for trade, and they don't want to confiscate it."

"Oh!" Old Gu looked at him in surprise, trying to read more proof of it in his face.

Hutai drew him along homewards, saying: "There's nothing to worry about! Haven't you finished here yet? People like us, they just say we're rich peasants, and hold a meeting asking us to offer a little of our own free will. I gave up sixty *mu* of land. They didn't want either of my carts, and left me the draught animals too so that I could go on doing business. They left me my sheep too. What about you? You're far below the mark because you never had a regular hired hand."

"I'm not clear. They haven't said anything yet. They took my fruit, and someone called me a working landlord." However he felt a gleam of hope, because Hutai's family was much richer than his. The Communists would surely apply the same standard everywhere!

He took Hutai home, and they talked well into the night. Hutai said it would not hurt a family like his to give up a few land. If they had too much land they couldn't cultivate it all themselves and would have to hire labourers, and now wages were high, it wasn't worth it. Since the Eighth Route Army's arrival business had been good. Being allowed to keep the cart was the best thing that could have happened to him. He hadn't oppressed anyone in the past, and so no one would bully him now. Formerly taxes had been high, and there had been so many bad people whom good people dared not offend — they had had a lot to put up with. But now equality was the word, and people could say what they liked. It was very fine. They had classified him as a rich peasant, but what did that matter, as long as he was

323

not a landlord? And Hutai advised Old Gu to go and have a talk with the work team, to get things straightened out. They couldn't consider him a landlord when all his family worked so hard. He couldn't even be called a rich peasant. Hutai also advised him to offer some land, saying not to do so was wrong, some poor people didn't have any at all. He had started as a poor man himself, and he ought to help the poor. Old Gu agreed with all he said. He listened happily, and promised to take Hutai's advice.

Then they spoke of the fighting. Hutai said he had seen a number of soldiers with his own eyes, travelling by train to Datong, taking some heavy artillery. Everybody said Datong was sure to be taken and everybody in Zhangjiakou was busy preparing for its capture. Every single person had sent comforts, and those who could write had written to the troops. Once Datong was captured business would be good. He also said that the people in his village had been timid before, but after overthrowing two local despots and beating and imprisoning a rumour-monger who was in league with the Kuomintang, nobody was afraid any more. Before that nobody dared speak, for fear lest if by any chance Chiang Kai-shek were to come back, they should be under their thumb again. Hutai also said Chiang Kai-shek was no good, he couldn't come back. They had the Eighth Route Army men in their village who were in high spirits, both men and horses were in fine fettle. All the Kuomintang troops were conscripted to fight against their will, and were no good. The Kuomintang regular army in the Qinglong Bridge area was no match even for our guerrillas!

As soon as it was light the next day, Old Gu got out the cart and saw Hutai off, accompanying him to the river. And as he watched White Nose drawing the cart into the river he remembered how things had been a month before. He trusted the Communists not to treat him badly. They were right to help the poor. If only all this had happened when he was young and poor! He shouted out good wishes for his business to Hutai who was already in mid-stream. Hutai turned his head to look at him, and said something in reply which he could not catch, but he understood its intention. Their life in the new society could only be easier. Then he went back, stretching his neck to look at his land not far off. And when he saw the plot he intended to give up, it no longer made him feel bad. He simply felt relaxed like a man who has just put down a heavy load.

5 2

WHEN Old Gu went to the peasants' association to offer some of his land, the co-operative was packed tightly with people. The courtyard was overcrowded and there were rows of people standing outside the gate. Each person had his own particular request, and all wanted to see the cadres, hoping to have their problems settled right away. One could not make oneself heard inside. When he saw how many people there were Old Gu felt rather alarmed, but screwing up his courage he squeezed his way in. He asked if Yumin were there or not, but no one answered him. He asked for Young Cheng, but again there was no answer. It had been hard enough squeezing his way in, but now there was no one responsible to be seen, only Bugao was sitting on the *kang*, surrounded by people telling him how much land they had.

"We've made a record," said Bugao. "We know."

But still they would tell him again: "My land's arid soil! And it's far off, can't you give me another piece in exchange?" Then Bugao wrote down the request so that he could pass it on to the land assessment committee. Another was explaining how he rented land from another village, asking what would happen to that land. Then Bugao wrote him a letter of introduction telling him to go to the other village to ask for the title deeds, because once he had the deeds everything would be plain sailing.

Old Gu stood there for quite a time, but no one paid any attention to him. Bugao was too busy even to look at him, so he was again at a loss. He was afraid of saying something wrong in front of all these people which would antagonize them. What could he do then? He squeezed his way out again, and when he got to the street he began to hesitate. Seeing a number of people walking towards the primary school, he followed them.

The bare side-court had been cleaned up, and all the members of the land assessment committee were there. This place was crowded too with people, some of whom had business, some of whom had not; but they hung about out of curiosity. Still Old Gu dared not go over, but watched for some time from a distance. He knew all the people there. They were all good people, and he would not have been afraid to speak to any one of them alone. But now they were together in a group, with some of the comrades from the district backing them up, and they seemed suddenly to have increased in stature, to have become real powerful executives, not too timid or humble but chatting and laughing. None of them had seen him. They let him go on standing at a distance, and he felt now even Orchard-keeper Li looked down on him. So he started growing nervous again, and walked slowly back, thinking: "Well, leave it to fate. I'm ready to do what you want."

Actually the men in the courtyard were just discussing him. The previous evening the cadres and land assessment committee members had held another meeting to determine the class status of all the families in the village again. There were altogether eight landlord families. In the past a few had been wrongly classified. The masses were disputing his category, some of them still thinking he ought to be classified as a landlord, while others said he should be a well-to-do middle peasant. Judging by the amount of labour he hired he should only have been classified as a well-to-do middle peasant, but in the end he was carelessly put down as a rich peasant. They ought to take part of his land, but as to which part, whether good land or bad, that was left to the land assessment committee to decide. So now the land assessment committee was busy estimating the acreage of the landlords and at the same time calculating what land to take from the rich peasants, Old Gu included.

Over the question of the differentiation of class status the work team and cadres had had some argument. Yang advocated leaving the peasants' association to decide, but there was no time for that. Comrade Pin had said that the distribution of land ought to be completed within from five days to a week before the mid-autumn festival, because if the work were not finished by then it would delay the harvest. Besides there was a bigger problem to consider — the war situation on the Beijing-Suiyuan Railway. So this matter, important as it was, could only be decided by a meeting of new and old cadres. Not waiting to find out reactions to their decisions, they began to take action. Naturally some mistakes were made. Some people had no chance to express their views, while some, obsessed with their own affairs, kept accosting the cadres and the land assessment committee, until the noise and confusion in the courtyard were extreme.

Tenant Hou had come too today, bringing two title deeds to show Yumin. His eyes were dancing as he looked at them.

Without giving him a chance to speak, Young Hou called out: "Go home! What did you come here for?" He thought his father was looking for him to forbid him to serve on the committee, and to call him home.

The old man only chuckled, and mumbled: "Oh, who could have thought it! What's the world coming to!" Everybody asked him what the matter was, telling him to explain slowly, whereupon he told them of his adventure that morning.

Early that morning he had just left his room, when he became aware of someone standing outside the house, and asked: "Who's there?" There was no answer, so he asked again, and the man walked in. It was someone who had never called on him before, so he was surprised and at once asked him in, greeting him: "Oh! Uncle Hou! Uncle . . . please come in and sit down."

Landlord Hou said not a word but followed him inside and instead of sitting on the *kang* forced Tenant Hou to sit there instead, then hurriedly kowtowed to him, and begged him: "Cousin! You must save me! In the past all my family has done injustice to you. Please be generous. I'm old now, I can't stand being attacked. You can have whatever you like." He sighed.

Tenant Hou was frightened, and quickly took hold of him to lift him up, but couldn't raise him, so he said: "Sit down and tell me about it, sit down!" With great difficulty he managed to make the old man get up, but the latter definitely refused to sit on the *kang*. He squatted on the ground, so Tenant Hou squatted down with him. They were both getting on in years and couldn't squat long, so presently they sat down on the ground. Seeing how excessively humble the other was, Tenant Hou felt ill at ease and said reassuringly: "What are you afraid of? We're all one family. After all these years the old ties count. I would never make things

328

difficult for you. Don't be afraid, that son of mine is a bad fellow."

By this time Tenant Hou's wife had come in. Landlord Hou kowtowed to her too till she was quite bewildered, and leant dumbfounded against the door. Then Hou apologized again for having done injustice to them in the past, speaking them fair while demanding a great deal of them and never lifting a finger to help them, letting them live virtually as beggars. He thrust two title deeds at Tenant Hou for over twelve *mu* of land, insisting on his accepting them, saying he was old and begging them to let him off, to put in a good word for him to the cadres. Tenant Hou dared not keep the title deeds, but Landlord Hou knelt down again and refused to get up till he accepted them.... The old rogue even cried. After putting on this act he finally left, to visit another of his tenants, intending to plead from house to house and so get through this difficult period safely, because he had been frightened by the trial the previous day. He realized the masses had arisen, and that if he made the least false step they could crush him like a bedbug.

After Landlord Hou had left, Tenant Hou and his wife looked at each other, afraid it was all a dream. They turned the title deeds over and over, then hurried to the door to look, and both laughed, laughed till they cried. Tenant Hou sat on the steps wiping his tears as he remembered all the hardships of his life. He had led camels in the desert, buffeted by wind and snow, he had trudged innumerable sand-dunes in the wilds, and as he plodded along his hopes had faded away like the horizon at evening. He remembered how when he fell ill and nearly died, he had thought it would be better to die, but he had recovered, and that was worse than dying. Gradually he had become fatalistic and looked for truth in a future life, comforting himself with this illusion. But now the future life was being realized in the present, his reward had come so quickly! He had never dreamed of this, never dared think of it. He ought to be happy, and indeed he was, only this happiness was more than he could bear, so that he was shedding tears of joy. He had come to life again, he could feel like a human being again, he was no longer a cranky old devil.

However his wife was muttering by his side: "Are you giving them back to him? Going to give them back to him?"

With a great effort Tenant Hou controlled himself and walked out with the title deeds, his agitated wife following him, still saying: "Are you still so stubborn! You still don't dare take them! Do you still believe that religious talk of his?"

"No," he said. "I'm going to the peasants' association. I want to tell them. I want to tell a lot of people, the world's really changed! Ho!..."

When they had heard his account, everybody laughed, and said, "Why didn't you ask him whether he was rich because that was his fate?" Another said: "Uncle Hou, you won't be going to heaven with him now!" Someone else praised him: "He's too straightforward, this old fellow. He's been trampled on all his life, but now at last he's coming to his senses!"

Young Hou laughed too and said, "Dad, Buddha has nothing to do with us. We burned incense every year, but he never paid the least attention. Yet as soon as Chairman Mao gave the order, people came here to give us land. Chairman Mao's our Buddha. In the future if we worship anyone it should be Chairman Mao. Don't you agree, Dad?"

Tenant Hou only grinned silently. Finally somebody asked him, "You'll have your share of the land. Will you give it back again?"

He shook his head vigorously, and answered: "No! No! Didn't that mass meeting yesterday bring me to my senses?" He chuckled.

News of these happenings spread to encourage the peasants and increase their confidence.

53

THE peasants did not go to the fields that day, but wandered about in groups to look for the village cadres or the work team. Or else, having discussed things among themselves, they went to tell the village cadres of their discussion, or repeated some confused opinions they had heard; and in this way they kept interrupting the work of the land assessment committee. The cadres grew desperate, and shouted: "Now you're on your feet, are you going to do without law and order? If so, you come and do this job yourselves." They proposed ignoring the masses, and pasted a notice on the door: "No admittance except on business." Yang said that was no good, they ought to listen to the people's views. The cadres did not like to contradict him, and just said: "It's no good being too democratic. That way nothing'll get done. There's no end to views."

Then Yang talked it over with Yumin, and they opened up another place for office work and meetings. They cleared up Landlord Jiang's three north rooms. There was a big locust tree in his courtyard through which not a ray of sun could penetrate, and under which a crowd might gather. Landlord Jiang and his woman had moved back to their old quarters. Most of the place was empty. There was only a poor relative living there to look after the house for him, although Jiang still asked him for rent. The peasants' association started working here, Yang and Hu remodelling the organization, dividing people into groups and choosing new group leaders. All problems had to be brought to these group meetings. When anyone spoke the others judged whether his view was right or wrong, and the group leaders reported it, and when there was any business they held a meeting of group leaders. Thus everyone was satisfied, saying this was better than going one by one to find Yumin.

Bugao could not look after all the details of organization by himself, so Young Han helped him. Yang and Hu went in turns to the different groups, and Yumin attended when he had time. Wen spent all his time with the land assessment committee, helping them divide up the land, until he saw how lively the group meetings were, and then he sometimes went over to join them. The group membership increased daily, and it was no longer a case of only one from each family. Then they set up additional groups, including women's groups, and the women held meetings too. After the meal they tidied up and gathered together. Yang wanted each to speak of her past grievances and sufferings. It seemed as if they would never finish, and each one cried, speaking of her hard lot.

Gui had no reservations now. Her husband Vineyard Li had told her: "When there's nothing to do, spend all the time you can at the meeting. I've got a meeting too. Landlord Xu won't be coming back, or even if he does I'm not afraid. If he does come we'll deal with him as we did with Schemer Qian, and if he's really re—re—reactionary, he won't get off with his life! Comrade Pin says we should check up thoroughly on his connections. Why, even Tenant Hou isn't scared. We needn't be afraid of anything."

Not only the women but the men too, the older men in particular, liked to talk about the past and describe their

332

hard lot. Some had regretted not speaking at the mass meeting and now they spoke in the groups. There was no longer any sympathy for the landlords, and Li's wife no longer dared to stand at the head of the street. If she showed her face outside men laughed at her: "Oh, even if she pays we're not interested! Making eyes at people all the time, wanting to make a cuckold of her husband!" And Landlord Hou was like a field-mouse, no longer daring to sit in the sun at the foot of the wall.

The landlords had lost all their power to awe, while their running dogs were calling on people right and left, smiling servilely and admitting their faults. Landlord Xu's confederate Rong, afraid he could not escape being attacked, voluntarily sent a letter of repentance to the peasants' association.

The more the peasants thought of their sufferings, the more they hated their oppressors, and the more united they became among themselves. However, they could not spend all their time attacking Some relatively minor offences were overlooked. People still had to concern themselves with their own affairs. Not all the fruit had been sold, and teams had to be organized to handle the work. Co-op Tian, Young Hou, and Orchard-keeper Li were all at the land assessment committee, so other people had to be found. However that was not difficult; everybody was glad of a chance to help. The few small traders and pedlars in the village were brought in to take part. Then things went even more smoothly, and in two or three days everything was finished. The apples and pears had not been sold, but the sweet-apples alone had realized between seven and eight million dollars. Some people suggested this money be used to buy draught animals for the poor, some proposed sinking a proper well. However everybody was afraid not to have a share, and finally in accordance with the wishes of the majority the money was divided up. Yang judged they would soon be leaving this village and unless they settled the matter now, there was bound to be trouble later, so he agreed to the general wish, and the money was divided up according to each family's size and situation. The land assessment committee was so busy that it entrusted this work to the group leaders.

Only a little of the furniture, implements and grain of the eight landlord families was left them. All the rest was taken out, registered and numbered. In the small groups people discussed their own needs and how these things should be distributed. It was easy for them to see eye to eye in attacking local despots, but when their own interests were involved, they wanted too much and got worked up, each hoping for a good share. So the group meetings were held more often and became more heated. Problems had to be solved there. Day by day they were learning one lesson — that in attacking an enemy one must be firm and ruthless, while among comrades there must be mutual consideration. That was the only way to achieve unity and not make a laughing-stock of themselves to the landlords.

Some people realizing this, said: "Yes, it's impossible to have absolute justice. The river water's comparatively level, but the river bed is still irregular, and the surface is ruffled with waves. We're all on the same hand, even though the fingers are of different lengths." Some could talk all right, but in their hearts they were still calculating how they could get on good terms with the land assessment committee, in order to get a little more land, or better land.

The militiamen intensified their training. They were all poor men who left their own work to stand guard or serve as sentries day and night, and attended meetings too. They despised selfishness and greed, and cursed these people: "The poor can be blinded by possessions too. Once you're rich see if you don't squeeze other people, and then we'll attack you too!" They had a glorious history, they had formed the front line in the war of resistance against Japan, had caught traitors, and now they wanted to be the people's guard, so that not a single bad man dare stir in their village. More and more militiamen were joining the Party. Their small corps was a strong bulwark for the village.

Swarthy Guo was the militiamen's model. When there was no grain at home he went secretly to borrow some, afraid that if the work team knew they might give him some of the victory grain. Later Yang came to hear of this, and questioned him, and Swarthy Guo blushed all over his face but stubbornly refused to admit it. He was thinking: "What a nuisance that Comrade Yang has found out. I wasn't trying to get a good name for myself."

However, among certain of the cadres there grew a tendency to selfishness. And a lively scene was enacted at the land assessment committee.

54

AFTER the small group meetings started being held, fewer people had gone to the land assessment committee. So the committee members were able to carry out the preparatory work of land distribution quite smoothly, estimating the amount of land available for distribution and classifying it, also estimating the number of families to distribute it to and classifying them. All the committee members were honestly disinterested and anxious to play fair. This was particularly true of Quan, who had no children of his own while Yumin, the nephew he had brought up, was already a grown man and had become a village cadre. With a few fruit trees of his own he was quite contented. His one thought was: "Chairman Mao is concerned for us so far away. How can we neglect our own village affairs? If we make everyone live better, Chairman Mao needn't worry so much!" He was a good old man, but his memory was faulty. He wanted to give everyone some good land, so whenever he went home to eat peasants often came to see him, and he would reassure them: "Don't worry, folks, you won't be left out. I promise to put in a word for you; but it's not for me to decide. It's everybody's business." However when they came to distribute land he would say: "Give him irrigated land, his family's short of hands." Or else: "Oh, he's a poor chap, he's never had anything good. Let it be irrigated land." Yumin often scolded him: "See here, do we have anyone here who isn't poor? There's only so much land. The good and bad all have to be matched." Or he would simply exclaim: "Heavens, you'd better rest for a while, Uncle."

Few people dropped in on the land assessment committee now, only the cadres still came regularly. The success of their mass accusation meeting had given the cadres confidence. They felt themselves the masters of the whole village with power to do anything, hence they stopped paying much attention to Wen's advice. Since they were all brothers together, Young Cheng and Yumin found it very difficult to send them away. They would come and stand about for a while listening or putting in a few words, which sometimes were helpful. Only because they were always around, each time the question of their share of land came up, the land assessment committee felt they must give them good land, regardless of their families' condition. The cadres themselves did not say anything, that is, they did not object. At such times Wen would say earnestly: "Uncle Quan, don't always be so soft. Of course the cadres are all our own people but you've got to see whether they're badly off or not. Don't make people say we show favouritism. That would mean our work was in vain."

Quan would tug at his beard in embarrassment and look at everybody, while no one said a word. Young Guo was the keenest of them all, but even he said: "The cadres are a little different. They're caring for us year in and year out, working away harder than anyone, sacrificing hours of their time! I think we ought to let it go at that."

And Orchard-keeper Li would join in: "Yes, they're good servants of the state. They ought to be rewarded for their labours. . . ."

Yumin often attended the group meetings. He realized the masses were watching the cadres carefully, and all business would have to be passed by them, but he spent little time at the land assessment committee and could not supervise the work. It was Young Cheng who should have played a decisive part there. But ever since that evening when Young Cheng had made up his mind to overcome his former scruples and exposed Schemer Qian's plot at the meeting, proving his own honesty and thereby doing much to arouse the masses, everybody felt he was a stout fellow, and he was pleased with his popular support, feeling he had not let the masses down. He wanted to do his job even better, he wanted to do as the comrades of the work team said. And so indeed he did. He attended meetings punctually, did not quarrel with anyone and swept the place himself. But he did not like talking, and at times when he should have upheld certain views he remained silent. As to the reason for this, no one knew or paid any attention. Since the mass meeting, along with his positive ideas he had felt a certain uneasiness. He often gritted his teeth secretly, thinking: "Oh, hang it all, anyway I've let her down!" He was thinking of Heini. He did not know how she was getting on these days with her uncle Qian. She must hate him. He was sorry he had forgotten to look out for her at the mass meeting, and wondered where she had been standing. Probably with the women's class. He wondered what she had felt when her uncle was hooted and cursed and beaten by the crowd. She was a poor orphan. She'd had a hard life of it with her bad uncle, and now things must be even worse for her. For him, Young Cheng, to attack Schemer Qian was right, but he had not helped her, in fact he had forced her into an unpleasant position. He felt very bad about this, but had not the courage to ask after her. Nor could he put her out of his mind. He was in a dilemma and it hampered his keenness in work. He was not as strong as he had hoped. He often followed the crowd.

Originally there was one man here who was firm and not affected by friendship or face. That was Liuman. But because of his anxiety and irregular life for the last three weeks and because he had used up his energy in the fight acting as a shock trooper, when victory was won he was exhausted. He felt tired out, his head and chest ached, sitting down for a short time made him uncomfortable, and he had to slip out to the porch at the back to sleep. It was shady under the tree and quiet, so he made his mind a blank like someone who has been ill for a long time, staring at the sky between the branches. If others criticized him, he would just rub his chest gently, answering without words. He had to rest. It was the only way to restore his nerve.

One day they came to discuss Organization Zhao's share of land while he happened to be there, and allotted him two *mu* of orchard and two *mu* of irrigated land on the hill. But Zhao did not want the orchard, so they found him two and a half *mu* of irrigated land instead. Zhao thought it was too little, and kept complaining, so Quan told him it was good land, the water channels were good too, and advised him to accept it, because it was not easy to find anything just right. Still Zhao refused.

It happened that Trade Union Qian was there, and he said bluntly: "If he doesn't want it, I do. You give it to me." They agreed, and after looking for a long time found another bigger piece of irrigated land for Zhao. Then Zhao was delighted and hurried to see what it was like. But when he saw it he was annoyed again: this plot of land was not bad, but it was too near the river, part of it was submerged, and part was in danger of submersion. He lost his temper and rushed back, shouting as he came in:

"What kind of fool do you think you're making of me?" Then he wanted the land they had given Trade Union Qian. They urged him to take the orchard land, but he refused. They talked it over with Trade Union Qian, but he would not give up his plot, saying:

"Do you think land reform is only for your benefit? That you can pick any land you please?"

Zhao had never thought much of this simple fellow, so now he said fiercely: "Why won't you give it to me? Are you still counting on your cousin's influence? Before, just because you were relatives we couldn't attack him. Now that we've carried it off you want land too, but you don't deserve any!"

At this Trade Union Qian saw red. Furious at having the truth distorted, he shouted: "Fine! All right, let's exchange our land! Let's exchange all we've got, and see who's really poor! Last year you got half a *mu* of Landlord Xu's orchard land and bought nearly six *mu* of vineyard. This spring you got one and four-fifths *mu* of land, and you had three *mu* of irrigated land on the hill to begin with. Yet you call yourself a poor peasant! Didn't I join in the struggle the same as you? This spring I got four-fifths of a *mu* of land and a picul of grain. Let's exchange! If we exchange, exchange everything, or else nothing at all!"

"You say I'm not a poor peasant — am I a landlord? All right, you come and attack me. You want to take my land, fine! You want to avenge your cousin!"

"Damn you! Don't try to bully people!" Trade Union Qian rushed over to hit him.

Orchard-keeper Li and Quan grabbed them both and urged: "Don't quarrel. You'll have people laughing at you."

Young Guo took hold of Trade Union Qian, while Young Hou restrained Zhao. Co-op Tian was a taciturn type but even he could not help being angry now. He pushed away his abacus, threw down his brush, and cursed: "We're working for the whole village, not for selfish people like you. I'm quitting. Let's have a meeting and re-elect officers. I'm quitting!"

Young Cheng lost his temper too: "It really is disgraceful! Comrade Wen said we shouldn't let you in, but you insisted on coming, just worrying about your bits of land. You've made us cadres lose face! Get out, all of you, this is no place for you to fight! Go outside to fight!" Then, changing his tune: "Friends, have we forgotten that we're brothers to death? How did we come to quarrel? We must be of one heart. If our unity is destroyed for an inch or so of land, can we be said to have risen up? Let's say no more about it. When Comrade Wen comes back he'll criticize us. We cadres must be content with whatever piece of land we're given, and if we're not given any we'll not ask for any. Look at Yumin. He's never been given a single piece of land. He got a picul of grain this spring which he finished up long ago, but he didn't say anything. We ought to learn from him." Like Yumin, he received only one picul of grain.

The two of them took the others' advice and stopped

340

quarrelling. Organization Zhao knew that he was in the wrong and that nobody sympathized with him, so he slipped away, saying, "Don't give me any land. I don't want anything. I've lived all these years without standing up, and without starving to death. It doesn't matter if I don't stand up."

Trade Union Qian did not go, but sat down fuming. He did not say anything, but thought: "I suppose I shall suffer all my life on account of my cousin."

News of this spread before Wen came back from the groups. One person told another, until it spread to different households. Discussion started in lanes and courtyards, one person urging another: "We can't leave this in the hands of a few land assessment committee members. If they won't report to us let's all refuse land, and let just the cadres stand up. We won't attend any meetings in future, and see whose cadres they are!"

Only when Wen and Yang announced that land distribution would have to be approved by the peasants' association, did the villagers become cheerful again. They also helped the group leaders to divide up the portable property without delay.

55

LIKE ants moving to a new home, the villagers were carrying furniture through various lanes to different households, assembling things according to their kind. They carried, shouted, laughed and cursed, squabbling together like children, some of them chewing dried fruit from other people's courtyards. Women stood in the street watching the fun, and children tagged along. When all the things had been collected, people were allowed to look at them. Every family went to have a look. The women followed the men, daughters-in-law behind their mothers-in-law, daughters with their mothers, mothers carrying their babies. They pointed at the things. The mothers pointed at the brand-new wardrobes, red lacquer chests and a pair of big flower vases, which would be fine things for their daughters' dowry. They fell in love with the tables, then with the chairs. That clock was a beauty, and it would strike the hours so cheerfully every day! Then they coveted the clothes; they had never seen such pretty coloured materials. It would be nice to buy one length for their daughters, one for their daughters-in-law, everything fair. Of course the young wives liked these things too. They would like to have a gown each, so they need not worry about clothes at New Year. Some old women just wanted a big jar or pitcher. Then with another container, sieve and bamboo basket, they'd have a complete set.

The men were quite indifferent to these things. They went to look at the big ploughs, wooden ploughs, boxes, grain sifters and harrows. After looking at one category of goods in one courtyard they went to look at another category in another courtyard. The not-so-poor went to look too, and the militiamen kept a watch, not allowing anyone to touch anything. When they got home, old couples would say: "Oh, you can't have everything you want. There's only a limited amount of things. We can only ask for what we need, not for anything we can get along without. If we ask for more they won't give it."

"Right, there are too many people, and everybody'll have to get something."

People hurried to look and to comment, and were in a hurry to divide the things. The group leaders made an inventory of everything, and allotted so much to each group.

The members of each group consulted together over their lists of requirements and the goods allotted. Everybody discussed it together, and when nobody had any more to say, the group leaders distributed slips they had brought, with the names of goods and their numbers, which people were to take to the appointed place to collect the goods. There was no possibility of mistake. This had been thought out by the whole community, because all lacked experience. The small groups had been rather slack at first, with poor attendance and a good deal of back-biting. But after this business came up, they felt it was best to speak out in the meetings, so more and more people attended, and were punctual. There were many different opinions which had to be discussed by the whole group before they could be passed. Thus the group meetings began to be taken more seriously. Nobody dared be casual, and the business went ahead swimmingly. In a few days their preparations were complete, and they were just waiting for the word to collect the things.

Wen and Yang saw pretty well eye to eye by now. The power and wisdom of the masses had corrected much of Wen's self-importance and self-righteousness. As he sat in the land assessment committee listening to arguments he might speak on a matter of principle, but he could not settle specific problems. The villagers were familiar with the acreage. When one person mentioned a plot of land the others knew what he was talking about: where it was, how it should be classified, how large it was, whose land it abutted on, where the water channels were and how big a crop could be raised. They knew the people too: who cultivated the land, what the landlord was like, what the peasant was like and whom the plot would suit. It was difficult for Wen to join in their animated discussions. He thought of helping with records, but did not know people's names; he thought of helping with reckoning, but although he knew a little geometry and trigonometry, Co-op Tian's abacus was much faster than his calculations. It was the same with the division of goods. At first he did not know how they should be distributed, and was afraid everybody would quarrel, all fighting for the same thing. However, together they had thought out a way; this improved the people's morale, and no one was dissatisfied.

He also overcame some of his prejudice against Yang and Hu. They enjoyed better prestige among the masses than he because they acted more like the people, while he could never rid himself entirely of his offensive intellectual's airs. He thought the masses difficult to approach and often did not know what to say to them. There was no barrier, however, between Comrade Pin and the masses; he understood them and could make decisions for them. Although so young he was remarkably able. This was the outcome of his knowledge of the mass movement and his firm stand. When no longer dared to dismiss him as a mere youngster; he had to accord him respect. Of course Wen was still very easy-going, subjective and prone to give himself airs, but he was gradually reforming himself and learning to get on with other people. That day he praised the masses' intelligence with the other cadres, and went to see each place where goods were kept, laughing and smiling with everybody else.

The distribution of land was nearly finished, and lists had been posted up in the main street for everyone to comment on. They decided to distribute things on the fourteenth of the eighth lunar month, and to discuss land distribution in the evening, to issue land tickets on the fifteenth, together with the money from the sale of fruit. On the evening of the fifteenth everyone would rest, on the sixteenth they would measure the land, and as soon as that was done it would be time to harvest the crops. The harvest could not be delayed; all the hurry had been on account of this. And after that Yang and the others could go back to report on their work to the county authorities, and then return to their old jobs.

On the fourteenth, people who had slips prepared what was necessary to remove the goods. Some had brought rope and poles; some brought sacks and had arranged for help. When the time came, the women turned out too. This time the distribution was very general. A number of families who ought to be considered middle peasants got a jar or a mirror, so there were a great many going to collect. The group leaders were responsible at the different centres to check the slips and see the goods taken away. The numbers and names must tally. To leave the courtyard people must have a new slip with a chop on it. With everything in good order nothing could go wrong.

All the members of the work team and the land assessment committee were there. Having finished their distribution of land they had nothing to do. Some of them also came to take their shares of things. Yang and Hu helped a good many of the people who had come to move things, asking as they did so: "Is there any more?" The place swarmed with people, and as the slips had to be checked the passage was often blocked. The women crowded round the clothes, bedding and kitchen utensils. Because they could not read, they just handed in their slips. If they were not satisfied with what they got they would look at something better, and shout: "That's wrong! I don't want this, this gown is too old." Women who got good clothes beamed with happiness, holding the gown up against themselves to see how it would look. Those who got old-fashioned, embroidered red gowns doubled up with laughter, while the bystanders started cracking jokes. The distribution of this pile of things was no easy matter. Two men group leaders who could read, as well as some women, stood supervising the distribution.

Yue, the shepherd's wife, was standing here in a broken straw hat, still wearing her old man's white vest, issuing directions with half a kaoliang stalk in her hand. In the mass accusation meeting she had led the other women to beat Schemer Qian. She was pointing here and there in the crowd, giving directions, the red bracelets with artificial pearls on her wrist flashing as she moved. Those rough women's hands had always been busy with pots and pans, stoves and troughs, steeped in water or working on the land; those hands roughened by wind and rain had been raised to beat the cruel representative of the ruling class! It had been a moving sight, and she herself had been moved. After that action she seemed less easily angry than before, and lost her temper with the shepherd less, becoming gentler; while the shepherd, because he was concerned in the distribution of land, spent more time at home. She was not so sharp with other people either. In this distribution of things a good many of the women worked very hard, and Yue had proved her ability again.

Two gowns fell to the share of Vice-Head Zhao's wife too. She put on one of blue cotton which fitted her all right and looked very well, carrying another white one in her hand, as well as a length of patterned material. Patting the smooth cloth over her breast as she walked she asked everyone she met, "What cloth is this? Look how fine it is, how even!"

Young Cheng went from place to place to watch the fun, rejoicing to see people going home with their arms full. He himself had been given some implements and grain, and Freckles Li was helping him carry them back. Freckles Li had four large flower vases himself. As they were striding out they bumped into Hu, who said: "What do you want those for?"

Freckles Li shook his head and said smiling: "Nobody wanted them, so I said I'd have them."

Someone in the crowd laughed and said: "Aren't you getting them for your half pint? Why didn't you ask for a pretty dress for the wedding this winter?" Li's freckled face turned red, but he strode off without answering.

"Who's the half pint?" asked Hu.

"His little wife-to-be," answered the other, laughing.

"The half pint!" Hu laughed too.

They saw Sheng's mother in the crowd carrying a brace of fowl, hobbling this way and that, looking for people to talk to. When she saw Wen she hurried over, and greeted him: "Comrade! You've taken so much trouble, and you've thought of everything. This way everybody's got something."

Wen smiled back and asked her: "Do you have any hens? I see you've got a cock here!"

"Hens! Oh yes, I have several. I bought them as chicks and raised them, but these, well, these are revolutionary fowl." This made a lot of people laugh.

"Didn't you get anything else?" Wen asked.

The woman came closer and said with a wink: "Oh, of course I did. I'm an army dependent, I got five pecks of grain same as all army dependents. When the crops are gathered in I shan't lack. You see, Comrade Wen, I had to take it. They only give it to army dependents. It's for face, isn't it?"

Yang standing by felt very amused, and laughed: "Hurry up home! Bring up your two revolutionary fowl properly!"

There were some people squeezing past carrying big containers. Strong youngsters could carry them single-handed, but some were so large it took two people to carry them.

Inside, an old man was circling round a black water-container, trying to think of a way to carry it off, but in vain. Young Cheng could not make out who it was. He decided to go and help him, but he had only taken a few steps when he heard a familiar voice at his side, saying: "Uncle, we've still got a vase. Come and see, isn't it a beauty! It's white porcelain!" Young Cheng stopped, and saw Heini squeezing through the crowd, still wearing the same blue gown. She had not seen him, and hurried happily over, lifting up a vase to show her uncle. Wenfu laughed with her, nodded and said: "Heini! First think of a way to take this container. We thought it was a small one, so we didn't bring any rope."

"I'll carry it on my back, Uncle," Heini answered. "You take the vase." So saying she picked up the container, laughed again heartily, and said: "This container's from our house, Uncle. I know it quite well, Uncle Qian bought it that year from the county town. It's a good container. See how thick the glaze is. . . ."

"Well, Heini, don't keep chattering, put it on my back."

"No, I'll take it."

"Come on . . . let me have it."

"It's too heavy for you, Uncle, better let me. . . ."

Young Cheng stood dazed. This unexpected encounter bewildered him for a moment. He thought, "Why, she's still so happy! What's she happy about?" Then he realized, as if suddenly waking up from a dream, how ridiculous his past worries had been. "Why shouldn't she be happy? She used to be a poor child. When Schemer Qian was attacked, the people he had oppressed were liberated. Wasn't she one of the liberated? How could she be in the same boat with him?"

Then Young Cheng felt like a released fighter. He rushed over to Wenfu, and said loudly: "Uncle, let me carry it for you." Without waiting for his consent, he hoisted the container on to his back. The old man looked at him, spreading his hands, not knowing what to say, while Heini turned her face away as if to dissociate herself from them. Then Wenfu followed him slowly out, muttering to himself: "Well, well!" Heini had stopped smiling, and walked some distance behind them in silence. And a crowd of people pressed after them.

Presently all the things had been taken away, but what a scene in the courtyards and hitherto empty rooms of the peasants' houses! Some small rooms were stuffed with red lacquer furniture. In the peasants' own houses these things naturally looked much better than in the place for distribution, much more delightful. Every lane or street was filled with happy laughter.

56

THAT evening, during the meeting of the peasants' association, Old Dong came back from the district sweating from his walk, presenting a strange appearance for a cool autumn evening. Without waiting for the meeting to finish he took Wen out and gave him a letter. He had brought news of the raising of the siege of Datong. The attack on Datong was being excellently carried out, and in a few days the city should be taken. Only Fu Zuoyi had brought up reinforcements, and although the Communists had wiped out some of his men at Zhuozishan and another division at Fengzhen, still he had led his cavalry into Fengzhen. Zhangjiakou lay between two battlefronts, and the capture of Datong would not solve this problem. Confronted with this predicament, their main forces would have to move east to prevent the enemy from advancing west from Qinglong Bridge. They had the strength to throw back the attacking forces of Chiang Kaishek and Fu Zuoyi. The men's morale was excellent, many troops who had not had a chance to fight at Datong were delighted now. Each man swore he would capture several dozen American rifles. The fortifications at Yanqing were not bad, quite strong, but it was imperative to send all available manpower at once to the Huailai region to build more. This was an urgent task, and even though the next day would be the Moon Festival, that could not be helped, men would have to be sent off at once!

Naturally this news did not throw Wen and the others into a panic, but it was quite unexpected. Living in the country, at some distance from any city, the newspapers they saw were all two days old. They were not well-informed about the situation, and now that there was a sudden change in the military situation they had to consider the future work in the village carefully. However, at the same time Old Dong had brought them additional instructions, namely: "When this phase of land reform is finished, you need not return to Zhangjiakou for the time being, but should go to the Eighth District of Zhuolu where you will be assigned work." The nature of their new work need not concern them now. The one thing certain was that they must leave the village very soon. Naturally nothing could go wrong with the work in the village, because the village cadres and active elements were well able to shoulder the responsibility. Only at this juncture it was very possible rumours might arise, and the fear that the country would change hands. That was something they could not help worrying about.

The meeting went with a swing. Organization Zhao, called to account by the masses, was rather indignant, and shouted: "What land do you accuse me of getting! I haven't got any-

350

thing, and if I haven't got anything why should you criticize me?" Quan acknowledged his mistake to the whole community, saying he had been an incompetent fool. He announced that in the past they had given the cadres some good land, but after the quarrel Wen had called all the cadres and land assessment committee members to a meeting, and criticized certain people, and after that they had stopped, realizing their mistake. Previously he had thought the cadres deserved special treatment on account of their past services, but that was wrong, he had been wrong. . . .

Some people raised questions in connection with their own land. Young Cheng, Co-op Tian and Freckles Li explained matters, then everybody was free to speak. Whenever possible to remedy a mistake in distribution, they exchanged land. At first a great many people were dissatisfied, but gradually they stopped being so. The meeting did not last unduly long, and everybody left feeling relaxed, now that three weeks and more of tension were practically at an end. They were looking forward to the festival the next day, the Moon Festival, the festival of emancipation. Someone said: "This is easy to remember: I shall tell my children and grandchildren they mustn't forget. It was the mid-autumn festival this year our family got land, got a start so that we could really stand up." And they calculated with delight what preparations they ought to make for the harvest. Truly it was a brave new world.

Yumin and the others went back to Wen's courtyard, feeling their work had been successful. Freckles Li in particular was singing happily, while Young Cheng was smiling his rare smile. They brought with them bunches of ripe grapes — the grapes of their district were famous, sweeter than honey. They ate themselves and invited others to eat. Freckles Li wanted to fetch his fiddle, however presently they realized there was something in the air, and asked Old Dong: "Has something happened?"

"Nothing serious," Wen reassured them, "only we must discuss the work in the village thoroughly this evening. A new job has come up!"

Yumin had joined the Party during the White Terror, and was not easily disconcerted, so he said: "Never mind, whatever job we're given we'll do it! Tell us."

They made very detailed plans for the harvest and for sending porters and assigned tasks. The porters should leave by the following afternoon at the latest, and since the fighting made it more imperative to speed up the harvest they ought to organize shock troops. Women and old people would have to be incorporated in the harvesting teams, the grain should be distributed according to their new plots of land. They also reorganized the militia, accepted a number of new members, inspected the rifles and ammunition. Old Dong and Wen, in the name of the district authority, appointed Ex-soldier Zhang deputy captain. Since Zhang was a veteran soldier, the Nuanshui militia was strengthened by his appointment.

They also appointed Liuman in place of Security Officer Zhang. The security officer's work was very important at this period, when landlords and bad elements had to be strictly watched, and this had to be done with reliance on the masses. Liuman was firm and would make a good security officer whom the masses would support. They checked upon the number of new Party members too. There were now thirty-nine in all, new and old. They talked about how to improve their education and give them some practical work, who should be helped, guided or watched. The matters were left to Freckles Li and Organization Zhao who were told to try their best to fulfill their duty. They must not allow the blackboard news to lapse, and must find a crier to broadcast news.

The former village head Jiang had been removed. Vice-Head Zhao became village head with Orchard-keeper Li and Young Guo as his deputies. Later there might be rear service work, in which case there would be too much for one man to do. The peasants' association was still headed by Young Cheng, who had to speed up the harvest and maintain the new allocation of land, not letting people return some of it as they had done that spring. There must be more group meetings to express the views of the community and to educate them. Only by unity and stubborn opposition to the forces of feudalism could they safeguard their victory.

Matters had been precipitated. They had not expected to be leaving so soon. All felt an indescribable emotion, but there was no time for regrets at parting. It was very late and they had to prepare for the next day.

57

AS soon as it was light, things started humming outside the primary school. Men had brought pine branches cut from the hills, the stage was filled with people working, who stacked the planks here. Red paper flowers had appeared too, woven into a bright archway where hung a big red cotton banner on which was written: "Celebrate the return of the land to its owners." On both sides at the back hung rush mats cn which were pasted red and green slips of paper with slogans written on them: "Destroy feudalism root and branch", "Support land reform", "The land returns to its rightful owners, everybody will have food", "In unity is strength", "Chairman Mao is our Saviour", "Forever follow Chairman Mao", "Support the Eighth Route Army", "Long live the Communist Party!" Then the gongs and drums from the primary school were brought out and sounded triumphantly on the stage. Some people came to watch the fun, others hurried home for a meal. Many people were drinking wine and eating meat dumplings.

Wen and the rest had dumplings too, and their host said: "Oh, so sorry, we didn't buy meat, it's calabash." Wen strolled out to see several families, some of whom were eating very well. The worst-off at least had pumpkin dumplings. Many villagers brought them fruit: pears, apples, and grapes. When they refused to take them the givers were angry, so they let them leave them there. Before breakfast they had held a meeting of cadres and prepared all the porters. After the meeting one hundred able-bodied men would set out, to return in three days.

Everybody in the village knew what the meeting that day was for, and meant to enjoy themselves. They had put on their new clothes and put their houses in order early. Some of them knew of the change in the situation, but were not alarmed. Gunpowder had been bought from Shacheng, and their old rifles which had not been used for quite a few years were to be let off too. These rifles were kept for birthdays and weddings and made a loud, sharp report, good to hear. Some of the villagers could perform. They got together and formed an orchestra, regretting they had been so busy the last few days they had not thought of it before. If there had not been a meeting the previous evening they could have put on an opera without difficulty. These people cleared up a corner of the stage and started playing on their instruments. The men in the street knew they liked fun, and surrounded them asking if they would sing or not.

Tenant Hou came to watch the fun too. All the old people remembered what he had been like as a youngster and told the others how handsome he had looked dressed up, his voice was strong and his acting good: he was the best performer Nuanshui ever had. The young people laughed, looking at his wizened, monkeyish face and said: "Uncle! Give us a demonstration. Work off your bad luck by singing. Wash out all these years of disappointment! What about it?" The old man said nothing, just smiled, but he kept standing by the stage, listening to the music.

When everybody had arrived some pedlars set up stalls at the back by the wall, and had a good many customers for fruit and melon seeds.

Presently the primary school dancers came out, and danced through some of the lanes and the big streets, ending up before the stage where they gave a skilful performance of whip dances, followed by so many songs and such a variety of dances, that the audience was amazed and marvelled at the children's good memories.

Villagers were greeting each other as if it were New Year.

When they had finished their meeting all the cadres came, bringing a portrait of Chairman Mao which had just been painted. It was a fair likeness, and they pasted it on a board and stood it on a table at the back. Some people wanted to light incense before it, but the majority disagreed, saying: "Chairman Mao doesn't like superstition." People stood on their toes to look, and the school children pushed their way to a corner in front and sang:

> From the red east rises the sun,
> There appears in China Mao Zedong!

There were now over fifty militiamen, all wearing plain white shirts, towels on their heads and leather belts at their waists, each with a cartridge belt over his shoulder and a hand grenade belt containing two hand grenades. These two belts crossed over their chests, and made them look very martial. Ex-soldier Zhang was similarly equipped. He and Swarthy Guo directed the others and they formed a column, standing together during the meeting. They sang the *Eighth Route Army March* with its heroic and impressive air.

All the cadres crowded onto the stage. Young Cheng stepped forward and declared the meeting open, saying: "Elders! Neighbours! Our meeting today is to celebrate the return of the land to its rightful owners! We suffered, generations of our ancestors lived like beasts, because we had no land, nothing to eat and nothing to wear — where had our land gone?"

"Stolen by the exploiting landlords!" answered several voices from below.

"Now the Communist policy is that every peasant shall have land of his own to till. The land is for those who have suffered. Do you approve or not?"

"Yes!"

"In a moment we're going to distribute tickets, stating where the land is. The old title deeds are no longer valid. We're going to burn them."

Excited murmurs swept the assembly.

"Chairman Mao thought of this for us," Young Cheng went on. "Chairman Mao is the champion of the poor. There in Yan'an he is thinking of us and working for us day and night. Today we've invited him here. See, here's his portrait. We ought to bow to him to express our thanks."

"Bow to Chairman Mao!" came the response from below the stage.

"It's right for us to bow to Chairman Mao!"

Young Cheng turned round and called out very respectfully in front of Chairman Mao's portrait: "Bow!" There was not a sound from the men and women below as they all bowed their heads after him. They bowed three times. Then Young Cheng turned round again to go on, but the crowd had started shouting slogans: "Support Chairman Mao! Long live Chairman Mao!"

Next Orchard-keeper Li reported on the distribution of land and problems connected with it, explaining to the masses why they must leave Schemer Qian and the others enough to live on: "As long as they submit and mend their ways, and are willing to work, they should be given land. You don't want to drive them to become thieves or beggars, do you? If we don't give them land to cultivate, they'll have nothing to do, and if they beg, won't that mean eating our food?" When he explained this everyone laughed, and no one insisted on their original idea of leaving nothing to the landlords.

When the land slips were distributed, all the villagers listened carefully as one cadre announced the size of each plot of land and its boundaries. The eyes of all the crowd eagerly followed each one who went up to take a slip. When he came back the people nearby craned their necks to look, while he held the red paper slip tightly, as if it weighed a hundred-weight. Some put it in the wallet of their belt, and kept their hands outside. Some quietly showed their slips to people who could read and asked if what had just been announced was right or not.

The names were called out one after the other. The proceeds from the fruit were divided too, taking a considerable time, but nobody felt impatient. Even when the slips had all been given out, nobody left, and Young Cheng called out: "Sound the drums and let off guns to celebrate."

Once more Freckles Li led the others in shouting slogans, which echoed far and wide. Gongs and drums were beaten frenziedly, whistles were blown, the old rifles were let off one after the other, the people shouting all the while. Then the school children sang again. Nobody could quite make out what they were singing, but all the grown-ups seemed to have become children again, enjoying this tumult of noise. Their extreme happiness and deep emotion impelled them to rejoice wildly.

However Young Cheng called out again from the stage, and a number of cadres shouted with him: "Stop talking please! Be quiet! Don't sing!" The noise still continued for a moment, but presently the crowd quietened down, and they heard the order: "Start the demonstration!"

The red banner on the stage was mounted on two bamboo poles and lifted down to be carried at the head of the procession. Immediately behind it came the band, next the militiamen, then all the villagers, the men in front, then the women and last the school children. They proceeded from the main street to the lanes, from the lanes to outside of the village, forming a long procession, and a few people left at home stood in the street to watch them go by. Whenever they passed a landlord's house they shouted: "Down with the feudalistic landlords!" with voices like thunder. The gates of the landlords' houses were wide open, but nobody came out. Only a few families had one or two standing by the door to stare round-eyed at the angrily shouting masses.

When the procession passed Schemer Qian's house they roared out: "Down with the local despot!" Qian's wife did not hide, but stood there nervously, watching with a blank face as they marched by, as if she had no special feeling but were just watching the fun, as if the demonstrators had nothing to do with her but were all strangers. Suddenly, however, she seemed struck with astonishment, she shook her head in amazement, her hand trembled, and she called out towards the procession: "Heini!" But no one answered. The column passed rapidly forward, and scratching her head she hobbled back inside. She felt the world had turned topsy-turvy.

The procession made a tour outside the village, and just as they reached the point for turning back Liuman and a group of men stood out from the column. Liuman had recovered from his exhaustion and regained the energy he had displayed at the mass trial. He shouted: "Those going to Huailai to dig trenches, this way!"

The procession stopped, a number of men went over to where he was, among them some cadres and some militiamen.

"Have you brought your things?" Liuman asked.

They lifted up their mattocks; they had come prepared.

"If you don't take bedding, why not take padded clothes? The evenings are very cool," Yumin said to some who he saw only wore lined clothes.

"Fall in!" shouted Liuman. "Look sharp!" They immediately formed a small column, over a hundred strong, all sturdy young men.

"We're going to build fortifications to defend our land! March!" Liuman marched at their head to the big road outside the village. They shouted slogans. Those left behind did not stir, only followed them with their eyes, while Yumin and Freckles Li led them in shouting: "Defend our land, down with the reactionaries! Three cheers for the Eighth Route Army!" The children started singing again. The small column receded into the distance, sturdy, quick and in high spirits. When they were out of sight, the villagers turned back and returned to the stage. By now there were fewer of them. Yumin spoke of the plans for going into the fields the next day. Everybody must join a harvesting team, everybody must work as directed. They listened contentedly, feeling that the plan was thoroughly drawn up. Only a very few asked quietly: "What does it mean? Is there going to be fighting in the east too?" However, most people had confidence. After the meeting had dispersed, they went home to eat dumplings and celebrate the festival.

58

AFTER eating an early supper Wen and the two others, as well as Old Dong, put on their packs and let Yumin, Young Cheng, Zhao and Swarthy Guo see them off to the east of the village. They were all racking their brains to think if there were any business they had forgotten in the village, hoping that they had prepared for all eventualities. Although they seemed to have said all there was to say, the village cadres kept asking: "Is there anything else?" Or saying regretfully: "Oh! We'd only just got to know each other! You must come again when you have time! Come to help us with the work!" Wen asked them not to come any further, but they insisted, and when at last the time came to part, all Yang could find to say was: "Keep close to the masses. That's the only way to be strong. If the masses aren't awakened, try to arouse them. When the masses do rise don't be afraid, but take your stand firmly among them to lead them. Be firm with your enemies but united among yourselves. You know all this quite well. Just carry it out with all your might!"

When they had said good-bye, Wen and the others headed for the county town and their new work. Along the road they met group after group of porters going to dig fortifications, all of them peasants from villages which had had land reform, all filled with a new spirit, brimming over with happiness, all seeming to say: "The land is ours, it's the result of our hard struggle for emancipation. Do you want to come and invade it, Chiang Kai-shek, you dog? It's no use! We have our people's army, the Eighth Route Army. We have millions of liberated peasants. We are united in one common aim, to defend our land!"

Halfway, Old Dong left them to go to the district, while the others continued on their way. They were like the porters headed for the front, full of self-confidence and satisfaction! Just as they were about to ford the river before reaching the city, the bright moon started rising behind them. They turned to look at its brightness, and at the villages under the moonlight. Over there was Nuanshui, where they had spent three weeks — what were the villagers there doing? Celebrating the Autumn Festival, celebrating the festival of their emancipation. Willow tendrils along the road stirred lightly. They pressed forward, waded into the water and across the Sanggan River, and the villagers across the river, no, not only the villagers but the peasants at the south gate of the city also were sounding gongs and drums. It was the same everywhere! Everywhere there had been a complete change during the last month or more! Now the world belonged to the toilers. There were no difficulties that could not be surmounted.

That evening they reached the county town and reported on their work. The next day when the sun was just rising over the Sanggan River they set out again, headed for a new post in the Eighth District where they would help in the work of political training.

On *The Sun Shines over the Sanggan River*

Feng Xuefeng[*]

This is a novel about land reform. The novel starts with Old Gu, a well-off middle peasant who is "carelessly classed as a rich peasant". In him the author gives us an excellent picture of a prosperous middle peasant. Then there is Hutai, related to Old Gu by marriage, a rich peasant who runs a small business. Although he plays only a small part in the novel, his character is clearly delineated. These two men — a rich and a well-to-do middle peasant — form one class of characters described by the author. At the start we see Old Gu coming back with his elder daughter from Hutai's house to Nuanshui, his own village, riding in a cart with rubber tyres. This cart not only gives an indication of Hutai's and Old Gu's class ideology, but also of the background and the time. Hutai, hearing that land reform was imminent, was afraid his cart would be confiscated, so he had asked Old Gu to take it back and keep it for him; moreover, Chiang Kai-shek was planning to attack the Liberated Areas, and the land reform we had just begun in this region had to be rapidly concluded. The second thing we notice about this middle peasant is the way he talks, all the way back, about the rich soil and crops on either side of the road. We realize

* Feng Xuefeng (1906-1976) is a well-known Chinese literary critic, writer and poet. — *Tr.*

how much he longs to own more land here. The third thing we note is Old Gu's relationship by marriage to the village despot, Schemer Qian, which shows up the conflict between them.

Beginning, then, with this well-to-do middle peasant, and while she is laying bare his heart to us, the author creates an atmosphere which pervades the whole novel and makes us realize the close relationship of landlords, rich, middle and poor peasants and farm labourers to the land and the class conflict between them. We sense the atmosphere of the place and time (land reform started slightly later in Nuanshui than in the villages around, so when the novel starts the peasants there are conscious of an impending storm, and it is in this atmosphere of fearful expectancy that the characters of different classes make their appearance).

Schemer Qian, landlord and local despot, is an important character because he represents the landlord class and is the chief object of the peasants' struggle. He is connected with all the villagers, and the current situation is reflected in his actions. To unfold this Machiavellian landlord's character and actions, the author has created the primary school teacher, Ren. As an individual, this intellectual who acts as running dog for the landlords is quite successfully drawn; but he is created largely to throw light on Schemer Qian and, to a lesser degree, Landlord Li. Again, Schemer Qian's niece, Heini, is introduced largely for the sake of the hired hand, Young Cheng, but also for Schemer Qian. Landlord Jiang and the loose woman, White Snake, also derive their importance from their connection with Schemer Qian. In her description of these characters, Ding Ling presents not only the main conflict between the peasantry and the landlord class, but also the conflict between the landlords themselves, and their home life.

Particularly noteworthy, however, is the fact that Ding Ling has not made a caricature of this landlord, Schemer Qian, nor has she described him as an out-and-out villain. Her treatment of him is true to the actual facts about this type of local despot, and she attempts to make her description strictly realistic. Ding Ling's success with this character is proof of her profound observation and analysis of village life, for this crafty landlord has taken steps in good time to cope with the changed situation by becoming an "army dependent" and winning allies among the village cadres. Outwardly, he appears quite calm and "enlightened". At the same time, his estate is a small one, and his secret sabotage is not of the most vicious type, so that even Comrade Wen of the work team considers him as a middle peasant. Yet the villagers are so afraid of him that they dare not mention his name. It is Schemer Qian who symbolizes the age-old rule of the landlord class. It is he too who constitutes a connecting link with the Kuomintang reactionaries. The peasants' scruples, fear of the reactionaries' return, and fatalism are on account of him. And these scruples and fears on the part of the peasants increase the landlords' actual power. Hence, although Schemer Qian is not one of the greatest despots, his power is by no means small.

This approach to problems, not only by describing facts, but by noting the psychological effect on the peasants of the landlords' power, is absolutely correct and shows great insight on the part of the author. In describing both Schemer Qian and the peasants, Ding Ling pays special attention to these psychological factors and goes into them very deeply, and this is one of the chief reasons for the success of this novel and the delineation of its characters. Only towards the very end does the struggle between the peasants and Qian become an open one. The peasants do not realize at first that Schemer

Qian is carrying out sabotage, but from the very beginning they feel in their hearts that he is their chief enemy. So, psychologically speaking, the class struggle begins early, to grow more and more intense as time goes on. This method of presenting the struggle is in keeping with actual fact, and artistically effective. Moreover, by using the analysis of characters and the creation of atmosphere to unfold her main theme, the author is able to give a really penetrating picture of the development of the class struggle.

Landlord Jiang and his place in the landlord class are also clearly depicted. He belongs to Qian's camp, not just because they are members of the same class, but because they are in league together.

The loose woman, White Snake, who does not come from a landlord family herself, is introduced not simply to give a picture of one aspect of the old society and throw light on the landlords, but also to describe the struggle and the peasant masses. She fits organically into the novel because she is connected with both landlords and peasants, and she plays her part too in the struggle. Her position is the same as that of Teacher Ren.

Though little is written about Landlord Li, readers understand what he is like. And his wife is one of the most striking and successfully drawn characters in the whole novel.

However, Heini — Schemer Qian's niece — does not strike one as too well depicted. Ding Ling seems to have shown some bias in her treatment of Heini, evidently wanting to portray a sweet girl who should win the hearts of readers as well as of the characters in the novel. But she pays too little attention to the contradictions in Heini's relationship to Schemer Qian, the social roots of such a character and the contradictions in the girl herself and makes too little attempt to analyse them. In general, however, the author is able to describe the contradictions in a character as a reflection of the contradictions in objective reality, so that she rarely expresses the development of character in isolation from the development of the conflict in real life. This method is the basic reason for her success in characterization. Nearly all Ding Ling's characters are portrayed in this realistic manner; Heini, however, is something of an exception.

The third group of characters are the men of the work team sent by the county Party committee. Comrade Wen, who leads the work team, is an impractical, high-flown intellectual, unable to get close to the masses and hence quite unable to understand them. The other two youngsters, Yang and Hu, although inexperienced, are able to mingle more closely with the masses, and gradually come to understand the village cadres and peasants and the actual conditions of the village as a whole. The author uses the work team to present the stages of the mass struggle of the peasants, but also makes use of the differences of opinion between Yang, Hu and Comrade Wen to bring out the ideas and emotions of the peasants and the chief difficulties of the struggle.

These three cadres are described to the life, and from Ding Ling's criticism of Comrade Wen and her description of the other two, we can learn much about the actual work of land reform. However, it is clear that her main purpose in writing the novel is not to describe the cadres, and they are relegated to a secondary position.

The most important set of characters in the book is, of course, the village cadres — Yumin (secretary of the Nuanshui Party Branch), Young Cheng (chairman of the peasants' association), Vice-Head Zhao, Swarthy Guo (captain of the militia), Gui (chairman of the women's association) and many other cadres. It is they who lead the peasant masses. These cadres and the ordinary peasants are the chief characters of the book. The author gives a graphic description of all the village cadres and many of the peasants connected with them.

Ding Ling gives us a clear picture of what is the ideology of Yumin, Young Cheng and the other cadres, and makes them wage a struggle of ideas with the peasant masses; and in her eyes the victory won in this struggle of ideas is just as important as the victory over the landlords. The author's central aim is to describe the peasants, or, it would be more correct to say, to describe how the peasants in the course of their struggle overcome their ideological weaknesses and develop and grow in stature. Here, on a broad social basis, she describes the strength engendered when the peasants become class conscious. We know it is not easy in places where the reactionaries still reign for the peasants to rise up and struggle, largely because they are too weak by themselves. But in liberated areas where several struggles have already taken place, although they have strength to spare to overthrow the landlord class, it is still difficult to start the struggle. It is easy to understand the true nature and power of the personal scruples, fear of the reactionaries' return, fatalism and other anxieties that beset the peasants at this time. There is undoubtedly a historical reason for these anxieties, but they are also a reflection of the continuing existence of the landlords' power. Hence, in order to expel these anxieties, the real cause for them must be uprooted — the landlord class must be overthrown. Must be overthrown, though, by the peasants themselves. Unless the peasants are awakened and use their own strength against the landlords, even if the latter are overthrown, fear of their return will still linger in the peasants' minds. The landlords' power will still hold sway over their hearts.

So to overthrow the landlord class is no easy matter. In the first place, the peasants themselves must act, nobody else can act for them. In the second place, if the peasants are to act, not only must they wage a class struggle in actual practice, they must also wage a class struggle in their own minds. Only when this class struggle in their minds has been won, will they be truly awakened and able to overthrow the landlord class. The author has a deep understanding of village society and its class relations, as well as of the peasant mentality. She also shows profound understanding of the Party's directives on the mass line in land reform. So, taking as her basic point of departure the relationships to the land which determine the village class relationships, she can give us concrete and penetrating analyses and descriptions of the extent of the villagers' dependence on the land, the various aspects of the landlords' influence over and enslavement of the peasants, the rise of the peasants' struggle and the source of their strength, and the complexity of the relationships between different classes and groups of individuals. The author's deep understanding of the peasants arises from her understanding of the complexity and importance of the class struggle in land reform. From a broad social and historical basis and amid complex human relationships, she observes the unfolding of the class struggle and the peasants' own ideological struggle; then the peasant masses and their very real strength are displayed so vividly to us, and so convincingly, we can detect no exaggeration or falsification.

Comrade Pin, propaganda director of the county Party committee, has an important role towards the end of the novel. Although he comes to Nuanshui very late and stays only for a very short time, it is he who sets a match, as it were, to the pile of fuel already prepared. That is to say, the author uses Comrade Pin's words to point out the real historic victory of the peasants. Thus, although Comrade Pin plays a part of the utmost importance in guiding Nuanshui's land reform struggle, and the author sketches his admirable qualities and likable character in a few vivid strokes, he is not one of the chief figures in the novel — the chief figures are the village cadres and peasants, as already mentioned.

In characterization too, the author pays most attention to the village cadres and peasants. To mention specific cases, the chief characters, like Yumin, Young Cheng, Vice-Head Zhao, Swarthy Guo and Freckles Li, impress us as strongly individual figures, true to life. While, of the peasant women, we cannot but admire the lifelike and striking figures of Gui and Yue. It is clear, however, that the author is less intent on individual characterization than on depicting a group of people. We are given a relatively detailed analysis of Yumin and Gui, but with the other peasants we feel the author is analysing and describing the development of the struggle rather than depicting characters. Yet, even in the case of Yumin and Gui, it is only because the plot requires them to appear relatively often that the author has occasion to devote more space to them. It is not because the author wants to go into greater detail with these figures that she makes them appear more often. However, although the author does not write more fully about any particular character, practically all the cadres and peasants in the book, regardless of their importance and the space devoted to them, make a marked impression on us. That is to say, virtually all the characters have distinctive individuality, and this is undoubtedly one reason for the author's success.

It is clear that the author describes people in order to describe the struggle, to describe society and life. This means the portrayal of characters is subordinated to the portrayal of society and life. Here, that is to say, it is subordinated to the portrayal of the class struggle in the countryside (land reform). Works of literature must describe people; if there are no people, the value of such works will be very low. But the description of characters, while it is not the aim, is an indispensable method. People are the agents of all that takes place in society. Without the description of people, there can be no description of society in literature. Hence both the aim and method of literature demand that, on the basis of society and life, from the development of the struggle, authors must write of people. This is a fundamental rule. It is in fact the method of realism in creating types. In *The Sun Shines over the Sanggan River*, Ding Ling in her creation of characters may be said to have succeeded, in general, in using the method of realism.

To my mind, the fact that the author has achieved such success in this direction is due to her relatively deep understanding of life, her study of society, her knowledge of many people, of their life and struggle, of how they act and think in the struggle, and what part they play. Hence she can write of people in the framework of society and life, during the course of the struggle. Her characters develop step by step following the development of the struggle, in the closest connection with the struggle. Individual characteristics are chosen for their importance and social significance, and all actions, words or ideas which fail to accord with or are not necessary to the laws of development of the struggle are not forced upon the characters, for they would be unsuitable and superfluous. This does not mean, however, that her characters are placed in a passive position, for the struggle is waged by people who develop in the struggle of contradictions. And then the author is always on the alert to see that her characters are realistically portrayed.

All Ding Ling's characters have individuality and yet are,

to a greater or lesser degree, types. What is typical in them is expressed through their individuality, which is, of course, the only way it can be expressed. There is nothing mysterious about the fact that characters can be both individuals and types. When you have seen many people, you can distinguish both their individual features and what they have in common (that is, what makes them typical. Class character is the main factor here). Then, no matter whether you describe an individual or a type, in each case the description will be based on actual people. And so long as this is the case, your characters will naturally have both individuality and typicalness; while, the better you write, the more striking and penetrating these features well be. Our basic demand is for characters true to life, and this applies whether we write of individuals or types.

It is true that in this novel the author has not given us any types so outstanding that we are absolutely bowled over by them. But she has skilfully and realistically created real people, and some of her characters, we must admit, are unforgettable types.

Moreover, these real people are peasants. If Ding Ling could write only of intellectuals like Comrade Wen, and not of peasants, she would not have won so much praise. Similarly, if she could paint successful pictures of Schemer Qian, Landlord Li's wife, Old Gu and his two daughters, but not of Yumin, Young Cheng, Vice-Head Zhao, Swarthy Guo, Gui, Yue and the others, we should not be paying such tribute to her today.

To consider this work from another angle, we should take the author's outstanding achievement in this work as representative of the achievements in our literature in recent years. During the last ten years our socialist realist literature has been growing. A number of writers have created or are beginning to create real people. This novel of Ding Ling's is only an outstanding example of this. We should note this achievement, and the achievement of all our best writers, in order to affirm and develop the realism already growing in our literature.

Another point we should note is the way in which Ding Ling, in this novel, links up the leadership of the Party (*i.e.*, leadership of the proletariat) with the peasants' own struggle, according to the inner relations of the class struggle in the villages, presenting this as one historical condition of the peasants' demand for land and the development of the revolutionary struggle. This means that the Party leadership cannot be described as an outside force, unconnected with the peasants. This is another very important feature of this book. Many people recognize superficially that without the leadership of the Party the peasants cannot stand up, so they often consider the peasants quite simply as being liberated by an outside force, as if the peasants themselves were unable to revolt or struggle. They fail to realize that the peasantry is a revolutionary fighting class, and that the leadership of the proletariat and the Communist Party is one of the historical conditions which enabled the peasants in this period to rise up and struggle. Hence the leadership of the proletariat and the Communist Party has an inner historical connection with the peasants' revolutionary struggle. Thus, to recognize the necessity for Party leadership, one must recognize the inner historical relationship of the proletariat and peasantry. That is to say, one must recognize that the leadership of the proletariat and the worker-peasant alliance are historically inevitable, and not view this alliance as the juxtaposition of two forces which have no inner historical connection.

When I think back to the contents of the book as a whole,

I am struck by the author's mastery of artistic expression. Without a highly developed artistic technique, the book could not have been what it is. In this novel Ding Ling has painted a great canvas, but on this canvas beauty of scenery is relegated to second place. What takes first place is characterization, penetrating and correct analysis of ideas, and a rich atmosphere woven of poetic sensibility and the joy of living. I hope the author will pay more attention in future to polishing her language and making use of popular expressions — although this must not be done at the expense of the artistic qualities already mentioned. I was most struck by the large canvas covered in this novel, and the poetic character of the book. And all readers must, I think, have admired the poetic prose of the chapter describing the orchard, where the language achieves a standard seldom attained hitherto by our young literature.

In brief, the faithfulness to life and artistry already observed in this work make it an epic of our great land reform, small although its scale may be, and in spite of the fact that it was written before most of China had been liberated, and before land reform had been carried out in most parts.

Of course, if we say there should be epics to record our great land reform movement, this work cannot be considered the most brilliant or greatest epic it deserves. For our country is so vast, land reform has been carried out over such wide areas since liberation, such complex social relationships have been involved, and the historical significance of the movement is so great, it is understandable if readers are still waiting for a more comprehensive work to appear to reflect all the relationships and aspects of this great movement with wider vision and deeper insight. This is a sign of the increased demands our people are making on literature.

Several works on land reform have already appeared and

won the respect of readers. And the fundamental reason for this is the people's respect for this great historical period. All works that can reflect this era in our history will have epic significance and will be acclaimed by the public. And so we prize a work like *The Sun Shines over the Sanggan River,* not just because it is one of the best books on land reform and gives a good picture of this movement but because it shows that our literature has already achieved the power to reflect reality, and is growing in stature.

Beijing, May 14, 1952

About the Author

Ding Ling was born in 1904 in Lingli, Hunan Province, and spent her childhood at Changde. Her original name was Jiang Bingzhi or Ding Bingzhi, and she first wrote under the pen-names Bingzhi and Congxuan. Her father died while she was still a child. She received her education at Changde, Changsha, Beijing and Shanghai. She started writing in 1927.

Her first works were published in the *Fiction Monthly*. These were her stories "The Dream", "In Summer Vacation", "Miss Sophie's Diary" and "The Girl Amao". They were later included in a collection titled *In the Dark*, published in 1928. That same year she organized, together with Shen Congwen and Hu Yeping, the Literary Society of Red and Black, which published the fortnightly *Red and Black*. She published the stories "The Diary of Suicide" in 1929 and "A Woman and Wei Hu" in 1930. She joined the League of Left-wing Writers in 1931, and soon became editor of its magazine, *The Dipper*. In the same year her story "The Birth of a Man" was published.

In 1932, she joined the Communist Party, and published the story "Flood". The following year, she became the Party secretary of the League of Left-wing Writers, and published a novel, *Mother*, and other stories. In 1933, she was thrown into jail, in Shanghai, by the Kuomintang authorities, to be released only in 1936, thanks to the efforts of the Party. She then went to the Northern Shaanxi Central Soviet Area, and became the Deputy Political Commissar of the Central Guards Regiment of the Red Army.

After the outbreak of the War of Resistance Against Japanese Aggression, in 1937, she went to Yan'an, where she headed the Northwest War Service Corps and edited the literary supplement of the Party paper, *Liberation Daily*. In 1942, Ding Ling participated in the Party's Rectification Movement while she was at the Central Party School. Guided by Comrade Mao Zedong's *Talks at Yan'an Forum on Literature and Art*, she took great interest in the movement for a new literature, initiated in Yan'an, and spent a lot of time in living among the workers, peasants and soldiers. During this period, she published the drama, "A Reunion"; well-known travel reports, "The 129th Division and the Shanxi-Hebei-Shandong-Henan Border Region" and "Notes in March"; and the short novels, *Faith Through Tear-blurred Eyes, When I Was at Xia Village* and *An Unfired Shell*.

In 1946, she spent many months as a member of land reform work teams in north China. She wrote *The Sun Shines over the Sanggan River* in 1948, a novel reflecting the life of the peasants during the land reform. The novel won a Stalin Prize in 1951 and has been translated into 13 languages.

After the founding of the People's Republic of China, Ding Ling was appointed to head of the Department of Literature and Art of the Propaganda Department of the Party Central Committee. She was also Vice-Chairman of the Union of Chinese Writers, Secretary of the Party Group of the Union, Chief Editor of the *Literary Gazette* and *People's Literature*, and head of the Central Institute of Literature. Her works during this period include the essays, "Step into the New Era", and "Settle Down Among the Masses", a collection of prose titled *Notes on the Travel to Europe* and several short stories, such as "The Man in Charge of Grain".

In 1957, Ding Ling was wrongly labelled a Rightist and her works were banned. She was then sent to work on a farm

378

in northeast China for 12 years and was jailed for five years during the "cultural revolution". Though living in extremely difficult conditions for two decades, Ding Ling still maintained her confidence in the future and continued to do creative writing. Part of her novel *In the Coldest Days*, published in *Qingming* magazine in 1979, was written under such conditions.

After she was rehabilitated in 1978, she was elected to be a member of the Fifth National Committee of the Chinese People's Political Consultative Conference, in 1979, and to be a member of the Fourth National Committee of the Federation of Chinese Writers and Artists, and Vice-Chairman of the Union of Chinese Writers. She published "Du Wanxiang" and a dozen other stories in the year after returning to Beijing. Her novels *The Sun Shines over the Sanggan River* and *Mother* have been reprinted by the People's Literature Publishing House.

太阳照在桑干河上

丁　玲著

杨宪益、戴乃迭译

＊

外文出版社出版

（中国北京百万庄路24号）

外文印刷厂印刷

中国国际书店发行

（北京399信箱）

1984年（34开）第一版

编号：（英）10050—1099

00305

10—E—124P